維 克 斐 牧 師 傳 譯 註

THE

VICAR OF WAKEFIELD

BY

OLIVER GOLDSMITH

TRANSLATED AND ANNOTATED

BY

WU KWANG-KIEN

THE COMMERCIAL PRESS, LIMITED

SHANGHAI, CHINA

ADVERTISEMENT

There are an hundred faults in this Thing, and an hundred things might be said to prove them beauties. But it is needless. A book may be amusing with numerous errors, or it may be very dull without a single absurdity. The hero of this piece unites in himself the three greatest characters upon earth; he is a priest, an husbandman, and the father of a family. He is drawn as ready to teach, and ready to obey, as simple in affluence, and majestic in adversity. In this age of opulence and refinement, whom can such a character please? Such as are fond of high life, will turn with disdain from the simplicity of his country fireside. Such as mistake ribaldry for humor, will find no wit in his harmless conversation; and such as have been taught to deride religion, will laugh at one, whose chief stores of comfort are drawn from futurity.

OLIVER GOLDSMITH.

自　　序

我這本書有一百處的毛病、也有一百處的好處、這却都不相干、大凡一本書、雖然有許多毛病、也許有許多興趣、又有一本書、只有一處的毛病、却索然無味、此中自有分別、我這本書的英雄（即主要人物）、一人而具三種世人最尊重的資格、他爲人師、爲人夫、爲人父、好教導人、又能守法、處富厚能單簡、處貧賤能尊嚴、我們現在的繁華世界、能歡喜這種人嗎、慕浮華的人、是看不起他田家園爐的樂境、誤把淫詞粗語當作趣語的人、看不出他平常談話的滋味、又有一種人、受過蔑視宗教的教育、就要笑他靠將來以安心、終恐難以索解也、歌士米序

譯　者　序

愛爾蘭人歌士米、所著維克斐牧師傳、久爲歐美兩洲人所好讀、德國大文豪葛特 (Goethe) 暮年日記曰、偶然又檢出維克斐牧師傳、不免從頭至尾、又讀一遍、不禁回憶七十年前、余之獲益於此書者最多、作者措語冷峭、而命意高遠、存心愷悌、對於人事之過失、公平寬恕、受禍不減其馴良、遇變不失其常度、此皆余當少年正在構成人格之時所得最善最美之教育也(下略)、英國大文豪司葛德 (Sir Walter Scott) 曰、我輩好讀維克斐牧師傳、少年時喜讀之、老年時又喜讀之、作者善以最妙之文、達最眞最美之情感、又能以人之貞淫善惡、一歸於天性、使讀者氣舒以平、尤使人追慕作者之爲人(下略)、英國大小說家提喀利(Thackeray)、謂英國文章家多矣、以歌士米之爲人最爲人所愛、又謂歐洲王公第宅、窮鄉僻壤、無不有歌士米維克斐牧師傳者(下略)、富士德 (John Forster) 爲大小說家狄金士(Charles Dickens) 作傳、謂狄金士善描性情、用筆輕妙、不獨能令讀者讚美、且能令人愛作者之爲人、以作者爲可與歌士米爲伍 (下略)、作者自序、謂是書有一百處毛病、其實是美不勝收、故至今英美兩國、仍作爲英文課本、法國人之學英文者亦然、余前爲商務印書館編英文讀本、已採若干段、少年親友、多嗜讀歌士米此作、但作者善於選字造句、語淺意深、其天懷和易、卽敍瑣事亦往往語帶詼諧、順手拈來、多成趣語、易爲讀者所忽略、故略爲批出、以期隅反、又書中所引典故及成語單詞之不易解者、亦擇尤加注、以便讀者、初譯時在二十年前、或作或止、積有歲時、今全書告成、聊記數語於篇首、民國十四年大暑新會伍光建序

4

CONTENTS

CONTENTS

x CONTENTS

CONTENTS

THE
VICAR OF WAKEFIELD

THE VICAR OF WAKEFIELD
維 克 斐 牧 師 傳

CHAPTER I

THE DESCRIPTION OF THE FAMILY OF WAKEFIELD, IN WHICH A KINDRED LIKENESS PREVAILS, AS WELL OF MINDS AS OF PERSONS.

第 一 回

敍 維 克 斐 牧 師 家 庭　這 一 家 人 面 貌
思 想 大 略 相 同
(老 牧 師 閒 享 家 庭 樂)

I was ever[1] of opinion,[2] that the honest man who married and brought up a large family, did more service[3] than he who continued single and only talked of population.[4] From this motive, I had scarce taken orders a year, before I began to think seriously of matrimony, and chose my wife, as she did her wedding gown, not for a fine glossy surface, but

我常常以爲．凡一個誠實人．娶了親．教養許多兒女．比不娶親的人空談生齒戶口的．比較上爲有功於世．我因爲有這個意思．故此我受戒{借用}之後．不到一年．就認眞的想到娶親的事．我選我的女人．要有彼此永遠可以相得的資格．就如同我女人選

---

1. Ever, 永遠；常常． 2. I was of opinion, 我有這個意思；我以爲．
3. Service, 事功；did service, 立過功；有功；辦過事． 4. Population. 戶口；生齒；通國的人數．

11

such qualities as would wear well. To do her justice, she was a good-natured, notable woman; and as for breeding, there were few country ladies who could show more. She could read any English book without much spelling; but for pickling, preserving, and cookery none could excel her. She prided herself also upon being an excellent contriver in housekeeping; though I could never find that we grew richer with all her contrivances.

However, we loved each other tenderly, and our fondness increased as we grew old. There was, in fact, nothing that could make us angry with the world or each other. We had an elegant house, situated in a fine country, and a good neighborhood. The year was spent in a moral[1] or rural amusement,[2] in visiting our rich neighbors, and relieving such as were poor. We had no revolutions to fear, nor

不要只求外面光滑細膩，要穿結婚禮服的材料一樣，專求可以耐久經穿。我替我的女人說一句公道話，他脾氣好，又說到婦人家。鄉下女人比他強的不多。英文書他也能讀〔此人不識字不多〕，若是製酸菜蜜餞，烹調醃臘，他卻無人管得，他自命為最妙的祕訣。他對於治家務自許多妙，我們卻並未因此富出〔此語諷諧言其女人想出治家方法也〕。

雖是這樣說，我們兩人相愛，越上向年紀，愛情越加。按事實，我們夫婦兩人不懷怨怒，即對世界也不懷怨怒。我們坐落四圍鄉下之內，有一所好房子，風景雅的鄉下人都是良鄉。一年之內，就學樂而不淫。有錢的鄰人，我們有時往來，有時周濟貧的鄰人。我們無革命可怕，也不受

---

1. Moral, 合禮; 不淫亂.　2. Moral or rural amusement, 此處 moral amusement 有作 救濟貧民解 者.

THE VICAR OF WAKEFIELD

fatigues to undergo; all our adventures were by the fireside, and all our migrations from the blue bed to the brown.

As we lived near the road, we often had the traveler or stranger visit us to taste our gooseberry wine, for which we had great reputation; and I profess with the veracity of an historian, that I never knew one of them to find fault with it. Our cousins, too, even to the fortieth remove, all remembered their affinity, without any help from the herald's office,[1] and came very frequently to see us. Some of them did us no great honor by these claims of kindred, as we had the blind, the maimed, and the halt amongst the number. However, my wife always insisted that as they were the same *flesh and blood*, they should sit with us at the same table. So that if we had not very rich, we generally had very happy, friends about us;

着辛苦. 我們冒險的事. 不過是圍爐閒談. 遷徙之事. 也不過是從藍色的牀遷到棕色的牀 {圍爐閒談本無冒險之可言從此牀搬到彼一牀更無遷徙之可言此語反射成趣亦言安居樂業不好遠出也}.

因爲我們住近大路. 常有旅行人或異鄉人來訪. 嘗我們很出名的家釀果子酒. 我敢說. 嘗過的人. 向來沒有不喜歡我的家釀. 我這句話. 也有歷史家的話那樣可靠 {敍家庭瑣事而借重歷史家略帶譏諷歷史家之好鋪敍無關重要之事也亦譏諷歷史家之敍事不可靠}. 我們的堂兄弟表兄弟們. 那怕遠推到十餘代. 也不用翻族譜. 都認親戚. 常來探訪. 有些來認親戚的人. 却也不甚體面. 因爲內中也有瞎子. 也有跛的. 也有殘廢的. 但我的女人當他們都是親骨肉. 一定要他們同我們同一桌子吃飯. 故此我們雖無富翁光降. 却來探訪的朋友. 無一個不

---

1. Herald's office, 國家設官專管譜系.

for this remark will hold good through life, that the poorer the guest, the better pleased he ever is with being treated; and as some men gaze with admiration at the colors of a tulip, or the wing of a butterfly, so I was by nature an admirer of happy human faces. However, when any one of our relations was found to be a person of a very bad character, a troublesome guest, or one we desired to get rid of, upon his leaving my house I ever took care to lend him a riding coat, or a pair of boots, or sometimes a horse of small value, and I always had the satisfaction of finding he never came back to return them. By this the house was cleared of such as we did not like; but never was the family of Wakefield known to turn the traveler or the poor dependent out of doors.

Thus we lived several years in a state of much happiness, not but that we sometimes had those little rubs[1] which Providence

是很歡喜的. 我有一句話. 是永遠不可廢的. 就是越貧窮的朋友. 受了我們的款待是越歡喜. 有許多人喜歡看花的顏色或蝴蝶的翼. 我却喜歡看高興人的臉. 雖然. 人有良莠不齊. 親戚中也有品行極壞的. 也有很麻煩的. 也有我們不願同他來往的. 我當他臨走出門的時候. 我總要留意借給他一件騎馬用的長褂. 或一雙靴子. 有時借給他一匹不甚值錢的馬. 從此以後. 他們再也不來還借去的東西. 這等人不再來也罷了. 我倒覺得心安. 用了這個法子. 我們家裏沒有我們不喜歡的客. 但是我們維氏一家人. 對於旅行人或窮親戚. 向無閉門不納的事.

如是者我們過了好幾年快樂的日子. 這話並不是說我們沒有不幸的事. 例如我的果園.

---

1. Rubs, 磨; 小折磨; 小不如意之事.

sends to enhance[1] the value of its favors. My orchard was often robbed by school-boys, and my wife's custards plundered by the cats or the children. The Squire would sometimes fall asleep in the most pathetic parts of my sermon, or his lady return my wife's civilities at church with a mutilated courtesy. But we soon got over the uneasiness caused by such accidents, and usually in three or four days began to wonder how they vexed us.

My children, the offspring of temperance,[2] as they were educated without softness, so they were at once well formed and healthy; my sons hardy and active, my daughters beautiful and blooming. When I stood in the midst of the little circle, which promised to be the supports of my declining age, I could not avoid repeating the famous story of Count Abensburg, who, in Henry II's progress through Germany, while other courtiers

我被們教得鄉牧是爲瞠不鄉對完還小之事過裏一過得種

來儁有時兒女我說時候寫以講令怠時裏描自宣讚之有時教堂禮還這上如都下芥了倒於

生點心有時被當時候聽動着了命知自不寫眞也雕在躬離但是正得這當些去我們對介意呢

學的有時講切哀却牧師聽亦聽實太人鞠躬半的人寶之得就後我爲什麼還異事

小被作吃了宜睡處能也煩矢的女備不不不不所之是雖回三詫小

時人偸吃宜哀却師動描其鄉紳之最睡耐一紳我

常女貓搶堂最紳之最睡耐一紳

不令固子兒到持候出的二向不強兒女來扶時伯爵說的第

我們飲食一切教養兒女四肢健的勞花靠他們前本述亞這故事理顯

過文身們美垂故不名是弱體活麗暮於免的日耳曼帝故不名是

1. Enhance, 加增. 2. Offspring of temperance, 此句太泛, 近來 temperance 專指不飲酒, 其實此字泛指凡事得中不過度也.

came with their treasures, brought his thirty-two children, and presented them to his sovereign as the most valuable offering he had to bestow. In this manner, though I had but six, I considered them as a very valuable present made to my country, and consequently looked upon it as my debtor. Our eldest son was named George, after his uncle who left us ten thousand pounds. Our second child, a girl, I intend to call after her aunt Grissel; but my wife, who during her pregnancy had been reading romances, insisted upon her being called Olivia. In less than another year we had another daughter, and now I was determined that Grissel should be her name; but a rich relation taking a fancy to stand godmother,[1] the girl was, by her directions, called Sophia, so that we had two romantic names in the family; but I solemnly protest I had no hand in it.

出巡時.所有大臣皆輦寶物進獻.惟有這位伯爵獻的是他夫婦所生的三十二個兒子.他對皇帝說.這就是他進貢的至寶.我雖然只有六個兒女.我也當是獻與國家的至寶.我以爲國家當感激我.應該待我是個債主{此二段與開章第一句說娶親多生子相應}.我的大兒子叫佐之.這是他伯伯的名字.伯伯有遺產一萬鎊分給他.第二個是女兒.原要用他伯母的名字.但是我的女人懷孕的時候讀小說.他一定要叫他奧維雅.再過不到一年.又得一個女兒.這趟我立定主意要他用伯母的名字.誰知有一位有錢的親戚.要作他乾娘.這位乾娘就替他起名字叫素緋雅.故此我們家裏有兩個小說裏頭人物的名字.我却要莊重的說明.這兩個的命名.都同我無干{此寫維牧師不

1. Godfather and godmother, 此是中國所無,借用乾爹乾娘作解,奉耶教孩子之 godfather 和 godmother, 是擔任小孩耶教教育之責.

Moses was our next, and after an interval of twelve years we had two sons more.

It would be fruitless to deny exultation when I saw my little ones about me, but the vanity[1] and the satisfaction of my wife were even greater than mine. When our visitors would say, "Well, upon my word, Mrs. Primrose,[2] you have the finest children in the whole country."— "Ay, neighbor," she would answer, "they are as heaven made them, handsome enough, if they be good enough, for handsome is that handsome does." And then she would bid the girls hold up their heads, who, to conceal nothing, were certainly very handsome. Mere outside is so very trifling a circumstance with me, that I should scarce have remembered to mention it, had it not been a general topic[3] of conversation in the country. Olivia, now about

往下是個兒子叫摩西。再過十二年。又得兩個兒子。

我看見我的一羣兒女在身邊。我非常得意。這是不必隱諱不認的。而我女人之自鳴得意。比我更甚{比我}甚以爲然也{讀小然也}說{甚以讀小}。有時來客對我的女人說道。普太太。你的兒女是國內最好看的。我却不是說恭維話。我的女人就答道。好鄰居。他們是生成這樣的。相貌好。還要行爲好。他們只要行爲好。就算是好。說完就叫女兒們擡起頭來{越是客氣}{越客氣}話越顯得是得意話描寫普太太得意之極}。我不瞞衆位說。他們長得果然好看。我以爲外貌好看原算不了什麼。着不是鄉下裏人人都說他們長得好看。我也忘記提起這句話了。奧維雅

eighteen, had that luxuri-
ancy of beauty with which
painters generally drew
Hebe, open, sprightly, and
commanding. Sophia's
features were not so strik-
ing at first, but often did
more certain execution, for
they were soft, modest, and
alluring. The one van-
quished by a single blow,
the other by efforts suc-
cessfully repeated.

The temper of a woman
is generally formed from
the turn of her features—
at least, it was so with my
daughters. Olivia wished
for many lovers, Sophia to
secure one. Olivia was
often affected from too
great a desire to please.
Sophia even repressed ex-
cellence from her fears to
offend. The one entertained me with her vivacity
when I was gay, the other
with her sense when I was
serious. But these quali-
ties were never carried to
excess in either, and I have
often seen them exchange
characters for a whole day
together. A suit of mourn-
ing has transformed my

今年快十八歲.長得艷
麗.神釆煥發.如畫師所
繪的希臘仙女希畢.繪
出坦白活潑而又動人.
素緋雅的面貌.乍看不
如他姊姊的動人.而柔
媚幽閒.有潛移之力.往
往尤能動人.大女兒能
使男子一見立刻傾倒.
二女兒能使男子屢見
必定傾倒.

大概而論.女人脾氣
隨面貌而定.我的兩個
女兒更甚.奧維雅願意
有許多人愛他.素緋雅
只要拿定一個.奧維雅
惟恐人不歡喜.故有造
作.素緋雅惟恐得罪人.
故往往矜持.處處不露
所長.我高興的時候.看
見大女兒的活潑.使我
覺得有味.我嚴重的時
候.則覺得我二女兒端
莊爲有意思.但是他們
行爲雖然不同.從來却
不過火.也有終日之間.
活潑的變了端莊.端莊
的反變了活潑.大女兒
若穿了素服.就變活潑

coquette into a prude,[1] and a new set of ribands has given her younger sister more than natural vivacity. My eldest son, George, was bred at Oxford, as I intended him for one of the learned professions. My second boy, Moses, whom I designed for business, received a sort of miscellaneous education at home. But it is needless to attempt describing the particulars of young people that had seen but very little of the world. In short, a family likeness prevailed through all, and properly speaking, they had but one character — that of being all equally generous,[2] credulous,[3] simple,[4] and inoffensive.[5]

為寡言寡笑的女子. 若二女兒衣服上添幾條花邊或帶子. 則又變作異常活潑. 我要大兒子學文藝. 故叫他入牛津大學. 我要二兒子作生意. 留在家中受雜湊教育. 但少年人未曾出門涉世. 也用不着說他們的品格. 總而言之. 他們都有家風. 個個都一樣的慷慨. 老實. 純良. 易於上當 {此句照應回目}.

---

1. Prude, 過裝貞節之婦女. 2. Generous. 慷慨; 大度; 疏財仗義.
3. Credulous, 易於信人; 易於上當. 4. Simple, 老實; 腦筋單簡
5. Inoffensive, 純良.

CHAPTER II

FAMILY MISFORTUNES — THE LOSS OF FORTUNE ONLY
SERVES TO INCREASE THE PRIDE OF THE WORTHY.

第 二 回

家 庭 不 幸　君 子 不 為 貧 賤 所 移
(好 辯 論 兩 親 家 失 和)

The temporal concerns of our family were chiefly committed to my wife's management; as to the spiritual, I took them entirely under my own direction. The profits of my living, which amounted to but thirty-five pounds a year, I made over to the orphans and widows of the clergy of our diocese,[1] for, having a fortune of my own, I was careless of temporalities, and felt a secret pleasure in doing my duty without reward. I also set a resolution of keeping no curate, and of being acquainted with every man in the parish,[2]

且說我們的家事.大約歸我的女人管.宗教的事.全歸我指揮.我的教職所入.每年有三十五鎊.拿去周濟我教職所管地面已故教士的孤兒寡婦.因為我自己的私財.尚稱足用.家人生產的事.我就不留心.我辦事不領薪俸.私心覺得快樂.我又決意不用人幫助.教區裏面的

---

1. Diocese, ｝教士所管地面 ｛此字所包地面廣.
2. Parish, ｝　　　　　　 ｛此字所包地面狹.

exhorting the married men to temperance, and the bachelors to matrimony; so that in a few years it was a common saying that there were three strange wants at Wakefield — a parson wanting pride, young men wanting wives, and alehouses wanting customers.

Matrimony was always one of my favorite topics, and I wrote several sermons to prove its happiness; but there was a peculiar tenet which I made a point of supporting, for I maintained with Whiston, that it was unlawful for a priest of the Church of England, after the death of his first wife, to take a second; or, to express it in one word, I valued myself upon being a strict monogamist.

I was early initiated[1] into this important dispute, on which so many laborious[2] volumes have been written. I published some tracts upon the subject myself, which, as they never sold,

人. 我沒一個不認識. 勸娶過親的人不要多吃酒. 勸未娶妻的人娶親. 過了幾年. 大家都說維克斐鄉有可怪的三無一. 牧師無驕傲氣. 二. 少年人無不娶親. 三. 酒店無主顧.

嫁娶的事. 是我最喜歡談的話柄. 我寫過好幾首宣講文證明嫁娶的歡樂. 其中有一層主義. 是我最用心維持的. 就是韋先生所主持的道理. 說是奉英國宗教的教士. 凡有斷弦的. 不應再娶. 若是再娶. 就是違律. 一言以蔽之. 我很自重. 我自己是一個篤守一夫一妻主義的人.

這一層道理. 已經有人費了許多精神. 寫過許多本書. 我很早就有人指教我這個易遭反對的問題. 我自己也曾印行幾篇我的拙作. 可惜一本也賣不出去. 我

---

1. Initiated, 發起；指導；指教.　2. Laborious, 費事；吃力.

I have the consolation of thinking were read only by the happy *few*. Some of my friends called this my weak side; but alas! they had not like me made it a subject of long contemplation. The more I reflected upon it, the more important it appeared; I even went a step beyond Whiston in displaying my principles; as he had engraven upon his wife's tomb that she was the *only* wife of William Whiston, so I wrote a similar epitaph for my wife, though still living, in which I extolled her prudence, economy, and obedience, till death, and having got it copied fair, with an elegant frame, it was placed over the chimney piece, where it answered several very useful purposes. It admonished my wife of her duty to me, and my fidelity to her; it inspired her with a passion for fame, and constantly put her in mind of her end.

It was thus, perhaps, from hearing marriage so often recommended, that my oldest son, just upon

只好說曲高和寡．自己安慰自己〔此種冷問題實寶一本實寶，自然是一本實寶以爲曲高和寡，出去反自以爲曲高和寡，見牧師於此種處顆自鳴得意，如此描寫可謂能用曲筆〕．有幾個朋友說．這是我的弱點．可惜他們對於這個問題．向來未曾試過．同我一樣的用過許多苦心．我越要緊想這個問題．越覺得〔這種問題也去用許多，又說越想越覺得要緊，寫得牧師迂腐有趣又是，原是牧師的弱點他反不認好笑〕．我表示我的主義．比韋先生更進一步．韋先生刻他太太的墓碑．說他是韋威廉的獨一太太．我的太太現在還活着．我替他預作同樣謹慎好看的墓碑．恭維他怎樣聽話．作配上省儉．至死都聽話．用恭楷寫好．好看的架子．擺在爐臺上．這樣布置．有幾樣用處．一來可以提醒我的太太對於我應盡應盡婦職信．二於他．應起留記名常常記得的．可使他發熱衷．常常記得〔替太預太〕．世的熱衷．一天總是要死的〔作墓誌更好笑〕．

大約因爲我常常勸人嫁娶．故此我的大兒子．一離開大學．就看中

leaving college, fixed his affections upon the daughter
of a neighboring clergyman,
who was a dignitary in the
Church, and in circum-
stances to give her a large
fortune, but fortune was
her smallest accomplish-
ment. Miss Arabella
Wilmot was allowed by all
(except my two daughters)
to be completely pretty.
Her youth, health and
innocence were still height-
ened by a complexion so
transparent, and such a
happy sensibility[1] of look,
as even age could not gaze
on with indifference. As
Mr. Wilmot knew that I
could make a very hand-
some settlement on my son,
he was not averse to the
match, so both families
lived together in all that
harmony which generally
precedes an expected
alliance. Being convinced
by experience that the days
of courtship are the most
happy of our lives, I was
willing enough to lengthen
the period; and the various
amusements which the

了 鄰 鄉 教 士 的 女 兒. 這
位 教 士. 名 位 頗 高. 可 以
給 他 的 女 兒 很 厚 的 妝
奩. 這 位 小 姐 不 獨 有 妝
奩. 而 且 人 人 都 說 他 長
得 全 美. 只 有 我 的 兩 個
女 兒 單 不 附 和 {輕輕寫 兩位小
姐忌他 人之美}. 這 位 小 姐. 正 在
妙 年. 身 體 壯 健. 智 識 純
正. 面 貌 不 獨 晶 瑩. 並 且
富 於 知 覺. 就 是 老 年 人
見 了 也 不 免 動 心. 這 位
教 士. 名 叫 威 勒 謨. 曉 得
我 力 量 可 以 分 豐 厚 的
家 產 給 我 的 大 兒 子. 却
也 不 反 對 我 們 兩 家 作
親. 故 此 兩 家 來 往 和 氣.
大 凡 兩 家 將 來 要 作 親
的 都 是 這 樣. 我 從 閱 歷
得 來. 曉 得 求 親 的 時 候.
是 男 女 最 樂 的 時 候. 我
很 願 把 求 親 的 日 子

---

1. Sensibility, 知覺.

young couple every day
shared in each other's company seemed to increase
their passion. We were
generally awaked in the
morning by music, and on
fine days rode a-hunting.
The hours between break-
fast and dinner the ladies
devoted to dress and study;
they usually read a page,
and then gazed at them-
selves in the glass, which
even philosophers might
own often presented the
page of greatest beauty.
At dinner my wife took the
lead, for as she always
insisted upon carrying
everything herself, it being
her mother's way, she gave
us upon these occasions the
history of every dish.
When we had dined, to
prevent the ladies leaving
us, I generally ordered the
table to be removed, and
sometimes, with the music
master's assistance, the
girls would give us a very
agreeable concert. Walk-
ing out, drinking tea,
country dances, and forfeits
shortened the rest of the
day, without the assistance
of cards, as I hated all
manner of gaming except

拖長. 這一對少年人.
每日互相陪伴. 同作
各種的消遣. 那相愛
之情自然是日見其深.
我們早上被音樂喚醒.
遇着好天. 出門打獵.
早餐與大餐之間. 女眷
們專打扮及讀書. 讀一
頁書就要照照鏡子
｛活描女孩／兒態度｝. 鏡子這件東
西. 那怕是哲學家也說
是最好看的一頁書
｛讚世上人無論男女／無不喜歡照鏡也｝. 吃大
餐的時候. 我的女人領
頭先行他作母親的擺
場. 一定要自己割肉分
菜. 他還要把每樣菜的
歷史對我們說一遍. 吃
完大餐我不願女眷們
就走. 我往往吩咐將餐
桌挪開有時請敎音樂
的先生幫忙. 兩個女兒
就同唱. 此後出門散步.
飲茶. 作鄉下跳舞. 處罰
遊戲. 這樣日子過得極
快. 不必靠賭錢助興. 因
我最恨各種賭博. 却有

backgammon, at which my old friend and I sometimes took a twopenny hit. Nor can I here pass over an ominous circumstance that happened the last time we played together; I only wanted to fling a quatre, and yet I threw deuce ace five times running.

Some months were e-lapsed in this manner, till at last it was thought con-venient to fix a day for the nuptials of the young couple, who seemed ear-nestly to desire it. During the preparations for the wedding, I need not describe the busy importance of my wife, nor the sly looks of my daughters; in fact, my attention was fixed on another object — the com-pleting a tract which I intended shortly to publish in defense of my favorite principle. As I looked upon this as a masterpiece, both for argument and style, I could not in the pride of my heart avoid showing it to my old friend Mr. Wilmot, as I made no doubt of receiving his approbation; but not till too late I discovered that

一件. 我同我的老友有時擲骰子. 只作兩個銅子的輸贏. 說起這件事. 我却不能忘了末後一次賭錢的預兆. 我心裏只要擲個四. 誰知一連擲么二擲了五次.

過了數月. 兩個少年人很想結婚. 遂預定日期. 當備辦一切的時候. 我的女人是忙的了不得. 我的兩個女兒臉上都是偷笑的神情. 這都不必細說. 那時我全副精神都注在另一件事上. 這事就是要作完一篇短論. 辯護我平生維持的主義. 這篇文章是我的傑作. 文境同議論都好. 我覺得很得意 {國語 中俗} 文章總是自己的好原來老牧師也犯此病} . 禁不住給我的親家威先生看. 我以為他一定以為然的. 誰知他非常的反對. 堅持異議. 等到我曉得了. 後悔已來不及了.

he was most violently attached to the contrary opinion, and with good reason, for he was at that time actually courting a fourth wife. This, as may be expected, produced a dispute attended with some acrimony, which threatened to interrupt our intended alliance, but on the day before that appointed for the ceremony, we agreed to discuss the subject at large.

It was managed with proper spirit on both sides: he asserted that I was heterodox — I retorted the charge; he replied, and I rejoined. In the meantime, while the controversy was hottest, I was called out by one of my relations, who, with a face of concern, advised me to give up the dispute—at least till my son's wedding was over. "How!" cried I; "relinquish the cause of truth, and let him be a husband, already driven to the very verge of absurdity! You might as well advise me to give up my fortune, as my argument."—"Your fortune," returned my

我的親家爲什麼反對呢.因爲這個時候.他正在忙的要娶第四次親作續絃.因爲我這篇文章.我們兩個人大擡其槓.兩個人頗鬧意見.幾乎阻礙兩家結婚的事.我們預定於吉期前一日.兩人再澈底討論這個問題.

到了那一天.我們兩個辯論.眞是旗鼓相當.他說我所持的是異端.我反駁他這話.他再駁過來.我再駁過去.我們兩人正在辯駁得最熱鬧的時候.有一個親戚把我喊出去.他滿面不快.勸我不要辯駁.就是一定要辯駁.不如等兒子結婚之後再駁.我就喊道.什麼呀.叫我不維持正理麼.他已經快做到毫無道理的地位了.還讓他第四次結婚麼.你勸我拋棄正理.倒不如

friend, "I am now sorry to inform you, is almost nothing. The merchant in town, in whose hands your money was lodged, has gone off, to avoid a statute of bankruptcy, and is thought not to have left a shilling in the pound. I was unwilling to shock you or the family with the account till after the wedding, but now it may serve to moderate your warmth in the argument, for I suppose your own prudence will enforce the necessity of dissembling, at least, till your son has the young lady's fortune secure."— "Well," returned I, "if what you tell me be true, and if I am to be a beggar, it shall never make me a rascal, nor induce me to disavow my principles. I'll go this moment, and inform the company of my circumstances, and as for the argument, I even here retract my former concessions in the old gentleman's favor; nor will I allow him now to be a husband in any sense of the expression."

勸我拋棄我的財產了（雖是寫老牧師之迂亦自任兼寫其以道義自任）那人說道．你說到財產．我的財產人就告訴你罷．你的財產幾乎全完了．倫敦商人替你存款的．規避破產律．已經逃走了．欠人的款二十分償不了一分．我原意非等到你兒子這事結婚之後．我不把我告訴你能少了產驚嚇你全家．現在我這爲不至結財再答訴你．你可以不必以你手．我的話熱鬧的辯駁．我不盤些假．變能能我爲自己打算的裝子．至於前讓了的．尤不也勉強等到兒子嫁到兩步了我次寫牧師之一生末稱感婚．把新娘的陪手於前步第四夫生之句爲穩穩當當的到了辯駁．我本人稱感同道．你的親家告訴我的話變能能我去辯的尤結牧師之一句爲是了倘若有其事子．倘若我也不義形人步．我次寫牧師之末稱感了變使個叫一化個光也主情兩讓了我第四夫本人稱感立告成我拋棄我把人．至從步了他本段先欲此稱感駁訴的話．我現在不讓讓爲人欲此稱直意段先我其的話現不能自稱偶強咄咄逼意直段先欲人稱感婚．還強自稱偶言姦也夫．

It would be endless to describe the different sensations of both families when I divulged the news of our misfortune; but what others felt was slight to what the lovers appeared to endure. Mr. Wilmot, who seemed before sufficiently inclined to break off the match, was by this blow soon determined; one virtue he had in perfection, which was prudence, too often the only one that is left us at seventy-two.

產的說可．受從意了麼了之其
破家也尤所生的打意完　年盤　人及
運兩這覺女先婚的主極算到什剩
倒後．同感少威拆次定件會年時　老算
的之不的男有一拿一是老的有　燕打
我有人少最很這就有們歲沒盤　寫好
把布各別個覺乎有單他德我二都算
我宣兩感似然婚美約十德打之然
我事盡兩感似因婚美然自拆的大七道會老在　戒得誠然
的感盡這的前思．自拆的大七道會

CHAPTER III

A MIGRATION — THE FORTUNATE CIRCUMSTANCES OF OUR LIVES ARE GENERALLY FOUND AT LAST TO BE OF OUR OWN PROCURING.

第 三 回

移 居　幸 福 原 是 自 召
（白 且 爾 客 店 遇 牧 師）

The only hope of our family now was that the report of misfortune might be malicious[1] or premature; but a letter from my agent in town soon came with a confirmation of every particular. The loss of fortune to myself alone would have been trifling; the only uneasiness I felt was for my family, who were to be humble without an education to render them callous[2] to contempt.

Near a fortnight had passed before I attempted to restrain their affliction, for premature consolation is but the remembrancer of

且說這時候我們一家人只盼望那朋友來報告我們不幸的事是存壞意造謠言．或者是還沒有到時候．誰知我們倫敦的經手辦事人來信．說明詳細情形．證實那報告是確實的．我個人對於破財．原算不了什麼大事．但是我很替家裏的人難過因爲他們見理不透．不能使他們對於世人欺侮貧窮的態度不受感覺．

若是安慰他們太早．反使他們更忘不了他們的憂愁．故此我等到

---

1. Malicious, 存 壞 心; 意 存 陷 害.　2. Callous, 無 知 覺.

sorrow. During this interval, my thoughts were employed on some future means of supporting them, and at last a small cure of fifteen pounds a year was offered me in a distant neighborhood, where I could still enjoy my principles without molestation. With this proposal I joyfully closed, having determined to increase my salary by managing a little farm.

Having taken this resolution, my next care was to get together the wrecks of my fortune; and all debts collected and paid, out of fourteen thousand pounds, we had but four hundred remaining. My chief attention therefore was now to bring down the pride of my family to their circumstances, for I well knew that aspiring[1] beggary is wretchedness itself. "You cannot be ignorant, my children," cried I, "that no prudence of ours could have prevented our late misfortune, but prudence

差不多過了兩星期之後.才想法節制他們的痛苦.這個當口.我用心想將來怎麼樣養家的法子.到後來離我們頗遠的地方.有人商量請我當一個小教職.每年薪俸有十五鎊.我在那個地方.還可以享受我所持的主義.沒得人來騷擾我.我很歡喜的答應了.我同時立定主意作農家事業加些進款.

打定了主意之後.第二件的事體.就是收束破產後的餘財.把一切人欠欠人的債務.清結之後.我原有的一萬四千鎊.只剩了四百鎊.於是我第一件留意的事.就是把我家裏人擺慣的架子拖下來.使他們同現在的光景相稱.因爲我曉得叫化子擺闊架子.是最難受的事.我就對兒女們說道.

---

1. Aspiring, 發大口氣; 有大志; 想闊; 想擺大架子.

may do much in disappointing its effects. We are now poor, my fondlings, and wisdom bids us to conform to our humble situation. Let us then, without repining, give up those splendors with which numbers are wretched, and seek in humbler circumstances[1] that peace with which all may be happy. The poor live pleasantly without our help, why then should not we learn to live without theirs? No, my children, let us from this moment give up all pretensions to gentility; we have still enough left for happiness if we are wise, and let us draw upon content for the deficiencies of fortune."

As my eldest son was bred a scholar, I determined to send him to town, where his abilities might contribute to our support and his own. The separation of friends and families is, perhaps, one of the most distressful circumstances attendant on penury. The day soon arrived on which

新們也事破許們是該該多,不裏得不快不女派要的樂雖知多個他可家.的分人

我們怕謹慎我們.那受我們若應應還了.境求用過麼兒關只下快產是許原意本助幫難朋於第一次家裏

曉得.那十分是好算自貝了.我們乎上場窮可窮也為我後開法.們的我們補我以

該破怎樣的.盤苦的寶窮的行界排在原心幫我們呢.以丟得我們富可.

應幸先不了.若是的困我在知識賤世把悔人人得我日學呀一們財日不那就乏.

你們近當防後產多.現有素曉我要頭個着樂能們頭我餘的然足缺乏.

我的大兒子主定他靠並窮過我們第一次

學者.我打倫敦.自顧個人無往以一是離.

---

1. Circumstances, 環境.

we were to disperse for the first time. My son, after taking leave of his mother and the rest, who mingled their tears with their kisses, came to ask a blessing from me. This I gave him from my heart, and which, added to five guineas, was all the patrimony I had now to bestow. "You are going, my boy," cried I, "to London no foot, in the manner Hooker, your great ancestor, traveled there before you. Take from me the same horse that was given him by the good Bishop Jewel, this staff, and take this book too, it will be your comfort on the way; these two lines in it are worth a million: *I have been young, and now am old; yet never saw I the righteous man forsaken, or his seed begging their bread.* Let this be your consolation as you travel on. Go, my boy; whatever be thy fortune, let me see thee once a year; still, keep a good heart, and farewell." As he was possessed of integrity and honor, I was under no apprehensions from throwing him

分離的日子到了．我的兒子．同他母親姊弟們辭別．他們又哭．又同他接吻．他走來求我保佑．我很高興的保佑他．不過我的保佑．和五個金錢．就是我現在力量所能嗀分給他的家產．我對他說道．我的兒子呀．你步行至倫敦．從前你的闊遠祖．也是這樣步行．某主教曾贈他一匹馬．我今日也給你一匹．這條手杖你拿去〈贈他一匹馬給你一匹馬都是指一條手杖當作馬並非眞馬也〉．這本書你也拿去．你在路上看看這書．也可以安慰安慰．書裏頭有兩句話值得一百萬塊錢．這兩句話說道．我從前年少．現在老了．我却未見過正派人爲天所棄．也未見過正派人的兒女作叫化子．你旅行的時候．就可以拿這兩句話安慰自己．兒子呀．你去罷．無論你的遭遇怎樣．讓我一年見你一次．不要灰心．你去罷．他爲人誠實．顧體面．他雖然一點披掛也沒有．我就

naked into the amphi-
theater of life; for I knew
he would act a good part,
whether vanquished or
victorious.

His departure only pre-
pared the way for our own,
which arrived a few days
afterwards. The leaving a
neighborhood in which we
had enjoyed so many hours
of tranquillity, was not
without a tear which
scarce fortitude itself
could suppress. Besides, a
journey of seventy miles to
a family that had hitherto
never been above ten from
home, filled us with ap-
prehension, and the cries of
the poor, who followed us
for some miles, contributed
to increase it. The first
day's journey brought us
in safety within thirty miles
of our future retreat, and
we put up for the night at
an obscure inn in a village
by the way. When we
were shown a room, I
desired the landlord, in my
usual way, to let us have
his company, with which
he complied, as what he
drank would increase the
bill next morning. He
knew, however, the whole

叫他登世界的戲場.我
卻很放心.我却曉得.無
論他或勝或敗.必能唱
好戲.

我大兒子去後.過了
幾天.就是我們走.我們
住在這個地方.過了許
多安樂日子.現在要辭
別.遷居別處.無論怎麼
樣.也捨不得.禁不住灑
淚而別.況且我們有的
出外.至多也不過離家
二三十里.現在遷居.要
走二百餘里.心裏總覺
得有些不放心.鄰居的
貧人.依依不捨.遠送多
少里.都不肯回去.更叫
我們心裏難過.第一天
走的路.離所居還有百
里.當晚在小店住宿.店
主人把我們領到一間
房.我請店主人同我們
一桌吃飯.這是我向來
的習慣.店主人自然是
願意的.因為他所吃所
喝的.都算在我帳上.我
們的新居鄰近.店主全

neighborhood to which I was removing, particularly Squire Thornhill, who was to be my landlord, and who lived within a few miles of the place. This gentleman he described as one who desired to know little more of the world than its pleasures, being particularly remarkable for his attachment to the fair sex. He observed that no virtue was able to resist his arts and assiduity, and that scarce a farmer's daughter within ten miles round but what had found him successful and faithless. Though this account gave me some pain, it had a very different effect upon my daughters, whose features seemed to brighten with the expectation of an approaching triumph; nor was my wife less pleased and confident of their allurements and virtue. While our thoughts were thus employed, the hostess entered the room, to inform her husband that the strange gentleman, who had been two days in the house, wanted money, and could not satisfy them for

曉得.那裏有位鄉紳.名叫唐希爾.就是我們的房東.店主人更曉得清楚.他住的大宅.離我的新居.不過十餘里.他說這位鄉紳.除了尋樂之外.不大留意世事.平生最喜歡親近婦女.我聽了.心裏有些難過.我兩個女兒聽了.臉上很高興.以為很有使這位鄉紳一見便傾倒的希望.我的女人也很高興.相信兩個女兒的品貌.確有這種的希望.我們正在各人心裏想這件事的時候.店主婆進來.告訴他的男人說.住在店裏有兩天的一位異鄉客人.不能給房錢.店主

his reckoning. "Want money!" replied the host, "that must be impossible: for it was no later than yesterday he paid three guineas to our beadle to spare an old broken soldier that was to be whipped through the town for dog stealing." The hostess, however, still persisting in her first assertion, he was preparing to leave the room, swearing that he would be satisfied one way or another, when I begged the landlord would introduce me to a stranger of so much charity as he described. With this he complied, showing in a gentleman who seemed to be about thirty, dressed in clothes that once were laced. His person was well-formed, and his face marked with the lines of thinking. He had something short and dry in his address, and seemed not to understand ceremony, or to despise it. Upon the landlord's leaving the room, I could not avoid expressing my concern to the stranger at seeing a gentleman in such circumstances,

人說道.怎麼沒得錢.這不能彀.他昨天看見一個殘廢老兵偷狗.被人捉了.要遊街.鞭打示衆.他心裏不忍 就拿出三個金鎊交給地保{借用}.把那兵放了.為什麼沒得錢還帳.那店主婆還說.這客人是沒得錢.店主人正要走出去.還說.無論怎麼樣.一定要客人還帳.我就說.這個客人疎財仗義.請介紹我們相見.店主人把客人領了來.原來是三十上下年紀.穿的舊衣裳.身材甚好.臉上露出是個好用心的人.說話甚單簡乾脆.似乎不大懂得俗套禮節.也許是他看不起虛文.店主人走出去.我禁不住對這客人說.一位斯文人.為環境

and offered him my purse to satisfy the present demand. "I take it with all my heart, sir," replied he; "and am glad that a late oversight in giving what money I had about me, has shown me that there are still some men like you. I must, however, previously entreat being informed of the name and residence of my benefactor, in order to repay him as soon as possible." In this I satisfied him fully, not only mentioning my name and late misfortunes, but the place to which I was going to remove. "This," cried he, "happens still more luckily than I hoped for, as I am going the same way myself, having been detained here two days by the floods, which I hope by to-morrow will be found passable." I testified the pleasure I should have in his company, and, my wife and daughters joining in entreaty, he was prevailed upon to stay supper. The stranger's conversation, which was at once pleasing and instructive, induced me to wish for a continuance

所迫.不能還帳.我聽見難過.請他不必客氣.我可以代還.他答道.我很謝你幫助.我一時不小心.把錢用完.却想不到世界上.還有你這樣的人.我心裏歡喜.但是我先要請教你尊姓大名.寓居何處.我將來可以如數奉還.我才可以受你的幫助.我逐一的詳告他.把我如何不幸.新近破產.及現在正遷居某處的話.都告訴他.他說道.這更巧了.我也是往某處去.我們同路.我因爲被水潦所阻.停留這裏兩天.大約明天水退.可以去咧.我告訴他.我極喜歡與他同路走.我的女人女兒同我.都勸他同我們吃晚飯.這位異鄉人的談吐.令人聽了.歡喜而且受益.我很想接連暢談.但爲時

of it; but it was now high
time to retire and take
refreshment against the fatigues of the following day.

The next morning we all
set forward together; my
family on horseback, while
Mr. Burchell, our new companion, walked along the
footpath by the roadside,
observing, with a smile,
that, as we were ill-mount-
ed, he would be too generous to attempt leaving us
behind. As the floods were
not yet subsided, we were
obliged to hire a guide,
who trotted on before, Mr.
Burchell and I bringing up
the rear. We lightened the
fatigues of the road with
philosophical disputes,
which he seemed to under-
stand perfectly. But what
surprised me most was,
that though he was a
money borrower, he de-
fended his opinion with as
much obstinacy as if he
had been my patron. He
now and then also informed
me to whom the different
seats belonged that lay in
our view as we traveled the
road. "That," cried he,
pointing to a very magnificent house which stood at

已晚.吃點東西之後.都
去歇宿.以便明天走路.
　第二天早上.我們一
齊起行.我的眷屬騎馬.
我們的新交名叫白且
爾.在路邊步行.他微笑
的說.我們的牲口走的
慢.他不便快走.丟我們
落後.因爲大水還沒有
退.我們不能不雇一個領
路的.他自然在前走.我
同白且爾押後.我們兩
個人.因爲減少行路勞
頓.一面走一面辯論哲
學{老牧師總是好辯}.他對於哲
學.很曉得完全.我覺得
最奇怪的是他雖然是
欠我錢的人.到了力辯
他自己的主義時候.他
好像是我的債主{此寫白且爾亦是偏強}.當我們在路上
走的時候.他有時指給
我看.這是某人的產業.
有一次他指着遠遠的

some distance, "belongs to Mr. Thornhill, a young gentleman who enjoys a large fortune, though entirely dependent on the will of his uncle, Sir William Thornhill, a gentleman, who, content with a little himself, permits his nephew to enjoy the rest, and chiefly resides in town."—"What!" cried I, "is my young landlord then the nephew of a man whose virtues, generosity, and singularities,[1] are so universally known? I have heard Sir William Thornhill represented as one of the most generous, yet whimsical,[2] men in the kingdom; a man of consummate[3] benevolence."—"Something, perhaps, too much so," replied Mr. Burchell; "at least, he carried benevolence to an excess when young; for his passions were then strong, and as they were all upon the side of virtue, they led it up to a romantic[4] extreme. He early began to aim at the

一座大宅.說道.這是唐希爾的.他是個少年.享有很大的財產.却是全憑他叔叔的遺囑分派.他的叔叔就是威廉唐希爾爵士 ｛此兩節介紹唐威廉白且爾希爾．｝廉唐希爾爵士是書中要人全書線索布局皆從此兩節發端讀者宜留意．這個人自己却不花錢.剩下的讓他姪子去花.自己住在倫敦.

我聽了.說道.原來我的房東.就是爵士的姪子麼.這個爵士.人人都曉得是有道德.疏財仗義.有些古怪脾氣.我聽說.這位爵士是國內最疏財仗義而有怪癖的人.這個人絕頂的喜歡行善.

白且爾答道.太過疏財仗義了.他少年的時候.未免行善太過些.後來稍好.那時候他是個很有血性的人.好在都是偏於道德一方面他爲血氣所用.走到意想所到的極端.他早年就立意做一個出色的武官

---

1. Singularity, 獨一無二; 非常; 反常; 奇特. 2. Whimsical, 有無故發生之思想或舉動; 有突如其來之異想; 有怪癖. 3. Consummate, 絕頂. 4. Romantic, 意造; 全憑意想; 不適用.

qualifications of the soldier and scholar; was soon distinguished[1] in the army, and had some reputation among men of learning. Adulation ever follows the ambitious:[2] for such alone receive most pleasure from flattery. He was surrounded with crowds, who showed him only one side of their character; so that he began to lose a regard for private interest in universal sympathy. He loved all mankind; for fortune prevented him from knowing that there were rascals. Physicians tell us of a disorder in which the whole body is so exquisitely sensible,[3] that the slightest touch gives pain; what some have thus suffered in their persons, this gentleman felt in his mind. The slightest distress, whether real or fictitious, touched him to the quick, and his soul labored under a sickly sensibility of the miseries of others. Thus disposed

和出色的文士。不久居然在陸軍中就很出類拔萃。在學問界中。亦頗有名。大凡一個好出色的人。自然就有許多人恭維他。這種人惟有受恭維巴結才快活。左右前後有許多人包圍他。這班人自然是只讓他看見他們的一方面。於是因博愛就不及想到自己的私利。他以爲世界上的人都是好的。這也有個道理。因爲他富有貲財。不讓他曉得世界上原有許多騙子。醫生們說。有一種病。通身的知覺。變作異常的靈醒。只要一摸。便覺得痛。別人犯的。不過是皮膚知覺過於靈醒。這位爵士犯的。却是良心的知覺異常靈醒。見了人家的困苦。無論是眞的或是假裝的。一見就動心。覺得非常之難過。同得了病差不多。他旣然這

---

1. Distinguished, 出類拔萃. 2. Ambitious, 好出色；有大志. 3. Sensible, 善知覺；有知識；sensitive, 易感動；兩字大有分別，作者却用顛倒了，此章 sensible. sensibility 應改作 sensitive, sensitiveness.

to relieve, it will be easily conjectured, he found numbers disposed to solicit; his profusions[1] began to impair his fortune, but not his good-nature; that, indeed, was seen to increase as the other seemed to decay—he grew improvident[2] as he grew poor: and though he talked like a man of sense, his actions were those of a fool. Still, however, being surrounded with importunity, and no longer able to satisfy every request that was made him, instead of *money* he gave *promises*. They were all he had to bestow, and he had not resolution enough to give any man pain by a denial. By this he drew round him crowds of dependents, whom he was sure to disappoint, yet wished to relieve. These hung upon him for a time, and left him with merited reproaches and contempt. But, in proportion as he became contemptible to others, he became despicable to himself. His mind

樣存心好周濟. 自然就有許多人求他周濟. 於是胡亂花錢. 不久他的家產. 就日見其損. 但是他好善的心. 却不少減. 他的財產. 雖然日見其消. 他的好善的心. 反日見其長. 等到他窮了. 還是不打算. 你聽他說話. 是個明白人. 你看他作事. 却是糊塗人. 到了這個地步. 他還是不改. 不過求他的人還有許多. 這時候他無錢給人. 只好口頭的答應. 他只剩了這口頭答應的虛惠給人. 又不能拿定主意不答應人. 恐怕求他的人難過. 故此對於許多包圍他倚靠他的人. 他心裏很想援助他們. 却是有心無力. 總是令他們大失所望. 這班人跟隨他幾時. 後來散了. 却無一個不罵他看他不起的. 人家旣然看不起他. 他慢慢的也就看不起自己. 他從前原靠

---

1. Profusion, 亂花錢. 2. Improvident, 不打算；不防備.

THE VICAR OF WAKEFIELD 31

had leaned upon their adulation, and, that support being taken away, he could find no pleasure in the applause of his heart, which he had never learned to reverence. The world now began to wear a different aspect; the flattery of his friends began to dwindle into simple approbation. Approbation soon took the more friendly form of advice, and advice when rejected produced their reproaches. He now therefore found that such friends as benefits had gathered round him, were little estimable; he now found that a man's own heart must be ever given to gain that of another. I now found, that—that—I forget what I was going to observe; in short, sir, he resolved to respect himself, and laid down a plan of restoring his falling fortune. For this purpose, in his own whimsical manner, he traveled through Europe on foot; and now, though he has scarce attained the age of thirty, his circumstances are more affluent than ever. At present, his

人家恭維.後來無人恭維他.他的心向來以爲善爲樂.他旣無力爲善.心裏自然是失了樂境.這是由於他向來不曉得尊敬他的熱心的緣故.由此他世情就大變了.從前人家恭維他.後來慢慢人家不恭維他.對他不過是唯唯是是的.再後來人家要敎訓他.敎訓他.他不聽人家就埋怨他.他這才曉得以利合的朋友是無甚價值的.才曉得交朋友是要拿肝膽換肝膽的.我才曉得 { 自己閱歷這故綻 且說這一個 爾原是自字驚出破口更正 我字快快改 } .我忘了我說什麼.總而言之.他這時候就拿定主意.作自愛的工夫.想出計策來恢復他的破落財產.因爲這樣.因要順着他自己的怪脾氣走.徒步旅行歐洲.他現在雖然尚未到三十歲.他的景況.比從前好得多.現在他還是周濟人.但

bounties are more rational and moderate than before; but still he preserves the character of a humorist, and finds most pleasure in eccentric virtues."

My attention was so much taken up by Mr. Burchell's account, that I scarce looked forward as we went along, till we were alarmed by the cries of my family, when turning, I perceived my youngest daughter in the midst of a rapid stream, thrown from her horse, and struggling with the torrent. She had sunk twice, nor was it in my power to disengage myself in time to bring her relief. My sensations were even too violent to permit my attempting her rescue; she must have certainly perished had not my companion, perceiving her danger, instantly plunged in to her relief, and, with some difficulty, brought her in safety to the opposite shore. By taking the current a little farther up, the rest of the family got safely over; where we had an opportunity of joining our acknowledgments to hers.

是方法比從前有分寸. 所花的錢. 比從前較少. 但是他詼諧玩世的品格. 還是保存不改. 總是喜歡不合中道的美德〔白且爾所說的一篇話亦是作者自寫其品格及閱歷〕.

我全副精神聽白且爾說話. 一路走來. 却未曾往前頭看. 忽然我們聽見女眷們叫喊一聲. 往前一看. 才看見我的小女兒丟下馬來. 落在急流中間. 抵抗那急溜. 淹沒兩次. 我來不及去救他. 心裏非常着急. 也無法救他. 白且爾立刻跳入水裏. 費了些氣力. 才把我女兒救出來. 放在對岸. 我們遶了些路. 平安的都到了對岸. 我們和我的女兒. 借這機會. 謝那白先生. 我的女兒謝那救他的人. 易於意

Her gratitude may be more readily imagined than described: she thanked her deliverer more with looks than words, and continued to lean upon his arm, as if still willing to receive assistance. My wife also hoped one day to have the pleasure of returning his kindness at her own house. Thus, after we were refreshed at the next inn, and had dined together, as Mr. Burchell was going to a different part of the country, he took leave, and we pursued our journey; my wife observing as he went, that she liked him extremely, and protesting that if he had birth and fortune to entitle him to match into such a family as ours, she knew no man she would sooner fix upon. I could not but smile to hear her talk in this lofty strain; one almost at the verge of beggary thus to assume the language of the most insulting affluence might excite the ridicule of ill nature; but I was never much displeased with those harmless delusions that tend to make us more happy.

話少。他謝意深而難於言傳。他還是靠在他手上。好像是還要他援助的意思。我的女人也說。擇一天。請他到我們家裏。報答他拯救之恩。於是到了最近的客店歇息。吃了飯。白且爾與我們不同路。與我們分手。走他的。我們走我們的。我們在路上。我的女人對我說。他很喜歡這位白先生。又很認真的說。假使這位先生是個富貴人。配同我們這樣的家結親。他一定趕快的挑選白先生作女壻〔牧師爲先生，以自白口氣好大，仍看不起，盡看不起白先生，太貴人，太富，意在言外。〕。我聽他這樣的大口氣。禁不住微笑。一個人轉眼就快要討飯〔中國俗語所謂隔壁窮也。〕。還要說這種自居富貴欺侮貧賤人的話〔白難明，有以人欺人，自欺欺人，太甚，令人不能不高興。〕。若是欠涵養的聽見。是自然要恥笑的。但是這種無害的糊塗見解。能令人快樂些〔涉世往往以糊塗得之，世往往亦不難，言之古人所以樂此。〕。

CHAPTER IV

A PROOF THAT EVEN THE HUMBLEST FORTUNE MAY GRANT
HAPPINESS, WHICH DEPENDS NOT ON CIRCUMSTANCES,
BUT CONSTITUTION.

第 四 回

貧 賤 亦 可 以 快 樂 快 樂 視 心 境 不 視 環 境
(老 牧 師 苦 口 戒 浮 華)

The place of our retreat was in a little neighborhood, consisting of farmers, who tilled their own grounds, and were equal strangers to opulence and poverty. As they had almost all the conveniences of life[1] within themselves, they seldom visited towns or cities in search of superfluity.[2] Remote from the polite, they still retained the primeval[3] simplicity of manners; and frugal by habit, they scarce knew that temperance was a virtue. They wrought with cheerfulness on days of

且 說 我 們 退 隱 的 地
方. 隣 近 都 是 自 食 其 力
的 種 田 人 家. 不 曉 得 什
麼 叫 作 富. 什 麼 叫 作 貧.
因 為 他 們 人 生 日 用 所
必 需 的. 自 己 都 有. 不 必
仰 給 於 外. 他 們 很 少 的
入 城. 找 那 些 多 餘 不 等
用 的 東 西. 離 那 些 富 貴
好 繁 文 的 人 家 很 遠. 他
們 還 保 存 太 古 時 樸 素 的
風 氣. 習 慣 省 儉. 不 曉 得
不 奢 不 侈. 凡 事 適 中. 是
個 美 德. 遇 工 作 的 日 子.
他 們 高 高 興 興 的 作 工.

---

1. Conveniences of life, 人生所必需.　2. Superfluity, 多餘之物.
3. Primeval, 太古時代的.

labor, but observed festivals as intervals of idleness and pleasure. They kept up the Christmas carol, sent true love knots on Valentine morning, ate pancakes on Shrovetide, showed their wit on the first of April, and religiously cracked nuts or Michaelmas Eve.[1] Being apprised[2] of our approach, the whole neighborhood came out to meet their minister, dressed in their finest clothes, and preceded by a pipe and tabor. A feast also was provided for our reception, at which we sat cheerfully down, and what the conversation wanted in wit was made up in laughter.

Our little habitation was situated at the foot of a sloping hill, sheltered with a beautiful underwood behind, and a prattling river before; on one side a meadow, on the other a green. My farm consisted of about twenty acres of excellent land, having given a

遇着佳節．就作爲休息尋樂的日子．耶穌聖誕節是要舉行的．二月十四日是要送同心結｛借用｝的．懺悔日是要吃煎餅的．四月一號是要耍點小聰明的．九月廿九｛或云是十月末日｝是要燒果子仁的．這條村裏的人．聽見我們到．都穿新衣裳．吹笛子．打小鼓．走來接新牧師．還預備了飲食款待．我們很高興的坐下來．大眾談話．雖然聽不見俏皮話．卻聽見好幾次大笑｛寫鄉下人淳樸鳳氣令人神往｝歐美久已不見矣東方則尚有之｝．

我們小宅坐落一個山坡脚下．宅後是佳樹．宅前是潺潺如語的河流．一邊是牧場．一邊是草地．原有良田約二十畝．我花了一百鎊．同前

---

1. Michaelmas Eve, 或云此節在九月念九，或云在十月末日，是日燒果子仁以卜婚事之成否． 2. Apprised, 告知．

hundred pounds for my predecessor's goodwill. Nothing could exceed the neatness of my little inclosures, the elms and hedgerows appearing with inexpressible beauty. My house consisted of but one story, and was covered with thatch, which gave it an air of great snugness; the walls on the inside were nicely whitewashed, and my daughters undertook to adorn them with pictures of their own designing. Though the same room served us for parlor and kitchen, that only made it the warmer. Besides, as it was kept with the utmost neatness, the dishes, plates, and coppers being well scoured, and all disposed in bright rows on the shelves, the eye was agreeably relieved, and did not want richer furniture. There were three other apartments, one for my wife and me, another for our two daughters, within our own, and the third, with two beds, for the rest of the children.

任盤過來．那裏也比不上我這個小田園的清雅．還有高榆小樹．說不出無限的美觀．這住宅有樓一層．蓋的是草頂．是很舒服的住宅．房裏的牆．都刷過白粉．我的兩個女兒．擔任自己出意作畫．裝飾粉牆．有一間房子作廚房．兼作客廳．雖略有不便．然而暖些．況且收拾得很乾淨．所有盃盤碟子銅鍋無不好好的磨洗過．一排排擺在櫥上．眼見了也並不討厭．我們也就可以不用富麗家具了．另外還有三間房．我夫婦住一間．內裏一間套房．住我兩個女兒．其餘一間．擺兩個鋪．住孩子們

The little republic[1] to which I gave laws was regulated in the following manner—by sunrise we all assembled in our common apartment, the fire being previously kindled by the servant. After we had saluted each other with proper ceremony — for I always thought fit to keep up some mechanical[2] forms of good breeding, without which freedom ever destroys friendship—we all bent in gratitude to that Being who gave us another day. This duty being performed, my son and I went to pursue our usual industry abroad, while my wife and daughters employed themselves in providing breakfast, which was always ready at a certain time. I allowed half an hour for this meal, and an hour for dinner; which time was taken up in innocent mirth between my wife and daughters, and in philosophical arguments between my son and me.

歸我執行法律的這個小共和國．是這樣治理．太陽出來．我們齊集客廳．由僕人生好火．我們彼此相見行合宜禮節．我以爲這種俗禮．雖嫌太板．是必要保存實行的．太過隨便自由．恐傷情誼．見過禮之後．就祈禱．謝上帝饒我們多活一日．禱謝完了．我同兒子到外面作事．我的女人同女兒預備早飯．到了一定時候．是要預備好的．吃早飯限半點鐘．大餐限一點鐘．這一點鐘裏頭．女人同女兒尋無害的快樂．我同兒子辯論哲學{老牧師有}{好辯辯}．

---

1. Republic, 共和國 (此處指家庭). 2. Mechanical, 呆板.

As we rose with the sun, so we never pursued our labors after it was gone down, but returned home to the expecting family; where smiling looks, a neat hearth, and pleasant fire, were prepared for our reception. Nor were we without guests; sometimes farmer Flamborough, our talkative neighbor, and often the blind piper, would pay us a visit, and taste our gooseberry wine; for the making of which we had lost neither the receipt nor the reputation. These harmless people had several ways of being good company; while one played, the other would sing some soothing ballad, Johnny Armstrong's Last Good Night, or The Cruelty of Barbara Allen. The night was concluded[1] in the manner we began the morning, my youngest boys being appointed to read the lessons of the day, and he that read the loudest, distinctest, and best, was to have a halfpenny on

我們既然是日出就起來.到了日入之後.向不操作.我們回家.免家人盼望.一入家門.就有笑臉和整齊雅潔的家庭.還有令人起興的小火歡迎我們.偶然也有客人來訪.有時是種地的最多話的法林巴.來得次數多些的是一個吹笛子的瞎子.嘗嘗我們的家釀果子酒.釀酒的法子.也還未曾忘記.這家釀的名譽.也還保全.這幾位良善人也有幾樣長處.可以作良伴.這一個奏樂.那一個唱歌.唱的歌名是末一夜.或是阿蘭之苛虐.晚上睡前是同早上起後一樣的.該派是小兒子們讀聖經.那一個讀得最響最清楚最好聽的.我給他一個小銅錢.到了

---

1. Concluded, 結束.

Sunday to put in the poor's box.

When Sunday came, it was indeed a day of finery, which all my sumptuary edicts[1] could not restrain. How well soever I fancied my lectures against pride had conquered the vanity of my daughters; yet I still found them secretly attached to all their former finery: they still loved laces, ribands, bugles, and catgut; my wife herself retained a passion for her crimson paduasoy, because I formerly happened to say it became her.

The first Sunday, in particular, their behavior served to mortify me; I had desired my girls the preceding night to be dressed early the next day; for I always loved to be at church a good while before the rest of the congregation. They punctually obeyed my directions; but when we were to assemble in the morning at breakfast, down

星期那一天.把這個小銅錢.放在濟貧櫃內.

到了星期日.是我家裏女眷們出風頭的日子.無論我頒行什麼禁止奢華的諭旨.也禁不了.我妄想以為我對兩個女兒宣講反對繁華的道理.已經把他們好穿好戴好虛榮的思想打倒了.誰知他們還是喜歡花邊線帶繡貨的女人.從前穿過大紅緞子衣服.我偶然曾說過好看.誰知他現在還是非常喜歡穿大紅緞子.

到了這裏第一個星期.他們的行為.幾乎把我氣死.我早一天晚上就吩咐我的女兒.叫他們明天一早就要打扮好.因為我向來喜歡比衆人先到教堂.他們很聽我的話.很按時候.到了早上聚會吃早飯的

---

1. Sumptuary edicts, 古時羅馬帝, 後來大查理帝, 英王愛都華第三, 皆訾定律, 禁止飲食衣服奢侈, 英國此律, 至一八五六年始廢.

came my wife and daughters, dressed out in all their former splendor: their hair plastered up with pomatum, their faces patched to taste, their trains bundled up in a heap behind, and rustling at every motion. I could not help smiling at their vanity, particularly that of my wife, from whom I expected more discretion. In this exigence, therefore, my only resource was to order my son, with an important air, to call our coach. The girls were amazed at the command; but I repeated it with more solemnity than before.—"Surely, my dear, you jest," cried my wife; "we can walk it perfectly well: we want no coach to carry us now."— "You mistake, child," returned I; "we do want a coach; for if we walk to church in this trim, the very children in the parish will hoot after us."—"Indeed," replied my wife; "I always imagined that my Charles was fond of seeing his children neat and handsome about him."—"You

時候.我的女人.帶着兩個女兒下來.打扮得同從前我們未破產的時候一樣.頭髮是搽滿油脂.臉上照着最時路的樣子.粘的黑紬.長裙摺起一個大包.堆在背後.走路都聽見響.我看見他們這樣好打扮.不免微笑.我原盼望我的女人有些分寸.誰知也是一樣的好打扮.更覺得好笑.我到了這個緊急當口.無他法可想.只好露出很頂眞的樣子.命我的兒子套家裏的大車.女兒聽見我這樣吩咐.大驚.我再把我吩咐兒子的話.更頂眞的再說一遍.我的女人對我說道.你別開玩笑了.我們很可以步行那點兒路.我們不要大車載我們去.我答道.你錯了.我們一定要大車.假使我們這樣打扮步行到教堂.這鄉裏的孩子們看見我們.必定要跟在後頭.喝倒釆的.我的女人答道.我向來以爲你喜歡看見兒女們穿得

may be as neat as you please," interrupted I, "and I shall love you the better for it; but all this is not neatness, but frippery. These ruffings, and pinkings, and patchings, will only make us hated by all the wives of our neighbors. No, my children," continued I, more gravely, "those gowns may be altered into something of a plainer cut; for finery is very unbecoming in us, who want the means of decency. I do not know whether such flouncing and shredding is becoming even in the rich, if we consider, upon a moderate calculation, that the nakedness of the indigent world may be clothed from the trimmings of the vain."

This remonstrance had the proper effect; they went with great composure, that very instant, to change their dress; and the next day I had the satisfaction of finding my daughters, at their own request, employed in cutting up their trains into Sunday waistcoats for Dick and Bill, the

清楚好看.我攔住道.你喜歡怎麼清楚.就打扮到怎麼清楚.我看見更愛你.但是你們現在的打扮.不叫清楚.叫作拖掦.這些堆疊和尖角.緣邊.貼臉.反令鄉下女人恨我們.我更嚴厲的說道.這些衣裳.可以改清雅些.我們現在要過個稍為像樣的日子.還作不到.反去打扮得這樣華麗.是很不對的.我們畧爲算算看.世上奢華人家衣服的欄杆緣邊.足彀衣被天下無衣無褐的人.那怕就是有錢人家.也不應該穿這裏拖一條那裏拖一塊的華麗衣服.

我這一番責難的話.却有效果.他們立刻很安靜的走去換衣服.第二天.我很滿意的看見女兒們自己要把長裙剪短了.把剪下來的料子替我兩個小兒子.一個叫狄克.一個叫比勒.

two little ones, and, what
was still more satisfactory,
the gowns seemed im-
proved by this curtailing.

作星期日穿的衣服. 我
尤其滿意的. 是長裙剪
短了更好看.

CHAPTER V

A NEW AND GREAT ACQUAINTANCE INTRODUCED — WHAT WE PLACE MOST HOPES UPON, GENERALLY PROVES MOST FATAL.

第 五 回

介紹一位新認得的闊人　我們以爲極有希望的事往往是致命傷的事
（唐希爾初識奧小姐）

At a small distance from the house my predecessor had made a seat, overshaded by a hedge of hawthorn and honeysuckle. Here, when the weather was fine and our labor soon finished, we usually sat together, to enjoy an extensive landscape, in the calm of the evening. Here, too, we drank tea, which was now become an occasional banquet; and as we had it but seldom, it diffused a new joy, the preparations for it being made with no small share of bustle and ceremony. On these occasions our two little ones read to us, and they were regularly served

且說離我們的住宅不遠.我的前任製一個長椅.在一大叢金銀花山查樹陰之下.遇着好天氣.我們工作完了.將近黃昏時候.我們常常同坐在這裏享受眼前的遠景.也在這裏吃茶點.也不過偶然享一次盛席.因爲並不常吃.到了要吃的時候.倒是算作一件大事.費不少的事.擺不少的排場.每逢吃茶.兩個小兒子讀書給我們聽.我們吃過.他

53

after we had done. Some times, to give a variety to our amusements, the girls sung to the guitar; and while they thus formed a little concert, my wife and I would stroll down the sloping field, that was embellished with bluebells and centaury, talk of our children with rapture, and enjoy the breeze that wafted both health and harmony. In this manner we began to find that every situation in life may bring its own peculiar pleasures: every morning waked us to a repetition of toil; but the evening repaid it with vacant hilarity.

It was about the beginning of autumn, on a holiday—for I kept such as intervals of relaxation from labor — that I had drawn out my family to our usual place of amusement, and our young musicians began their usual concert. As we were thus engaged, we saw a stag bound nimbly by, within about twenty paces of where we were sitting, and by its panting, it seemed pressed by the hunters.

們才吃. 有時變通消遣辦法. 兩個女兒彈六弦琴唱歌. 當他們彈唱的時候. 我同我的女人在那有紅花藍花點綴的斜坡上散步. 談談我們的兒女. 談到十分高興. 同時清風徐來. 令人心悅神怡. 這才曉得一個人. 無論處的什麼境遇. 都有隨境遇而來的快樂. 每早起來都有事操作. 到了晚上快樂無事. 就是操作的報酬.

有一日正是初秋時候. 是個放假日. 我照例停止操作. 我帶領全家到這消遣的地方. 兩個女兒起首彈唱. 有一隻鹿在旁邊很快跑過. 離我們坐處不過二十步. 那鹿跑過的時候. 我們聽見他喘氣. 大約打獵的人在後緊追. 我們沒

We had not much time to reflect upon the poor animal's distress, when we perceived the dogs and horsemen come sweeping along at some distance behind, and making the very path it had taken. I was instantly for returning in with my family; but either curiosity or surprise, or some more hidden motive, held my wife and daughters to their seats. The huntsman, who rode foremost, passed us with great swiftness, followed by four or five persons more, who seemed in equal haste. At last, a young gentleman, of a more genteel appearance than the rest, came forward, and for a while regarding us, instead of pursuing the chase, stopped short, and giving his horse to a servant who attended, approached us with a careless, superior air.[1] He seemed to want no introduction, but was going to salute my daughters as one certain of a kind reception; but they had early learned the lesson

得多少時候替那受窘的鹿擔憂.不久就看見獵狗同打獵的人.一陣風像的追過來.向鹿走的路追趕.我要立刻回家.也不曉得爲的是好奇.抑或是來得突兀.抑一時動不得.或有別的用意.使我女人同女兒坐在椅上不動.第一個打獵人騎馬.很快的跑過去了.隨後有四五個.也一樣的跑得很快.最後是一個少年.面貌比那先跑過的人斯文些.跑過來.看了我們一會子.勒住韁不往前追.把馬交給僕人.走到我們跟前.很帶從容高傲的神氣.他不等介紹.要同我的女兒見禮.好像是曉得我的女兒一定歡迎他的.但是我的女兒很曉得拿冷淡態度對付這種預存成見的舉動.不同他招呼.他一見

---

1. Air, 神氣; 氣象.

of looking presumption out of countenance.[1] Upon which he let us know his name was Thornhill, and that he was owner of the estate that lay for some extent around us. He again, therefore, offered to salute the female part of the family; and such was the power of fortune and fine clothes, that he found no second repulse. As his address,[2] though confident,[3] was easy, we soon became more familiar; and perceiving musical instruments lying near, he begged to be favored with a song. As I did not approve of such disproportioned acquaintances, I winked upon my daughters in order to prevent their compliance; but my hint was counteracted by one from their mother; so that, with a cheerful air, they gave us a favorite song of Dryden's. Mr. Thornhill seemed highly delighted with their performance and choice, and then took up the guitar

這個樣.就自己先通名姓說他是唐希爾.是這裏一帶地方的業主.於是再又要同女眷們見禮.果然錢財同華麗衣服.很有力量.女眷們也就同他招呼.他的言談舉動.雖然果於自信.却是從容不迫.我們慢慢就熟習.他看見旁邊放着樂器.就求賞奏一曲.我却並不以不平等的結交為然.就對女兒們使眼色.叫他們不必敷衍他.誰知我使的眼色.被我女人使的眼色反對.女兒們就很高興的唱衆人都愛聽的詩人德氏所製的歌.唐希爾好像是聽了這曲子很高興.自己把六弦琴拿

---

1. Looking out of countenance, 不假以辭色. 2. Address, 言談舉動的神氣. 3. Confident, 自信.

himself He played but very indifferently; however, my eldest daughter repaid his former applause with interest, and assured him that his tones were louder than even those of her master. At this compliment he bowed, which she returned with a courtesy. He praised her taste, and she commended his understanding: an age could not have made them better acquainted; while the fond mother, too, equally happy, insisted upon her landlord's stepping in and tasting a glass of her gooseberry. The whole family seemed earnest to please him: my girls attempted to entertain him with topics they thought most modern, while Moses, on the contrary, gave him a question or two from the ancients, for which he had the satisfaction of being laughed at: my little ones were no less busy, and fondly stuck close to the stranger. All my endeavors could scarce keep their dirty fingers from handling and tarnishing the lace on his clothes and lifting up the flaps of

樣恭兒彈些．鞠腰清知像幾樣房鐘很。我許多的兒子書他是以他摩氣緊事他們裳褸要

怎樣恭兒彈些．鞠躬清知像幾一位這一嘗的人．都歡喜．我想出鮮時的我從古來．他們摩恭維{此處稚之西}

見力女他響又說話．也女兒他認得像幾{寫得躍躍／躍在紙上}

不極維我說生話．也女兒大女維他就像是認得幾{躍得躍在紙上}

並女兒恭些先生恭維大女兒恭兩個人好像的老朋友的母親．一定要我們家裏全家的．要使女兒最酬他不然．幾句話大知笑．是{此處稚之西}我兩個最小的兒子的愛的費然他衣線幾乎緊事他們裳褸要

彈得的大女他比過火些．教琴了這大女兒恭女兒恭兩個好．的老朋友母親．一定要到我們家裏酒的女兒以應卻出眾無家說俏皮話我兩個最小的兒子的親愛的緊事他們裳褸要

得我比聽回禮．他女兒恭兩個初交．愛的喜歡．到我酒的兩個為柄卻幾人大知他．是十年的溺喜一定酒的女兒最新酬不然句人大知笑．是{此處西維寫稚之}我忙着這客人．我不摸金線要把小

他躬還大他們初年那的東果踴躍的兩以柄西找出被摩西家人說俏皮話{無知}也忙着這客他們快要把小金線

起來好維他還得他躬還雅識是十那的東果踴躍的自話摩中卻笑為會無知子．靠的的上了．也忙着干預小手的金線快要把小金線那幾隻小手的金線那幾隻小

了．

his pocket holes, to see what was there. At the approach of evening, he took leave, but not till he had requested permission to renew his visit, which, as he was our landlord, we most readily agreed to.

As soon as he was gone, my wife called a council on the conduct of the day. She was of opinion that it was a most fortunate hit, for that she had known even stranger things than that brought to bear. She hoped again to see the day in which we might hold up our heads with the best of them, and concluded, she protested she could see no reason why the two Miss Wrinkles should marry great fortunes and her children get none. As this last argument was directed to me, I protested I could see no reason for it neither, nor why Mr. Simkins got the ten thousand pound prize in the lottery and we sat down with a blank. "I protest, Charles," cried my wife, "this is the way you always damp my girls and me when we are in spirits. Tell me, Sophy, my dear,

裏天色將晚. 許為自然

看天色將晚. 許他.

他一走後. 我的女人召集家裏的人. 開一個會議. 議論今日的事. 他以為今日這件事. 是個巧相逢. 他曉得這種事. 到後來有極奇的結果. 他盼望我們再有出頭之日. 可以同最闊的人比肩. 末後. 他很鄭重的說爾錢就{描吞}快. 小姐的人. 應寫婦人不就呢{則言痛之}. 因為

開客人的口袋. 看些什麼. 臨走要求許再來探訪. 我們因是我們的房東.

他一個克有家. 林與女人段. 兩着見不離. 他末後對着重什麼萬該應{冷水澆背話}: 我同我的女兒起興的時候. 你這樣的冷水澆背. 素

他一個人的克有兒家. 前牛段後牛段. 即不末後. 他是很鄭出重出得了一應{冷水澆背}: 我查理{牧師名小}. 我同我的女兒總是回頭對女兒們說道. 素

what do you think of our new visitor? Don't you think he seemed to be good-natured?"—"Immensely so, indeed, mamma," replied she. "I think he has a great deel to say upon everything, and is never at a loss; and the more trifling the subject, the more he has to say."—"Yes," cried Olivia, "he is well enough for a man, but for my part I don't much like him— he is so extremely impudent and familiar; but on the guitar he is shocking." These two last speeches I interpreted by contraries. I found by this that Sophia internally despised, as much as Olivia secretly admired him.—"Whatever may be your opinions of him, my children," cried I, "to confess the truth, he has not prepossessed me in his favor. Disproportioned friendships ever terminate in disgust, and I thought,, notwithstanding all his ease, that he seemed perfectly sensible of the distance between us. Let us keep to companions of our own rank. There is no character more contemptible

緋.你看我們這位新朋友怎麼樣.你看他是不是一個好脾氣的人.女兒答道.媽媽.他很是個好脾氣的人.他無論對於什麼東西.都有一番話說.沒有說不出來的.那題目越不相干.他越有得說.奧維雅說道.可不是.這樣男人也就罷了.專由我一方面看.我不甚喜歡他.他太過臉皮厚.太過不客氣.他彈琴簡直是可怕.我解說這兩個女兒的話.是用反襯法.我曉得素緋雅心裏是極看不起唐希爾.奧維雅心理却稱讚他.我就說道.兒女們.我不問你們對於這個人的意見怎樣.我對你們說實話.我不喜歡他.凡是貴賤結交.後來的結果.總是彼此相厭.我看他雖然覺得很自如的.他很曉得彼此兩家的分際.相差得太遠.我們還是同階級相等的人作朋友罷.世界上最令人瞧不起的.無過於趨

than a man that is a
fortune hunter, and I can
see no reason why fortune-
hunting women should not
be contemptible too. Thus,
at best, we shall be con-
temptible if his views are
honorable; but if they be
otherwise! I should shud-
der but to think of that!
It is true I have no apprehensions from the conduct
of my children, but I think
there are some from his
character."—I would have
proceeded, but for the
interruption of a servant
from the squire, who, with
his compliments, sent us a
side of venison, and a promise to dine with us some
days after. This well-
timed present pleaded more
powerfully in his favor
than anything I had to say
could obviate. I therefore
continued silent, satisfied
with just having pointed
out danger, and leaving it
to their own discretion[1] to
avoid it. That virtue
which requires to be ever
guarded is scarce worth the
sentinel.

炎鄙思們是光到曉會唐紳把
打還他巧．我論他不所滿事凡時就於此是者善如類讀
炎頂們是光到曉會唐紳把打還他巧．我論他不所滿事凡時就於此是者

附勢之好若尙他明．這得失希還

的女人．這樣看面說大為意思．光人不樣女的．可就難下說．那

人．自然也在來．他明所是呢．寒兒的．難個差就下說．

趨可從意我若大想我不那鄉來．

炎鄙思們是光到曉會唐紳把打還他巧．

1. Discretion, 相機行事.

CHAPTER VI

THE HAPPINESS OF A COUNTRY FIRESIDE.

第 六 回

鄉 下 家 庭 之 快 樂
（素緋雅無意露眞情）

As we carried on the former dispute with some degree of warmth, in order to accommodate matters, it was universally agreed that we should have a part of the venison for supper, and the girls undertook the task with alacrity. "I am sorry," cried I, "that we have no neighbor or stranger to take a part in this good cheer; feasts of this kind acquire a double relish[1] from hospitality."—"Bless me," cried my wife, "here comes our good friend Mr. Burchell, that saved our Sophia, and that run you down fairly in the argument."—"Confute me in argument, child!" cried I. "You mistake there, my

且說我們辯論前回的問題. 辯得很熱鬧. 於是通融起見. 大衆議決. 割一塊鹿肉作晚餐. 女兒很高興的去烹調. 我說道. 有這樣好菜. 應該有客人同享. 那就加倍的有味. 可惜無鄰居. 無客人來同享. 我女人說道. 好呀. 打救素緋雅的好朋友白先生來了. 這可把你的辯論駁倒了. 我說道. 把我的辯論駁倒了麼. 我的寶貝. 你錯

---

1. Relish, 好滋味.

61

dear. I believe there are but few that can do that: I never dispute your abilities at making a goose pie, and I beg you'll leave argument to me."—As I spoke, poor Mr. Burchell entered the house, and was welcomed by the family, who shook him heartily by the hand, while little Dick officiously reached him a chair.

I was pleased with the poor man's friendship for two reasons: because I knew that he wanted mine, and I knew him to be friendly as far as he was able. He was known in our neighborhood by the character of the poor Gentleman that would do no good when he was young, though he was not yet thirty. He would at intervals talk with great good sense; but in general he was fondest of the company of children, whom he used to call harmless little men. He was famous, I found, for singing them ballads, and telling them stories; and seldom went out without something in his pockets for them, a

了.有限的幾個人能殼駁倒我{寫牧師自以爲是未能破除積習}.善烤鵝排.是你的本事.我向來不同你辯.說到辯駁.你不要管我罷.我說話的時候.白且爾進來.人人都歡迎他.很慇勤同他拉手.狄克好多事.端把椅子請他坐.

這個窮人.我倒是很喜歡他同我作朋友.內中有兩層緣故.一來是我曉得他要同我作朋友.二來是他極力同我要好.我們這裏鄉下.都曉得他是一個窮人.少年時候不要好.這時候他還不到三十歲.有個時候.他的談論也還有道理.大概說的話.他最喜歡小孩子.說他們是無害的小把戲.他最出名的是唱歌給小孩們聽.告訴他們故事.總帶些東西給他們.也許是

THE VICAR OF WAKEFIELD 53

piece of gingerbread, or a halfpenny whistle. He generally came for a few days into our neighborhood once a year, and lived upon the neighbor's hospitality. He sat down to supper among us, and my wife was not sparing of her gooseberry wine. The tale went round, he sang us old songs, and gave the children the story of the Buck of Beverland, with the history of Patient Grissel, the adventures of Catskin, and then Fair Rosamond's Bower. Our cock, which always crew at eleven, now told us it was time for repose; but an unforeseen difficulty started about lodging the stranger: all our beds were already taken up, and it was too late to send him to the next alehouse. In this dilemma, little Dick offered him his part of the bed, if his brother Moses would let him lie with him; "and I," cried Bill, "will giv. Mr. Burchell my part, if my sisters' will take me to theirs."—"Well done, my good children," cried I; "hospitality is one of the first Christian duties. The

塊餅．也許是個小叫子．每年總來一次．住幾天．住在我們的隣居家．他這次來了．同我們坐下吃晚飯．我的女人很勸他喝我們的果子酒．他說些故事．唱幾個老曲子．告訴我的小孩子們鹿的故事．吉力塞的歷史．克士京冒險記．羅沙曼草亭記．我們家裏養的公雞．向來是晚上十一點鐘啼．這個時候雞啼．我們就曉得應該歇宿．才想起來沒得牀鋪安頓這位客人．又不能半夜叫客人去小酒店住宿．狄克先說．倘若他的哥哥讓他同牀．他願意讓地方給客人．比勒說道．倘若姊姊讓我同牀．我願意把我睡的地方給白先生．我聽了．說道．好孩子們．你們讓得好．招待異鄉人．是基督教徒應盡義務中之

beast retires to its shelter, and the bird flies to its nest; but helpless man can only find refuge from his fellow creature. The greatest stranger in this world was He that came to save it. He never had a house, as if willing to see what hospitality was left remaining amongst us. Deborah, my dear," cried I, to my wife, "give these boys a lump of sugar each, and let Dick's be the largest, because he spoke first."

In the morning early I called out my whole family to help at saving an after-growth of hay, and our guest offering his assist-ance, he was accepted among the number. Our labors went on lightly; we turned the swath to the wind. I went foremost, and the rest followed in due succession. I could not void, however, observing the assiduity of Mr. Bur-chell in assisting my daugh-ter Sophia in her part of the task. When he had finished his own, he would join in hers, and enter into a close conversation; but

一．走獸有穴可歸．飛鳥有巢可住．無告之人．只能彀在同類中尋棲止

｛前頭已說過兩次白且爾是
個窮人這裏當面且說無告
之人豈不令白
且爾難堪耶｝

這世界上．最偉大無告之人．就是來救世的人．他向無棲身之所．彷彿是要看世界上還剩有幾個肯收留無告的人．我又對我的女人說道．我的至愛．給小孩子一人一塊糖．狄克先說的．應該給一塊大些的糖．

第二天一早．我把全家人喊出門．幫忙最後收的乾草．我們的客人．願意幫忙．我們就讓他幫我們作工、作得很寫意．把草排好吹風．我前行．餘人跟我走．我禁不住看見白且爾．很費力的．幫我女兒素緋雅作他那一部分的事．他先把自己的作完．就去幫我的女兒．兩個人談得很密．我却曉得這女兒

I nad too good an opinion of Sophia's understanding, and was too well convinced of her ambition, to be under any uneasiness from a man of broken fortune. When we were finished for the day, Mr. Burchell was invited as on the night before but he refused, as he was to lie that night at a neighbor's, to whose child he was carrying a whistle. When gone, our conversation at supper turned upon our late unfortunate guest. "What a strong instance," said I, "is that poor man of the miseries attending a youth of levity and extravagance. He by no means wants sense, which only serves to aggravate his former folly. Poor forlorn creature, where are now the revelers, the flatterers, that he could once inspire[1] and command? Gone, perhaps, to attend the bagnio pander, grown rich by his extravagance. They once praised him, and now they applaud the pander: their former raptures at his wit

心地明白. 我又曉得我女兒立志非凡. 我對這個窮漢却無不放心. 這一天的工作完了. 我們仍舊留他. 他辭謝. 說是當晚要住在鄰居人家. 帶一個小叫子給那家的孩子. 他走了之後. 我們吃晚飯時候. 就談到這個不幸的客人. 我說道. 這就是少年輕浮奢侈. 後來困苦的好榜樣. 他這個人. 並不是無知識. 却用知識去加重他從前的過惡. 你這困窮無賴的人呀. 從前你能慫恿使奔走的一班吃喝玩樂的朋友. 同那一班好巴結你的人. 現在都那裏去了. 從前他們恭維他聰明機靈. 現在

---

1. Inspire, 授意使人作事; 說話使人會意.

are now converted into sarcasms at his folly: he is poor, and perhaps deserves poverty; for he has neither the·ambition to be independent, nor the skill to be useful." Prompted perhaps by some secret reasons, I delivered this observation with too much acrimony, which my Sophia gently reproved "Whatsoever his former conduct may have been, papa, his circumstances should exempt him from censure now. His present indigence is a sufficient punishment for former folly; and I have heard my papa himself say that we should never strike one unnecessary blow at a victim over whom Providence holds the scourge of its resentment."—"You are right, Sophy," cried my son Moses, "and one of the ancients finely represents so malicious a conduct, by the attempts of a rustic to flay Marsyas,[1] whose skin, the fable tells us, had been wholly stripped off by another. Besides, I don't

挖苦他是個傻瓜. 他現在窮了. 也許是應該窮的. 因為他旣無獨立的志氣. 又無用世的本事 {此種 neither … nor … 句可學}. 也許我是心懷私見 {老牧師不願與 其女與白且深交也} 爾 故此把這番痛罵他的話說得太過. 不留餘地. 索緋雅就很溫和的駁我道. 爸爸. 無論他從前行為怎麼樣. 他現在所處的環境. 應該可以免了他受人指摘. 他現在所受的困苦. 足彀罰他從前的過惡. 我曾聽爸爸說過. 上帝旣操罰惡之權. 我們就不應該再加一下無謂的打擊 {這番話說得極寬厚也 娓娓動聽如見其人}. 我的兒子摩西對他姊姊說道. 姊姊你說得對有一個古人說過一段古事. 勸人不可報恨太過. 說的是有一個人已經被人剝完了皮. 一個鄉愚還要再剝. 這報怨

---

1. Marsyas, 此事見古代神話.

know if this poor man's situation be so bad as my father would represent it. We are not to judge of the feelings of others by what we might feel if in their place. However dark the habitation of the mole to our eyes, yet the animal itself finds the apartment sufficiently lightsome. And to confess a truth, this man's mind seems fitted to its station; for I never heard any one more sprightly than he was to-day, when he conversed with you." This was said without the least design; however, it excited a blush, which she strove to cover by an affected laugh, assuring him, that she scarce took any notice of what he said to her; but that she believed he might once have been a very fine gentleman. The readiness with which she undertook to vindicate herself, and her blushing, were symptoms I did not internally approve; but I repressed my suspicions.

As we expected our landlord the next day, my wife went to make the venison

的手段未免太毒了.況且父親說這個人怎樣怎樣的困窮.或者尚不至於窮到這樣.我們不能拿我們設身處地的感覺.去判斷他人的感覺.我們的眼睛看見隱鼠所住地方是很黑暗.難保那隱鼠不看見是很敞亮光的.我照實說.這個人的心境.同他的處境很合拍.他今天同你說話.再高興也沒有.摩西這句話.原出無心.他姊姊却是有意.聽了臉上一紅.裝出一笑.蓋過去了.還說他並未留意白希爾說的什麼{神筆之傳}.不過相信他從前是個上等人.我女兒急於要表明自己.又加臉上這一紅.我心裏很不以這種現象為然.但是我把我的疑團按住.

明天是房東來.我的女人去作鹿排.摩西坐

pasty. Moses sat reading, while I taught the little ones: my daughters seemed equally busy with the rest; and I observed them for a good while cooking something over the fire. I at first supposed they were assisting their mother; but little Dick informed me in a whisper, that they were making a *wash* for the face. Washes of all kinds I had a natural antipathy to; for I knew that instead of mending the complexion, they spoiled it. I therefore approached my chair by sly degrees to the fire, and grasping the poker as if it wanted mending, seemingly by accident, overturned the whole composition, and it was too late to begin another.

下讀書. 我教兩個小兒子. 兩個女兒像是很忙. 我留心許久的看他們在火上煑東西. 其初我以為他們幫母親作菜. 狄克在耳邊告訴我. 他們製膏子塗臉. 我天生的最惡無論什麼膏子. 因為我曉得膏子不獨不能補臉. 反能害臉 {老牧師從何處得此閱歷應用潤字而用補字牧師未免挖苦}. 我於是把我坐的椅子慢慢的挪近火邊. 以為火不旺. 裝作通火偶然失手的樣子. 把兩個女兒煑的東西推翻. 這時候想再作也來不及了 {老牧師很淘氣然而卻用點苦心}.

CHAPTER VII

A TOWN WIT DESCRIBED — THE DULLEST FELLOW MAY
LEARN TO BE COMICAL FOR A NIGHT OR TWO.

第 七 回

叙 城 裏 的 小 機 靈 人　頂 蠢 的 人 也
能 學 會 耍 一 兩 夜 的 小 丑
（奧 維 雅 鍾 情 唐 希 爾）

When the morning arrived on which we were to entertain our young landlord, it may be easily supposed what provisions were exhausted to make an appearance.[1] It may also be conjectured that my wife and daughters expanded their gayest plumage upon this occasion. Mr. Thornhill came with a couple of friends, his chaplain and feeder.[2] The servants, who were numerous, he politely ordered to the next alehouse; but my wife, in the triumph of her heart, insisted on entertaining them all; for

且說我們請房東吃飯那天早上.讀者可以意會.我們什麼食物都使完了去裝面子.也可以意會.我的女人和我兩個女兒趕這個機會穿上頂華麗的衣裳.招待貴客.唐希爾帶着兩個人來.一個是家裏的牧師.一個是不上不下的清客之類.跟來的還有許多家人.他要打發到酒店去.我的女人得意的了不得.一定要連這班家人都招待.到後

1. To make an appearance, 裝面子. 2. Feeder, 或云是清客篾片之流,或云是管事,或云是專管喂養鬪雞者.

69

which, by the bye, our family was pinched for three weeks after. As Mr. Burchell had hinted to us the day before, that he was making some proposals of marriage to Miss Wilmot, my son George's former mistress, this a good deal damped[1] the heartiness of his reception; but accident, in some measure, relieved our embarrassment; for one of the company, happening to mention her name, Mr. Thornhill observed with an oath that he never knew anything more absurd than calling such a fright a beauty: "For strike me ugly,"[2] continued he, "if I should not find as much pleasure in choosing my mistress by the information of a lamp under the clock at St. Dunstan's." At this he laughed, and so did we: the jests of the rich are ever successful. Olivia, too, could not avoid whispering loud enough to be heard, that he had an infinite fund of humor.

來我們因為這事. 受了三星期的窘｛貧窮人拼命家款要｝. 因為｛富貴客無不受窘待者雖受窘而仍以為樂｝. 因為白且爾早日曾露出口風. 他要向威小姐求親. 這就是我的大兒子求過親而打散的. 故此他來我們都不甚歡迎. 但是無意中出一小事. 把我們難為情的意思打散了. 因為座中有一位. 偶然提及威小姐. 唐希爾頗粗口的說. 這種醜怪東西. 還說是美人. 太沒道理了. 假使我拿一個燈籠. 在某教堂鐘樓底下. 挑選我的太太. 還得不着許多快樂. 我不相信. 他說完大笑｛唐希爾眞是粗俗不堪｝. 我們也都笑了. 闊人說笑話. 自然是人人都要陪笑的. 我的女兒奧維雅. 禁不住竊竊私語. 聲音却令人聽見. 說的是. 他有無限的詼諧.

---

1. Damped, 冷水澆背. 2. Strike me ugly, 賭嘴語.

THE VICAR OF WAKEFIELD 61

After dinner, I began with my usual toast,[1] the Church;[2] for this I was thanked by the chaplain, as he said the Church was the only mistress of his affections.[3] "Come, tell us honestly, Frank,"[4] said the squire, with his usual archness, "suppose the Church, your present mistress, dressed in lawn sleeves,[5] on one hand, and Miss Sophia, with no lawn about her,[6] on the other, which would you be for?"—"For both, to be sure," cried the chaplain.—"Right, Frank," cried the squire; "for may this glass suffocate me, but a fine girl is worth all the priestcraft in the creation. For what are tithes and tricks but an imposition[7]—all a confounded imposture,[8] and I can prove it."—"I wish you would," cried my son Moses; "and I think," continued he, "that I should be able to answer you."—"Very well, sir,"

吃過飯. 我說頌詞. 我的老例頌的是宗教. 唐家的牧師謝謝我. 他還說. 我愛的惟一女情人就是宗教. 那鄉紳很刁蛋的說道. 法朗克. 你老實說. 譬如一方面你所愛的情人. 穿細竹布袍袖子. 一方面是素緋雅小姐. 一絲竹布也不穿. ｛此句之意直云裸體也可謂淫褻極矣｝. 你愛誰呢. 唐家牧師答道. 一定兩方面都愛. 鄉紳說道. 法朗克不錯. 那怕這鍾酒把我嗆死. 我也要說. 一個美女子. 比世界上什麽宗教把戲都好. 什麽是宗教稅. 什麽是宗教禮節. 都是騙人的. 亂七八糟騙人的事 ｛對着兩位牧師肆口漫罵宗教寫得唐希爾棄蔑禮教淋漓盡致｝. 我並且可以證實. 摩西說道. 請你證實. 我

---

1. Toast, 頌詞. 2. Church, 宗教; 宗教職官. 3. Mistress of his affections, 家庭尋常宴客, 往往先頌婦女, 故唐家牧師, 因譬牧師不先頌婦女而先頌宗教, 故說到婦女也. 4. Frank, 唐家牧師小名. 5. Lawn sleeves, 主教袍袖以細白竹布爲之, 此句語帶雙關. 6. With no lawn about her, 婦女多以竹布作內衣, 此處謂不著內衣. 7. Imposition, 騙人行爲. 8. Imposture, 騙人之事.

cried the squire, who immediately smoked him,[1] and winking on the rest of the company, to prepare us for the sport; "if you are for a cool argument upon that subject, I am ready to accept the challenge.[2] And first, whether are you for managing it analogically or dialogically?"[3]—"I am for managing it rationally," cried Moses, quite happy at being permitted to dispute.—"Good again," cried the squire, "and firstly, of the first. I hope you'll not deny that whatever is, is. If you don't grant me that, I can go no further."—"Why," returned Moses, "I think I may grant that, and make the best of it."—"I hope too," returned the other, "you'll grant that a part is less than the whole."—"I grant that too," cried Moses; "it is but just and reasonable."—"I hope," cried the squire, "you'll not deny that the two angles of a triangle are

可以駁你.鄉紳一聽.曉得摩西老實.一面對衆人使眼色.叫衆人預備聽笑話.於是答摩西道.你若是要平心靜氣的辯論這個問題.我預備同你闢.第一層.你還是用比喻的方法.還是用問答的方法.摩西因爲讓他辯駁.很高興說道.我是用有理的方法.鄉紳答道.又是好的.第一層中之第一層.你不能駁.無論什麼是的.就是是的.你如果不以這個爲然.我就不能往下再辯了.摩西答道.我想我可以答應這一層.我就儘着這層駁你.鄉紳說道.全大於分.你也不能駁的.摩西道.這是公道合理的話.我不駁.鄉紳又說道.一三角形的兩

1. Smoked him, 曉得他老實.　2. Challenge, 挑戰.　3. Analogically or dialogically, 此兩字用得不甚通,唐希爾以艱深文淺陋也.

equal to two right ones."[1]—
"Nothing can be plainer,"
returned the other, and
looked round with his usual
importance.—"Very well,"
cried the squire, speaking
very quick, "the premises[2]
being thus settled, I proceed to observe, that the
concatenation[3] of self-ex-
istence, proceeding in a
reciprocal duplicate ratio,
naturally produces a prob-
lematical dialogism, which
in some measure proves that
the essence of spirituality
may be referred to the
second predicable."—
"Hold—hold," cried the
other, "I deny that. Do
you think I can thus
tamely submit to such
heterodox doctrines?"—
"What," replied the squire,
as if in a passion, "not
submit! Answer me one
plain question: Do you
think Aristotle right when
he says, that relatives are
related?" — "Undoubted-
ly," replied the other.—
"If so, then," cried the

個角.相加等於兩直角
{此是幾何原本公理
內之一條原無可駁}.摩西
很鄭重的四圍一看.說
道.這一層道理再淺顯
也沒有了.鄉紳於是很
快嘴的說道.很好.前提
已經定了.我就要說.把
自然存在.貫串起來.用
反置雙比例法.自然生
出可以作問題的問答.
也可以證明精神歸在第
二個本題{此段東扯西拉
胡說巴道胡亂
串起許多哲學算學字眼
大言欺人讀之大發一笑}.
摩西說道.慢着慢着.我
不以你所說的為然.你
這種異端道理.能服我
麼{雖摩西也曉
得鄉紳胡扯}.鄉紳好
像生氣的說道.你不服
麼.你且先答我一句淺
白的話.阿理斯德說.有
關係的就是有關係
{此句無
理可辯}.你看對不對.
摩西答道.自然是對的.
鄉紳說道.旣是這樣.我

---

1. Two angles of a triangle are equal to two right ones, 鄉紳全錯
了, 幾何原題云, 凡平面三角形內之三角相加等於兩直角, 摩
西不曉得駁. 2. Premises, 前提 (名學名詞). 3. Concatenation, 貫
串; 聯貫.

squire, "answer me directly to what I propose: Whether do you judge the analytical investigation of the first part of my enthymeme[1] deficient secundem quoad, or quoad minus,[2] and give me your reasons; give me your reasons, I say, directly."— "I protest," cried Moses, "I don't rightly comprehend the force of your reasoning; but if it be reduced to one simple proposition, I fancy it may then have an answer."— "O, sir," cried the squire, "I am your most humble servant. I find you want me to furnish you with argument and intellects too. No, sir, there I protest you are too hard for me." This effectually[3] raised the laugh against poor Moses, who sat the only dismal figure in a group of merry faces: nor did he offer a single syllable more during the whole entertainment.

But though all this gave me no pleasure, it had a

有一個提議.你直接的答我.我提議的是.請你判斷用解析法研究我第一部分 ｝此處不通此一段用幾個希臘字更是胡扯 ｝請你把道理說給我聽.把道理說給我聽.我說.你簡直的答我.摩西說道.我不明白你的理.你倘能把你所說的.作成一個簡單的提議.我想.我可以答你.鄉紳說道.呀.先生.我對不起你.原來你旣要我把辯駁法子給你.還要我把知識也給你.先生.你要得太多.我供給不起.這一番話很有力量.叫衆人笑摩西.這時候人人都是高興的.惟有摩西.一個人.坐在那裏最難受.終席他也再不說一句話.

我聽見唐希爾說的話.心中不快.奧維雅却

---

1. Enthymeme, 辯論之只有一前提者(名學語). 2. Secundem quoad, or quoad minus, 拉丁文,如此用法,不成意義. 3. Effectually, 有效;有力.

very different effect upon Olivia, who mistook it for humor, though but a mere act of the memory. She thought him, therefore, a very fine gentleman; and such as consider what powerful ingredients[1] a good figure, fine clothes, and fortune are in that character, will easily forgive her. Mr. Thornhill, notwithstanding his real ignorance, talked with ease, and could expatiate upon the common topics of conversation with fluency. It is not surprising then that such talents should win the affections of a girl, who by education was taught to value an appearance[2] in herself, and consequently to set a value upon it in another.

Upon his departure, we again entered to a debate upon the merits of our young landlord. As he directed his looks and conversation to Olivia, it was no longer doubted but that she was the object that induced him to be our

大不然.他誤作是詼諧.其實不過是專靠記性.他以為唐希爾是個極上等人.凡是男人長得身材好.穿的衣服好.又是富有貲產.女人總當他是上等人.我們也就不能單怪奧維雅（不是小瞽／姐出脫是挖苦世上女子之無見識也）.唐希爾雖然全無學問.但是嘴却會說.平常談話.他却是口若懸河的.女孩子受的教育.原重在表面上好看.自然也重男子的表面好看.唐希爾這種人.自然可以贏得女子愛情.也無足怪.

客人走了之後.我們又討論他的長處.因為他兩眼愛看奧維雅.又愛同奧維雅說話.他之

---

1. Ingredients, 作料. 2. Appearance, 外觀.

visitor. Nor did she seem to be much displeased at the innocent raillery of her brother and sister upon this occasion. Even Deborah herself seemed to share the glory of the day, and exulted in her daughter's victory as if it were her own. "And now, my dear," cried she to me, "I'll fairly own, that it was I that instructed my girls to encourage our landlord's addresses. I had always some ambition, and you now see that I was right; for who knows how this may end?" — "Ay, who knows that, indeed," answered I, with a groan; "for my part I don't much like it; and I could have been better pleased with one that was poor and honest, than this fine gentleman with his fortune and infidelity; for, depend on't, if he be what I suspect him, no freethinker shall ever have a child of mine."

"Sure, father," cried Moses, "you are too severe in this; for Heaven will never arraign him for what he thinks, but for what he does. Every man has a

所以光降．自然是意在奧維雅．毫無疑義的了．他的兄弟同妹妹都笑他．他也並無不喜歡．我的女人以為今天是極有榮耀的日子．他的女兒得勝．就同自己得勝一樣．他還要居功．對我說道．我說句公道話．原是我叫女兒們鼓勵我們的房東求親的．我向來有大志．你現在才曉得我不錯．誰能料到這事的結果呢．我哼了一聲答道．誰知道結果怎麼樣呢．據我看來．我很不喜歡這件事．可惜他是個闊少．有錢無行．假使他是個貧窮而誠實的人．我更喜歡．倘若我疑他疑的不錯．我萬不能把女兒嫁給蔑視宗教的人｛牧師有先見之明｝．

摩西說道．父親責備他太嚴厲了．天不責人的思想．只責人的行為．人人都有一千個惡思

thousand vicious thoughts, which arise without his power to suppress. Think-ing freely of religion may be involuntary with this gentleman; so that allow-ing his sentiments to be wrong, yet as he is purely passive in his assent, he is no more to be blamed for his errors, than the governor of a city without walls for the shelter he is obliged to af-ford an invading enemy."

"True, my son," cried I; "but if the governor invites the enemy there, he is justly culpable. And such is always the case with those who embrace error. The vice does not lie in assenting to the proofs they see; but in being blind to many of the proofs that offer. So that, though our erroneous opinions be invol-untary when formed, yet as we have been willfully corrupt, or very negligent in forming them, we deserve punishment for our vice, or contempt for our folly."

My wife now kept up the conversation, though not the argument: she observed, that several very prudent men of our acquaintance

想.無力壓制他不發生.我們房東蔑視宗教.也許是自然而然的.他的思想雖然不對.但是尚未見於行事.我們不能怪他.如同地方官無城可守.怎能怪他不能抵禦敵軍呢.

我答道.兒子.你說的不錯.若是地方官把敵軍請來.他還無罪嗎.凡是抱住背理宗旨的人.都是這樣.他們的壞處.不在只信眼見的證據.在乎還有許多證據.他閉眼不看.這就同貪官判案一樣.只憑聽見的證據.其餘還有許多證據.他都不聽.就判案.是以我們不對的思想成立時候.雖是不由自主.但是我們立意存壞思想.或是隨隨便便.不加選擇.放任壞思想成立.後來作出惡行為.自然應該受罰.或犯過失.亦應受人看不起.

我的女人.雖然不辯駁.却也湊着談話.他說我們認得幾位小心謹慎的人.也不信教.却是

were freethinkers, and made very good husbands; and she knew some sensible girls that had skill enough to make converts of thier spouses; "And who knows, my dear," continued she, "what Olivia may be able to do? The girl has a great deal to say upon every subject, and to my knowledge is very well skilled in controversy."

"Why my dear, what controversy can she have read?" cried I. "It does not occur to me that I ever put such books into her hands: you certainly over-rate her merit."—"Indeed, papa," replied Olivia, "she does not: I have read a great deal of controversy. I have read the disputes between Thwackum and Square;[1] the controversy between Robinson Crusoe and Friday[2] the savage, and I am now employed in reading the controversy in Religious Courtship."[3] "Very well," cried I, "that's a good girl; I find

很好的丈夫.他還說.有些有知識的女子.有本事叫丈夫奉教.又說道.誰曉得奧維雅的力量可以作到什麼地步呢.無論談什麼.他都有些話說.據我所知.他很有辯駁的本事.

我問道.他曾經讀過什麼辯駁書.我却記不得我給過他什麼辯駁書看過.你把他的本事.看得太大了.奧維雅答道.爸爸.母親並沒把我的本事看得太大.我曾經讀過許多辯駁.我曾經讀過圖華同斯括的辯駁.也讀過魯濱孫同他的黑奴辯駁.我現在正在讀奉教人之求親這本書裏頭的辯駁.我答道很好.好女兒.我

---

1. Thwackum and Square, 小說書內兩個人物. 2. Robinson Crusoe and Friday, 魯濱孫與黑奴 (見魯濱孫飄流記). 3. Religious Courtship, 此書是 Defoe 所著, 卽著魯濱孫飄流記者.

you are perfectly qualified for making converts, and so go help your mother to make the gooseberry pie."

曉得你有完全資格勸人入教. 你去幫你的母親去作果子糕罷﹛敢得冷僑﹜.

CHAPTER VIII

AN AMOUR, WHICH PROMISES LITTLE GOOD FORTUNE, YET MAY BE PRODUCTIVE OF MUCH

第 八 回

男女相愛不望富貴將來却生出大關係
（白且爾談詩砭流俗）

The next morning we were again visited by Mr. Burchell, though I began for certain reasons to be displeased with the frequency of his return; but I could not refuse him my company and my fireside. It is true his labor more than requited[1] his entertainment, for he wrought among us with vigor, and either in the meadow or at the hayrick put himself foremost. Besides, he had always something amusing to say that lessened our toil, and was at once so out of the way, and yet so sensible, that I loved, laughed at, and pitied him.

且說白且爾第二天早上又來訪我們．我有我的一番道理．雖然起首不喜歡他屢次去而復來．但是我不能不陪他在火爐邊談談．他替我們用力的工作．抵得過我們的招待．因爲無論在草場．或是堆乾草地方．他都是第一個出力况且他常常說幾句有趣味的話．減輕我們的辛苦．他說的都是我們想不到的話．却頗有道理．我又可憐他．又笑他

---

1. Requite, 相抵.

My only dislike arose from an attachment he discovered to my daughter; he would, in a jesting manner, call her his little mistress, and when he bought each of the girls a set of ribands, hers was the finest. I knew not how, but he every day seemed to become more amiable, his wit to improve, and his simplicity to assume the superior airs of wisdom.

Our family dined in the field, and we sat, or rather reclined round a temperate repast, our cloth spread upon the hay, while Mr. Burchell gave cheerfulness to the feast. To heighten our satisfaction, two blackbirds answered each other from opposite hedges, the familiar redbreast came and pecked the crumbs from our hands, and every sound seemed but the echo of tranquillity. "I never sit thus," says Sophia, "but I think of the two lovers, so sweetly described by Mr. Gay, who were struck dead in each other's arms. There is something so pathetic in the description,

他的為作送一份
他很愛我作女兒邊
歡喜不我就為他作送
又愛他．我不喜歡他的
一件事．就為他很愛我
的女兒．有時候他作
頑笑的話．喊我女兒作情
人．他有時買花那一份
我兩個女兒．把那一份
頂好的送與我小女兒．
我不曉得是怎麼樣．只
覺得他一天比一天的
和藹．俏皮話說得日見
進步．他從前是很老實
的．現在他的智慧一日
比一日高 ｛可見得是善而
敬之｝．與人交久而

我們吃飯．全家都坐
在田上．斜靠着地．桌布
鋪在乾草上．不多的幾
樣飯菜．擺在中間．白且
爾自己很高興的．也鼓
勵我們高興．有．兩座籬
笆．一方一座．小鳥對唱．
我們見慣的紅脖子．飛
來在我們手上啄麵包
屑．所聽見的聲音．都是
安樂的迴響 ｛好一幅
田家樂｝．
素緋雅說道．詩人蓋先
生說得媚媚可聽的．一
雙相愛的少年男女．為
雷所擊．相抱而死．我每
次坐在樹下的時候．總
要想到這故事．蓋先生
說得凄楚動人．我讀過

that I have read it a hundred times with new rapture."[1]—"In my opinion," cried the son, "the finest strokes[2] in that description are much below those in the Acis and Galatea of Ovid. The Roman poet understands the use of *contrast*[3] better, and upon that figure[4] artfully managed all strength in the pathetic[5] depends."—"It is remarkable," cried Mr. Burchell, "that both the poets you mention have equally contributed to introduce a false taste into their respective countries, by loading all their lines with epithet.[6] Men of little genius found them most easily imitated in their defects, and English poetry, like that in the latter empire of Rome, is nothing at present but a combination of luxuriant images,[7] without plot or connection; a string of epithets that improve the

一百遍.每讀一遍.都是歡喜欲狂的.我的兒子說道.那段故事裏頭.寫得最好的.也還趕不上羅馬詩人奧維所作的阿西士同加拉提的故事.這位羅馬詩人.比蓋先生善用反襯.修辭學裏頭這個法子.只要布置得清.寫來就有力量.能動人悲哀.白且爾說道.你們兩人所說的兩位詩人.都一樣的好多用字眼.行行都布滿了.因是把不正不雅的風氣灌入兩國.凡是缺少眞才的人.覺得他們的毛病易學.故此英國現在的詩.好似羅馬帝國季年的詩.不過是堆砌許多借用的富麗字眼.其中却一無所有.無布局.無貫串.就好像一條長繩子.貫串許多聲調鏗鏘的字.裏頭却無一

---

1. Rapture, 歡喜欲狂. 2. Finest strokes, 文字之最能 (打擊) 動人處; 一篇之醫策. 3. Contrast, 作文反襯法. 4. Figure, 修辭學之反常達意法. 5. Pathetic, 悲哀動人. 6. Epithet, 字眼; 陪襯字眼 (adjective). 7. Images, 狀貌; 樣子 (修辭學借喻法比較法所用之字).

THE VICAR OF WAKEFIELD 73

sound, without carrying on the sense. But perhaps, madam, while I thus reprehend others, you'll think it just that I should give them an opportunity to retaliate; and indeed I have made this remark only to have an opportunity of introducing to the company a ballad, which, whatever be its other defects, is, I think, at least free from those I have mentioned."

點意思 {陋往往頹
文體卑 各國皆
落至極點

然不獨英國羅馬也清水出芙
藥天然去雕飾雖外國亦有同
尚 {.瑪當.你心裏想我
焉

這樣貶他人.我就應該
給他人一個機會報復.
我所以說這句話.就是
乘機把一篇歌介紹衆
位一聽.這首歌什麼短
處都許有.却無我剛才
所說的毛病.

A BALLAD *

離合歌

"Turn, gentle Hermit of the dale,
 And guide my lonely way,
To where yon taper cheers the vale
 With hospitable ray.

"For here forlorn and lost I tread,
 With fainting steps and slow;
Where wilds immeasurably spread,
 Seem length'ning as I go."

"Forbear, my son," the Hermit cries,
 "To tempt the dangerous gloom;
For yonder faithless phantom flies
 To lure thee to thy doom.

"Here to the houseless child of want
 My door is open still;
And though my portion is but scant,
 I give it with good will.

我遠遠見有燭
光.請煩你這位隱
者.回頭領我到那
裏.我迷了路.走
得疲乏了.眼前都
是荒野.越走越走
不完.那隱者答
道.好孩子.那是
靠不住的鬼火陷
人於險的.你不要
上當.不必向那裏
去.寒舍雖然無什
麼設備.却是很歡
迎無家可歸的人.

*此歌另有文言翻譯見卷末.

"Then turn to-night, and freely share
   Whate'er my cell bestows;
My rushy couch and frugal fare,
   My blessing and repose.

"No flocks that range the valley free,
   To slaughter I condemn;
Taught by that Power that pities me,
   I learn to pity them.

"But from the mountain's grassy side ·
   A guiltless feast I bring:
A scrip with herds and fruits supply'd
   And water from the spring.

"Then, pilgrim, turn, thy cares forego;
   All earth-born cares are wrong;
Man wants but little here below,
   Nor wants that little long."

Soft as the dew from Heav'n descends,
   His gentle accents fell:
The modest stranger lowly bends,
   And follows to the cell.

Far in a wilderness obscure
   The lonely mansion lay,
A refuge to the neighb'ring poor
   And strangers led astray.

No stores beneath its humble thatch
   Requir'd a master's care;
The wicket, op'ning with a latch,
   Receiv'd the harmless pair.

And now, when busy crowds retire
   To take their ev'ning rest,
The Hermit trimm'd his little fire
   And cheer'd his pensive guest:

And spread his vegetable store,
   And gayly prest, and smil'd;
And skill'd in legendary lore
   The ling'ring hours beguil'd.

你今晚不如請到我的茅舍.有什麼我同你分.有的是蔬食蘆菻.你可以暫時休息.因爲上天憐憫我.我也憐憫牛羊.我隨他們自由遊戲於山谷.我是不肯殺以爲食的.我食的是山邊的野菜鮮果.飲的是山泉.你這位遠行的香客.不如轉向我那裏.請你破除憂慮.世上的事值不當去憂他.我人生在世.原用不着要多少東西.不到幾時.連這要的東西也可不必要了.這位隱者說的話.溫柔如天降的露水.那謙退的異鄉客人低頭跟着隱者走.遠遠的荒野間隱隱的有一所住處.鄰近的貧人或迷路的過客可以投宿.那屋裏沒得什麼東西.用不着人保管.關了柴門.兩人進去.這時候勞苦的人都回家歇宿.隱者撥火.使那懷憂的過客振振精神.他攤開蔬果.含笑的勸客人吃.又說了許多古事消遣長夜.貓兒在旁戲

84

THE VICAR OF WAKEFIELD

Around in sympathetic mirth
  Its tricks the kitten tries,
The cricket chirrups in the hearth,
  The crackling faggot flies.

But nothing could a charm impart
  To soothe the stranger's woe;
For grief was heavy at his heart,
  And tears began to flow.

His rising cares the Hermit spied,
  With answ'ring care opprest;
"And whence, unhappy youth," he cried,
  "The sorrows of thy breast?

"From better habitations spurn'd,
  Reluctant dost thou rove?
Or grieve for friendship unreturn'd,
  Or unregarded love?

"Alas! the joys that fortune brings,
  Are trifling and decay;
And those who prize the paltry things,
  More trifling still than they.

"And what is friendship but a name,
  A charm that lulls to sleep;
A shade that follows wealth or fame,
  But leaves the wretch to weep?

"And love is still an emptier sound,
  The modern fair-one's jest;
On earth unseen, or only found
  To warn the turtle's nest.

"For shame, fond youth, thy sorrows hush,
  And spurn the sex," he said;
But while he spoke, a rising blush
  His love-lorn guest betray'd.

Surpris'd he sees new beauties rise,
  Swift mantling to the view;
Like colors o'er the morning skies,
  As bright, as transient, too.

蟋蟀在爐邊歌唱. 柴火畢剝畢剝的響. 火星四處的飛. 這種娛人的情景. 不獨不能解那客人的憂愁. 又令他傷心滴淚. 隱者看見了. 不由得問他爲何這樣愁苦. 問他是不是原本富貴人家. 不爲所容. 不得已漫遊至此. 抑或是朋友負義. 抑或因戀愛見棄. 隱者又勸他說道. 富貴帶來的歡樂. 原算不了什麼. 又不能耐久. 其餘的更不足數了. 說到朋友交情. 更是有名無實. 不過是種安神藥. 受了迷當是安睡. 朋友原是跟着富貴勢力走的. 無勢利就無朋友. 說到愛情更是虛擊. 不過是新派女人拿來同男人開頑笑的. 地球上沒得愛情. 只有斑鳩巢裏還有. 糊塗孩子呀. 把你的愁苦壓下去罷. 把你所愛的美女撇開罷. 當隱者說話的時候. 不料那位爲情寃所害的客人. 不覺臉通紅了. 他看見客人臉上忽然露出如朝暉的美麗.

The bashful look, the rising breast,
　　Alternate spread alarms:
The lovely stranger stands confest,
　　A maid in all her charms.

"And, ah! forgive a stranger rude,
　　A wretch forlorn," she cried;
"Whose feet unhallow'd thus intrude
　　Where Heav'n and you reside.

"But let a maid thy pity share,
　　Whom love has taught to stray;
Who seeks for rest, but finds despair
　　Companion of her way.

"My father liv'd beside the Tyne,
　　A wealthy lord was he:
And all his wealth was mark'd as mine,
　　He had but only me.

"To win me from his tender arms,
　　Unnumber'd suitors came;
Who praised me for imputed charms,
　　And felt or feign'd a flame.

"Each hour a mercenary crowd
　　With richest proffers strove:
Among the rest young Edwin bow'd,
　　But never talk'd of love.

"In humble, simplest habit clad,
　　No wealth nor power had he:
Wisdom and worth were all he had,
　　But these were all to me.

"And when, beside me in the dale,
　　He carol'd lays of love,
His breath lent fragrance to the gale,
　　And music to the grove.

客含起他貌說一個的的你你情他一路憂父是他一個就來恭美．我一班而貴中名對都既勢有這重他情都林開降上天光地

他貌說一個的的你你情他一路憂父是他一個就來恭美

餓人羞落跟女道可異兩這可而原孤愁是個只家人有求維他每人來獻獨愛我到是無力實都的的他

頃這時胸脯就前歎請憐鄉隻個憐失為行同泰有生產獨無親我們點臺爭富有特鞠愛在是山我邊我香是鮮露這

又不見帶點站的是你饒無人汗脚踏路的求休只他晤錢我享限若干大約怎樣怎樣都鐘臺我先恐貴一位文字他平財有值我所嵌風仙花晚都個

不停供口氣恕留賀入但一女息有地方錢我的因此來的愛富後於少也却穿常衣無知然最看得得聽樂上人了．在站氣恕收賀踏地．一望．行作地方我一我都的的恐我却躬字．常衣財．得滿滿白這人

了點美恕留踏求女息作錢我此人來愛的恐少穿衣然得比人

86

"The blossom opening to the day,
　The dews of Heav'n refin'd,
Could nought of purity display
　To emulate his mind.

"The dew, the blossom on the tree,
　With charms inconstant shine:
Their charms were his, but woe to me,
　Their constancy was mine.

"For still I try'd each fickle art,
　Importunate and vain;
And while his passion touch'd my heart,
　I triumph'd in his pain.

"Till quite dejected with my scorn,
　He left me to my pride:
And sought a solitude forlorn,
　In secret where he died.

"But mine the sorrow, mine the fault,
　And well my life shall pay;
I'll seek the solitude he sought,
　And stretch me where he lay.

"And there forlorn, despairing, hid,
　I'll lay me down and die:
'Twas so for me that Edwin did,
　And so for him will I."

"Forbid it Heav'n!" the Hermit cried,
　And clasp'd her to his breast:
The wond'ring fair one turn'd to chide,—
　'Twas Edwin's self that prest.

"Turn, Angelina, ever dear,
　My charmer, turn to see
Thy own, thy long-lost Edwin here,
　Restor'd to love and thee.

明清潔。但是枝上的花葉上的露是不能久的。他雖愛我，我愛他却不能久。他只管懇求我，我却不該無定性的一味用手段去對付他。他的愛情雖然動我的心，我却播弄他，使他心痛，我反以爲樂。後來他見我看他不起，很愁苦的走了，叫我一個人去得意。他私下裏找了一個極荒涼的地方，就死在那裏。他一去之後，我才後悔，心裏極其愁苦。我只好去償他的命。去找他去的那個地方，同他在那一個荒涼無人理的地方，作一個荒涼無希望的人。就死。我以死報之。愛特文而一死，我只死報之。聽了兩女子說道，那女子不許過臉來。要抱我。原來抱住愛特文。一看就是愛特文說道。我的愛林納，你轉過臉來看你的愛特文。你已失蹤的愛特文在這裏。仍如從前，讓我抱你，把什麼愁苦都撇開了。我

"Thus let me hold thee to my heart,
　And ev'ry care resign:
And shall we never, never part,
　My life—my all that's mine?

"No, never from this hour to part,
　We'll live and love so true;
The sigh that rends thy constant heart,
　Shall break thy Edwin's too."

While this ballad was reading, Sophia seemed to mix an air of tenderness with her approbation. But our tranquillity was soon disturbed by the report of a gun just by us, and immediately after a man was seen bustling through the hedge, to take up the game he had killed. This sportsman was the squire's chaplain, who had shot one of the blackbirds that so agreeably entertained us. So loud a report, and so near, startled my daughters; and I could perceive that Sophia in the fright had thrown herself into Mr. Burchell's arms for protection. The gentleman came up, and asked pardon for having disturbed us, affirming that he was ignorant of our being so near. He therefore sat down by my youngest

們從此永不分離.從此以後我們永不分離.眞誠相愛.你歎一口氣.不獨傷你的心.連我的心也傷了.

素緋雅聽他唱這歌.一面稱讚.一面露出一段柔情.我們正在很安閒的時候.忽然聽見槍聲.隨卽看見有一個人.竄進小樹叢裏.去捉打落的東西.這打獵的原來就是鄉紳家裏的教士.把那唱得很好聽的鳥.打死一個{大煞風景}.這槍聲又響又近.我兩個女兒嚇了一跳.我看見素緋雅受驚的時候.倒在白且爾身上.白且爾兩手抱住他.那獵人走上來告罪.說是並不曉得他同我們相離這樣近.說完坐在我的小女

daughter, and, sportsman-
like, offered her what he
had killed that morning.
She was going to refuse,
but a private look from her
mother soon induced her
to correct the mistake, and
accept his present, though
with some reluctance.   My
wife, as usual, discovered
her pride in a whisper,
observing that Sophy had
made a conquest of the
chaplain, as well as her
sister had of the squire.   I
suspected, however, with
more probability, that her
affections were placed upon
a different object.   The
chaplain's errand was to
inform us that Mr. Thorn-
hill had provided music and
refreshments, and intended
that night giving the young
ladies a ball by moonlight
on the grass plot before our
door.   "Nor can I deny,"
continued he, "but I have
an interest in being first to
deliver this message, as I
expect for my reward to be
honored with Miss Sophy's
hand as a partner."   To
this my girl replied that
she should have no objec-
tion, if she could do it with

兒身邊. 照着打獵派頭.
把那早上打的東西. 送
我女兒. 我女兒正要辭
謝. 他的母親使眼色. 我
女兒立刻改過來. 收了
這份禮. 却仍帶着有些
不甚願意受的樣子. 我
女人很得意向我耳邊
說. 素緋雅收服了這位
教士. 同奧維雅收服那
鄉紳一樣. 我却疑心素
緋雅的愛情. 別有所屬.
我曉得我疑得倒有幾
分對. 原來那教士奉鄉
紳命來說. 預備音樂茶
點. 意欲當晚請兩位小
姐. 在我們門前草地上.
月夜跳舞. 他接着說道.
我老實供認. 我是第一
個來送信. 却有點私心.
因為我要求素緋雅小
姐. 同我跳舞. 作為給我
送信的酬謝. 我女兒答
道. 假使面子上過得去.
我並無什麼不願意. 隨
卽對白且爾接着說道.

honor. "But here," continued she, "is a gentleman," looking at Mr. Burchell, "who has been my companion in the task for the day, and it is fit he should share in its amusements." Mr. Burchell returned her a compliment for her attentions, but resigned her up to the chaplain, adding that he was to go that night five miles, being invited to a harvest supper. His refusal appeared to me a little extraordinary,[1] nor could I conceive how so sensible a girl as my youngest could thus prefer a man of broken fortune to one whose expectations[2] were much greater. But as men are most capable of distinguishing merit in women, so the ladies often form the truest judgments of us. The two sexes seem placed as spies upon each other, and are furnished with different abilities, adapted for mutual inspection.

但是這位先生.今天陪我操作.陪了一天.到了消遣游戲.他應該也有一份.白且爾謝謝我女兒的一番好意.說情願讓與教士.因爲有人請他吃收穫晚飯.卽晚還要走十幾里路到那裏去.我覺得他這一辭.有點反常.再說我的小女兒是很有知識的.爲什麼偏喜歡一個破產的人.不喜歡前程大有希望的人呢.女人的好醜.男人最會分別.男人的好醜.自然是女人斷得最確.好像是男人是偵探女人的.女人是偵探男人的.各有本能.互相偵察.

---

1. Extraordinary, 反常；出乎尋常之外. 2. Expectations, 前程；希望.

CHAPTER IX

TWO LADIES OF GREAT DISTINCTION INTRODUCED — SUPERIOR FINERY EVER SEEMS TO CONFER SUPERIOR BREEDING.

第 九 回

介 紹 兩 位 極 闊 女 人　俗 見 以 爲 衣 服 好
就 是 家 教 好
（唐 希 爾 月 夜 宴 佳 人）

Mr. Burchell had scarce taken leave, and Sophia consented to dance with the chaplain, when my little ones came running out to tell us that the squire was come, with a crowd of company. Upon our return we found our landlord, with a couple of under-gentlemen, and two young ladies richly dressed, whom he introduced as women of very great distinction and fashion from town.[1] We happened not to have chairs enough for the whole company; but

且說白且爾才告辭走了.素緋雅答應同那教士跳舞.我的兩個小兒子從屋裏跑來報告說.鄉紳帶了許多人來了.我們進屋看見鄉紳帶了兩位篾片.還有兩位穿得頂闊的少年女人.鄉紳介紹說是京裏最闊最時髦的女人.可巧我們椅子不彀.唐希

---

1. Town, 此字指倫敦.

91

Mr. Thornhill immediately proposed that every gentleman should sit in a lady's lap. This I positively objected to, notwithstanding a look of disapprobation from my wife. Moses was therefore dispatched to borrow a couple of chairs; and as we were in want of ladies to make up a set at country dances, the two gentlemen went with him in quest of a couple of partners. Chairs and partners were soon provided. The gentlemen returned with my neighbor Flamborough's rosy daughters, flaunting with red topknots. But an unlucky circumstance was not adverted to: though the Miss Flamboroughs were reckoned the very best dancers in the parish, and understood the jig and the roundabout to perfection, yet they were totally unacquainted with country dances. This at first discomposed us; however, after a little shoving and dragging, they at last went merrily on. Our music consisted of two fiddles, with a pipe and tabor. The moon shone

爾就立刻出主意說.每個男人坐在每個女人身上{可見唐希爾之放蕩無檢}.我簡直的不答應.我的女人還使眼色.不以我爲然.我們打發摩西去借椅子.因爲女客不彀數.不能.作某種跳舞.兩個箆片.就同摩西同去找女客.不久椅子已彀了.女客已彀了.兩個箆片把我們鄰居法林巴兩位小姐請來.這兩位臉色像玫瑰花.髮上飄兩個大紅結.却有一件不湊趣的事.這兩位法小姐.雖然會好幾種跳舞.但是某種跳舞却不會{行文至此故作一折}.起初衆人都有點不舒服.後來推推拉拉的.也就跳得很高興.用的樂器.是兩個提琴.一把笛子.一個小鼓.

bright; Mr. Thornhill and my eldest daughter led up the ball, to the great delight of the spectators; for the neighbors, hearing what was going forward, came flocking about us. My girl moved with so much grace and vivacity, that my wife could not avoid discovering the pride of her heart by assuring me, that though the little chit did it so cleverly, all the steps were stolen from herself. The ladies of the town strove hard to be equally easy,[1] but without success. They swam, sprawled, languished, and frisked; but all would not do: the gazers indeed owned that it was fine; but neighbor Flamborough observed, that Miss Livy's feet seemed as pat to the music as its echo. After the dance had continued about an hour, the two ladies, who were apprehensive of catching cold, moved to break up the ball. One of them, I thought, expressed her sentiments upon this occasion

月色光明. 鄉紳同我的大女兒領班跳. 鄉近的人來了好些看熱鬧. 無不個個高興. 我的女兒腳步. 又大方. 又活潑. 我女人看見了. 非常得意. 告訴我說這小寶貝聰敏. 跳得好看. 那腳步都是偷學我的〔老太太好居功卻是極得意語〕. 那京裏來的兩位女人. 極力也要學腳步從容. 怎麼樣也學不來. 無論身子怎麼樣扭. 兩隻手怎麼樣轉來轉去. 身子怎麼樣忽然軟下來. 怎麼樣忽然亂動亂跳. 總也跳不出好樣來. 旁觀的人. 雖然說好. 鄰居法林巴說. 總趕不上奧維雅小姐. 跳得合拍. 兩腳拍地. 如同音樂的迴響. 跳了有一點鐘. 京裏來的兩個女人. 怕受涼. 請停止跳舞. 內中有一位說話. 說得很粗. 說

---

1. Easy, 從容; 不勉強.

in a very coarse manner, when she observed that *by the living jingo, she was all of a muck of sweat.* Upon our return to the house, we found a very elegant cold supper, which Mr. Thornhill had ordered to be brought with him. The conversation at this time was more reserved than before. The two ladies threw my girls quite into the shade; for they would talk of nothing but high life, and high-lived company, with other fashionable topics, such as pictures, taste, Shakespeare, and the musical glasses. 'Tis true they once or twice mortified us sensibly by slipping out an oath; but that appeared to me as the surest symptom of their distinction (though I am since informed that swearing is perfectly unfashionable). Their finery, however, threw a veil over any grossness in their conversation. My daughters seemed to regard their superior accomplishments with envy; and what appeared amiss was ascribed to tiptop quality breeding.

是出了一身臭汗.我們進屋子.看見擺着很出色的冷食.是鄉紳帶來的.這時候的談話.却不似從前的隨便.我的兩個女兒.却都落後了.京裏來的兩個女人.說的都是闊話.最時髦的話.不是談畫.就是談京裏的時尚.或大詩人沙士比.又談當日最時髦的.是拿玻璃杯搓出樂音.有一兩次.他們說的極粗的話.當時我以爲是時髦(後來才曉得不是的).但是穿上華麗衣裳.也就把語言粗鄙蓋過去了{善於}{挖苦}.我的女兒以爲是他們有上等才藝.很羨慕他們.雖然曉得他們很有不對的地方.反以爲是受過超等的教養.這兩位京裏來的女人.對於我兩個

But the condescension[1] of the ladies was still superior to their other accomplishments. One of them observed, that had Miss Olivia seen a little more of the world, it would greatly improve her. To which the other added, that a single winter in town would make little Sophia quite another thing. My wife warmly assented to both; adding, that there was nothing she more ardently wished than to give her girls a single winter's polishing. To this I could not help replying, that their breeding was already superior to their fortune; and that greater refinement would only serve to make their poverty ridiculous, and give them a taste for pleasures they had no right to possess.—"And what pleasures," cried Mr. Thornhill, "do they not deserve to possess, who have so much in their power to bestow? As for my part," continued he, "my fortune is pretty large;

女兒.特爲的降格客氣.更超過他們別的才藝〔亦是極力挖苦凡此等降格客氣的派頭往往令旁觀者肉麻〕.有一位說.倘若奧維雅小姐.多見些世面.當然更有進步.那一位接着說道.只要在京裏過一個冬.素緋雅自然就會變作另外一個人.我的女人都很以這話爲然.又說他很熱心的要兩個女兒受一冬的打磨擦光.我禁不住回答這話.說道.論我們的家世.他們的教育已經是過分了.若是踵事增華.不過令人更笑他們窮.反叫他們多添好些彀不上辦不到的好尙.唐希爾說道.他們既然很有力量叫人快樂.爲什麼就不應該享受無論何種的快樂呢.就我本人說.

---

1. Condescension, 俯就；屈尊；富貴人對貧賤人特爲降格.

95

love, liberty, and pleasure are my maxims; but, curse me, if a settlement of half my estate could give my charming Olivia pleasure, it should be hers; and the only favor I would ask in return would be to add myself to the benefit." I was not such a stranger to the world as to be ignorant that this was the fashionable cant to disguise the insolence of the basest proposal, but I made an effort to suppress my resentment. "Sir," cried I, "the family which you now condescend to favor with your company has been bred with as nice a sense of honor as you. Any attempts to injure that may be attended with very dangerous consequences. Honor, sir, is our only possession at present, and of that last treasure we must be particularly careful."—I was soon sorry for the warmth with which I had spoken this, when the young gentleman, grasping my hand, swore he commended my spirit, though he disapproved my suspicions.

我廣有財產.倘若我拿一半給奧維雅小姐.可以使他快樂.我就給他.我所要求的.不過是我要同享利益〔唐希爾言外不懷好意無怪牧師面斥他〕.我對於世情.不是個完全外行.聽了唐希爾這不中聽的時髦話.很生氣.只好用力壓住.不發怒.我就答道.先生.你今天屈尊光降我家.我家裏的人受過教育.曉得愛名譽.顧面子.同你一樣.若是設法傷害我們的名譽.就有危險的結果.先生我們財產雖然沒有.却曉得顧體面.體面就是我們最後剩卞來的至寶.我們是要特別留心保存的.我說了這一番嚴厲的話.有點後悔太過火.那鄉紳抓住我的手.矢誓的說.他很恭維我的氣概.却不以我懷疑爲然.

The two ladies now began a very discreet and serious dialogue upon virtue: in this my wife, the chaplain, and I soon joined; and the squire himself was at last prought to confess a sense of sorrow for his former excesses. We talked of the pleasures of temperance, and of the sunshine in the mind unpolluted with guilt. I was so well pleased, that my little ones were kept up beyond the usual time to be edified by so much good conversation. Mr. Thornhill even went beyond me, and demanded if I had any objection to giving prayers. I joyfully embraced the proposal, and in this manner the night was passed in a most comfortable way, till at last the company began to think of returning. The ladies seemed very unwilling to part with my daughters, for whom they conceived a particular affection, and joined in a request to have the pleasure of their company home. The squire seconded the proposal, and my wife added her entreaties; the girls too looked

這時候那京裏來的兩個女人．起首很見機很莊重的講道德．我的女人．和那個教士．和我．不久都同他們交談．後來鄉紳供認慚愧．說話太過火．我們談到凡事適中的快樂．又談到凡一個人他心地不爲罪惡所汙．自然光明．我很喜歡叫兒女們聽許多這樣的話．可以使他們道德上有進步．不由得讓兒女們久坐．過了他們該歇宿的時候．唐希爾比我還要進一步．問我對於這時候祈禱．有什麼反對．我很高興的依照他的話祈禱｛寫唐希爾同京裏來的女人善於見風轉舵忽然祈禱起來未免可笑｝．這晚上過得很舒服．後來客人想起回家．京裏來的兩位女人．很特別的愛上我的兩個女兒．很不願意分手．兩個一齊要求我讓兩個女兒同到他們家裏．鄉紳也是這樣的求我．我的女人也求我．兩個女兒眼看

upon me as if they wished
to go.　In this perplexity
I made two or three ex-
cuses, which my daughters
as readily removed; so that
at last I was obliged to
give a peremptory refusal,
for which we had nothing
but sullen looks and short
answers the whole day
ensuing.

着我.也願意同去.我也
沒了主意.託故說了幾
句不能去的話.兩個女
兒却答我幾句可以去
的話.到後來.我不得不
說一定不準去.第二天
一整天.他們臉上都是
很不高興.答我的話.都
是很短的.

CHAPTER X

THE FAMILY ENDEAVORS TO COPE WITH THEIR BETTERS — THE MISERIES OF THE POOR WHEN THEY ATTEMPT TO APPEAR ABOVE THEIR CIRCUMSTANCES.

第 十 回

我們家裏人要同有錢的人比　貧人
試擺富人架子之可憐
（出風頭大煞風景）

I now began to find that all my long and painful lectures upon temperance, simplicity, and contentment were entirely disregarded. The distinctions lately paid us by our betters awaked that pride which I had laid asleep, but not removed. Our windows again, as formerly, were filled with washes for the neck and face. The sun was dreaded as an enemy to the skin without doors, and the fire as a spoiler of the complexion within. My wife observed that rising too early would hurt her daughters' eyes, that working after dinner

且說。我這時候才看出來。我費了許多工夫。宣講道理。講節制、簡樸、知足幾件的事。我家裏人簡直不理會。我屢次把他們勸。不發盡。近來有錢的人來訪。待他們驕奢。把我壓除好了的驕傲。又發作了。我禁不住又想。又塗臉。門家了。我們的窗子又同從前一樣。擺滿了膏子。出門怕太陽曬。有傷皮膚。在裏頭怕火。蹧蹋了臉色。我的女人說。女兒起得太早。恐怕傷了眼晴。吃過飯作

would redden their noses, and she convinced me that the hands never looked so white as when they did nothing. Instead, therefore, of finishing George's shirts, we now had them new modeling their old gauzes, or flourishing upon catgut. The poor Miss Flamboroughs, their former gay companions, were cast off as mean acquaintances, and the whole conversation ran upon high life and high-lived company, with pictures, taste, Shakespeare, and the musical glasses.

But we could have borne all this, had not a fortune-telling gypsy[1] come to raise us into perfect sublimity. The tawny sibyl no sooner appeared than my girls came running to me for a shilling apiece to cross her hand with silver.[2] To say the truth, I was tired of being always wise, and could not help gratifying their request, because I loved to see them happy. I gave each of them a

事. 又恐怕紅了鼻子. 還說了許多話要我相信. 若要兩隻手白. 無過於不作事. 故此現在他們. 不替佐之把內衣縫完. 反去改造他們自己的紗製舊衣裳. 不然. 就是弄胡琴. 可憐隔壁的兩位法林巴小姐. 從前我是的兩個女兒. 和他們是有頑有笑的. 現在嫌人家窮. 都摔開不理人家了. 終日談的都是闊人家的生活. 闊朋友. 又談繪畫. 和最時髦的穿戴. 沙士比的戲. 玻璃盃發樂音 {未後兩句是 / 拾人牙慧}.

他們若是摹仿闊人作到這裏爲止. 也還罷了. 誰知來了一個行脚算命的婆子. 把他們一吹. 吹到天頂上去了. 有了一天. 這黑臉婆子來了. 兩個女兒立刻走來. 每人向我要一個先令去算命. 我老實說. 我勸他們勸得太多. 好像是我不全是對的. 他們都是不好對的. 我也厭煩了. 只是心裏也讓他們高興. 我覺得快樂. 於是每個女

1. Gypsy, 外來遊民皮膚黃色相傳是埃及人. 2. Cross her hand with silver, 先用銀錢橫劃算命者手掌才會算得準.

shilling; though, for the honor of the family, it must be observed, that they never went without money themselves, as my wife always generously let them have a guinea each to keep in their pockets; but with strict injunctions never to change it. After they had been closeted up with the fortune teller for some time, I knew by their looks, upon their returning, that they had been promised something great.— "Well, my girls, how have you sped? Tell me, Livy, has the fortune teller given thee a pennyworth?"— "I protest, papa," says the girl, "I believe she deals with somebody that's not right; for she positively declared that I am to be married to a squire in less than a twelvemonth!"— "Well, now, Sophy, my child," said I, "and what sort of a husband are you to have?"—"Sir," replied she, "I am to have a lord soon after my sister has married the squire."— "How," cried I, "is that all you are to have for your two shillings! Only a lord

兒給一個先令.爲我的家庭體面起見.我要說明白.他們並不是沒得錢.因爲我的女人總要每個女兒給一個金錢.放在口袋裏.却不許換輔幣零用｛給錢與不給等寫來好笑｝.他們拿了先令.同那算命老婆子關在屋裏好一會.後來走出來.我一看他們的臉.就曉得算命老婆子答應了他們極闊的前程.我問道.好呀.我的女兒們.怎麼樣啦.奧維雅.你告訴我.算命的告訴你的話.值得一個銅子嗎.他答道.爸爸.我恐怕他是同魔鬼來往有魔術.因爲他很頂真的說.我到不了一年.就嫁一位鄉紳.我又問道.素緋雅.我的孩子.你將來嫁什麼人呢.他答道.老爺子.算命的說.我姊姊嫁與鄉紳之後.不久我就嫁與一位爵爺.我說道.什麼呀.兩個先令.不過換得這一點東西嗎.花了兩個先令.

and a squire for two shillings! You fools, I could have promised you a prince and a nabob for half the money."

This curiosity of theirs, however, was attended with very serious effects; we now began to think ourselves designed by the stars to something exalted, and already anticipated our future grandeur.

It has been a thousand times observed, and I must observe it once more, that the hours we pass with happy prospects in view are more pleasing than those crowded with fruition. In the first case, we cook the dish to our own appetite; in the latter, nature cooks it for us. It is impossible to repeat the train[1] of agreeable reveries[2] we called up for our own entertainment. We looked upon our fortunes as once more rising; and as the whole parish asserted that the squire was in love with my daughter, she was actually so with him; for they

不過得一位爵爺.一位鄉紳嗎.你們真是傻子. 我只要一個先令.可以答應你們一位王爺.一位大富翁 {奚落得｜痛快}.

他們這一算命要預知將來.却生出極要緊的效果.我們自此以後.相信走極高極貴的命運.預望將來大關.

有一句話.是前人說過一千遍的.我再說一遍.說的是我們盼望將來好光景所過的時候.比實收效果所過的較為快樂.第一層.我們所盼望的.是照着合我們自己的口味去作菜.第二層.是天作好給我們吃的.我們自己接二連三幻想造出來的空中樓閣.有寫不出來的樂境.我們這時候.以為重新走好運.因為通村都說鄉紳戀愛我的女兒. 我的女兒就居然實行

---

1. Train, 一串. 2. Reveries, 幻想；妄想；似夢非夢.

persuaded her into the passion. In this agreeable interval my wife had the most lucky dreams in the world, which she took care to tell us every morning, with great solemnity and exactness. It was one night a coffin and cross-bones—the sign of an approaching wedding; at another time she imagined her daughters' pockets filled with farthings—a certain sign they would short-ly be stuffed with gold. The girls themselves had their omens. They felt strange kisses on their lips; they saw rings in the candle, purses bounced from the fire,[1] and true love knots lurked in the bottom of every teacup.

Towards the end of the week we received a card from the town ladies, in which, with their compli-ments, they hoped to see all our family at church the Sunday following. All Saturday morning I could perceive, in consequence of

戀愛鄉紳. 彷彿就是通村的人. 勸他發動愛情的. 這個當口. 我的女人作的夢. 都是世界上別人夢不到的好夢. 每早起來. 他很鄭重很小心的把昨夜的夢告訴我們. 所有詳細的夢境. 說得極清楚. 一點兒也不漏. 有一晚上. 他夢的是棺材同兩條交加大腿骨. 這是快辦喜事的預兆. 又有一晚. 他夢的是女兒的幾個口袋. 都裝滿了小銅錢. 這是一定不久口袋裏裝滿金錢的預兆. 女兒們也有他們的預兆. 他們覺得有人同他接吻. 又看見燭光成暈. 火裏有煤塊像錢口袋. 從火裏跳出來. 茶碗底藏着同心結.

快到星期那一天. 接到京裏兩位女人的請帖. 盼望我們全家星期那一天在教堂相見. 因為這一請. 我看見星期

---

1. Purses bounced from the fire, 發財預兆.

this, my wife and daughters in close conference together, and now and then glancing at me with looks that betrayed a latent[1] plot.[2] To be sincere, I had strong suspicions that some absurd proposal was preparing for appearing with splendor the next day. In the evening they began their operations[3] in a very regular manner, and my wife undertook to conduct the siege. After tea, when I seemed in spirits, she began thus:—"I fancy, Charles, my dear, we shall have a great deal of good company at our church tomorrow."—"Perhaps we may, my dear," returned I; "though you need be under no uneasiness about that, you shall have a sermon whether there be or not."— "That is what I expect," returned she; "but I think, my dear, we ought to appear there as decently as possible, for who knows what may happen?"—"Your precautions,"[4] replied

六那一天. 我的女人同兩個女兒. 秘密會議. 有時拿眼偷看我. 露出來他們商議什麼詭計. 我很疑心他們預備實行極無理的事. 明天要大出風頭. 到了晚上. 他們就依次的發兵. 我的女人擔任圍城. 吃過了茶. 當我很高興的時候. 我的女人就開始攻擊. 說道. 查理{牧師小名}. 我的寶貝. 明天教堂裏闊人必多. 我答道. 我的寶貝. 也許有的. 不過你不必爲這事煩心. 毋論闊人或多或少. 我一定有一篇好宣講文. 給你聽. 他答道. 這一層我很曉得. 不過我想. 我們必定要穿得像樣好見人. 誰料得會發生什麼事呢. 我答道. 你先事預防. 我很贊成.

---

1. Latent 隱藏不露. 2. Plot, 詭計；陰謀. 3. Operations, 動作；動兵. 4. Precautions, 先事預防.

THE VICAR OF WAKEFIELD · 95

I, "are highly commendable. A decent[1] behavior and appearance in church is what charms me. We should be devout and humble, cheerful and serene."—"Yes," cried she, "I know that; but I mean, we should go there in as proper a manner as possible; not altogether like the scrubs about us."— "You are quite right, my dear," returned I, "and I was going to make the very same proposal. The proper manner of going is, to go there as early as possible, to have time for meditation before the service begins."—"Phoo, Charles," interrupted she, "all that is very true; but not what I would be at. I mean we should go there genteelly. You know the church is two miles off, and I protest I don't like to see my daughters trudging up to their pew all blowzed and red with walking, and looking for all the world as if they had been winners at a smock race. Now, my

我最喜歡看見人在教堂裏行為及外貌.都要莊重像樣.要虔誠.卑下.高興.沉靜.他答道.這個我曉得.但是我的意思說的是.我們到教堂去.應該殼樣子.不要學窮苦人的樣子.我答道.你說的很對.我正要告訴你同樣的意思.凡到教堂去要殼樣子.是越早去越好.教儀未起之先.可以有時候用心思想. {此段夫婦一問一答一個要說却不敢卽說一個心裏很明白一味裝糊塗好像捉迷藏}.他攔住說道.咳.查理.你所說的都不錯.不過不是我的意思.我說的是.我們到教堂去.要特別好看些.你曉得的.我們家裏離教堂還有六七里路.我老實說.我很不喜歡女兒們步行走多少路.走到教堂裏的坐位.滿臉通紅.好像是賽跑得頭彩的.我的意思.是我們有

1. Decent, 不瀣涅；不輕佻；莊重；過得去；令人起敬；像樣.

dear, my proposal is this: there are our two plow horses, the colt that has been in our family these nine years, and his companion, Blackberry, that has scarce done an earthly thing for this month past. They are both grown fat and lazy. Why should not they do something as well as we? And let me tell you, when Moses has trimmed them a little, they will cut a very tolerable figure."

To this proposal I objected, that walking would be twenty times more genteel[1] than such a paltry conveyance, as Blackberry was wall-eyed, and the colt wanted a tail: that they had never been broke to the rein; but had a hundred vicious tricks; and that we had but one saddle and pillion in the whole house. All these objections, however, were overruled;[2] so that I was obliged to comply. The next morning I perceived them not a little busy in collecting such

兩個種地的馬．一匹是小馬．在我們家裏有九年了．一匹是他的同伴．叫黑果．在這一個月內．什麼事也沒作過．這兩匹馬懶到發胖了．我們都忙的作事．爲什麼馬就不派作點事呢．我告訴你．只要摩西把馬洗刷修剪．還是很可以見人的｛牧師太太急了｝｛索性說出來｝．

我反對這個條陳．用這種牲口上路．更寒酸．不如步行却大方幾十倍．況且黑果是兩隻白眼．那小馬又欠一條尾巴．這兩個馬向來不曾教練上過轡．當坐馬騎上了．不曉得要鬧多少壞脾氣．況且我們家裏只有一副鞍．一副後墊．我這幾句反對的話．他們全不聽．我只好依了．第二天早上．我看見他們在那裏收拾各種應用東西．預備出發．我

---

1. Genteel (*adj.*)，合於上等人之身分；大方．　2. Overruled，反對；不以爲然；駁倒；推翻．

materials as might be necessary for the expedition; but as I found it would be a business of time, I walked on to the church before, and they promised speedily to follow. I waited near an hour in the reading desk for their arrival; but not finding them come as expected, I was obliged to begin, and went through the service[1] not without some uneasiness at finding them absent. This was increased when all was finished, and no appearance of the family. I therefore walked back by the horse-way, which was five miles round, though the footway was but two; and when got about halfway home, perceived the procession marching slowly forward toward the church; my son, my wife, and the two little ones exalted on one horse, and my two daughters upon the other. I demanded the cause of their delay; but I soon found by their looks they had met with a thousand

曉得他們要忙得好一會.我先行.去教堂.他們答應趕快的隨後來.我到了之後.在書桌旁坐下.等了幾乎一點鐘.等他們來.越等越不來.我只好起首祈禱講經.看見他們不來.心裏很有點不安.等到禮拜都作完了.他們還不來.我心裏更加不安.於是我從馬路走回去.回到半路.才看見他們同擺儀仗像的.慢慢向教堂來.我的兒子.我的女人.還有兩個小的.堆在一個馬上.兩個女兒.又在一只馬上.我責問他們.爲什麼躭擱.一看他們的臉.就曉得他們在路上出了許多事.第一件.兩匹

1. Church service, 祈禱; 講經; 作禮拜.

misfortunes on the road. The horses had at first refused to move from the door, till Mr. Burchell was kind enough to beat them forward for about two hundred yards with his cudgel. Next, the straps of my wife's pillion broke down, and they were obliged to stop to repair them before they could proceed. After that, one of the horses took it into his head to stand still, and neither blows nor entreaties could prevail with him to proceed. He was just recovering from this dismal[1] situation when I found them; but perceiving everything safe, I own their present mortification[2] did not much displease me, as it would give me many opportunities of future triumph, and teach my daughters more humility.[3]

馬呆站在家門口.不肯走.後來白且爾郭忙.拿棍子敲馬.敲了有二百碼遠.那兩匹馬才走的.第二件.馬背上墊子的皮帶斷了.只好停住.修理好了再往前走.後來有匹馬意想情願的.站住不動.勸他也不成.打他也不成.他總是個不走{此一段偏有許多不漢趣的事寫得好笑}.我碰着他們.正是敗興剛有轉機的時候.我看見他們都平安.受了這一番折磨.心裏暗暗的並無什麼不高興.因為怎麼一來.給我將來許多機會說話.贏他們.我的女兒受了一番教訓.以後可稍斂迹些.不再出風頭. .

---

1. Dismal, 敗興; 慘淡; 寂寞. 2. Mortification (*mortis*, 拉丁文, 死也), 冷水澆背或令人敗興之事; 受折磨. 3. Humility, 卑下; 甘居人下; 斂迹.

CHAPTER XI

THE FAMILY STILL RESOLVE TO HOLD UP THEIR HEADS

第 十 一 回
家 裏 的 人 還 是 要 出 風 頭
（唐 希 爾 設 計 害 善 良）

Michaelmas Eve happening on the next day, we were invited to burn nuts and play tricks at neighbor Flamborough's. Our late mortifications had humbled us a little, or it is probable we might have rejected such an invitation with contempt; however, we suffered ourselves to be happy. Our honest neighbor's goose and dumplings were fine, and the lamb's wool, even in the opinion of my wife, who was a connoisseur,[1] was excellent. It is true, his manner of telling stories was not quite so well. They were very long, and very dull, and all about himself, and we had

且說第二天就到了
九月廿九的節．鄰居法
林巴請我們去過節．燒
果仁｛不知／所謂｝．頑把戲．我
們受過一番折磨．壓住
我們的風頭少出些．不
然的話．大約一定看人
不起．不肯去的．但是我
們勉勉強強尋些快樂
｛還是看不也／起鄰居也｝．鄰居的燒
鵝和包子很好吃．那雜
釀的甜酒．據我的女人
是個行家說．是釀得非
常之好．法林巴說故事．
却說得不甚好．說得太
長．又無趣味．又說的都
是自己所說的笑話｛席上／｝
｛閒談最忌／總說自己｝．我們從前都

---

1. Connoisseur, 行家；善看古董字畫者．

109

laughed at them ten times before; however, we were kind enough to laugh at them once more.

Mr. Burchell, who was one of the party, was always fond of seeing some innocent amusement going forward, and set the boys and girls to blind man's buff. My wife, too, was persuaded to join in the diversion,[1] and it gave me pleasure to think she was not yet too old. In the meantime, my neighbor and I looked on, laughed at every feat,[2] and praised our own dexterity when we were young. Hot cockles succeeded next, questions and commands followed that, and last of all, they sat down to hunt the slipper. As every person may not be acquainted with this primeval pastime, it may be necessary to observe that the company at this play plant themselves in a ring upon the ground, all except one who stands in the middle,

聽過. 笑過有十輪了. 我們却是很客氣的再笑一輪 {是勉強敷衍仍看不起人也}.

席上原有白且爾. 他向來是喜歡有些正當無害的遊戲進行. 就叫少年男女們捉迷藏. 還勸我的女人也同他們去開心. 我倒很歡喜看見他還不太老. 我和法林巴旁觀看熱鬧. 看見耍得好. 就大笑. 談我們少年遊戲的本事. 隨後頑的是閉住眼猜誰來打. 又頑請令遵令的遊戲. 最後是坐下頑搶鞋. 這一個是太古時候的遊戲. 不是個個人都曉得的. 我不能不解說. 頑的時候. 衆人都坐下. 圍成一個圈子. 有一個站在圈子中間. 四圍的人. 傳遞

---

1. Diversion, 開心或解悶的事. 2. Feat, 膽量過人的事; 他人所作不到的事; 出色的技藝或游戲.

whose business it is to catch a shoe, which the company shove about under their hams from one to another, something like a weaver's shuttle. As it is impossible, in this case, for the lady who is up to face all the company at once, the great beauty of the play lies in hitting her a thump with the heel of the shoe on that side least capable of making a defense. It was in this manner that my eldest daughter was hemmed in, and thumped about, all blowzed, in spirits, and bawling for fair play, fair play, with a voice that might deafen a ballad singer, when, confusion on confusion, who should enter the room but our two great acquaintances from town, Lady Blarney and Miss Carolina Wilelmina Amelia Skeggs! Description would but beggar, therefore it is unnecessary to describe, this new mortification. Death! To be seen by ladies of such high breeding in such vulgar attitudes! Nothing better could ensue from such a vulgar play of

一隻鞋子. 如織布穿梭一樣. 鬧笑的地方. 就在站在中間的女人. 不能同時轉身. 四面八方的對着這一圈子人. 人家就拿鞋子對那防備不到的地方拍他. 我的大女兒正在身入重圍. 被人用鞋子拍的塌塌的響. 滿臉通紅. 在那裏喊. 說他們不公道. 他喊的聲音很吵. 幾乎可以把唱大曲的壓下去. 正在亂中加亂的時候. 誰知兩個京裏的女人. 一個有爵的叫巴拉尼. 一個叫很長名字的斯克小姐. 走進來. 我寫也寫不出來我女兒那種自覺難堪的光景〔廝作者寫得出可謂熱鬧之極〕. 該死呀. 種種俗態. 被受過高等教養的闊女人看見了. 法林巴發起的粗俗遊戲. 是不會

Mr. Flamborough's propos-
ing. We seemed stuck to
the ground for some time,
as if actually petrified with
amazement.

The two ladies had been
at our house to see us, and
finding us from home, came
after us hither, as they
were uneasy to know what
accident could have kept
us from church the day
before. Olivia undertook
to be our prolocutor, and
delivered the whole in a
summary way, only saying,
"We were thrown from our
horses." At which account
the ladies were greatly con-
cerned; but being told the
family received no hurt,
they were extremely glad;
but being informed that
we were almost killed by
the fright, they were vastly
sorry; but hearing that we
had a very good night,
they were extremely glad
again. Nothing could ex-
ceed their complaisance to
my daughters; their professions the last evening were
warm, but now they were
ardent. They protested a
desire of having a more last-
ing acquaintance. Lady
Blarney was particularly

有好結果的. 我們有好
一會. 被這兩個女人高
貴的氣勢壓倒. 好像是
變了石頭生根在地上.
動也動不得.

原來這兩位女人. 先
到我們家裏看我們. 見
我們不在家. 找到這裏.
因爲昨天我們未到教
堂. 要打聽我們到底遇
了什麼事故. 奧維雅替
我們說. 騎馬跌下來. 兩
位聽了. 說很關切. 奧維
雅又說. 都沒受傷. 兩位
說. 聽了很高興. 奧維雅
又說. 我們幾乎嚇死. 兩
位聽了說. 很難過. 奧維
雅說. 晚上却睡得很好.
兩位說. 聽了極高興
﹛描寫應酬場中俗態﹜. 這兩位總
要我兩個女兒高興. 樣
樣遷就. 無以復加. 早一
天晚上. 這兩位說的話.
不過是親熱而已. 這時
候說的話. 簡直是熱到
燒人. 說是要同我兩個
女兒作永久的朋友. 巴
拉尼是特別的同奧維

attached to Olivia; Miss Carolina Wilelmina Amelia Skeggs (I love to give the whole name) took a greater fancy to her sister. They supported the conversation between themselves, while my daughters sat silent, admiring their exalted breeding. But as every reader, however beggarly himself, is fond of high-lived dialogues, with anecdotes of lords, ladies, and Knights of the Garter, I must beg leave to give him the concluding part of the present conversation.

"All that I know of the matter," cried Miss Skeggs, "is this, that it may be true, or it may not be true; but this I can assure your ladyship, that the whole rout[1] was in amaze; his lordship turned all manner of colors, my lady fell into a swoon,[2] but Sir Tomkyn, drawing his sword, swore he was hers to the last drop of his blood."

"Well," replied our peeress, "this I can say, that the duchess never told me

雅親熱．那位名字很長的斯克小姐．尤其喜歡素緋雅．他們兩位彼此交談．我的兩個女兒不響．在那裏羨慕他們的高貴派頭．但是讀者無論窮到是個叫化子．也喜歡聽高貴人談話．貴族及貴婦高等爵士們的逸事 {此處旁帶一挖苦讀者}．我不揣冒昧．把這兩位高貴女人末後一段的談話．寫下來給讀者看．斯克小姐說道．這件事．我也不曉得到底是怎麼樣．也許是真的．也許是假的．那晚上大宴會的人．都大為驚異．那位貴族臉上．變各種顏色．貴婦是暈倒．那唐金爵士拔出刀來說．只有流剩一滴血．他還是衛護貴婦．還是貴婦的人．

　那一位答道．我能說我相信公爵夫人．無論什麼祕密．都告訴我的．

---

1. Rout, 晚上的大宴會. 2. Swoon, 初版作 sound, 後來坊刻有作 swoon 者，有作 sound 者，從前此兩字寫異音同.

a syllable of the matter, and I believe her grace would keep nothing a secret from me. This you may depend upon as a fact, that the next morning my lord duke cried out three times to his valet de chambre, 'Jernigan, Jernigan, Jernigan, bring me my garters.'"

But previously I should have mentioned the very impolite behavior of Mr. Burchell, who, during this discourse, sat with his face turned to the fire, and at the conclusion of every sentence would cry out *Fudge!*—an expression which displeased us all, and in some measure damped the rising spirit of the conversation.

"Besides, my dear Skeggs," continued our peeress, "there is nothing of this in the copy of verses that Dr. Burdock made upon the occasion." *Fudge!*

"I am surprised at that," cried Miss Skeggs, "for he seldom leaves anything out, as he writes only for his own amusement. But can your ladyship favor me

對於這件事. 他却一字沒對我說過. 第二天. 公爵喊他的家人. 喊了三次. 說查尼干. 查尼干. 查尼干. 你把我的襪帶拿來. 這一件却是事實 {可見所謂受過高貴教育的高貴女人所說的話不過如此都不相干} 毫無道理 }.

但我先應說明白且爾之無禮. 當這兩位高貴女人交談的時候. 他的臉向着火. 他們說完一句. 他就喊一聲胡說. 我們聽了. 都很不喜歡. 那兩位的談話. 也就不甚高興 {白且爾看破兩位高貴女人的破綻忍受不住故} 壓喊胡說 }.

巴拉尼接着說道. 我的親愛斯克小姐. 況且巴博士. 拿這個題目作的詩. 却無一字提及. (又聽喊胡說.)

斯克小姐說道. 這却奇怪. 他作詩是為自己消遣. 很少的漏去不說

with a sight of them?"
Fudge!

"My dear creature,"
replied our peeress, "do
you think I carry such
things about me? Though
they are very fine, to be
sure, and I think myself
something of a judge; at
least, I know what pleases
myself. Indeed, I was ever
an admirer of all Doctor
Burdock's little pieces: for
except what he does, and
our dear countess at Han-
over Square, there's nothing comes out but the most
lowest stuff in nature; not
a bit of high life among
them." *Fudge!*

"Your ladyship should
except," says t'other,
"your own things in the
Lady's Magazine. I hope
you'll say there's nothing
low-lived there? But I
suppose we are to have no
more from that quarter?"
Fudge!

"Why, my dear," says
the lady, "you know my
reader and companion
has left me, to be married
to Captain Roach; and as
my poor eyes won't suffer
me to write myself, I have
been for some time looking

的. 你能給我看看嗎.
（又聽喊胡說）

巴拉尼答道. 我的寶
貝. 我身上還帶這種東
西嗎. 我以爲我懂得詩.
我曉得我喜歡什麼. 他
的詩是不錯. 我向來喜
歡他的短篇. 除了他的
著作. 還有住在某處的
伯爵夫人的詩. 其餘的
都是最下等的貨. 毫無
富貴派頭.（又聽喊胡說）

斯克小姐答道. 你應
該把你的著作剋在婦
女雜誌的除外. 那裏頭
沒得下等東西. 我猜以
後再不見有你的東西
在那雜誌咧.（又聽喊
胡說）

巴拉尼答道. 我的文
學陪伴走了. 嫁了某大
佐. 因爲寫東西傷我的
眼睛. 我曾經另外再找

out for another. A proper
person is no easy matter
to find; and to be sure
thirty pounds a year is a
small stipend for a well-
bred girl of character, that
can read, write, and behave
in company; as for the
chits about town, there is
no bearing them about
one." *Fudge!*

"That I know," cried
Miss Skeggs, "by experi-
ence. For of the three
companions I had this last
half year, one of them refused to do plain work an
hour in the day; another
thought twenty-five guineas
a year too small a salary,
and I was obliged to send
away the third, because I
suspected an intrigue with
the chaplain. Honor, my
dear Lady Blarney, honor
is worth any price; but
where is that to be found?"
Fudge!

My wife had been for a
long time all attention to
this discourse, but was particularly struck with the
latter part of it. Thirty
pounds and twenty-five
guineas made fifty-six
pounds five shillings
English money, all which

人.合式人是不容易找
得着.每年不過三十鎊
束修.難找着受過好教
育.品行又好.能讀能寫.
能應酬的人.京裏的女
孩子們.我受不了常時
擺在身邊.(胡說){此段慢慢
露出}
陰謀.

斯克小姐說道.我有
過閱歷.我曉得.這後半
年.我有過三個陪伴.一
個不肯每天作一點鐘
的平常事.一個嫌每年
二十五個金錢薪水太
少.第三個.我疑心他有
祕密愛情的事.我辭退
他.我的巴拉尼.知廉恥
顧體面.是最要緊的.那
裏去找呢.(胡說)

我的女人.聚精會神
的聽他們兩個人談話.
對於後來這段話.尤其
動心.三十金鎊.二十五
個金錢.合計是五十六
鎊五先令.在那裏等人

was in a manner going a-begging, and might easily be secured in the family. She for a moment studied my looks for approbation; and, to own a truth, I was of opinion that two such places would fit our two daughters exactly. Besides, if the squire had any real affection for my eldest daughter, this would be the way to make her every way qualified for her fortune. My wife, therefore, was resolved that we should not be deprived of such advantages for want of assurance, and undertook to harangue for the family. "I hope," cried she, "your ladyships will pardon my present presumption.[1] It is true we have no right to pretend to such favors, but yet it is natural for me to wish putting my children forward in the world. And I will be bold to say my two girls have had a pretty good education, and capacity, at least the country can't show better. They can read, write, and cast

承受.我們家裏可以拿過來.他看我的臉.看了一會.意思要我答應.我老實說.我以爲這兩個席位.很合兩個女兒身分.況且鄉紳倘或眞愛我的大女兒.這個席位可以使他有嫁與富貴人家的資格.於是我的女人.打定主意不客氣.不.使這種利益出我們的家門.就擔任替我們家裏說話.於是對那兩位高貴女人說道.我要說點過於自信的話.請你饒我.實在我們不應得這樣恩惠.但是我自然想把我的兒女們見見世界.我大膽說.我兩女兒受過頗好的教育.也還能作事.無論如何.鄉下裏沒有好過他們的.他們會讀.會寫.會

---

1. Presumption, 過於自信或果於自信之語意;自以爲是.

accounts; they understand their needle, broadstitch,[1] cross[2] and change,[3] and all manner of plain work; they can pink, point, and frill, and know something of music; they can do up small clothes, work upon catgut; my eldest can cut paper, and my youngest has a very pretty manner of telling fortunes upon the cards." *Fudge!*

When she had delivered this pretty piece of eloquence, the two ladies looked at each other a few minutes in silence, with an air of doubt and importance. At last Miss Carolina Wilelmina Amelia Skeggs condescended to observe that the young ladies, from the opinion she could form of them from so slight an acquaintance, seemed very fit for such employments; "but a thing of this kind, madam," cried she, addressing my spouse, "requires a thorough examination into characters, and a more perfect knowledge of each

算. 又會針線. 各種縫級. 上下針. 還有其他平常活計都會. 他們還會打眼. 穿孔. 綠邊. 又會音樂. 作短衣裳. 作繡活. 我的大女兒會剪紙花. 我的小女兒會拿紙牌算命. (胡說)

他把這篇好演說說完了 {好演說三字 / 意帶挖苦}. 那兩個女人面面相看. 不響. 有幾分鐘. 帶着鄭重懷疑的神氣. 後來那長名字斯克小姐屈尊的說. 兩位小姐同他不過是初交. 却很像能稱作陪伴之職. 又對着我女人說道. 瑪當. 但是這種事體. 須要嚴查品格. 彼此都要很深的相知. 瑪當.

1. Broadstitch, 此縫級法今已失傳.　2. Cross, 似是上下針.
3. Change, 此法恐亦失傳或云是臀骨縫法.

other. Not, madam," continued she, "that I in the least suspect the young ladies' virtue, prudence, and discretion;[1] but there is a form in these things, madam, there is a form."

My wife approved her suspicions very much, observing that she was very apt to be suspicious herself; but referred her to all the neighbors for a character; but this our peeress declined as unnecessary, alleging that her cousin Thornhill's recommendation would be sufficient, and upon this we rested our petition.

我對於兩位小姐行為謹慎機靈.斷無絲毫懷疑.不過這種事體.有照例的正式規則.

我女人很以他懷疑為然.還說他自己也易於懷疑.只好請兩位女人向各鄰居查問.但是那位貴人不肯.還說不必.只要有他老表唐希爾保薦就彀了.我們求事.說到這裏為止.

---

1. Discretion 有應付之能; 隨機應變; 有分寸; 機靈.

CHAPTER XII

FORTUNE SEEMS RESOLVED TO HUMBLE THE FAMILY OF WAKEFIELD — MORTIFICATIONS ARE OFTEN MORE PAINFUL THAN REAL CALAMITIES.

第 十 二 回

運 氣 不 佳 還 要 把 我 們 打 下 去　志 氣 頹喪 比 實 禍 難 受
(麽 西 賣 馬 受 局 騙)

When we were returned home, the night was dedicated[1] to schemes of future conquest. Deborah exerted much sagacity in conjecturing which of the two girls was likely to have the best place, and most opportunities of seeing good company. The only obstacle to our preferment[2] was in obtaining the squire's recommendation; but he had already shown us too many instances of his friendship to doubt of it now. Even in bed, my wife kept up the usual theme: "Well, faith, my

且 說 我 們 回 家 之 後. 那 天 晚 上 全 用 在 策 畫 將 來 的 勝 算. 狄 波 拉 {牧師太太小名} 費 了 許 多 聰 明 去 猜 那 一 個 女 兒 得 頂 好 的 席 位. 有 最 多 的 機 會 同 闊 人 應 酬. 要 得 這 優 差. 惟 一 的 為 難. 是 求 得 鄉 紳 的 保 薦. 但 是 他 已 經 屢 次 同 我 們 拉 交 情. 這 個 時 候 不 用 疑 他 不 保 薦. 上 牀 睡 覺. 我 的 女 人 還 要 談 這 件 事.

---

1. Dedicated, 全用在. 2. Preferment, 升階；優差.

dear Charles, between ourselves, I think we have made an excellent day's work of it."—"Pretty well," cried I, not knowing what to say.—"What, only pretty well!" returned she. "I think it is very well. Suppose the girls should come to make acquaintances of taste in town! This I am assured of, that London is the only place in the world for all manner of husbands. Besides, my dear, stranger things happen every day; and as ladies of quality are so taken with my daughters, what will not men of quality be! *Entre nous*, I protest I like my Lady Blarney vastly—so very obliging.[1] However, Miss Carolina Wilelmina Amelia Skeggs has my warm heart. But yet, when they came to talk of places in town, you saw at once how I nailed them. Tell me, my dear, don't you think I did for my children there?"— "Ay," returned I, not knowing well what to think

說道. 我的寶貝查理. 我對你說. 我們今天辦了一天頂好的事. 我不曉得說什麼. 答道. 還好. 他答道. 什麼. 不過還好就完了嗎. 我看是很好. 譬如兩個女兒在京城認識些富貴朋友. 我曉得的. 只有倫敦一個地方. 什麼丈夫都有. 況且天天都有奇事出現. 高貴女人極喜歡我們兩個女兒. 高貴的男子. 更不必說了. 我對你說. 我頂喜歡巴拉尼. 他興肯替人辦事. 令人感激. 然而很長名字的斯克小姐. 最得我的心. 他們一談起京城有席位的話. 你看見的. 我立刻把他們釘住了. 你告訴我. 我能替女兒出力罷. 我對於這事. 想不出什麼來. 只好答. 噯. 我求老天保佑

---

1. Obliging, 使人感激.

of the matter; "Heaven grant they may be both the better for it this day three months!" This was one of those observations I usually made to impress my wife with an opinion of my sagacity; for if the girls succeeded, then it was a pious wish fulfilled; but if anything unfortunate ensued, then it might be looked upon as a prophecy. All this conversation, however, was only preparatory to another scheme, and indeed I dreaded as much. This was nothing less than that, as we were now to hold up our heads a little higher in the world, it would be proper to sell the colt, which was grown old, at a neighboring fair, and buy us a horse that would carry single or double upon an occasion, and make a pretty appearance at church or upon a visit. This at first I opposed stoutly, but it was as stoutly defended. However, as I weakened, my antagonists gained strength, till at last it was resolved to part with him.

他們．這三個月內比從前更好．這一句話．我向來對我的女人說．印在他心裏．使他曉得我的聰明．這原是一句騎牆話．倘或兩個女兒得意．那是應了我們虔誠希望的心．倘或遇有不幸的事．我的話算是句預言．但是我恐怕這番談話．不過都是預備第二件事．這第二件．並非他事．就是我們現在要抬起頭來．稍爲出些風頭．不能不在附近的市集．把那匹小馬賣了．他已經老了．不如另外買一匹可以一個人或兩個人騎的．有時騎了到教堂．或拜客．好看些．我起初極力反對他．他極力的反對我．一定要賣．我反對力稍弱．敵人攻擊更猛．後來商定只好賣馬．

THE VICAR OF WAKEFIELD

As the fair happened on the following day, I had intentions of going myself; but my wife persuaded me that I had got a cold, and nothing could prevail upon[1] her to permit me from home. "No, my dear," said she, "our son Moses is a discreet boy, and can buy and sell to very good advantage; you know all our great bargains are of his purchasing. He always stands out and higgles, and actually tires them till he gets a bargain."

As I had some idea of my son's prudence, I was willing enough to trust him with this commission; and the next morning I perceived his sisters mighty busy in fitting out Moses for the fair; trimming his hair, brushing his buckles, and cocking his hat with pins. The business of the toilet being over, we had at last the satisfaction of seeing him mounted upon the colt, with a deal box before him to bring home

第二天是集期.我原想自己去的.我女人說我傷風.勸我不要去.我怎樣說.他也不讓我去.他說道.摩西很會隨機應變.能買能賣.都佔便宜.他曉得的.我們買的便宜貨.都是他買的.他很能耐煩講價.他把人家講累了.得了便宜.才罷手.

我略為曉得我兒子有點把握.我很願意把這事付託給他辦.第二天早上.我看見他兩個姊姊.非常的忙着打扮他趕集.替他理髮刷鞋扣.拿別針同他別帽子.打扮好了.到末後我們很滿意的.看他騎上馬.前頭擺着一個木箱子.預備裝雜物帶回家.他身

1. Prevail upon, 贏; 勝; 勸回頭.

groceries in.　He had on a coat of that cloth they call thunder and lightning, which, though grown too short, was much too good to be thrown away.　His waistcoat was of gosling green, and his sisters had tied his hair with a broad black riband.　We all followed him several paces from the door, bawling after him good luck, good luck, till we could see him no longer.

He was scarce gone, when Mr. Thornhill's butler came to congratulate us upon our good fortune, saying, that he overheard his young master mention our names with great commendation.

Good fortune seemed resolved not to come alone.　Another footman from the same family followed, with a card for my daughters, importing that the two ladies had received such pleasing accounts from Mr. Thornhill of us all, that, after a few previous inquiries, they hoped to be perfectly satisfied.　"Ay," cried my wife, "I now see it is no easy matter to get

穿一件黑白柳條呢衣. 短了些. 我們却捨不得 摔了. 裏面是一件鵝黃 色背心. 兩個姊姊用一 大塊黑紬子同他結頭 髮. 我們一齊送他出大 門. 送好幾步. 在後面喊 道. 走好運. 走好運. 等到 看不見他. 我們才回頭.

他才走了. 唐希爾的 總管家來. 同我們道喜. 說是他聽見說我們的 名字. 極力說我們的好 話.

我們的好運又跟着 來. 接着唐家又有一個 家人來. 帶着片子. 說京 裏來的兩位女人. 探問 唐鄉紳幾句話. 鄉紳說 了我們許多好處. 他們 盼望可以滿意. 我的女 人說道. 唏. 我現在曉得 了. 要進大家的門. 是不

into the families of the great; but when once gets in, then, as Moses says, one may go to sleep." To this piece of humor—for she intended it for wit—my daughters assented with a loud laugh of pleasure. In short, such was her satisfaction at this message, that she actually put her hand in her pocket, and gave the messenger sevenpence halfpenny.

This was to be our visiting day. The next that came was Mr. Burchell, who had been at the fair. He brought my little ones a pennyworth of gingerbread each, which my wife undertook to keep for them, and give them by letters at a time. He brought my daughters also a couple of boxes, in which they might keep wafers, snuff, patches, or even money (when they got it). My wife was usually fond of a weasel-skin purse, as being the most lucky, but this by the bye. We had still a regard for Mr. Burchell, though his late rude behavior was in some measure displeasing; nor could we now avoid

容易的. 但是一踏進門以後. 就是摩西說的話. 我們可以安睡咧. 我女人的意思. 是要說句俏皮話. 我的女兒很以為然. 大笑一會. 我女人聽了這個喜信. 非常得意. 伸手到口袋裏. 掏出七個大銅錢. 一個小銅錢. 打賞來人 {只賞七個大銅錢一個小銅錢未免不大方不}.

今天原是我們招待客人的日子. 第二個客是白且爾. 從集上來的. 帶了餅來給小孩子. 一人一塊. 我女人收着. 每次拿一個字母給. 他們吃 {餅上有字母}. 又帶了兩個盒子 一個女兒送一個. 裝零碎. 也可以裝錢 (只要有) {這三字說他們身上無錢也}. 我女人向來喜歡黃鼠狼皮作的錢句以為是最吉利. 我說到盒子. 隨便帶說這一句. 白且爾前趟行為無禮. 我們有點不喜歡他. 然

communicating our happiness to him, and asking his advice; although we seldom followed advice, we were all ready enough to ask it. When he read the note from the two ladies, he shook his head, and observed that an affair of this sort demanded the utmost circumspection.[1] This air of diffidence[2] highly displeased my wife. "I never doubted, sir," cried she, "your readiness to be against my daughters and me. You have more circumspection than is wanted. However, I fancy, when we come to ask advice, we will apply to persons who seem to have made use of it themselves." — "Whatever my own conduct may have been, madam," replied he, "is not the present question; though, as I have made no use of advice myself, I should in conscience give it to those that will." As I was apprehensive this answer might draw on a repartee,

而也還關切他. 現在我們不免把喜信告訴他. 請教他. 我們常請教人. 却是很少聽人的話. 他讀了兩位女人來的信片. 就搖頭說. 這種事體. 要非常小心. 他這種懷疑的神氣. 很令我女人不高興. 我的女人說道. 我曉得. 你一來就反對我. 反對我的女兒. 你這個人. 未免太過慮. 雖然我們向人請教的時候. 我們要請教那種自己能遵照教人的話的人
{這是當面教訓白且罵教人小心自己却不小心}.
他答道. 瑪當. 現在的問題. 同我個人從前的行為好壞無干. 我雖不請教人. 遇着有人願意照行我教他的話. 我憑着良心. 不能不把話告訴他. 我恐怕他這一答. 要招對方用俏皮話駁過來. 答話說得旣無趣味.

---

1. Circumspection, 四面八方都要顧到. 2. Diffidence, 疑圖; 不自信.

making up by abuse what it wanted in wit, I changed the subject by seeming to wonder what could keep our son so long at the fair, as it was now almost nightfall. "Never mind our son," cried my wife; "depend upon it, he knows what he is about. I'll warrant we'll never see him sell his hens of a rainy day. I have seen him buy such bargains as would amaze one. I'll tell you a good story about that that will make you split your sides with laughing.—But, as I live, yonder comes Moses, without a horse, and the box at his back."

As she spoke, Moses came slowly on foot, and sweating under the deal box, which he had strapped round his shoulders like a peddler.—"Welcome, welcome, Moses! Well, my boy, what have you brought us from the fair?"—"I have brought you myself," cried Moses, with a sly look, and resting the box on the dresser.—"Ah, Moses," cried my wife, "that we know; but where is the horse?"—"I have

反要得罪人．我把別的話來打叉．裝作詫異樣子．說．天快黑了．爲什麼摩西在集上就擱許久．還不回來．我的女人說道．不要你管．你放心．他曉得他幹什麼．我可以擔保他決計不會下雨天賣母雞的〈牧師太怒態〈牧師太體可掬接着要說笑話遮掩過去母雞沽了雨最難看難賣脫也〉．我曾見他很買過極便宜的東西．你見了．也要驚倒．我要告訴你一段故事．叫你聽了大笑．笑到肚子都要炸．這不是摩西回來了嗎．馬是賣了．身後背着木箱．

他說話的時候．摩西慢慢步行而來．用皮帶穿着木箱．背在後面．同一個小販子一樣．滿臉是汗．我女人說道．好孩子．歡迎歡迎．你從集上．帶了什麼東西回來給我們．摩西臉上有點詭祕的神色．一面把木箱放在小桌上．說道．我自己帶回來給你．我女人說道．呀．摩西．我曉得．但

sold him," cried Moses, "for three pounds five shillings and twopence."— "Well done, my good boy," returned she; "I knew you would touch them off. Between ourselves, three pounds five shillings and twopence is no bad day's work. Come, let us have it then."—"I have brought back no money," cried Moses again. "I have laid it all out in a bargain,[1] and here it is," pulling out a bundle from his breast; "here they are; a gross of green spectacles, with silver rims and shagreen cases."—"A gross of green spectacles!" repeated my wife, in a faint voice. "And you have parted with the colt, and brought us back nothing but a gross of green paltry spectacles!"—"Dear mother," cried the boy, "why won't you listen to reason? I had them a dead bargain, or I should not have bought them. The silver rims alone will sell for double the money."—"A fig[2] for

是馬那裏去了.摩西答道.我把馬賣了三鎊五先令二便士.我女人說道.好孩子.辦得好.我早曉得你講價講贏他們.老實說.三鎊五先令二便士.這一天的事作得不錯.來來.把錢拿來.摩西從懷裏掏出一包東西來.說道.我把錢買了些便宜貨.這包就是的.是十二打綠眼鏡.銀邊.沙皮盒子.我女人氣得話幾乎說不出來.微微的聲音說道.十二打的綠眼鏡麽.他把馬賣了.什麽也沒買回來.只買回來十二打不相干的沒用處的綠眼鏡.摩西喊道.好母親.你爲什麽不聽我說出道理來.我買得極便宜.不然.我爲什麽買他呢.光是那銀邊.就不止值兩倍的買價.

---

1. Bargain, 便宜貨.　2. A fig, 一文不值; 無用.

the silver rims!" cried my wife in a passion: "I dare swear they won't sell for above half the money at the rate of broken silver, five shillings an ounce."— "You need be under no uneasiness," cried I, "about selling the rims; for they are not worth sixpence, for I perceive they are only copper varnished over."— "What," cried my wife; "not silver! the rims not silver!"—"No," cried I, "no more silver than your saucepan."—"And so," returned she, "we have parted with the colt, and have only got a gross of green spectacles, with copper rims and shagreen cases! A murrain[1] take such trumpery! The blockhead has been imposed upon, and should have known his company better."—"There, my dear," cried I, "you are wrong; he should not have known them at all."— "Marry,[2] hang the idiot," returned she, "to bring me such stuff; if I had them,

我女人大怒.說道.那銀邊一文錢也不值.我敢發誓說.若是賣出去當破銀賣.五先令一兩.也賣不了一半原價 {此段摹寫} {上當反觀上文說他會買便宜貨}.我說道.你不必白煩心.賣眼鏡邊.我看是銅的.外加一層銀色.值不了六便士.我女人喊道.什麼.不是銀的麼.那眼鏡邊子不是銀的麼.我說道.不是的.你的小湯汁鍋不是銀的.這也不是銀的.我女人說道.我們把馬賣了.只得了十二打的銅邊沙皮盒的綠眼鏡.讓疫鬼把這無用的東西拿走.你這個大傻子.上當了.你應該曉得同什麼人交易呀.我答道.我的寶貝.你錯了.他不應該認得這班人.我女人答道.簡直的把這獸子吊死了罷.買這種東西給我.假使我拿來.我把

---

1. Murrain, 瘟疫. 2. Marry, 實在; 簡直的.

I would throw them in the fire."—"There again you are wrong, my dear," cried I; "for though they be copper, we will keep them by us, as copper spectacles, you know, are better than nothing."

By this time the unfortunate Moses was undeceived. He now saw that he had indeed been imposed upon by a prowling sharper, who, observing his figure, had marked him for an easy prey. I therefore asked the circumstances of his deception. He sold the horse, it seems, and walked the fair in search of another. A reverend-looking man brought him to a tent, under pretense of having one to sell. "Here," continued Moses, "we met another man, very well dressed, who desired to borrow twenty pounds upon these, saying that he wanted money, and would dispose of them for a third of the value. The first gentleman, who pretended to be my friend, whispered me to buy them, and cautioned me not to let so good an offer pass.

那些東西摔在火裏. 我答道. 你又錯了. 雖然是銅邊眼鏡. 比沒有總好些. 我們應該留在家裏

〔老牧師的太太急於賣馬原要拿錢買匹好馬預備將來出風頭因摩西上了當自然是大生氣老牧師氣也不是笑也不是只好一味鎮靜冷譏熱諷寫來眞好看〕. 到了這時候. 摩西才曉得是上了當. 這才明白被一個在集上走來走去的騙子. 看見他可欺. 受了騙. 我於是問他被騙的情形. 他說把馬賣了之後. 要在集上另找一匹. 有一個像教士的人說. 他有一匹出賣. 帶他到一帳篷裏去. 摩西接着說道. 我們在帳篷裏. 遇着另一個人. 穿得很好. 要借二十鎊錢. 說是等錢使. 寧願把這些眼鏡. 打三折出賣. 第一個人裝作是我的好朋友. 附耳說道. 買了罷. 不要失了機會. 我把我

THE VICAR OF WAKEFIELD

I sent for Mr. Flamborough, and they talked him up as finely as they did me, and so at last we were persuaded to buy the two gross between us."

們的鄰居法林巴請過來. 那兩個人說了好些話騙他. 同騙我一樣. 於是我同法林巴兩人. 一人買十二打.

CHAPTER XIII

MR. BURCHELL IS FOUND TO BE AN ENEMY; FOR HE HAS
THE CONFIDENCE TO GIVE DISAGREEABLE ADVICE.

第 十 三 回

白且爾好進不入耳之言我們當
他是仇人
（白且爾直言被驅逐）

Our family had now made several attempts to be fine, but some unforeseen disaster demolished each as soon as projected.[1] I endeavored to take the advantage of every disappointment,[2] to improve their good sense in proportion as they were frustrated in ambition. "You see, my children," cried I, "how little is to be got by attempts to impose upon the world, in coping with our betters. Such as are poor, and will associate with none but the rich, are hated by those they avoid, and despised by those they

且說我們家裏．試了許多方法．要擺架子．不料一實行就出了意外．那方法就行不通．我看見他們好閣的意思越施行不出來．我越竭力的利用他們失望的機會．使他們醒悟．我對他們說道．孩子們我們已經窮了．還要裝出闊樣來．同富貴人相比．這種朦世的事體．沒得什麼效果．凡貧賤人若不同別人往來．專要同闊人往來．我們不同他往來

---

1. Projected, 實行．　2. Disappointment, 失望．

follow. Unequal combinations are always disadvantageous to the weaker side; the rich having the pleasure, and the poor the inconveniences that result from them. But come, Dick, my boy, and repeat the fable that you were reading to-day, for the good of the company."

"Once upon a time," cried the child, "a Giant and a Dwarf were friends, and kept together. They made a bargain[1] that they would never forsake each other, but go seek adventures. The first battle they fought was with two Saracens, and the Dwarf, who was very courageous, dealt one of the champions[2] a most angry blow. It did the Saracen very little injury, who, lifting up his sword, fairly struck off the poor Dwarf's arm. He was now in a woeful plight; but the Giant coming to his assistance, in a short time left the two Saracens dead on the plain, and the Dwarf

的人恨我們. 我們要同他往來的人. 瞧不起我們. 貧人與富人作朋友. 都是貧人吃虧. 富人取了樂. 貧人受拮据. 狄克. 好孩子. 你來把今天讀的一篇寓言. 說一遍我們聽.

狄克於是說道. 從前有一個高子. 和一個矮子作朋友. 常在一塊兒. 他們同盟. 同出混世. 彼此不相棄. 第一次. 同阿剌伯人打仗. 矮子膽大. 重重的打了敵人一下. 那阿剌伯人沒受大損傷. 却舉刀一砍. 把矮子的膀子斬下一條. 矮子自然是很受痛楚. 高子才走來幫忙. 不一會. 把兩個敵人打死. 矮子把

---

1. Made a bargain, 約好; 同盟; 議妥價. 2. Champion, 選手; 無敵; 敵手.

cut off the dead man's head out of spite. They then traveled on to another adventure. This was against three bloody-minded Satyrs,[1] who were carrying away a damsel in distress. The Dwarf was not quite so fierce now as before; but for all that, struck the first blow, which was returned by another that knocked out his eye; but the Giant was soon up with them, and had they not fled, would certainly have killed them every one. They were all very joyful for this victory, and the damsel who was relieved fell in love with the Giant, and married him. They now traveled far, and farther than I can tell, till they met with a company of robbers. The Giant, for the first time, was foremost now; but the Dwarf was not far behind. The battle was stout and long. Wherever the Giant came, all fell before him; but the Dwarf had liked to have been killed more than once. At last the victory

敵人的頭切下來洩忿. 兩個人又同行. 有一次遇着三個有野獸性的人. 搶一個女子. 這次矮子雖然不及上次的奮勇. 仍是第一個先動手. 敵人一還手. 打丟矮子一個眼睛. 高子走上來. 假使敵人不逃走. 一定都要被他打死. 兩個人打了勝仗. 非常高興. 那女子被救. 愛那高子. 嫁了他. 兩個人又同行. 我說不出來行了多遠. 碰見一羣強盜. 這是第一次高子先上前. 矮子也不甚落後. 這一次打仗. 打得又兇又久. 高子往前一衝. 敵人無有不被他打倒的. 矮子有好幾次幾乎送了命. 到後來.

---

1. Satyr, 牛人牛獸之怪; 人之有野獸性者; 色鬼; 有淫行之男人.

declared for the two adventurers; but the Dwarf lost his leg. The Dwarf was now without an arm, a leg, and an eye, while the Giant was without a single wound. Upon which he cried out to his little companion, 'My little hero, this is glorious sport; let us get one victory more, and then we shall have honor forever.' 'No,' cries the Dwarf, who was by this time grown wiser—'No, I declare off; I'll fight no more; for I find in every battle that you get all the honor and rewards, but all the blows fall upon me.'"

I was going to moralize[1] this fable, when our attention was called off to a warm dispute between my wife and Mr. Burchell, upon my daughters' intended expedition to town. My wife very strenuously insisted upon the advantages that would result from it; Mr. Burchell, on the contrary, dissuaded her with great ardor, and I stood neuter. His present dissuasions

還是這兩個人贏了. 但是矮子丟了一條腿. 現在矮子共總丟了一隻手. 一隻脚. 一個眼睛. 高子却並無一處受傷. 於是高子對矮子說道. 我的小英雄. 我們同出混世. 很好頑. 我們出去. 再打一仗. 我們的榮耀就永遠存在了. 矮子到了這時候. 比從前聰明些. 答道. 不. 我不幹了. 我不再打了. 每次打仗. 好處都是你的. 捱打都是我.

我正要把這段寓言包藏的教訓解說一番. 却被我女人同白且爾爭辯. 打了叉. 他們兩個人辯的是. 我兩個女兒入京的事. 我女人辯得很力. 說他們入京. 有多少利益. 白且爾反對. 竭力勸他不必叫女兒入京. 我守中立. 白且爾

---

1. Moralize, 從寓言發明其中所包含的教訓.

seemed but the second part of those which were received with so ill a grace in the morning. The dispute grew high, while poor Deborah, instead of reasoning stronger, talked louder, and at last was obliged to take shelter from a defeat in clamor. The conclusion of her harangue, however, was highly displeasing to us all. She knew, she said, of some who had their own secret reasons for what they advised; but for her part, she wished such to stay away from her house for the future.—"Madam," cried Burchell, with looks of great composure, which tended to inflame her the more, "as for secret reasons, you are right; I have secret reasons, which I forbear to mention, because you are not able to answer those of which I make no secret. But I find my visits here are become troublesome; I'll take my leave, therefore, now, and perhaps come once more to take a final farewell when I am quitting the country." Thus saying, he took up

現在勸阻我女人．是接着早起的議論再駁下去．早上我女人聽了．很生氣．現在爭論得更兇．我的女人雖然說不出更有力量的道理．聲音却更大起來｛無理的人只會大聲喊｝．末後輸了．說不出理來．只好亂喊來遮掩．他最後大聲說的話．叫我們都不高興．他說道．他曉得別人這樣勸他．是有私意．他盼望這種人．以後不必到他家裏來｛牧師太太急了下逐客令｝．白且爾極鎭靜的說道．瑪當．你說我有私意．你說的不錯．我是有私意．我所以不肯說出來者．因爲我明說的．你還不能答．但是我曉得你們討厭我來．我現在告辭．也許我往外國的時候．再來一次．作末後的辭行．一

his hat; nor could the attempts of Sophia, whose looks seemed to upbraid his precipitancy, prevent his going.

When gone, we all regarded each other for some minutes with confusion. My wife, who knew herself to be the cause, strove to hide her concern with a forced smile, and an air of assurance, which I was willing to reprove; "How, woman!" cried I to her; "is it thus we treat strangers? Is it thus we return their kindness? Be assured, my dear, that these were the harshest words, and to me the most unpleasing, that have escaped your lips!"—"Why would he provoke me then?" replied she; "but I know the motives of his advice perfectly well. He would prevent my girls from going to town, that he may have the pleasure of my youngest daughter's company here at home. But whatever happens, she shall choose better company than such low-lived fellows as he."— "Low-lived, my dear, do you call him?" cried I;

面說. 一面拿了帽子. 素緋雅眼睛看他. 像是責他性急. 意在留他. 也留不住.

他走過之後. 我們面面相看. 有幾分鐘. 心裏都有些亂了. 我女人知道這事由他發生. 勉強微笑. 故作冷靜態度. 遮掩他心理有些難受. 我却不以為然. 說道. 女人. 這是你對待客人的樣子麼. 這是我們報答他們的恩惠麼. 我的寶貝. 你剛才說的. 是你向來所未說過無情的話. 也是我最不喜歡聽的話. 他答道. 他為什麼要激怒我呢. 我很曉得他勸我那番話的用意. 他要攔阻我兩個女兒入京. 好叫我的小女兒在家陪伴他. 無論怎麼樣. 我一定要小女兒自己挑選好過那些下流人的作陪伴. 我答道. 你說他下流麼. 我們也許是把

"it is very possible we may mistake this man's character, for he seems upon some occasions the most finished gentleman I ever knew. —Tell me, Sophia, my girl, has he ever given you any secret instances of his attachment?"—"His conversation with me, sir," replied my daughter, "has ever been sensible, modest, and pleasing. As to aught else, no, never. Once, indeed, I remember to have heard him say he never knew a woman who could find merit in a man that seemed poor."—"Such, my dear," cried I, "is the common cant of all the unfortunate or idle. But I hope you have been taught to judge properly of such men, and that it would be even madness to expect happiness from one who has been so very bad an economist of his own. Your mother and I have now better prospects for you. The next winter, which you will probably spend in town, will give you opportunities of making a more prudent choice."

他看錯了.有時候我見他比我向來所認得的人還上等.

素緋雅.我的女兒.他私下裏曾否表示過他的愛情.素緋雅答道.他同我談話.向來都是有分寸.謙恭.令人樂聞的.別的話.向未說過.我還記得有一次.他說過.向來未見過女人見露出窮相的男人有什麼好處.我說道.這種話.都是不中用的人.或是倒運人的常談.我盼望你受過教訓.如何評判這路人.這個人處理自己財產.鬧到這樣精.除非是個瘋子.不然是不會希冀同這種人過快樂日子的.我同你母親.現在有好前程給你.下一個冬天.大約你總在京裏過.那時候你有機會可以挑選較好的人.

THE VICAR OF WAKEFIELD

What Sophia's reflections were upon this occasion I can't pretend to determine, but I was not displeased at the bottom that we were rid of a guest from whom I had much to fear. Our breach of hospitality went to my conscience a little; but I quickly silenced that monitor by two or three specious[1] reasons, which served to satisfy and reconcile me to myself. The pain which conscience gives the man who has already done wrong, is soon got over. Conscience is a coward, and those faults it has not strength enough to prevent, it seldom has justice enough to accuse.

素緋雅對於這事. 怎樣思前想後. 我却不得而知. 這一位客人. 我有點畏懼. 現在把他弄走了. 心裏也未嘗不喜歡. 我們這次有虧待客之禮. 我良心上有點過不去. 但是我却有兩三層說得過去的道理. 很快的把良心責問我的話. 搪塞過去了. 然後我覺得. 良心上還沒什麼過不去. 也覺得滿意 {文過遂非之／人往往如此}. 良心原是個懦夫. 犯了過失. 事前既無力量禁止. 事後更難公公道道的去告發 {作者往往／以佳句收}.

---

1. Specious, 可以說得去；說得過去.

CHAPTER XIV

FRESH MORTIFICATIONS, OR A DEMONSTRATION THAT SEEMING CALAMITIES MAY BE REAL BLESSINGS.

第 十 四 回

新 發 生 致 命 傷 的 事　似 是 禍 而 實 是 福 之 指 證

（老 牧 師 賣 馬 得 廢 紙）

The journey of my daughters to town was now resolved upon, Mr. Thornhill having kindly promised to inspect their conduct himself, and inform us by letter of their behavior. But it was thought indispensably[1] necessary that their appearance should equal the greatness of their expectations, which could not be done without expense. We debated therefore in full council what were the easiest methods of raising money, or, more properly speaking, what we could most conveniently sell. The deliberation was

且說. 我們已決定送兩個女兒入京. 唐希爾答應查考他們的行為. 用信通知我們. 但是他們前程既然遠大. 外觀就不能不相稱. 就不能不花錢. 我們故此大衆會議最容易籌款法子. 換而言之. 就是變賣什麼東西最便當. 不久就

---

1. Indispensably, 非此不可；少他不得.

soon finished; it was found that our remaining horse was utterly useless for the plow, without his companion, and equally unfit for the road, as wanting an eye; it was therefore determined that we should dispose of[1] him for the purposes above-mentioned, at the neighboring fair, and, to prevent imposition, that I should go with him myself. Though this was one of the first mercantile transactions of my life, yet I had no doubt about acquitting myself with reputation. The opinion a man forms of his own prudence[2] is measured by that of the company he keeps, and as mine was mostly in the family way, I had conceived no unfavorable sentiments of my worldly wisdom. My wife, however, next morning, at parting, after I had got some paces from the door, called me back, to advise me, in a whisper, to have all my eyes about me.

I had, in the usual forms, when I came to the fair, put my horse through all

商量好.我們剩下一匹馬.既然少了他的老伴.那馬又是一隻眼.既不能種地.又不能駄腳.我們就商定.在鄰近的一個集上.也把他賣了我親自去.就不會再上當.雖然這是我生平第一次作買賣.我自信總可以爭到點面子.凡一個人自己以為辦事有多少計劃.是要從他平日所交的什麼朋友計算的.因為我在家的時候多.我自己以為處世的智計.也還不錯{在家時候多則閱世淺}.我的女人.好像還有點不放心.到第二天早上.我離家的時候.我出門已經走了幾步.他還把我喊回來.附耳教我.要我十二分的留神{牧師太太有知人之明很怕他上當}.

我到了集上.也按着向來辦法.把我的馬溜走給人看.快走.慢走.不快

---

1. Dispose of, 賣去. 2. Prudence, 有策劃;小心謹慎;有步驟.

his paces; but for some time had no bidders. At last a chapman approached; and, after he had for a good while examined the horse round, finding him blind of one eye, he would have nothing to say to him: a second came up; but observing he had a spavin, declared he would not take him for the driving home: a third perceived he had a windgall, and would bid no money; a fourth knew by his eye that he had the botts: a fifth wondered what a plague[1] I could do at the fair with a blind, spavined, galled hack, that was only fit to be cut up for a dog kennel. By this time I began to have a most hearty contempt for the poor animal myself, and was almost ashamed at the approach of every customer; for though I did not entirely believe all the fellows told me, yet I reflected that the number of witnesses was a strong presumption that they were right, and St. Gregory, upon "Good

不慢的走.都作遍了.給眾人看了好一會.也無人問價.後來有一個生意人.或小販之類.查看我的馬好一會.看見那馬是一隻眼.一句不響就走了.第二個上來.看見那馬蹄子上腫了一塊.說道.若是買了這馬.恐怕走不到家.這馬就要壞了.第三個人來看.見那馬足節有一個瘤.不說價就走了.第四個人走上來.看看那馬的眼睛.曉得這馬患蟲病.第五個人見了我的馬.很詫異的說道.這個馬.旣瞎眼.又腳腫.又生瘤.沒什麼用處.只好宰了.切碎拿去喂狗.到了這個時候.我自己也很看不起我的馬.有買主走過來.我覺得很難爲情.那些人說那馬的壞話.我雖然不盡相信.但是說這話的人旣多.我又很相信他們說的不能都全靠不住.聖加力戈

---

1. What a plague, 粗人口頭話；粗話.

Works," professes himself to be of the same opinion.

I was in this mortifying situation, when a brother clergyman, an old acquaintance, who had also business at the fair, came up, and shaking me by the hand, proposed adjourning to a public house, and taking a glass of whatever we could get. I readily closed with the offer, and entering an alehouse, we were shown into a little back room, where there was only a venerable old man, who sat wholly intent[1] over a large book which he was reading. I never in my life saw a figure that prepossessed[2] me more favorably. His locks of silver gray venerably shaded his temples, and his green old age seemed to be the result of health and benevolence. However, his presence did not interrupt our conversation; my friend and I discoursed on the various turns of fortune we had met; the Whistonian controversy, my last pamphlet,

里著的書.也說過這意思.

我正在極難受的時候.有一個同行教士.久已認識的.也是到集上辦事的.走過來同我拉手.請我到一間小酒店歇歇.看店裏有什麼酒.喝一鐘.我就如他所請.進了一個皮酒店.店小二領我們進去後面一間小房.先有一個很端莊的老頭子.全副精神在那裏看書.我平生還未見過這樣令我喜歡的人.他一頭的白髮蓋着額.這個人.一定是身體壯健.存心慈善.故能享此高年.我們却不因爲他在跟前.不接下去談話.我同我的朋友談的是別後彼此的景況.又談到我主張一夫一妻的駁論{見前第二回}.和我末後所著的短論.

---

1. Intent, 很用心. 2. Prepossessed, 一見令人喜.

the archdeacon's reply, and
the hard measure that was
dealt me. But our atten-
tion was in a short time
taken off by the appear-
ance of a youth, who,
entering the room, respect-
fully said something softly
to the old stranger. "Make
no apologies, my child,"
said the old man, "to do
good is a duty we owe to
all our fellow creatures;
take this, I wish it were
more; but five pounds will
relieve your distress, and
you are welcome." The
modest youth shed tears
of gratitude, and yet his
gratitude was scarce
equal to mine. I could
have hugged the good old
man in my arms, his be-
nevolence pleased me so.
He continued to read, and
we resumed our conversa-
tion, until my companion,
after some time, recollecting that he had business
to transact in the fair,
promised to be soon back,
adding that he always
desired to have as much of
Dr. Primrose's company as
possible. The old gentle-
man, hearing my name
mentioned, seemed to look

副監督如何駁我.如何
的很同我過不去.談的
不久.有一個少年進來.
打了我們的叉.那少年
低低的同那老頭子說
話.那老頭子說道.好小
子.不必說抱歉話.我們
對於同胞作好事.是應
該盡的職分.你把這個
拿去.可惜不甚多.但是
五個金鎊.可以救你的
急.我很願意你拿去.那
少年感激流淚.但是我
感激這老頭子.也不亞
於那少年.老頭子這樣
的慈善.我眞可以摟抱
他.他還是讀他的書.我
們談我們的話.後來我
的同伴想起來.還要到
集上辦事.等一會再來.
臨走他還說.他很願意
同普博士｛老師也 牧也｝多多
的談話.那老頭子聽見
我的名字.很留神看我

at me with attention for
some time; and, when my
friend was gone, most re-
spectfully demanded if I
was in any way related to
the great Primrose, that
courageous monogamist,
who had been the bulwark[1]
of the Church. Never did
my heart feel sincerer rapture than at that moment.
"Sir," cried I, "the ap-
plause of so good a man,
as I am sure you are, adds
to that happiness in my
breast which your benevo-
lence has already excited.
You behold before you, sir,
that Dr. Primrose, the
monogamist, whom you
have been pleased to call
great. You here see that
unfortunate divine, who
has so long, and it would
ill become me to say, suc-
cessfully, fought against
the deuterogamy[2] of the
age."—"Sir," cried the
stranger, struck with awe,
"I fear I have been too
familiar, but you'll forgive
my curiosity, sir—I beg
pardon."—"Sir," cried I,
grasping his hand, "you

好一會子.等到我的朋
友走了.很恭敬的問我.
同那位很有膽子.主張
一夫一妻.護持宗教.偉
大的普牧師.有什麼瓜
葛｛好一串恭維話｝.我聽了.心
裏實在高興.到了極點.
爲向來所未試過的｛老牧師好恭維｝.我答道.先生.你的
慈善行爲.已經令我快
樂.我現在又蒙你這位好
人嘉獎.我更加快樂.先
生.現在站在你跟前的.
就是主張一夫一妻的
普博士.過蒙你稱爲偉
大.你看見的.就是那不
幸的教士 費了許多日
子.奮鬪妻死續絃的風
氣.我却不好意思說我
奮鬪成功.那老頭子大
驚.說道.先生.我恐怕
我太不客氣了.請你饒
恕我多嘴好問.先生.
求你恕罪.我拉他的手

1. Bulwark, 護牆. 2. Deuterogamy, 妻死續娶;續絃.

are so far from displeasing me by your familiarity, that I must beg you'll accept my friendship as you already have my esteem."—"Then, with gratitude, I accept the offer," cried he, squeezing me by the hand. "Thou glorious pillar of unshaken orthodoxy! and do I behold—" I here interrupted what he was going to say, for though as an author I could digest no small share of flattery, yet now my modesty would permit no more. However, no lovers in romance ever cemented a more instantaneous friendship. We talked upon several subjects; at first I thought he seemed rather devout than learned, and began to think he despised all human doctrines as dross. Yet this no way lessened him in my esteem, for I had for some time begun privately to harbor such an opinion myself. I therefore took occasion to observe, that the world in general began to be blamably indifferent as

說道. 先生. 我不獨不怪你太不客氣. 你已經得了我的恭敬心. 我請你收受我的交情. 他抓我的手說道. 我感激你. 我當你是朋友. 你是深信不疑篤守宗教正理的柱石. 我看見的 …. 我卻攔住他往下說. 我自命為著作家. 雖然吃了無限若干的恭維. 都能消化. 但是我謙退之心發作. 不能再容多少恭維了（老牧師也還知道 受恭維應有限制）. 雖然這樣說. 我們兩人. 立刻就作了朋友. 無論什麼小說上男女一見就相愛. 也沒有我們這樣快. 我們談好幾樣事. 起初我以為他. 是他學問之深不如他信教之篤. 以為他對於人類所想出的道理. 都當作精粕. 但我並不因此而少減我之恭敬心. 因為我已經有了幾時起首. 私下裏也存這種見解. 我故此乘機說. 世界上的人. 大概都起

THE VICAR OF WAKEFIELD 137

to doctrinal matters,[1] and followed human speculations too much. — "Ay, sir," replied he,· as if he had reserved all his learning to that moment, — "ay, sir, the world is in its dotage; and yet the cosmogony, or creation of the world, has puzzled philosophers of all ages. What a medley of opinions have they not broached upon the creation of the world? Sanchoniathon, Manetho, Berosus, and Ocellus Lucanus, have all attempted it in vain. The latter has these words: *Anarchon ara kai atelutaion to pan*,[2] which imply that all things have neither beginning nor end. Manetho, also, who lived about the time of Nebuchadon-Asser, Asser being a Syriac word usually applied as a surname to the kings of that country, as **Teglat Phael-Asser**, Nabon-Asser — he, I say, formed a conjecture[3] equally absurd; for as we usually say, *ek to biblion*

首把宗教道理看得很平淡. 人類的設想. 看得太重. 他好像這些時候把學問藏起. 到現在才顯露出來. 答道. 先生. 世界已經到了老糊塗的程度了. 然而世界是如何創造的. 歷來的哲學家. 都迷惑了. 說不出個道理來. 對於這個問題. 發表了一大堆東拉西扯. 七雜八湊的意見. 如非尼沙某人. 埃及某人. 加而狄某人. 希臘某人{胡拉一串古人名}. 都要解說世界創造的道理. 都不相干. 那位希臘人說{以下是雜湊希臘短句}. 其意以為世界無始無終. 瑪尼圖. 他是那卜沙當愛斯爾{一個長名字}時候人. 愛斯爾這個字. 是個西里阿字. 該國國王常有這個稱呼. 例如狄加拉非勒愛斯爾{又一個長名字}. 那邦愛斯爾. 他所猜的是一樣不合理. 因為我們常

---

1. Doctrinal matters. 宗教道理. 2. *Anarchon . . . pan*, 一串希臘文其中有一字希臘字典所無. 3. Conjecture, 猜.

kubernetes,[1] which implies that books will never teach the world; so he attempted to investigate—But, sir, I ask pardon; I am straying from the question."—That he actually was; nor could I for my life see how the creation of the world had anything to do with the business I was talking of; but it was sufficient to show me that he was a man of letters, and I now reverenced him the more. I was resolved, therefore, to bring him to the touchstone, but he was too mild and too gentle to contend for victory. Whenever I made any observation that looked like a challenge to controversy, he would smile, shake his head, and say nothing, by which I understood he could say much if he thought proper. The subject therefore insensibly changed from the business of antiquity to that which brought us both to the fair; mine, I told him, was to sell a horse, and very luckily indeed, his was to

說 ｛又攙一希
　　攏短臘句｝. 意謂書不
能教人. 他於是想研究
… ｛此句未
　　說完｝. 先生. 我求
你寬恕. 我走出題外了
｛老頭子東拉西扯語多費解
　欲以艱深文淺陋使人驚其
學問
淵博｝. 我曉得離題太
遠. 世界創造. 同我們
眼前所說的事. 毫無
相干. 但是他這一番
話. 足使我曉得他是個
有學問的人. 越加尊敬
他 ｛可見老牧師並不深於
　　古學被老頭子嚇倒｝.
我故此決定把試金石
拿出來. 但是他太和平
太溫厚. 不肯同我辯駁
爭勝. 只要我說一句話
帶點挑他辯論的意思.
他就微笑搖頭. 不說話.
我就明白他若是該說
的. 儘有得說. 並非不能
答我. 我們的話柄. 不知
不覺的從上古談到現
在趕集的事. 我告訴他
我來賣馬. 他說巧得很.

---

1. *Ek to biblion kubernetes*, 一串希臘文不成意義.

buy one for one of his tenants. My horse was soon produced, and, in fine, we struck a bargain. Nothing now remained but to pay me, and he accordingly pulled out a thirty-pound note, and bid me change it. Not being in a capacity of complying with this demand, he ordered his footman to be called up, who made his appearance in a very genteel livery. "Here, Abraham," cried he, "go and get gold for this: you'll do it at neighbor Jackson's, or anywhere." While the fellow was gone, he entertained me with a pathetic harangue on the great scarcity of silver, which I undertook to improve, by deploring also the great scarcity of gold; so that by the time Abraham returned, we had both agreed that money was never so hard to come at as now. Abraham returned to inform us, that he had been over the whole fair, and could not get change, though he had offered half a crown for doing it. This

他是替房客買馬．我把我的馬給他看．不一會．我們就議妥了價．我等他給錢．他掏出一張三十鎊的鈔票．叫我找他．我無錢找．他把跟人喊來．跟人走來．突的是很好號衣．他說道．阿伯拉罕．你去換金錢來．你可以同我們鄰居換．或什麼地方換都可以．他跟人去換錢的時候．他很感動的．大發議論．說現在銀子太缺．我改良他的議論．說現在金子太缺．很可惜．等到阿伯拉罕回來．我們兩人都說．現在現款太缺．阿伯拉罕回來說．走遍了一個集．也沒處換金錢．他願意貼二先令半的水．也換

was a very great disappointment to us all; but the old gentleman, having paused a little, asked me if I knew one Solomon Flamborough, in my part of the country. Upon replying that he was my next-door neighbor, "If that be the case, then," returned he, "I believe we shall deal. You shall have a draft upon him, payable at sight, and let me tell you he is as warm a man as any within five miles round him. Honest Solomon and I have been acquainted for many years together. I remember I always beat him at three jumps; but he could hop on one leg farther than I." A draft upon my neighbor was to me the same as money, for I was sufficiently convinced of his ability. The draft was signed and put into my hands; and Mr. Jenkinson, the old gentleman, his man Abraham and my horse, old Blackberry, trotted off very well pleased with each other.

After a short interval, being left to reflection, I

不出來．我們兩人都很失望．老頭子．停了一會．問我認得同村所羅門法林巴否．我答道．他就是我的鄰居．他說．旣然這樣．我們可以成交．我給你一張卽期支票．向所羅門支款．我告訴你．這裏周圍十餘里內．無人比得上他那麼熱心．我認得所羅門有許多年．我還記得我們兩人遊戲．若是跳三步．我總贏他．若是單脚跳．他却比我跳得遠〈老頭子故意說同所〉羅門法林巴是總角〈之交使牧師不犯疑〉．我以爲一張支票．向鄰居支款．同現錢一樣．我很相信法林巴有力量可以給錢〈上當了〉．老頭子把支票簽字．交給我．於是金京森〈老頭子名〉．阿伯拉罕．我的馬黑果子．高高興興的走了．

　過了一會．我一個人在那理細想．才起

began to recollect that I had done wrong in taking a draft from a stranger, and so prudently resolved upon following the purchaser, and having back my horse. But this was now too late: I therefore made directly homewards, resolving to get the draft changed into money at my friend's as fast as possible. I found my honest neighbor smoking his pipe at his own door; and informing him that I had a small bill upon him, he read it twice over. "You can read the name, I suppose," cried I, "Ephraim Jenkinson."— "Yes," returned he; "the name is written plain enough, and I know the gentleman too—the greatest rascal under the canopy of heaven. This is the very same rogue who sold us the spectacles. Was he not a venerable-looking man, with gray hair, and no flaps to his pocket holes? And did he not talk a long string of learning about Greek and cosmogony, and the world?" To this I replied with a groan. "Ay," continued he, "he

首想起來.不應該從生人手中受支票.於是想出妥當辦法.決意趕那買馬的人.把馬要回來.但是已經太遲了.只好一直回家.趕快向我的鄰居取·錢.我見他在大門口吃烟.就告訴他.我有一張小票.同他要錢.他把支票讀了兩次.我說道、你能讀那簽字麼.他答道.伊法雷金京森.名字是寫得很清楚.我認得他.他是天下頂大的一個光棍.賣眼鏡的也是這個光棍.他的相貌很尊嚴.白頭髮.衣裳口袋沒得蓋.談話總拖出一大串什麼希臘.什麼天地創造.什麼世界.是不是.我歎口氣說道.是的.我的鄰居說道.呀.他只有這麼一點

has but that one piece of learning in the world, and he always talks it away whenever he finds a scholar in company; but I know the rogue, and will catch him yet."

Though I was already sufficiently mortified, my greatest struggle was to come, in facing my wife and daughters. No truant was ever more afraid of returning to school, there to behold the master's visage, than I was of going home. I was determined. however, to anticipate their fury, by first falling into a passion myself.

But, alas! upon entering, I found the family no way disposed for battle. My wife and girls were all in tears, Mr. Thornhill having been there that day to inform them that their journey to town was entirely over. The two ladies, having heard reports of us from some malicious person about us, were that day set out for London. He could neither discover the tendency nor the author of these; but whatever they might be, or whoever might

學問只有碰見是個學者. 他就一串一串的拖出來. 我認得他. 總有一天我們把他捉着.

我這時候雖是十分難受. 但是最難受的還在後頭. 我怎樣見我的女人同兩個女兒呢. 我回家見他們. 比逃學的小學生回到學堂去見先生那副臉. 還要害怕. 我却決意比他們先發脾氣. 抵抗他們 {牧師這時候又可憐又可笑}.

可憐我一進家門. 才看見他們無意同我鬧發脾氣. 我的女人同我兩個女兒. 在那裏哭. 原來當天唐希爾來告訴他們. 不必進京. 因為京裏來的兩位女人. 聽見有個壞心眼的人. 造我們謠言. 當日就回京去了. 他又說不曉得誰造這謠言. 也不曉得是什麼意思. 但是無論什麼意思. 什麼人造. 他一定保

have broached them, he continued to assure our family of his friendship and protection. I found, therefore, that they bore my disappointment with great resignation, as it was eclipsed in the greatness of their own. But what preplexed us most was. to think who could be so base as to asperse[1] the character of a family so harmless as ours, too humble to excite envy, and too inoffensive to create disgust.

護我們. 同我們作朋友. 我家裏的人. 因爲這件事最失望. 掩過了我賣馬受騙的事. 只好隱受痛苦不響. 但是我一家人的品行是最純良的. 況且是貧賤. 不招人妒. 向來又不得罪人. 不會招人討厭. 究竟是誰這樣卑劣. 造謠蹧蹬我們. 眞令我們疑惑不解.

---

1. Asperse, 造謠言; 蹧蹬人.

CHAPTER XV

ALL MR. BURCHELL'S VILLAINY AT ONCE DETECTED — THE FOLLY OF BEING OVERWISE

第 十 五 回

探 出 白 且 爾 惡 劣 行 爲　太 聰 明 之 過
(責 負 義 牧 師 逐 客)

That evening and a part of the following day was employed in fruitless attempts to discover our enemies; scarcely a family in the neighborhood but incurred[1] our suspicions, and each of us had reasons for our opinion best known to ourselves. As we were in this perplexity, one of our little boys, who had been playing abroad. brought in a letter case, which he found on the green. It was quickly known to belong to Mr. Burchell, with whom it had been seen, and, upon examination, contained some hints upon different subjects; but what particularly

且說當天晚上和第二天大半天. 我們想法法打聽誰是我們仇人. 也打聽不出來. 凡是我們的街坊. 我們都疑心到了. 這個疑心這個. 那人疑心那個. 這是各人自己自有理由. 我們正在懷疑的時候. 我們的一個孩子在外頑耍. 在草地上拾着一個袖珍信夾拿進來. 我們見過白且爾有這東西. 就曉得是他的. 我們一看. 是講各種事務的都有. 最

---

1. Incurred, 走入; 陷入; 列入.

154

engaged our attention was a sealed note, superscribed *the copy of a letter to be sent to the two ladies at Thornhill Castle*. It instantly occurred that he was the base informer, and we deliberated whether the note should not be broken open. I was against it; but Sophia, who said she was sure that of all men he would be the last to be guilty of so much baseness, insisted upon its being read. In this she was seconded by the rest of the family, and, at their joint solicitation, I read as follows:

"LADIES,—The bearer will sufficiently satisfy you as to the person from whom this comes: one at least the friend of innocence, and ready to prevent its being seduced. I am informed for a truth, that you have some intention of bringing two young ladies to town, whom I have some knowledge of, under the character of companions. As I would neither have simplicity imposed upon nor virtue contaminated, I must offer it as my opinion, that the impropriety of

留神的是一件封口信.信面寫的是送與唐希爾府的兩位高貴女人.這就立刻現出來.造謠言的是白且爾.我們就商議應否拆這封信.我反對拆信.素緋雅說.無論什麼人.可以造這種謠言.惟有白且爾是萬萬不造這種謠言的.一定要拆信看.餘人都贊成.他們連合起來求我.我就拆讀那信道.

女士們.送這信的人足可以使你們知道寫這信的人是誰.這個人是保護良善的.有人告訴我一件實事.說你們有意帶兩位少年女人進京作陪伴.這兩位少年女人.我却有些曉得.我不願見兩個老實人受騙.也不願有人敗壞他們的道德.我告訴你.這種不規則的舉動.是

such a step will be attended
with dangerous conse-
quences.   It has never
been my way to treat the
infamous or the lewd with
severity, nor should I now
have taken this method
of explaining myself, or
reproving folly, did it not
aim at guilt.   Take, therefore, the admonition of a
friend, and seriously reflect
on the consequences of introducing infamy and vice
into retreats where peace
and innocence have hitherto resided."

Our doubts were now at
an end.   There seemed indeed something applicable
to both sides in this letter,
and its censures might as
well be referred to those to
whom it was written, as to
us; but the malicious meaning was obvious, and we
went no farther.   My wife
had scarce patience to
hear me to the end, but
railed[1] at the writer with
unrestrained resentment.[2]
Olivia was equally severe,

有危險結果的.我向來
不以嚴勵手段對待不
顧名譽的人.你們這種
舉動.若不是意圖陷害.
我就不必用現在這個方
法解說我的意思.或斥
你們這種妄動.請你們
聽朋友的警告.把不名
譽不道德的事引入一
個良善安樂人家的結
果.認眞想透.不可妄動.

這一封信.把我們的疑
團都解釋了.信裏的話
原是說到兩方面.語意
有點騎牆.那些責備的
話.可以指那兩位女人.
也可以指我們.但是用
意之陰險.一望而知
{匿名信固是語多騎牆牧師
們亦難免牽強誤會之咎}.
我們就不往下討論.我
的女人.幾乎不耐煩聽
我.讀到底.大罵寫信人.
盡情洩忿.奧維雅也一

---

1. Railed, 辱罵.   2. Resentment, 懷恨;懷怒;發怒;洩忿.

and Sophia seemed perfectly amazed at his baseness. As for my part, it appeared to me one of the vilest instances of unprovoked ingratitude I had met with. Nor could I account for it in any other manner than by imputing it to his desire of detaining my youngest daughter in the country, to have the more frequent opportunities of an interview. In this manner we all sat ruminating upon schemes of vengeance, when our other little boy came running in to tell us that Mr. Burchell was approaching at the other end of the field. It is easier to conceive than describe the complicated sensations which are felt from the pain of a recent injury, and the pleasure of approaching vengeance. Though our intentions were only to upbraid him with his ingratitude, yet it was resolved to do it in a manner that would be perfectly cutting. For this purpose we agreed to meet him with our usual

樣的嚴厲.素緋雅好像是極其驚異那寫人怎樣的卑劣.以我看起來.我們並未得罪他.他却這樣忘恩負義.險惡到這地步.我生平是第一次遇着.我想不出來.他爲什麽有這樣擧動.除非是他要把我小女兒留在鄉下.可以有機會常常相見.我們正在想法子報復.那一個小兒子跑進來告訴我們說.白且爾從那一頭來.快到了.我們這時候的心境.一面因剛才受害.心裏痛恨.一面眼前又可以報復.不是筆墨能殼寫出來的.我們的意思.雖然只要責他忘恩負義.但是決意要作出極斬截的樣子.因爲這樣.我們定計.還是照常的

smiles, to chat in the beginning with more than ordi-
nary kindness, to amuse
him a little; and then, in
the midst of the flattering
calm, to burst upon him
like an earthquake, and
overwhelm him with the
sense of his own baseness.
This being resolved upon,
my wife undertook to man-
age the business herself, as
she really had some talents
for such an undertaking.
We saw him approach; he
entered, drew a chair, and
sat down.—"A fine day,
Mr. Burchell."—"A very
fine day, Doctor; though I
fancy we shall have some
rain, by the shooting of
my corns."—"The shoot-
ing of your horns!"[1] cried
my wife, in a loud fit of
laughter, and then asked
pardon for being fond of a
joke.—"Dear madam,"
replied he, "I pardon you
with all my heart; for I
protest I should not have
thought it a joke had you
not told me."—"Perhaps

陪笑臉. 歡迎他. 同他說
說笑笑. 當很鎮靜恭維
他的時候. 忽然如山崩
地裂的. 把他的險惡說
出來. 壓倒他. 我們定計
之後. 我的女人擔任. 如
法辦理. 他原有這種
本事辦這件事. 我們
看見他走近. 他進門.
拉一把椅子坐下. 我
說道. 白且爾先生. 今
天天氣好. 他答道. 博
士. 天氣很好. 但是我覺
我脚上的雞眼. 一陣陣
的刺痛. 恐怕還要下雨.
我女人大笑道. 你出的
角麼 {將白且爾用的corns / 改作horns當笑話}.
接着說道. 我喜歡說笑
話. 請你勿怪. 白且爾答
道. 瑪當. 我眞不怪你. 我
實在說. 你不告訴我. 我
還不曉得是句笑話
{語帶/挖苦}. 我女人對我們

---

1. Shooting of my corns, shooting of your horns, shooting 原有數
義, 第一個似應作刺痛解, 第二個應作出解, 如出頭出角
之出.

not, sir," cried my wife, winking at us; "and yet I dare say you can tell us how many jokes go to an ounce."—"I fancy, madam," returned Burchell, "you have been reading a jest book this morning, that ounce of jokes is so very good a conceit;[1] and yet, madam, I had rather see half an ounce of understanding." — "I believe you might," cried my wife, still smiling at us, though the laugh was against her; "and yet I have seen some men pretend to understanding that have very little." — "And no doubt," returned her antagonist, "you have known ladies set up for wits that had none." — I quickly began to find that my wife was likely to gain but little at this business; so I resolved to treat him in a style of more severity myself. "Both wit, and understanding," cried I, "are trifles without integrity; it is that which gives value to every character. The ignorant

使眼色. 答道. 也許你不曉得. 但是我相信你可以告訴我們. 多少句笑話殼一兩重. 他答道. 我想你今早你讀笑話書. 拿分量去秤笑話. 却是個好意思. 然而我寧願看見半兩的知識 {牧師太識也 / 讚牧太無知} 這句話原是白且爾笑他. 他還是微微笑. 對着我們. 接着說道. 你也許有這種心願. 但是我見過有一種人. 自以爲有知識. 其實知識不多. 他的敵人答道. 你總該見過. 有些堂客以爲自己有說俏皮話的本事. 其實沒有. 我立刻就看見我的女人不是他的敵手. 我決計自己出馬. 把點利害給他看. 我就說道. 只有知識同說俏皮話的本事. 算不了什麼. 最要緊的還是忠信. 人格有了忠信. 就有價值. 無知無識的一個鄉愚. 沒犯過罪惡. 比犯

1. Conceit, 意思; 自大; 過量比喻.

peasant, without fault, is greater than the philosopher with many; for what is genius or courage without a heart? '*An honest man is the noblest work of God.*'"

"I have always held that hackneyed[1] maxim of Pope," returned Mr. Burchell, "as very unworthy a man of genius, and a base desertion of his own superiority. As the reputation of books is raised not by their freedom from defect, but the greatness of their beauties, so should that of men be prized, not for their exemption from fault, but the size of those virtues they are possessed of. The scholar may want prudence, the statesman may have pride, and the champion ferocity; but shall we prefer to these the low mechanic, who laboriously plods through life without censure or applause? We might as well prefer the tame, correct paintings of the Flemish school, to the erroneous but sublime animations of the Roman pencil."

過許多罪惡的哲學家．強得多．一個人有智有勇．而無心肝．算得個什麼呢．有一句詩說得好．忠信人是上帝創造最可寶貴之物．

白爾答道．普拍〔英國詩人〕這一句極平常的格言．我向來以爲他這樣多才的人．不應該說的．把自己高貴的身分降低了．世界上的著作．應該由於內裏有高貴的思想而享大名．不應因爲如是而得名．人亦實在應該因爲有大道德．然後享大名．不應因爲此瑕疵而享大名．由類推．一個學者也許欠謹慎．一個政治家也許過於驕傲．一個拳師也許帶兒暴．總比一個下等工匠辛辛苦苦無毀無譽的過了一世的好．我們豈應說畫理不合嗎．林米派的繪畫雖不如法．比羅馬派雖不合理而生氣勃勃的好嗎．〔論人論藝的名言與作者此書自序相發明〕

---

1. Hackneyed, 平常.

THE VICAR OF WAKEFIELl 151

"Sir," replied I "your present observation is just, when there are shining virtues and minute defects: but when it appears that great vices are opposed in the same mind to as extraordinary virtues, such a character deserves contempt."

"Perhaps," cried he, "there may be some such monsters as you describe, of great vices joined to great virtues; yet in my progress through life, I never yet found one instance of their existence; on the contrary, I have ever perceived that where the mind was capacious, the affections were good. And, indeed, Providence seems kindly our friend in this particular, thus to debilitate[1] the understanding where the heart is corrupt, and diminish the power where there is the will to do mischief. This rule seems to extend even to other animals; the little vermin race are ever treacherous, cruel, and

我答道. 先生. 你剛才說的話公道. 却是指高道德比較小瑕疵而言. 但是同一個人. 雖有非常之高道德. 亦有非常之大過惡. 這種人. 只配爲世人所不齒.

他說道. 世上也許有你所說的大善而兼大惡的怪物. 然而我生平却向未見過這樣的一個人. 我所見的. 却同這樣人相反. 我只見心廣的人. 他就有血性. 對於這件事. 上天實有愛人之意. 心腸腐敗的人. 就叫他欠知識. 存心爲害的人. 就叫他欠能力{作者以爲大惡之人往往無才以濟其惡 徵諸歷史殊屬不然}. 這一條例還推廣到動物界. 小蟲之類. 都是懦弱. 而陰險殘暴. 絕有力的. 往往有大量. 勇敢而柔和.

1. Debilitate, 減; 致弱.

cowardly; whilst those endowed with strength and power are generous, brave, and gentle."

"These observations sound well," returned I; "and yet it would be easy this moment to point out a man," and I fixed my eye steadfastly upon him, "whose head and heart form a most detestable contrast. Ay, sir," continued I, raising my voice, "and I am glad to have his opportunity of detecting him in the midst of his fancied security. Do you know this, sir—this pocketbook?"—"Yes, sir," returned he, with a face of impenetrable assurance; "that pocketbook is mine, and I am glad you have found it."—"And do you know," cried I, "this letter? Nay, never falter, man; but look me full in the face; I say, do you know this letter?"—"That letter," returned he; "yes, it was I that wrote that letter."—"And how could you," said I, "so basely, so ungratefully, presume to write this letter?"—"And how came you," replied he,

我答道. 這幾句話說得好聽. 然而我這時候. 可以指出一個人. 我說到這裏. 兩眼釘住他. 說道. 心與口相反. 極令人厭恨. 我接着高聲說道. 噯. 先生. 這個人自以為安穩. 不怕人知. 我現在很喜歡趁這個機會. 揭露出來. 先生. 你認得這個袖珍小本嗎. 他一點不動聲色. 毫無畏懼的答道. 這小本是我的. 你找着了. 我很喜歡. 我說道. 你認得這封信嗎. 你不必支吾. 抬頭看我的臉. 我問的是. 你認得這信封嗎. 他答道. 這封信嗎. 是我寫的. 我說道. 你怎麼能幹這樣卑劣. 這樣忘恩負義. 敢寫這封信. 他毫不知羞恥的問我

THE VICAR OF WAKEFIELD 153

with looks of unparalleled[1] effrontery, "so basely to presume to break open this letter? Don't you know, now, I could hang you all for this? All that I have to do is to swear at the next justice's that you have been guilty of breaking open the lock of my pocketbook, and so hang you all up at this door." This piece of unexpected insolence raised me to such a pitch, that I could scarcely govern my passion. "Ungrateful wretch, begone, and no longer pollute my dwelling with thy baseness: begone, and never let me see thee again; go from my door and the only punishment I wish thee is an alarmed conscience, which will be a sufficient tormentor!" So saying, I threw him his pocketbook, which he took up with a smile, and shutting the clasps with the utmost composure, left us quite astonished at the serenity of his assurance. My wife was particularly enraged

道. 你爲何這樣的卑劣. 敢於拆我的信. 你曉得嗎. 你犯這個罪. 我可以使你受死刑〈私拆人信可以治罪〉〈當時英國法律嚴重 往往小罪處以極刑〉. 我只要跑到最近的司法衙門. 發個誓. 告你們拆開我的小本子. 就可以把你們一夥子吊死在你自己家門口〈當時刑法重處 雖小竊亦以極刑〉. 他這幾句意料所不及的羞辱我們的話. 把我激怒到不可壓制. 我喊道. 你這個忘恩負義無良心的人. 你走你的罷. 不要把你的惡劣汚穢我的住宅. 走你的罷. 不要讓我再見你的面. 你出門罷. 我只願你良心發現. 使你難過. 就是你所受的刑罰. 說到這裏. 我把那小本子捽給他. 他微微一笑. 拿起來. 很鎮靜的關好了. 走出去. 我們見他這樣的鎮靜. 自信無他. 倒令我們詫異. 我的女人看

---

1. Unparalleled, 無比.

that nothing could make him angry, or make him seem ashamed of his villainies. "My dear," cried I, willing to calm those passions that had been raised too high among us, "we are not to be surprised that bad men want shame; they only blush at being detected in doing good, but glory in their vices."

"Guilt and Shame, says the allegory, were at first companions, and in the beginning of their journey inseparably kept together. But their union was soon found to be disagreeable and inconvenient to both: Guilt gave Shame frequent uneasiness, and Shame often betrayed the secret conspiracies of Guilt. After long disagreement, therefore, they at length consented to part forever. Guilt boldly walked forward alone, to overtake Fate,[1] that went before in the shape of an executioner: but Shame, being naturally timorous,

見無論我們怎樣他.他總是不生氣.也不覺得難爲情.反令他自己很生氣.我覺得我們的怒氣太盛.說道.我的寶貝.惡人不知羞恥.有什麼奇怪.揭露他們的善事.他們倒會臉紅.揭露他們的罪惡.他們反覺得意.

有一段譬喻的話說.罪惡同羞恥.起初是同伴.初出行的時候.兩個人同在一起.形影不離的.不久就覺得這種的聯合.彼此都不得意.彼此都不便.罪惡往往令羞恥難過.羞恥往往把罪惡的陰謀走漏出來.兩人彼此不相安.爲日已久.後來說好.彼此就分手.罪惡於是一個人勇往直前.至死才罷手.死就是罪惡的劊子手.

---

1. Fate, 定數；死.

returned back to keep company with Virtue, which, in the beginning of their journey, they had left behind. Thus, my children, after men have traveled through a few stages in vice, Shame forsakes them, and returns back to wait upon the few virtues they have still remaining."

羞恥本來膽怯. 回過頭來. 去同道德作朋友. 當初羞恥同罪惡結伴的時候. 原把道德丟在後頭. 兒女們要曉得. 凡人向為惡的路走. 走過幾站. 羞恥就回頭. 同剩下不多的幾樣道德作伴.

CHAPTER XVI

THE FAMILY USE ART, WHICH IS OPPOSED WITH STILL GREATER

第 十 六 回

我 們 用 計　反 對 我 們 的 人 更 用 計
（普 夫 人 巧 計 探 眞 情）

Whatever might have been Sophia's sensations, the rest of the family was easily consoled for Mr. Burchell's absence by the company of our landlord, whose visits now became more frequent and longer. Though he had been disappointed in procuring my daughters the amusements of the town as he designed, he took every opportunity of supplying them with those little recreations which our retirement would admit of. He usually came in the morning, and while my son and I followed our occupations abroad, he sat with the family at home, and amused them by describing the town, with every part of which he was

且說．無論白且爾這一去．素緋雅心緒怎麼樣．姑且不提．白且爾雖然走了．我們房東却常來．我們家裏的人．心裏稍安慰些．雖然他想法要我們的兩個女兒進京消遣．沒有辦到．很失望．但是他常趁機會．請他們遊戲．那些遊戲．却還合我．們退隱人家的身分．他通常是早上來．正當我同兒子在外辦事的時候．他陪我的眷屬．坐在家裏．同他們解悶．談談京城的情形．京裏什麼地方他都熟．所有

THE VICAR OF WAKEFIELD 157

particularly acquainted. He could repeat all the observations that were retailed in the atmosphere of the playhouses, and had all the good things of the high wits by rote long before they made their way into the jest books. The intervals between conversation were employed in teaching my daughters piquet, or sometimes in setting my two little ones to box to make them *sharp*, as he called it; but the hopes of having him for a son-in-law in some measure blinded us to all his imperfections. It must be owned that my wife laid a thousand schemes to entrap him; or, to speak it more tenderly, used every art to magnify the merit of her daughter. If the cakes at tea ate short and crisp, they were made by Olivia; if the gooseberry wine was well knit, the gooseberries were of her gathering; it was her fingers which gave the pickles their peculiar green; and in the composition of a pudding, it was her judgment that fixed the ingredients. Then the poor

戲園裏頭聽來的話.他都背得出.京裏最有名的俏皮話.他都記得.他告訴我們的時候.笑話書還未印出來.談話之間.他教我兩個女兒鬭牌.有時教兩個小孩子打拳.要他們練習麻俐.他原有許多不美備的地方.但是因爲要他作女壻.我們眼睛就瞎了.看不見他的許多短處.我的女人.想出一千個方法牢籠他.要他作女壻.換而言之.說得輕鬆些.我的女人.把女兒的好處不曉得鋪張多少倍.例如進茶點的時候.點心又酥又脆.他就說是奧維雅作的.果子酒味好.是奧維雅親手摘的果子.酸果顏色鮮綠.那是奧維雅手段好.甜糕製得好.是奧維雅把材料配合得法.有時

woman would sometimes tell the squire that she thought him and Olivia extremely of a size, and would bid both stand up to see which was tallest. These instances of cunning, which she thought impenetrable, yet which everybody saw through, were very pleasing to our benefactor, who gave every day some new proofs of his passion, which, though they had not arisen to proposals of marriage, yet we thought fell but little short of it, and his slowness was attributed sometimes to native bashfulness and sometimes to his fear of offending his uncle. An occurrence, however, which happened soon after, put it beyond a doubt that he designed to become one of the family; my wife even regarded it as an absolute promise.

My wife and daughters happening to return a visit to neighbor Flamborough's, found that family had lately got their pictures drawn by a limner, who traveled the country, and took likenesses for fifteen shillings a head. As this

我女人說．鄉紳同奧維雅．恰好一樣的高．叫他們站在一處比．看是誰高．我女人用這些詭計．自己以爲人家看不出．但是無人不看出來．我們的恩人 ｛指鄉紳｝．却很喜歡．每天都新表示他的愛情．雖然尚未到開口求親．我們以爲也相去不遠了．我們以爲他這樣拖長．老不開口．是由於他怕羞．有時以爲他恐怕得罪了他的叔叔．後來不久發現一件事．我們曉得他有意同我們家聯姻無疑了．我的女人並且當作他是的確無疑的答應要娶奧維雅了．

我且說這一件事．有一天．我女人同兩個女兒．回拜鄉居法林巴．看見他們家裏每人畫一幅相．是一個穿鄉過鎮行脚畫師畫的．每畫一個人．十五個先令．因爲鄰居家裏．同我

family and ours had long a sort of rivalry in point of taste, our spirit took the alarm at this stolen march upon us, and notwithstanding all I could say, and I said much, it was resolved that we should have our pictures done too. Having, therefore, engaged the limner—for what could I do?—our next deliberation was to show the superiority in our taste in the attitudes. As for our neighbor's family, there were seven of them, and they were drawn with seven oranges, a thing quite out of taste, no variety in life, no composition in the world. We desired to have something in a brighter style, and after many debates, at length came to a unanimous resolution of being drawn together in one large historical family piece. This would be cheaper, since one frame would serve for all, and it would be infinitely more genteel—for all families of any taste were now drawn in the same manner. As we did not immediately

們家裏. 對於穿戴音樂繪畫. 是向來要比賽的. 我們見了. 被他們搶了先着. 很不甘心. 一定也要畫. 我勸了許多. 也不聽. 我也沒法. 只好也請那畫師. 以後就是商量怎樣坐. 怎樣立. 怎樣布局. 要賽過鄰居. 我們的鄰居家裏. 共是七口. 畫了七張. 每個人. 手上都拿了. 一個橘子. 旣嫌太俗. 又嫌太板. 毫無布局. 我們要比他們的派頭新鮮些. 討論了好幾回. 後來衆人同意. 決定借古人的事. 畫一大幅家庭樂. 只用一個畫架. 價錢也省得多. 也高雅得多. 現時高雅人家. 都是這樣畫的. 因爲馬上想不出一件古事來. 可以

recollect an historical subject to hit us, we were contented each with being drawn as independent historical figures. My wife desired to be represented as Venus, and the painter was desired not to be too frugal of his diamonds in her stomacher and hair. Her two little ones were to be as Cupids by her side, while I, in my gown and band, was to present her with my books on the Whistonian controversy. Olivia would be drawn as an Amazon, sitting upon a bank of flowers, dressed in a green Joseph richly laced with gold, and a whip in her hand. Sophia was to be a shepherdess, with as many sheep as the painter could put in for nothing; and Moses was to be dressed out with a hat and white feather. Our taste so much pleased the squire, that he insisted on being put in as one of the family, in the character of Alexander the Great, at Olivia's feet. This was considered by us all as an indication of his desire to be introduced into the family,

把我們全家都包括在一幅畫裏頭. 我們都願意. 各人各代表一個古人{合幾個古人同畫在一幅上可謂不倫不類}. 我的女人要畫作女愛神. 吩咐畫師在頭髮上及胸前要多多畫些金剛鑽{牧師太太還要畫作少年美女還要戴許多金剛鑽未免太好笑}. 兩個小兒子畫作男愛神{即膀上長肉翅}一體小胖子{一手持弓稞}畫在他身邊. 把我的相畫上長袍. 白圍領. 手拿我著作的韋氏辯論. 送與女愛神. 奧維雅畫作好戰好獵的女神. 一手執鞭. 身穿綠色長服. 滿繡金花. 坐在花堆上. 素緋雅畫作牧羊女. 左右畫許多綿羊. 越多越好. 摩西則頭戴大帽. 上插白羽. 鄉紳很喜歡我們的見解. 也要畫在這一幅之內. 也算是我們家裏人. 他却要畫作亞力山大. 坐在奧維雅脚下. 我們以為他表示願意作我們家

nor could we refuse his request. The painter, therefore, set to work, and as he wrought with assiduity and expedition, in less than four days the whole was completed. The piece was large, and it must be owned he did not spare his colors, for which my wife gave him great encomiums. We were all perfectly satisfied with his performance; but an unfortunate circumstance had not occurred till the picture was finished, which now struck us with dismay. It was so very large that we had no place in the house to fix it. How we all came to disregard so material a point is inconceivable; but certain it is we had been all greatly remiss. The picture, therefore, instead of gratifying our vanity, as we hoped, leaned in a most mortifying manner against the kitchen wall, where the canvas was stretched and painted, much too large to be got through any of the doors, and the jest of all our neighbors. One compared it to Robinson Crusoe's long boat, too

裏的人. 我們不免答應他. 畫師於是動手. 很出力的畫. 畫得很快. 不到四天. 都畫完了. 幅頭是很大. 顏料用得眞不少. 我女人大稱讚他. 我們人人無不十分滿意. 不料發生一件極不幸的事. 是畫完了才曉得的. 我們都糊塗了. 想不出辦法. 就是這幅畫太大. 無處好掛. 這麼樣的一個要點. 不曉得爲什麼事前就未曾想到. 我們都太過忽畧了. 這幅畫我們原盼望掛起來. 增多少榮耀. 現在只好斜靠着廚房牆. 擺在那裏. 我們越看越難過. 畫得太大. 那個門也走不過. 我們所有的鄰居都曉得. 誰不當是笑話. 有人比作魯濱孫的長

large to be removed; another thought it more resembled a reel in a bottle; some wondered how it could be got out, but still more were amazed how it ever got in.

But though it excited the ridicule of some, it effectually raised more malicious suggestions in many. The squire's portrait being found united with ours was an honor too great to escape envy. Scandalous whispers began to circulate at our expense, and our tranquillity was continually disturbed by persons who came as friends to tell us what was said of us by our enemies. These reports we always resented with becoming spirit, but scandal ever improves by opposition.

We once again, therefore, entered into a consultation upon obviating the malice of our enemies, and at last came to a resolution which had too much cunning to give me entire satisfaction. It was this: as our principal object was to discover the honor of Mr. Thornhill's addresses,

艇.太大了.挪不動.有人比作瓶裏軸.不知怎樣放進去的.有人詫異.怎麼樣搬進屋的.也有人替我們發愁.怎麼樣搬出來 {寫得敗興 失望難堪}.畫了這幅畫.旣然被人笑.還着實的令許多人生出許多有心躓跎我們的揣度.鄉紳的相.畫在我們全家堆裏.太替我們增面子.逃不了被人妒忌.背後污衊我們的話.漸漸播傳.同我們交情好的人.走來把我們仇人躓跎我們的話告訴我們.我們聽了.人人不安.我們自然痛恨這種謠言.但是越反對.謠言越多.

於是我們又商量設法.破除我們仇人的懷恨.後來商定一個法子.不過這個法子.過於詭詐.我原不甚滿意.我且把法子細說.因爲鄉紳向我女兒表示愛

THE VICAR OF WAKEFIELD

my wife undertook to sound him by pretending to ask his advice in the choice of a husband for her eldest daughter. If this was not found sufficient to induce him to a declaration, it was then resolved to terrify him with a rival.[1] To this last step, however, I would by no means give my consent, till Olivia gave me the most solemn assurances that she would marry the person provided to rival him upon this occasion, if he did not prevent it by taking her himself. Such was the scheme laid, which, though I did not strenuously oppose, I did not entirely approve.

The next time, therefore, that Mr. Thornhill came to see us, my girls took care to be out of the way, in order to give their mamma an opportunity of putting her scheme into execution; but they only retired to the next room, whence they could overhear the whole conversation. My wife artfully introduced

情. 我們主要目的. 是要揭開他. 是否有真意. 我女人擔任探他口氣. 借徑於請教他怎樣替大女兒擇夫. 假使這樣還引不出他開口求親. 我們就決意拿出一位要求親的. 同他作勁敵. 嚇他. 末後這一步. 我原是一定不答應的. 後來奧維雅很莊重的說明. 倘若走出一個勁敵來求親. 鄉紳還不去禁止. 他願意嫁與這個勁敵. 我只好答應了. 這就是我們擺佈的計策. 我雖然未出全力反對. 却也並不甚以為然.

故此唐希爾下次到我們家裏來. 我兩個女兒躲開. 好叫他們母親趁機會. 施行這個妙計. 他們不過躲在隔壁房間. 這邊房裏說話. 他們聽得很清楚. 我的女人很巧妙的. 引

---

1. Rival, 勁敵.

it by observing that one of the Miss Flamboroughs was like to have a very good match of it in Mr. Spanker. To this the squire assenting, she proceeded to remark that they who had warm fortunes were always sure of getting good husbands. "But heaven help," continued she, "the girls that have none. What signifies beauty, Mr. Thornhill? or what signifies all the virtue and all the qualifications in the world in this age of self-interest? It is not 'What is she?' but 'What has she?' is all the cry."

"Madam," returned he, "I highly approve the justice as well as the novelty of your remarks, and if I were a king it should be otherwise. It should then, indeed, be fine times with the girls without fortunes: our two young ladies should be the first for whom I would provide."

"Ah, sir," returned my wife, "you are pleased to be facetious; but I wish I were a queen, and then I know where my eldest daughter should look for a

他上路.先說鄰居一位法林巴小姐.同某君很像是配對得好.鄉紳說句是的.我女人往下說.有資產的小姐們.向來一定嫁得好丈夫.窮人家的女兒.是嫁不着好丈夫的.只好求上天幫助.哎.唐先生.現在的世情.都是講自私自利的.管什麼女子面貌長得好看.管什麼道德.管什麼各種的長處呢.現在的人.開口就要問某小姐有多少賠嫁.那裏有人問這小姐好不好.

鄉紳答道.瑪當.你的說話.又新鮮.又公道.假使我作國王.我一定不許這樣.我作了國王的話.小姐們沒資產的.都要過好日子.我第一件.就是替我們這兩位小姐預備.

我女人答道.呀.先生愛說笑話.我很想作一國的女王.那嗎.我曉得在那裏替我的大

husband. But now that you have put it into my head, seriously, Mr. Thornhill, can't you recommend me a proper husband for her? She is now nineteen years old, well grown, and well educated, and, in my humble opinion, does not want for parts."

"Madam," replied he, "if I were to choose, I would find out a person possessed of every accomplishment that can make an angel happy. One with prudence, fortune, taste, and sincerity, — such, madam, would be, in my opinion, the proper husband."—"Ay, sir," said she, "but do you know of any such person?"—"No, madam," returned he; "it is impossible to know any person that deserves to be her husband; she's too great a treasure for one man's possession; she's a goddess. Upon my soul, I speak what I think—she's an angel."—"Ah, Mr. Thornhill, you only flatter my poor girl; but we have been thinking of marrying her to one of your tenants, whose mother is lately

女兒擇配. 但是你現在的話提醒我. 我認真的問你. 唐先生. 你能不能保薦一位好丈夫. 配我的大女兒. 他現年十九歲. 長得好. 教得好. 我的愚見. 以為他很有才能.

他答道. 瑪當. 假使我去替他挑的話. 我自然挑出一個人. 這個人是要有各種才能學問. 能彀使仙女快樂的. 這個人. 小心謹慎. 不亂來. 有財產. 又高雅. 又誠懇. 瑪當. 我以為這樣的一種人才. 配當他的丈夫. 我女人說道. 呀. 你可曉得有這樣的一種人麼. 他答道. 瑪當. 我不曉得. 誰配作他的丈夫. 是萬不能曉得的. 他是一個至寶. 斷不是一個人所能享的. 他是一位女神. 我實在是心裏怎樣想. 嘴裏怎樣說. 他是一位仙女. 我女人答道. 唐希爾先生. 你不過恭維我女兒. 我們正想把他嫁給你的一個住客. 那個人的母親. 新近才死.

dead, and who wants a manager; you know whom I mean, Farmer Williams; a warm man, Mr. Thornhill, able to give her good bread, and who has several times made her proposals" (which was actually the case); "but, sir," concluded she, "I should be glad to have your approbation of our choice."—"How, madam," replied he, "my approbation! My approbation of such a choice! Never. What? Sacrifice so much beauty, and sense, and goodness to a creature insensible of the blessing! Excuse me, I can never approve of such a piece of injustice! And I have my reasons!"—"Indeed, sir," cried Deborah, "if you have your reasons, that's another affair; but I should be glad to know those reasons."—"Excuse me, madam," returned he, "they lie too deep for discovery" (laying his hand upon his bosom); "they remain buried, riveted here."

After he was gone, upon general consultation, we could not tell what to make

得林.多情的女兒.經向我女兒提過幾次.(這却是事實).但是我要請教你.你說我們挑選得好不好.他答道.怎麼樣.你問我好不好麼.你們挑選這個女婿.我不以為然.我極端不以為然.小姐這樣美貌.兼有知識.都犧牲了.嫁給一個好怪.我起不且.我女人道理.你旣然有你的道理.那又當別論.但是我很願意聽聽你的道理.他答道.請你不要見怪.一面一手捫心.一面一道.我的道理.深藏在這裏.揭露不得.深埋在這裏.釘牢在這裏

曉得威林.是個多情的人.也還能殼給我女兒過安樂日子.他曾向我女兒提過幾次.這却像太{牧太海師一希他浹他却很像}

你理家.你說的是誰.就是威林.是個務農人家.也還能殼給我女兒過安樂日子.他曾

要我說的是個情的女兒經向我女兒(這却是事請教你.你得好不好.樣.你問我們挑選這個以為然.我然.小姐這的有知識.處.都犧牲不會領略的人願.萬你們不能你們小姐還有我的答道.你理.那又當很願意聽他答道.他一面一說一道.這裏.揭露這裏.釘牢深味上神　口氣的不三{越卽不逼近離的}{唐希他答却很}

他 走 過 之 後. 我 們
又 討 論 一 番. 摸 不 着
他 說 了 這 些 好 聽 的 話.

of these fine sentiments. Olivia considered them as instances of the most exalted passion; but I was not quite so sanguine;[1] it seemed to me pretty plain, that they had more of love than matrimony in them; yet, whatever they might portend,[2] it was resolved to prosecute the scheme of Farmer Williams, who, from my daughter's first appearance in the country, had paid her his addresses.

是什麽意思.奥維雅以爲是他表示最高度的愛情.我却不存這樣的好希望.我看得很明白的.愛是有的.結婚恐怕未必.毋論他這些話.是什麽見端.我們决定同威林拍合.因爲我女兒初到這裏.他是第一個求親的.

1. Sanguine, 有好希望;存望好之心. 2. Portend, 發見預兆.

CHAPTER XVII

SCARCELY ANY VIRTUE FOUND TO RESIST THE POWER
OF LONG AND PLEASING TEMPTATION

第 十 七 回

一 個 人 久 爲 令 人 歡 喜 的 外 物 所 誘
有 時 非 道 德 所 能 抵 抗
（奧 維 雅 棄 家 私 奔）

As I only studied my child's real happiness, the assiduity[1] of Mr. Williams pleased me, as he was in easy circumstances, prudent, and sincere. It required but very little encouragement to revive his former passion; so that in an evening or two he and Mr. Thornhill met at our house, and surveyed each other for some time with looks of anger; but Williams owed his landlord no rent, and little regarded his indignation. Olivia, on her side, acted the coquette[2] to perfection, if that might

且 說. 我 只 能 從 女 兒 的 終 身 快 樂 設 想. 威 林 的 懇 切 求 親. 我 却 喜 歡. 因 爲 他 環 境 尚 好. 人 也 謹 慎 誠 實. 只 要 些 微 鼓 勵 他. 他 的 愛 情 就 復 活. 有 一 兩 天 晚 上. 他 和 唐 希 爾 同 在 我 們 家 裏. 兩 人 相 見. 怒 目 而 視. 但 威 林 並 不 欠 房 租. 也 就 不 管 唐 希 爾 生 氣. 奧 維 雅 就 同 戲 子 登 臺. 挑 動 兩

---

1. Assiduity, 勤懇不懈.　2. Coquette, 女人之好引動男人者.

178

THE VICAR OF WAKEFIELD

be called acting which was her real character, pretending to lavish all her tenderness on her new lover. Mr. Thornhill appeared quite dejected at this preference,[1] and with a pensive air took leave, though I own it puzzled me to find him so much in pain as he appeared to be, when he had it in his power so easily to remove the cause, by declaring an honorable passion. But whatever uneasiness he seemed to endure, it could easily be perceived that Olivia's anguish was still greater. After any of these interviews between her lovers, of which there were several, she usually retired to solitude,[2] and there indulged her grief. It was in such a situation I found her one evening, after she had been for some time supporting a fictitious gayety.—"You now see, my child," said I, "that your confidence in Mr. Thornhill's passion was all a dream; he permits the

家調情. 本事十足. 其實他本性如此. 並非作戲. 他裝出一副假造作. 把柔情都使向威林一方面. 唐希爾見他偏重一方. 很不高興. 告辭的時候. 好像是很有所深念的神氣. 他原可以正式開口求親. 就可以立刻掃除阻礙. 他為何自尋煩惱. 我却不解. 但是毋論他受什麼煩惱. 我覺得我女兒的隱痛更甚. 這兩個人在我們家裏. 會過好幾次. 每次相會之後. 我女兒總是一個人到房中. 盡量的發愁. 有一天晚上. 他假作歡笑好一會. 獨自回到房裏納悶. 我見了. 對他說道. 好孩子. 你現在曉得. 你向來相信唐希爾愛你. 不過是一場大夢. 他

---

1. Preference, 偏愛. 2. Solitude, 獨居.

rivalry of another, every way his inferior, though he knows it lies in his power to secure you to himself by a candid declaration."— "Yes, papa," returned she; "but he has his reasons for this delay — I know he has. The sincerity of his looks and words convinces me of his real esteem. A short time, I hope, will discover the generosity of his sentiments, and convince you that my opinion of him has been more just than yours." — "Olivia, my darling," returned I, "every scheme that has been hitherto pursued to compel him to a declaration has been proposed and planned by yourself, nor can you in the least say that I have constrained you. But you must not suppose, my dear, that I will ever be instrumental[1] in suffering his honest rival to be the dupe of your ill-placed passion. Whatever time you require to bring your fancied admirer to an explanation shall be granted; but at

很曉得只要光明正大. 正式的開口求親. 就可以得你. 爲什麼甘讓諸事都不如他的人作勁敵呢. 我女兒答道. 爸爸. 他所以遲延不開口. 是有個道理. 我曉得的. 他的說話. 他的神氣. 都是誠懇. 我相信他是看重我. 我盼望再過不多幾時. 就可以揭露他的厚情. 使你相信我料他的意思. 比你的眞切. 我答道. 我的小寶貝. 我們所施行的各種強逼他開口求親的方法. 都是你想出來的. 你不能說我有絲毫強制過你. 你却不要妄想. 因爲你的愛情鍾於非人. 我就讓你愚弄那誠懇求親的人. 你以爲等到什麼時候. 愛你的人. 才可以明白解說他的意思. 毋論等到什麼時候. 我都可以答應. 但是一過了你所

---

1. Instrumental, 有助於.

the expiration of that term, if he is still regardless, I must absolutely insist that honest Mr. Williams shall be rewarded for his fidelity. The character which I hitherto supported in life demands this from me, and my tenderness as a parent shall never influence my integrity as a man. Name then your day—let it be as distant as you think proper—and, in the meantime, take care to let Mr. Thornhill know the exact time on which I design delivering you up to another. If he really loves you, his own good sense will readily suggest that there is but one method alone to prevent him losing you forever."—This proposal, which she could not avoid considering as perfectly just, was readily agreed to. She again renewed her most positive promise of marrying Mr. Williams, in case of the other's insensibility; and at the next opportunity, in Mr. Thornhill's presence, that day month was fixed upon for her nuptials with his rival.

定的期限.若是愛你的人還是不理.我一定要答應威林.報酬他歷久不移的誠懇.我生平敦品.逼我要這樣作法.我爲父要慈愛.爲人要忠信.不能因慈愛而侵犯忠信.你先定一個日期.你以爲應該定得很遠的.你就定很遠的期限.你要留心告訴唐希爾.一過期限.我要把你許配別人.他若是眞愛你.他的善知識自然會使他知道只有一個法子.可以免得你爲他人所有.我這個意思.他也不能不說是十分公道.我女兒願照行.他重新又說.倘若那一個人仍是無知無覺的.他答應一定嫁給威林.下次唐希爾到我們家裏.就當面說明.從當日起.一個月後.要同威林行結婚禮.

Such vigorous proceedings seemed to redouble Mr. Thornhill's anxiety: but what Olivia really felt gave me some uneasiness. In this struggle between prudence and passion, her vivacity quite forsook her, and every opportunity of solitude was sought and spent in tears. One week passed away; but Mr. Thornhill made no efforts[1] to restrain her nuptials. The succeeding week he was still assiduous, but not more open. On the third he discontinued his visits entirely, and instead of my daughter testifying any impatience, as I expected, she seemed to retain a pensive tranquillity, which I looked upon as resignation.[2] For my own part, I was now sincerely pleased with thinking that my child was going to be secured in a continuance of competence and peace, and frequently applauded her resolution, in preferring happiness to ostentation.[3]

唐希爾看見這樣認真的辦法. 像是加倍的着急. 但是奧維雅心裏. 究竟是怎麼樣的感覺. 使我不安. 因爲他心裏愛情同謹慎擇夫兩件交關. 就看不見他向來的活潑. 一有機會. 總是一個人走開去哭. 過了一星期. 唐希爾也不出力禁阻奧維雅與他人結婚. 第二個星期. 他還是照常的來. 但是他究竟什麼意思. 仍是絲毫不露. 第三個星期. 他簡直不來. 我以爲女兒要現出不耐煩的神色. 他却仍然是安閒的深念. 我以爲他是到了無可如何. 只好忍痛不響. 我以爲女兒將來可以終身過飽煖安樂日子. 心裏着實歡喜. 並且常常稱讚他能毅決意犧牲排場. 寧享快樂.

---

1. Made no efforts, 不出力; 不想法.　2. Resignation, 退讓; 辭職; 放任.　3. Ostentation, 出風頭; 擺架子; 炫耀.

It was within about four days of her intended nuptials that my little family at night were gathered round a charming fire, telling stories of the past, and laying schemes for the future. Busied in forming a thousand projects, and laughing at whatever folly came uppermost, "Well, Moses," cried I, "we shall soon, my boy, have a wedding in the family; what is your opinion of matters and things in general?"—"My opinion, father, is, that all things go on very well; and I was just now thinking, that when sister Livy is married to Farmer Williams, we shall then have the loan of his cider press and brewing tubs for nothing."—"That we shall, Moses," cried I; "and he will sing us 'Death and the Lady,'¹ to raise our spirits, into the bargain."—"He has taught that song to our Dick," cried Moses, "and I think he goes through it very prettily."—"Does he so?" cried I,

離喜期四天的晚上．家裏人圍爐說古事．打算將來．想出一千個計畫．對於許多行不通的．我們就大笑．我說道．摩西．好孩子．我們不久家裏就辦喜事．你對於各種事體．有什麼意思．他答道．父親．我看諸事進行都很順利．我剛才正在那裏想．姊姊嫁了威林之後．我們可以不花錢白借他的榨蘋果東西．和釀酒桶用用．我說道．摩西．我們是要借的．還要威林唱報死使者歌．舞鼓我們的精神．摩西說道．他把這歌教了狄克．狄克唱得還好．我說道．他

---

1. "Death and the Lady," 歌名，又名 "Messenger of Mortality," 報死使者歌.

"then let us have it. Where's little Dick? Let him up with it boldly."— "My brother Dick," cried Bill, my youngest, "is just gone out with sister Livy; but Mr. Williams has taught me two songs, and I'll sing them for you, papa. Which song do you choose, 'The Dying Swan,' or 'the Elegy on the Death of a Mad Dog'?"—"The elegy, child, by all means," said I; "I never heard that yet; and Deborah, my life, grief, you know, is dry; let us have a bottle of the best gooseberry wine to keep up our spirits. I have wept so much at all sorts of elegies of late, that, without an enlivening glass, I am sure this will overcome me: and Sophy, love, take your guitar, and thrum in with the boy a little."

唱得好嗎. 讓我們聽聽. 狄克在那裏. 讓他放膽唱. 最小的孩子說道. 哥哥才同奧維雅姊姊出去. 威林先生教我兩隻歌. 爸爸. 我唱給你聽. 一隻是叫作天鵝將死. 一隻是輓瘋狗歌. 我說道. 唱輓歌罷. 我向來未聽過. 又對我女人說道. 哀情是枯槁的. 我們來一瓶果子酒. 助助精神. 我近來聽哀歌流淚不少. 若不吃鍾酒. 提提精神. 恐怕聽了. 又要下淚. 素緋雅你奏提琴. 配小兄弟唱. 比勒於是唱道.

AN ELEGY ON THE DEATH OF A MAD DOG*

Good people all, of every sort,
　Give ear unto my song;
And if you find it wondrous short
　It cannot hold you long.

輓瘋狗歌§

所有的好人們聽我唱歌. 你們若是嫌歌短. 好在是不就攔你們的時候. 愛林頓地方有一個人.

*此歌另有文言翻譯見卷末.　§瘋狗能害人該殺瘋狗既咬人尤該殺今幸而瘋狗死而被咬之人生只應慶生人不應哀瘋狗此歌之作不獨譏世之好作諛墓文者殆倘有深意存焉.

184

THE VICAR OF WAKEFIELD

In Islington there was a man,
　Of whom the world might say,
That still a godly race he ran,
　Whene'er he went to pray.

A kind and gentle heart he had,
　To comfort friends and foes;
The naked every day he clad,
　When he put on his clothes.

And in that town a dog was found,
　As many dogs there be,
Both mongrel, puppy, whelp and hound,
　And curs of low degree.

This dog and man at first were friends;
　But when a pique began,
The dog, to gain some private ends,
　Went mad, and bit the man.

Around from all the neighboring streets,
　The wondering neighbors ran,
And swore the dog had lost his wits,
　To bite so good a man.

The wound it seem'd both sore and sad
　To every Christian eye;
And while they swore the dog was mad,
　They swore the man would die.

But soon a wonder came to light,
　That showed the rogues they lied,
The man recovered of the bite,
　The dog it was that died.

新媽的愛一裘都體的狗．小下中初好一麼那私了口巷奇看這瘋督那一一是那不得這的人那

去是人仁是衣天裸住多狗狗其當是有什原來爲那報瘋人的覺出狗咬是甚見看的定死曉出謊的的是

裏候好和仇敵穿與他許種獵有狗原來爲不要變人的覺出狗當眞奉看難痛狗面死曉出謊咬卻是

教堂時作人友的時給人方麼惡狗一這個人後不曉得他們忽然那鄰們都走那人當眞奉看難痛狗一必時才都被死咬卻

他禱力他對樣的要的地什狗流有同朋天事隻怨咬所鄰怪都個了教傷定面瘋個到奇班原不隻

"A very good boy, Bill, upon my word; and an elegy that may truly be called tragical. Come, my children, here's Bill's health, and may he one day be a bishop."

他唱完了．我說道．比勒．好孩子．這個哀歌．眞是悲哀．來來．孩子們．我喝一鍾酒．祝他將來作主教．

"With all my heart," cried my wife; "and if he but preaches as well as he sings, I make no doubt of him. The most of his family, by the mother's side, could sing a good song; it was a common saying in our country, that the family of the Blenkinsops could never look straight before them, nor the Hugginsons blow out a candle; that there were none of the Grograms but could sing a song, or of the Marjorams but could tell a story."—"However that be," cried I, "the most vulgar ballad of them all generally pleases me better than the fine modern odes, and things that petrify[1] us in a single stanza; productions that we at once detest and praise. Put the glass to your brother, Moses. The great fault of these elegiasts is, that they are in despair for griefs that give the sensible part of mankind very little pain. A lady loses her muff, her fan, or her lap dog, and

我女人道．我很高興說他．只要他講經同唱歌一樣的好．定可以作主教．他母親娘家裏的人都唱得好．我們鄉下裏有句通常話．說某氏一家的人．不會向前直看．某氏家的人．不會吹滅蠟燭．某氏家的人都會唱歌．某氏家的人都會說古事．我說道．雖然這樣．那怕是極俗的歌．我都喜歡聽．我却不喜歡聽近人的高調．和那每句同韻的．聽一章．就令人無精神．這種著作．有人討厭．有人稱讚．摩西．你把鍾酒給小兄弟．這班作哀歌的人．拿不悲痛的題目作哀歌．例如一個女人失了袖籠子．扇子．或失了一隻小狗．這些糊塗詩人．跑回

---

1. Petrify, 化爲石；使人廓木；不能動情.

so, the silly poet runs home to versify the disaster."

"That may be the mode," cried Moses; "in sublimer compositions; but the Ranelagh songs that come down to us are perfectly familiar, and all cast in the same mold. Colin meets Dolly, and they hold a dialogue together; he gives her a fairing to put in her hair, and she presents him with a nosegay; and then they go together to church, where they give good advice to young nymphs and swains to get married as fast as they can."

"And very good advice too," cried I; "and I am told there is not a place in the world where advice can be given with so much propriety as there; for as it persuades us to marry, it also furnishes us with a wife; and surely that must be an excellent market, my boy, where we are told what we want, and supplied with it when wanting."

"Yes, sir," returned Moses; "and I know but of two such markets for

家去. 拿來作題目. 作哀歌.

摩西說道. 那些好作大文章的. 許是這樣. 但是流傳下來的. 從前在某遊樂園唱的歌. 都是很通俗的. 同出一個模範. 例如某男子遇某女子. 兩人問答. 男的在市場買一樣東西送給女的作首飾. 女的送男的一朵花. 於是兩個人同到教堂行禮. 還勸少男少女. 趕快的結婚.

我說道. 這種勸人的話很好. 世界上第一好地方勸人嫁娶就是教室. 教堂不獨勸人嫁娶. 還供給妻室. 旣然告訴我們要什麼東西. 我們若是要. 就可以供給. 豈不是個好市場麼.

摩西答道. 是的. 父親. 在歐洲地方. 這種供給妻室的市場. 我只知道兩處. 一處是英國浪尼

wives in Europe—Rane-lagh in England, and Fontarabia in Spain. The Spanish market is open once a year, but our English wives are salable every night."

"You are right, my boy," cried his mother; "Old England is the only place in the world for husbands to get wives."—"And for wives to manage their husbands," interrupted I. "It is a proverb abroad, that if a bridge were built across the sea, all the ladies of the continent would come over to take pattern from _ours; for there are no such wives in Europe as our own. But let us have one bottle more, Deborah, my life, and Moses, give us a good song. What thanks do we not owe to Heaven for thus bestowing tranquillity, health, and competence! I think myself happier now than the greatest monarch upon earth. He has no such fireside, nor such pleasant faces about it. Yes, Deborah, we are now growing old; but the evening of our life is likely to be happy.

拉.一處是西班牙風泰拉別亞.西班牙的市場.每年只開一次.我們英國.每晚都可以得到妻室的.

我女人說道.我的兒子.你說得不錯.世界上.只有老英國是第一個男人找女人的好地方.我攔住說道.世界上.也只有這個地方.女人管男人.外國有一句諺語.說的是若在海上搭一座橋.所有歐洲大陸的女人.都要跑到我們英國來.跟我們女人學.因爲歐洲各國爲妻的.都不如我們英國.狄波拉.我們再喝一瓶酒.摩西再唱一個好歌我們聽.我們很要謝謝上蒼.賜我們的安樂強健飽煖.我覺得這時候.比世界上什麼帝王都快樂.帝王有這樣家庭圍爐快樂嗎.左右有這樣歡喜的臉嗎〔此師時夫牧婦快樂極矣下文即跌出極不快樂的事如此反襯在英文修辭學謂之 contrast 如黑白相托善惡悲喜相襯皆是〕.狄波拉.我們兩人是一年比一年老.但是我兩老的晚景.總當是快樂

We are descended from ancestors that knew no stain, and we shall leave a good and virtuous race of children behind us. While we live, they will be our support and our pleasure here; and when we die, they will transmit our honor untainted to posterity. Come, my son, we wait for a song; let us have a chorus. But where is my darling Olivia? That little cherub's voice is always sweetest in the concert."

Just as I spoke, Dick came running in. "Oh, papa, papa, she is gone from us—she is gone from us—my sister Livy is gone from us forever."

"Gone, child!"

"Yes; she is gone off with two gentlemen in a post chaise, and one of them kissed her, and said he would die for her; and she cried very much, and was for coming back; but he persuaded her again, and she went into the chaise and said, 'Oh, what will my poor papa do when he knows I am undone!'"

的. 我們祖上都是清白世家. 我們身後留下的都是有道德的兒女〔下文跌出一事幾乎玷辱家世矣〕. 我們兩老在世時. 有他們養老承歡. 我們死後. 兒女們把我們清白無瑕家世的體面. 傳於後代. 來. 來. 我們等你唱歌. 我們大家合唱. 我的寶貝奧維雅那裏去了. 這個小仙女的聲音. 在合唱中最好聽.

我正說這句話. 狄克跑進來喊. 爸爸. 爸爸. 他逃了. 他逃了. 奧維雅姊姊逃了. 再也不回來了.

我問道. 孩子. 逃了嗎.

狄克答道. 是的. 他同兩個男人在一馬車上逃了. 有一個男人同他接吻. 還說他甘願爲他死. 姊姊大哭. 要回來. 他勸姊姊. 姊姊上車. 說道可憐我父親知道. 我糟了. 不曉得怎麼樣了.

"Now then," cried I, my children, go and be miserable; for we shall never enjoy one hour more. And oh, may Heaven's everlasting fury light upon him and his! Thus to rob me of my child! And sure it will, for taking back my sweet innocent that I was leading up to heaven. Such sincerity as my child was possessed of! But all our earthly happiness is now over! Go, my children, go and be miserable and infamous; for my heart is broken within me!"

"Father," cried my son, "is this your fortitude?"

"Fortitude, child! Yes, he shall see if I have fortitude! Bring me my pistols. I'll pursue the traitor. While he is on earth, I'll pursue him. Old as I am, he shall find I can sting him yet. The villain!— the perfidious villain!"

I had by this time reached down my pistols, when my poor wife, whose passions were not so strong as mine, caught me in her arms. "My dearest,

我喊道. 兒女們呀. 你們去愁苦罷. 我們從此以後. 不能再有一點鐘的安樂了. 天呀. 求你永降禍殃於搶我女兒的人. 及其後代. 我領我的女兒升天堂 {以道德教女也}. 那個人. 把我的柔和老實女兒拉回頭 {陷其女於罪惡也}. 天一定降禍殃於那個人的. 我的女兒如此忠厚. 我們世界上的快樂. 是完了. 兒女們. 你們去受悲痛. 擔醜名罷. 我心要碎了 {此處悲極呼天上文樂極謝天善於反襯}.

我兒子喊道. 父親. 你隱忍的毅力. 就不過如此嗎.

我答道. 孩子. 毅力麼. 我把我的毅力給你看. 把我的手槍拿來. 我去追這個賣我的賊子. 只要他活在世上. 我是要追他的. 我雖老了. 有一天他總要曉得我還能螫他一下. 賊子呀. 無信的賊子呀.

我這時候已經把手槍伸手拿下來. 我女人生氣. 沒有我那樣盛. 抓住我兩隻膀子. 喊道.

dearest husband," cried she, "the Bible is the only weapon that is fit for your old hands now. Open that, my love, and read our anguish into patience, for she has vilely deceived us."

"Indeed, sir," resumed my son, afoer a pause, "your rage is too violent and unbecoming. You should be my mother's comforter, and you increase her pain. It ill suited you and your reverend character thus to curse your greatest enemy; you should not have cursed him, villain as he is."

"I did not curse him, child, did I?"

"Indeed, sir, you did; you cursed him twice."

"Then may Heaven forgive me and him if I did. And now, my son, I see it was more than human benevolence that first taught us to forgive our enemies! Blessed be His holy name for all the good He hath given, and for all that He hath taken away! But it is not, it is not a small distress that can wring tears from these old eyes, that have

我的丈夫.這時候你的兩隻手.只應該拿聖經.你打開聖經罷.他很騙了我們.請你把聖經一讀.把我們的慘痛.化作忍耐罷.

停了一會.我兒子又說道.當眞.父親的怒氣太猛.也不合你身分.你應該安慰我的母親.你現在這樣.反令他更加悲痛.你詛罵你的大仇人.也不合你作教士的品格.那人雖然是個賊子.你也不應詛罵他.

我說道.孩子.我曾詛罵他麼.

他答道.父親.你的確詛罵他兩次.

我說道.我若是詛罵過他.我求天赦宥我.赦宥他.我的兒子呀.我現在曉得.第一個教我們保佑我們的仇敵.眞是天心慈愛.上帝賜我們許多好處.謝謝上帝.上帝拿走的.我們也謝謝上帝.我這兩隻老眼.多年已不流淚

not wept for so many years.
My child!—to undo my
darling! May confusion
seize—Heaven forgive me,
what am I about to say!
You may remember, my
love, how good she was,
and how charming; till this
vile moment, all her care
was to make us happy.
Had she but died! But
she is gone—the honor of
our family contaminated;
and I must look out for
happiness in other worlds
han here. But, my child,
you saw them go off; per-
haps he forced her away?
If he forced her, she may
yet be innocent."

"Ah, no, sir," cried the
child; "he only kissed her,
and called her his angel,
and she wept very much
and leaned upon his arm,
and they drove off very
fast."

"She's an ungrateful
creature," cried my wife,
who could scarcely speak
for weeping, "to use us thus.
She never had the least
constraint put upon her
affections. The vile strumpet has deserted her parents
without any provocation—
thus to bring your gray

了.若不是極悲痛難過
之事.不能令我流淚
{讀之}.我的孩子呀.人
{傷心}
把你害了.我求昏亂…
{此句又是詛罵仇人只}.上
{說得一半又忍住不說}
天宥我.我快要說什麽
你們都記得.我這女兒.
怎樣的好.怎樣的令人
愛.他一向直到這刻.全
副心腸.都是使我們快
樂.他倒不如死了的好.
他逃了.我們家裏的名
譽受污辱了.我只好向
別的世界求歡樂了.
兒子呀.你看見他們走
的.多半是他們強逼他
走的.若是他們強逼他
走的.他還可以是個未
失足的貞潔人{此是從悲痛}
{極姑作萬一之}
{想以減輕悲痛}

那孩子答道.呀.父親.
不是的.他只是同姊姊
接吻.喊姊姊是他的仙
女.姊姊總是哭.靠在那
人的膀子.他們的車走
得很快.

我的女人哭到不能成
聲.說道.這孩子這樣待
我們.太是個沒良心的
東西.他愛什麽人.我們
向來不加過限制.父母
並沒什麽惹他生氣.他
為什麽這樣下賤.棄父

THE VICAR OF WAKEFIELL

hairs to the grave, and I must shortly follow."

In this manner that night, the first of our real misfortunes, was spent in the bitterness of complaint, and ill-supported sallies[1] of enthusiasm.[2] I determined, however, to find out our betrayer, wherever he was, and reproach his baseness. The next morning we missed our wretched child at breakfast, where she used to give life and cheerfulness to us all. My wife, as before, attempted to ease her heart by reproaches. "Never," cried she, "shall that vilest stain of our family again darken these harmless doors. I will never call her daughter more. No; let the strumpet live with her vile seducer; she may bring us to shame, but she shall never more deceive us."

"Wife," said I, "do not talk thus hardly: my detestation of her guilt is as great as yours; but ever shall this house and this heart be open to a poor,

母而逃. 催促白髮老父速死. 叫我不久也跟着死.

這是我們家裏第一次遭大不幸的事. 這天晚上. 就是這樣含怨叫苦的過. 又想了些行不通的救護方法. 我是決意無論他在那裏. 去找那害我們的人. 責他卑劣行爲. 早上是向來我的女兒使我們活潑快樂的時候. 第二天早上吃早餐. 沒得他在左右. 我們眞是難過. 我女人向來心裏難過. 就要責人. 這時候他說道. 我這個清白家門. 永遠不讓我們家裏的一個最下賤的汚穢來玷辱. 我永遠不再叫他是我的女兒. 一定不叫. 讓這賤婦與那誘拐者同居. 他可以羞辱我們. 他却不能再騙我們.

我說道. 妻呀. 你不可說這樣絕情的話. 我恨他騙我們. 也同你一樣. 只要他知罪知悔. 回到家來. 我的心同我的

---

1. Sallies, 衝出; 發出.　2. Enthusiasm, 熱心; 踴躍.

returning, repentant sinner.
The sooner she returns from
her transgression, the more
welcome shall she be to
me.　For the first time, the
very best may err; art may
persuade, and novelty
spread out its charm.　The
first fault is the child of
simplicity;[1] but every
other the offspring of guilt.[2]
Yes; the wretched creature
shall be welcome to this
heart and this house,
though stained with ten
thousand vices.　I will
again hearken to the music
of her voice—again will I
hang fondly on her bosom,
if I find but repentance
there.　My son, bring
hither my Bible and my
staff; I will pursue her,
wherever she is.''

家門.還是容他進來.他
越早回來.我越歡迎.最
好的人.第一次也許走
差一步.也許是受甘言
巧語所誘.新奇的情景
也能惑人.第一次的錯
是由於太老實.上人的
當.以後的錯.就是有心
爲惡.這個可憐的女子.
雖然犯了一千個過失.
我的心同我的家門.還
是很歡迎他回來.他回
來之後.我仍舊聽他說
話的樂音.我還很憐愛
他的.靠他胸前.只要我
曉得他胸內有一顆悔
過的心.我的兒子.你把
我的聖經同我的手杖
拿來.無論我女兒在那
裏.我去找他.

---

1. The child of simplicity, 由老實（無心爲惡）生出來的.　2. The offspring of guilt, 由有心爲惡生出來的.

CHAPTER XVIII

THE PURSUIT OF A FATHER TO RECLAIM A LOST CHILD TO VIRTUE

第 十 八 回

父 親 找 尋 失 足 女 兒
(牧 師 尋 女 遇 戲 子)

Though the child could not describe the gentleman's person who handed his sister into the post chaise, yet my suspicions fell entirely upon our young landlord, whose character for such intrigues was but too well known. I therefore directed my steps towards Thornhill Castle, resolving to upbraid him, and, if possible, to bring back my daughter: but before I had reached his seat, I was met by one of my parishioners, who said he saw a young lady resembling my daughter in a post chaise with a gentleman, whom, by the description, I could only guess to be Mr. Burchell, and that they drove very fast. This

且說我的兒子.雖然說不出那扶我女兒上車那個男人的身材面貌.我就疑到是我們房東幹的事.人人皆知他這個人性格.是會用這種詭計的.我就向唐希爾府去尋.決意斥責他.若能辦得到.我就把女兒帶回家來.我還沒有到唐府的時候.碰見一個我教職屬下的一個人.說看見一個少年女子.很像我的女兒.同一個男子同車.據他說那男子的面貌.我猜是白且爾.他還說那馬車走

information, however, did by no means satisfy me. I therefore went to the young squire's, and though it was yet early, insisted upon seeing him immediately. He soon appeared with the most open,[1] familiar air, and seemed perfectly amazed at my daughter's elopement, protesting upon his honor that he was quite a stranger to it. I now, therefore, condemned my former suspicions, and could turn them only upon Mr. Burchell, who, I recollected, had of late several private conferences with her: but the appearance of another witness left me no room to doubt of his villainy, who averred that he and my daughter were actually gone towards the Wells, about thirty miles off, where there was a great deal of company. Being driven to that state of mind in which we are more ready to act precipitately than to reason right, I never debated with myself

得很快.他告訴我的話. 我覺得不滿意.我還是 去見那少年鄉紳.時候 雖然還早.我一定要立 刻見他.他一會子走出 來.臉上是很從容坦白 的.聽說我女兒逃了.他 非常之詫異.說全不曉 得.我於是很怪責自己 不該疑心他.就猜是白 且爾幹的事.這時候我 想起來.白且爾有好幾 次同我女兒私下會商. 況且又有一個見證人 說.白且爾同我女兒同 去維爾地方.我就曉得 是白且爾的奸計.維爾 地方.離這裏還有一百 里地.那裏是個熱鬧所 在.我到了這個時候.方 寸已亂.辦事總是鹵莽 不會仔細的.也不會疑

---

1. Open, 坦白; 無隱.

whether these accounts might not have been given by persons purposely placed in my way to mislead me, but resolved to pursue my daughter and her fancied deluder thither. I walked along with earnestness, and inquired of several by the way; but received no accounts, till, entering the town, I was met by a person on horseback, whom I remembered to have seen at the squire's, and he assured me, that if I followed them to the races, which were but thirty miles farther, I might depend upon overtaking them; for he had seen them dance there the night before, and the whole assembly seemed charmed with my daughter's performance. Early the next day I walked forward to the races, and about four in the afternoon I came upon the course. The company made a very brilliant appearance, all earnestly employed in one pursuit — that of pleasure; how different from mine — that of reclaiming a lost child to virtue! I thought I

到人家特爲設出圈套給我假消息. 騙我. 我就決計向那方去. 找我女兒. 同那拐他逃走的人. 我很踴躍的向那方走. 路上還問了好幾個人. 都得不着消息. 後來到了那市鎮. 碰見一個人騎着馬. 我認得是在鄉紳府裏見過的. 他很切實的告訴我說. 離此有一百里. 有賽馬會. 到那裏一定可以趕得着他們. 他還說. 早一天晚上. 還看見我女兒跳舞. 在場的人. 都很稱讚我女兒跳得好. 第二天一早. 我往賽馬場走. 下午四點鐘走到. 看見許多穿得很華麗的人都在那裏尋樂. 惟有我是來找私逃的女兒. 心境同他們很不同 {樂同/悲不}. 我好像

perceived Mr. Burchell at some distance from me; but, as if he dreaded an interview, upon my approaching him, he mixed among a crowd, and I saw him no more. I now reflected that it would be to no purpose to continue my pursuit farther, and resolved to return home to an innocent family, who wanted my assistance. But the agitations of my mind, and the fatigues I had undergone, threw me into a fever, the symptoms[1] of which I perceived before I came off the course. This was another unexpected stroke, as I was more than seventy miles distant from home: however, I retired to a little alehouse by the roadside; and in this place, the usual retreat of indigence and frugality, I laid me down patiently to wait the issue[2] of my disorder. I languished[3] here for nearly three weeks; but at last my constitution prevailed,

遠遠的看見白且爾．他好像是怕見我．我趕快走到跟前．他閃在人隊裏．就不見了｛不獨令牧師疑惑讚　者也疑惑｝．這時候我細想．再追也無益．立意回家．因爲我全家都是老實人．總要我在家料理．誰知我心裏旣大受打擊．又飽受辛苦．害起熱病來．我快要離開賽馬場的時候．先覺得有些不舒服．這一病又是受一打擊．又是我料不到的．離家還有二百里地．只好走入路邊一個貧人所住的小客店暫歇．耐煩的等病愈．養了三星期病好了｛女兒已遠颺了｝．身

---

1. Symptoms, 病狀.　2. Issue, 結果.　3. Languished, 欠精神；乏氣力.

though I was unprovided with money to defray the expenses of my entertainment. It is possible the anxiety from this last circumstance alone might have brought on a relapse,[1] had I not been supplied by a traveler, who stopped to take a cursory refreshment. This person was no other than the philanthropic bookseller in St. Paul's Churchyard, who has written so many books for children: he called himself their friend, but he was the friend of all mankind. He was no sooner alighted, but he was in haste to be gone; for he was ever on business of the utmost importance, and was at that time actually compiling materials for the history of one Mr. Thomas Trip.

I immediately recollected this good-natured man's red-pimpled face; for he had published for me against the deuterogamists of the age, and from him I borrowed a few pieces, to be paid at my return.

邊却未帶錢開消房飯. 我若是因為欠房飯又着急. 難免病好了不復發. 幸虧遇着一位旅行的人. 入店暫歇吃飯. 他就是倫敦城聖保羅大教堂前面一個賣書的. 這個人向來好善. 著了許多給孩子們讀的書. 他自稱是孩子們的好朋友. 但是他這個人還是人類的好朋友. 這人是很忙的. 一入店. 不一會就要走. 那時候他正在收輯材料. 著一本書. 書裏有許多圖畫. 預備小孩子們讀的.

我一看見那滿臉的紅瘢. 就認得是他. 我反對教士續絃的書. 原是他發行的. 我就向他借了幾個錢. 回家後還他. 我病雖然

---

1. Relapse, 病好再病.

Leaving the inn, therefore, as I was yet but weak, I resolved to return home by easy journeys of ten miles a day. My health and usual tranquillity were almost restored, and I now condemned that pride which had made me refractory[1] to the hand of correction. Man little knows what calamities are beyond his patience to bear till he tries them; as in ascending the heights of ambition, which look bright from below, every step we rise shows us some new and gloomy prospect of hidden disappointment; so in our descent from the summits of pleasure, though the vale of misery below may appear at first dark and gloomy, yet the busy mind, still attentive to its own amusement, finds as we descend something to flatter and to please. Still, as we approach, the darkest objects appear to brighten, and the mental eye becomes adapted to its gloomy situation.

是好了. 身體還是虛弱. 只好慢慢回家. 一天不過走三十多里. 我身體也差不多復原. 心裏也就漸漸的安靜. 這時候我才怪責我的傲性未馴. 爲什麼不服從上天譴罰我呢. 一個人要遇着災禍. 才曉得自己忍耐性的限度. 凡慕富貴的人. 初往上爬的時候. 看見上頭都是一片光采. 再往上爬. 才看見有許多從前看不見的黑闇. 令人失望. 等到從享受快樂的最高頂跌下來的時候. 看見底下都是一片愁苦. 黑闇不堪. 然而那心裏還是忙不過要找事消遣. 一步一步往下降的時候. 也未嘗不找. 着很有些令我們得意快活的事. 後來走到平地. 頂黑闇的東西. 也顯出有光采. 那時候幽悶的情景心眼已經看慣了.

---

1. Refractory, 不服從; 倔強.

THE VICAR OF WAKEFIELD

I now proceeded forward, and had walked about two hours when I perceived what appeared at a distance like a wagon, which I was resolved to overtake; but when I came up with it, found it to be a strolling company's cart, that was carrying their scenes and other theatrical furniture to the next village, where they were to exhibit. The cart was attended only by the person who drove it, and one of the company, as the rest of the players were to follow the ensuing day. Good company upon the road, says the proverb, is the shortest cut; I therefore entered into conversation with the poor player; and as I once had some theatrical powers myself, I disserted on such topics with my usual freedom; but as I was pretty much unacquainted with the present state of the stage, I demanded who were the present theatrical writers in vogue,[1] who the Drydens and Otways of the day.

且說我往前走.遠遠的望見好像是一輛車.決意要趕上去.走到跟前.才曉得是一輛雲遊戲班的車.裝那佈景及戲臺用的家伙.到前村去演戲.那車上只有一個車夫.一個戲子押車.其餘的戲子.明日趕來.俗語說得好.路上有好遊伴.路程就不覺得遠.我於是就同那窮戲子談起來.因爲我從前有過演戲的本事.我就同他隨便談戲.但是現在戲界的情形.我全不懂.我就問他.現在誰編的戲最時髦.從前是德氏奧氏最有名.現在是誰呢.

---

1. In vogue, 時髦；入時.

"I fancy, sir," cried the player, "few of our modern dramatists would think themselves much honored by being compared to the writers you mention. Dryden's and Rowe's manner, sir, are quite out of fashion; our taste has gone back a whole century: Fletcher, Ben Jonson, and all the plays of Shakespeare, are the only things that go down."

"How!" cried I; "is it possible the present age can be pleased with that antiquated dialect, that obsolete humor, those overcharged characters, which abound in the works you mention?"

"Sir," returned my companion, "the public think nothing about dialect, or humor, or character; for that is none of their business; they only go to be amused, and find themselves happy when they can enjoy a pantomime[1] under the sanction of Jonson's or Shakespeare's name."

那戲子答道. 先生. 你把現在的編戲家. 比你所說的那幾位. 恐怕現在的編戲家. 說你瞧不起他們. 什麼德氏羅氏. 現在是很不時髦. 我們的好尚. 遠追一百年前. 只有法氏莊氏沙士比編的戲. 為大衆所喜歡.

我很驚怪的問道. 什麼呀. 他們的古老話語. 他們的趣語. 到現在都變了老古董了. 那戲中的人物. 都是太過火的. 能彀得現在的人喜歡嗎 {作者為名 尊崇沙士比心裏却不很恭維 他現在二十世紀的批評亦不很恭維 沙士比}.

他答道. 先生. 現在的人只管消遣. 不管什麼古老話. 不管什麼趣語. 不管什麼人物. 只要借莊氏或沙士比的名. 演啞巴戲. 他們就喜歡 {此寫時髦戲不過兒戲而已}.

1. Pantomime, (一) 啞巴戲, 只形容動作聳肩縮頸之類; (二) 演給孩子們看的戲, 布景顏多變化.

"So then, I suppose," cried I, "that our modern dramatists are rather imitators of Shakespeare than of nature."

"To say the truth," returned my companion, "I don't know that they imitate anything at all; nor, indeed, does the public require it of them: it is not the composition of the piece, but the number of starts and attitudes that may be introduced into it that elicits applause. I have known a piece, with not one jest in the whole, shrugged into popularity. No, sir, the works of Congreve and Farquhar have too much wit in them for the present taste; our modern dialect is much more natural."

By this time the equipage of the strolling company was arrived at the village, which, it seems, had been apprised of our approach, and was come out to gaze at us; for my companion observed, that strollers always have more spectators without doors

我說道怎麼看起來. 現在編戲的人. 不過是剽襲沙士比. 並不是描摹人情.

我的同伴說道. 我老實說罷. 現在編戲的. 簡直的是什麼也不描摹. 看戲的人. 也不要他們描摹什麼. 他們原不管一本戲怎麼結構. 只要裏頭有許多亂砌亂跳. 有許多怪狀. 看戲的人就喝采叫好 ｛退化的時 . 好尚往往如此比牧師說的話更淋漓盡致｝ . 我曉得有一本戲. 始終無一句笑話. 不過許多聳肩縮頸的怪狀. 却人人都喜歡看. 先生. 從前孔氏花氏的戲. 趣語太多. 不合時人口味. 現在的話語. 好像來得自然些 ｛原有此理不過話語稍微近時 古便不入時人眼亦可見時 人之｝ . 不學

這時候戲車已到了那村子. 村裏的人先已曉得快到. 走出來看. 我的同伴說. 雲遊的戲班. 在街上看的人多. 在場裏看的人少. 我起

than within. I did not
consider the impropriety of
my being in such company
till I saw a mob gather
about me. I therefore took
shelter as fast as possible
in the first alehouse that
offered; and being shown
into the common room,
was accosted by a very
well-dressed gentleman,
who demanded whether I
was the real chaplain of
the company, or whether
it was only to be my
masquerade character in
the play. Upon my in-
forming him of the truth,
and that I did not belong
in any sort to the company,
he was condescending
enough to desire me and
the player to partake in a
bowl of punch, over which
he discussed modern poli
tics with great earnestness
and interest. I set him
down in my own mind for
nothing less than a Parlia-
ment man, at least; but
was almost confirmed in
my conjectures, when,
upon asking what there
was in the house for supper,
he insisted that the player
and I should sup with him

初不覺得我在戲子堆
裏有點不像樣. 這時候
有許多人圍着我. 我才
明白過來. 我於是避入
一間小酒店. 有一個穿
得很好的人問我. 是不
是戲班的教士. 不然就
是戲子裝的教士. 我老
實告訴他. 我不是班子
裏的人. 他居然屈尊的
請我同那戲子吃甜酒.
他一面吃. 一面很頂眞
的談政事. 談得很有趣.
我以爲他至少也是一
位議員. 他還問店裏有
什麼東西作晚餐. 後來
一定請我同那戲子到
他家裏吃晚飯. 我以爲
十分有九猜着他是位

THE VICAR OF WAKEFIELD 195

at his house; with which request, after some entreaties, we were prevailed on to comply.

議員. 他請我們吃飯. 我們謙讓一會. 他一定請我們. 我們只好去.

CHAPTER XIX

THE DESCRIPTION OF A PERSON DISCONTENTED WITH THE PRESENT GOVERNMENT, AND APPREHENSIVE OF THE LOSS OF OUR LIBERTIES.

第 十 九 回

一個不以現政府爲然的人恐怕人民
失了自由
(老牧師戲園遇子)

The house where we were to be entertained lying at a small distance from the village, our inviter observed that, as the coach was not ready, he would conduct us on foot, and we soon arrived at one of the most magnificent mansions I had seen in that part of the country. The apartment into which we were shown was perfectly elegant and modern. He went to give orders for supper, while the player, with a wink, observed that we were perfectly in luck. Our entertainer soon returned, an elegant supper was brought in, two or

且說這個人的家. 離村子不遠. 他說車還未備好. 領我們步行. 不久就走到一所最闊的房子. 爲附近地所無的. 我們進出的屋子是很時路很華麗. 他出去吩咐預備晚飯. 那戲子對我使眼色. 說. 是我們運氣好. 一會子他進來. 晚飯隨即擺好. 他介紹兩位隨便裝束的女人大衆

THE VICAR OF WAKEFIELD

three ladies in easy dishabille were introduced, and the conversation began with some sprightliness. Politics, however, were the subject on which our entertainer chiefly expatiated: for he asserted that liberty was at once his boast and his terror. After the cloth was removed, he asked me if I had seen the last "Monitor" to which replying in the negative, "What? nor the 'Auditor' I suppose?" cried he.

"Neither, sir," returned I. "That's strange—very strange," replied my entertainer. "Now I read all the politics that come out. The 'Daily,' the 'Public,' the 'Ledger,' the 'Chronicle,' the 'London Evening,' the 'Whitehall Evening,' the seventeen magazines, and the two reviews; and though they hate each other, I love them all. Liberty, sir, liberty is the Briton's boast, and, by all my coal mines in Cornwall, I reverence its guardians."

"Then it is to be hoped," cried I, "you reverence the king."

談得很高興．主人大談其政治．他說他最好誇談的是自由．他最怕也是自由．撤了桌布之後．他問我最後的摩尼佗報．看見沒有．我答未看過．他又問道．什麼．你大約連奧狄佗報也沒看過．

我答道．我也沒看過他說道．這實在是奇怪是講政治的報．我都看．狄理報．普畢列報．利吉爾報．剛尼克報．倫敦晚報．懷特賀爾報．還有十七家雜誌．兩家評論報．我都看．雖然這各種報．都互相攻擊．我都喜歡．先生．萬事無過自由．我們不列顛人．最矜誇自由．我以所有亢倭爾的煤礦發誓{亢爾 倭地爾｝{方並無礦 其胡說可知｝．我最尊敬的是保護自由的人．

我說道．你自然是尊敬國王的．

"Yes," returned my entertainer, "when he does what we would have him; but if he goes on as he has done of late, I'll never trouble myself more with his matters. I say nothing—I think only. I could have directed some things better. I don't think there has been a sufficient number of advisers; he should advise with every person willing to give him advice, and then we should have things done in another guess[1] manner."

"I wish," cried I, "that such intruding advisers were fixed in the pillory. It should be the duty of the honest men to assist the weaker side of our constitution—that sacred power that has for some years been every ay declining, and losing its due share of in   e in the state. Bu   se ignorants still continue the same cry of liberty; and if they have any weight, basely throw it into the subsiding scale."

他答道. 只要國王聽我們吩咐他怎麼辦. 他就怎麼辦. 我是尊敬他的. 若是他往下作去. 還是同他從前一樣. 我就不過問他的事. 我也不說話. 不過我曉得. 若是我指揮諸事. 要比他強些. 我看他的顧問太少. 凡是願意替國王策劃的人. 我都願意指教. 若是能彀這樣. 國事總要又是一個樣子 { 談政治的人往往自以為政策高妙 }.

我說道. 我倒願意看見這種干預國事的人枷號示衆. 我們的憲法有弱點. 誠實的人. 都應該幫忙. 我說的弱點. 就是君權一天比一天縮小. 國家就失了許多力量. 有一班不懂事的人. 還在那裏不斷的喊自由. 這班人若果有了力量. 就要出力的縮小君權.

---

1. Another guess, 另是一樣.

THE VICAR OF WAKEFIELD 199

"How!" cried one of the ladies; "do I live to see one so base, so sordid, as to be an enemy to liberty, and a defender of tyrants?[1] Liberty, that sacred gift of Heaven, that glorious privilege of Britons!"

"Can it be possible," cried our entertainer, "that there should be any found at present advocates for slavery? Any who are for meanly giving up the privileges of Britons? Can any, sir, be so abject?"

"No, sir," replied I; "I am for liberty, that attribute of God's! Glorious liberty! that theme of modern declamation. I would have all men kings. I would be a king myself. We have all naturally an equal right to the throne; we are all originally equal. This is my opinion, and was once the opinion of a set of honest men who were called Levelers. They tried to erect themselves into a community, where all should be equally free. But alas! it would

有一位女人說道.怎麼樣.我活在世上.居然還看見一個這樣卑劣下流的人.同自由作仇敵.保護暴君惡霸麼.自由是天賜的.神聖不可侵犯.不列顛人.最有榮耀的權利.

主人說道.現在還看見有主張奴隸制度的人麼.還有願意把不列顛人的權利放棄的麼.先生.世上還有這種可憐的下流人嗎.

我答道.不然.我是講自由的.自由是上帝特質.榮耀自由.現在人滿嘴裏所說的.我願意人人都是國王.我自己也願意作國王.我們自然都有相等權利作國王.我們原始都是相等的.這是我的意思.從前有過一班誠實人.也是這個意思.當時稱他做剷平黨.他們當日要建設一種社會.所有的人.都享相等的自由.但

---

1. Tyrants, 暴君; 惡霸.

never answer; for there were some among them stronger, and some more cunning than others, and these became masters of the rest; for as sure as your groom rides your horses, because he is a cunninger animal than they, so surely will the animal that is cunninger or stronger than he, sit upon his shoulders in turn. Since then it is entailed upon humanity to submit, and some are born to command, and others to obey, the question is, as there must be tyrants, whether it is better to have them in the same house with us, or in the same village, or still farther off, in the metropolis. Now, sir, for my own part, as I naturally hate the face of a tyrant, the farther off he is removed from me, the better pleased am I. The generality of mankind also are of my way of thinking, and have unanimously created one king, whose election at once diminishes the number of tyrants, and puts tyranny at the greatest distance from the greatest number

是永遠行不通．因為人羣中．有許多比別人強的．有許多比別人詭詐的．這種人就作了主人．餘人就作了他們的奴隸．也就同你的馬夫騎馬一樣．你的馬夫．比馬詭詐．故此他騎馬．不是馬騎他．若別的動物比你的馬夫強．或比你的馬夫詭詐．他們就騎你的馬夫．因為世人有天生驅使別人的．有天生受人驅使的．人在世上．只好受着．要緊的問題．是世上旣然一定少不了強暴欺人的惡霸．我們還是願意這種人住在我們家裏．還是願意他們同我們同村．還是願意他們再走遠些．住在京城．先生．據我看來．我是天生的討厭惡霸人的臉．他們越離得我遠．我越喜歡．人性大約相同．故此同心一致．造出一個國王．選出一個國王之後．立刻就減少許多惡霸．把惡霸推到遠遠的地方．離開大多數

210

of people. Now the great, who were tyrants themselves before the election of one tyrant, are naturally averse to a power raised over them, and whose weight must ever lean heaviest on the subordinate orders. It is the interest of the great, therefore, to diminish kingly power as much as possible, because whatever they take from that is naturally restored to themselves; and all they have to do in the state is to undermine the single tyrant by which they resume their primeval authority. Now the state may be so circumstanced, or its laws may be so disposed, or its men of opulence so minded, as all to conspire in carrying on this business of undermining monarchy. For; in the first place, if the circumstances of our state be such as to favor the accumulation of wealth, and make the opulent still more rich, this will increase their ambition. An accumulation of wealth, however, must necessarily be the consequence, when, as at present, more riches

的良民.但是未選出一個惡霸之先.本來有許多惡霸.所謂當世偉人是也.這班偉人.自然不願意有人在他之上.他們先受國王的逼壓.這班偉人自然要減少君權.他們從國王手上奪得來的權.就是他們原有的.他們自然要從根本上.削奪這惟一惡霸的權.恢復他們原有的權力.一個國的環境.和他所定的法律.和國中富豪的思想.都可以同謀摧陷君權.第一層.因為這一國所處的環境.其勢可以積聚貨財.自然富者越富.越富則越想擴充權利.以現在情形而論.對外貿易.比國內工業.進財較多.自然

flow in from external commerce than arise from internal industry; for external commerce can only be managed to advantage by the rich, and they have also at the same time all the emoluments arising from internal industry; so that the rich, with us, have two sources of wealth, whereas the poor have but one. For this reason, wealth, in all commercial states, is found to accumulate, and all such have hitherto in time become aristocratical. Again, the very laws also of this country may contribute to the accumulation of wealth; as when by their means their natural ties that bind the rich and the poor together are broken, and it is ordained that the rich shall only marry with the rich; or when the learned are held unqualified to serve their country as counselors, merely from a defect of opulence, and wealth is thus made the object of a wise man's ambition; by these means, I say, and such means as these, riches will accumulate. Now the possessor

聚財. 因為對外貿易. 必要大資本. 同時並可以獲國內工業的利益. 故此我們的富人財源有二. 窮人財源只有一. 是以商業之國聚財. 能聚財的不久就變作貴族. 第二層. 我們的法律. 也是幫助聚財. 因為這種法律. 把窮富相維繫的根本破壞. 限制富室只能同富室聯姻. 又國中有知識的人. 因為財產不殼. 就無參預國政的資格. 於是有知識的人. 也只好以發財為目的. 這都是聚財的方法. 這

of accumulated wealth, when furnished with the necessaries and pleasures of life, has no other method to employ the superfluity of his fortune but in purchasing power. That is, differently speaking, in making dependents, by purchasing the liberty of the needy or the venal,[1] of men who are willing to bear the mortification of contiguous tyranny for bread. Thus each very opulent man generally gathers round him a circle of the poorest of the people; and the polity abounding in accumulated wealth may be compared to a Cartesian system, each orb with a vortex of its own. Those, however, who are willing to move in a great man's vortex are only such as must be slaves, the rabble of mankind, whose souls and whose education are adapted to servitude, and who know nothing of liberty except the name. But there must still be a large number of the people

種人致富之後. 日用和行樂. 所需無幾. 多餘的錢. 就拿去買權力. 換而言之. 他們拿錢去買窮人和貪財者的自由. 這兩路人. 因為飯碗起見. 甘心忍受惡霸切膚之痛. 故此凡是一個富人. 都招集一團人. 如同狄克論宇宙是無數漩渦. 一個富人就是一個漩渦的中心. 有多少被他收買的人. 跟着他旋轉. 凡是甘心跟着漩渦轉的人. 都是奴隸. 都是流氓. 他們的教育. 他們的性情. 宜於作奴隸. 只聽見自由之名. 全不曉得自由之實. 完全是一羣奴隸. 但是總還有許多人.

1. The venal, 受賄者.

without the sphere of the opulent man's influence, namely, that order of man that subsists between the very rich and the very rabble; those men who are possessed of too large fortunes to submit to the neighboring man in power, and yet are too poor to set up for tyranny themselves. In this middle order of mankind are generally to be found all the arts, wisdom, and virtues of society. This order alone is known to be the true preserver of freedom, and may be called the people. Now it may happen that this middle order of mankind may lose all its influence in a state, and its voice be in a manner drowned in that of the rabble; for if the fortune sufficient for qualifying a person at present to give his voice in state affairs be ten times less than was judged sufficient upon forming the constitution, it is evident that greater numbers of the rabble will thus be introduced into the political system, and they, ever moving in the vortex

不入富人漩渦裏的. 這種人. 上不及富人. 下不墮落至奴隸. 雖有貲財. 還穀不上施橫暴於窮人. 也不甘心受富有貲財者的橫暴. 大概有技藝有知識有道德的人. 都在這中等人之內. 只有這中等人. 是眞保留自由. 這才叫作人民. 但是這中等人. 往往無權過問國事. 他們要說話. 被流氓無賴淹沒了. 因為若把現在議員財產資格. 定輕十倍. 自然那班富人花錢. 買許多流氓無賴入議院. 這班無賴議員. 入了漩渦. 就聽富人指揮調度 {英國憲法及各種政

策秘奧被牧師這番話和盤託出　叉作

者論貴族與君主爭權政治家顧

地調不孤彈後世大政治家顧

214

THE VICAR OF WAKEFIELD 205

of the great, will follow where greatness shall direct. In such a state, therefore, all that the middle order has left, is to preserve the prerogative and privileges of the one principal governor with the most sacred circumspection. For he divides the power of the rich, and calls off the great from falling with tenfold weight on the middle order placed beneath them. The middle order may be compared to a town of which the opulent are forming the siege, and of which the governor from without is hastening the relief. While the besiegers are in dread of an enemy over them, it is but natural to offer the townsmen the most specious terms;—to flatter them with sounds, amuse them with privileges; but if they once defeat the governor from behind, the walls of the town will be but a small defense to its inhabitants. What they may then expect may be seen by turning our eyes to Holland, Genoa, or Venice, where the laws govern the poor, and the

採其說　又此篇大論計分三
層一對外貿易致富二法律鼓

勵聚財三富人
豪反抗君權 ｝·處這種情

形.那中等人只有用全力
運用那神聖不可侵犯的
謹慎.保護至尊國主的
權利.因為這國主.分富
人的權力.不許他們用
十倍的力量壓制在下
之中等階級.譬喻說的
話.中等階級.好比一座
城.富人是圍城的.國主
好比帶兵.從外來解圍
的.圍城的人.恐怕一有
大仇敵來.推倒他們.自
然同被圍的人說好話.
說得天花亂墜的.恭維
他們.拿權利的話.同他
們鬮樂.倘或背後解圍
的人.被圍城的兵打敗
了.那座城還能保護城
裏的人嗎.他們只要睜
大眼.看看荷蘭.熱那亞.
威尼斯.就明白了.這三

rich govern the law. I am then for, and would die for, monarchy, sacred monarchy; for if there be anything sacred amongst men, it must be the anointed[1] Sovereign of his people, and every diminution of his power in war, or in peace, is an infringement upon the real liberties of the subject. The sounds of liberty, patriotism, and Britons, have already done *much;* it is to be hoped that the true sons of freedom will prevent their ever doing *more.* I have known many of these pretended champions for liberty in my time, yet do I not remember one that was not in his heart and in his family a tyrant."

My warmth, I found, had lengthened this harangue beyond the rules of good breeding; but the impatience of my entertainer, who often strove to interrupt it, could be restrained no longer. "What!" cried he; "then I have been all

處地方.都是富人管法律.法律管窮人.我是要保護君權.甘爲君權死.君權是神聖不可侵犯的.世界上若是有神聖不可侵犯的.惟有正式君主.無論在和平時代.或在交戰時代.若是稍犯君權.就是奪人民的眞自由.自由.愛國.不列顚.這三個虛名.已經爲害不淺.我盼望凡眞愛自由的人.都要阻止.免令再生禍害.我很認得好幾位假擁護自由的人.却沒見過有一位.他心裏同他家裏.不是一個惡霸。

我曉得我說得太高興.這番話說得太長.在應酬場中.是不應該的.主人很不耐煩.屢次攔阻我.到了這時候.他再忍不住.喊道.什麼呀.

---

1. Anointed, 古時猶太族國王登位,先由教士以油敷身,英王加冕,尚行此禮.

THE VICAR OF WAKEFIELD

this while entertaining a traitor in parson's clothes; but by all the coal mines of Cornwall, out he shall pack, if my name be Wilkinson." I now found I had gone too far, and asked pardon for the warmth with which I had spoken.

"Pardon," returned he, in a fury, "I think such principles demand ten thousand pardons. What, give up liberty, property, and as the 'Gazetteer' says, lie down to be saddled with wooden shoes! Sir, I insist upon your marching out of this house immediately, to prevent worse consequences; sir, I insist upon it."

I was going to repeat my remonstrances, but just then we heard a footman's rap at the door, and the two ladies cried out, "As sure as death, there is our master and mistress come home."

It seems my entertainer was all this while only the butler, who, in his master's absence, had a mind to cut a figure, and be for a while the gentleman himself; and, to say the truth, he talked

原來我這些時候．款待一個穿教士衣服的反叛．我以所有亢倭爾煤礦發誓．你滾你的罷．不然．我就不是威金生．我才曉得說得太過火．我就求主人恕罪．

他很怒的說道．恕罪麼．你所說的主義．要求一萬次恕罪．什麼呀．放棄自由麼．放棄財產麼．如同那蓋賽報說的話．臥下來．讓穿木屐的人騎麼｛喻富貴人被貧賤人管轄也｝．你趕快滾出去．免受不好看．我要你立刻滾．

我正在要再往下抗辯．忽聽得有跟人敲門聲．那兩個女人喊道．這可真是我們的主人同太太回家了．

這才曉得．請我的人．不過是管家頭．趁主人不在家的時候．冒充主人．出出風頭．但是

politics as well as most
country gentlemen do.
But nothing could now
exceed my confusion upon
seeing the gentleman and
his lady enter, nor was
their surprise at finding
such company and good
cheer less than ours.

"Gentlemen," cried the
real master of the house
to me and my companion,
"my wife and I are your
most humble servants; but
I protest this is so un-
expected a favor, that we
almost sink under the ob-
ligation."

However unexpected our
company might be to them,
theirs, I am sure, was still
more so to us, and I was
struck dumb with the ap-
prehensions of my own
absurdity, when whom
should I next see enter the
room but my dear Miss
Arabella Wilmot, who was
formerly designed to be
married to my son George,
but whose match was bro-
ken off, as already related.
As soon as she saw me, she
flew to my arms with the
utmost joy. "My dear
sir," cried she, "to what
happy accident is it that

他談政治.有許多鄉下
的紳士也不過這樣
{雖是挖苦鄉紳其實
土讟員也不過如此}.我
看見主人夫婦進來.說
不出那十分忙亂.他們
兩夫婦看見我們這裏
大請客.這樣高興.也未
免詫異.

　那位眞主人對我.
和同席的人說道.諸
位.我夫婦想不到諸客
光臨.十分感謝.

　他們兩夫婦雖然想不
到我們在這裏歡宴.我
們更想不到他們突如
其來.我覺得我自己十
分難爲情.立刻變作個
啞巴.一句話也說不出.
誰知還有一位進來.這
進來的.不是別人.就是
威勒謨小姐.原是快要
嫁與我兒子的.後來解
除婚約.威小姐一看
見我.很高興的走上
來.說道.我們遇着什
麼好運氣.得到你老

we owe so unexpected a visit? I am sure my uncle and aunt will be in raptures when they find they have the good Dr. Primrose for their guest." Upon hearing my name, the old gentleman and lady very politely stepped up, and welcomed me with most cordial hospitality. Nor could they forbear smiling upon being informed of the nature of my present visit; but the unfortunate butler, whom they at first seemed disposed to turn away, was at my intercession forgiven.

Mr. Arnold and his lady, to whom the house belonged, now insisted upon having the pleasure of my stay for some days, and as their niece, my charming pupil, whose mind in some measure had been formed under my own instructions, joined in their entreaties, I complied. That night I was shown to a magnificent chamber, and the next morning early Miss Wilmot desired to walk with me in the garden, which was decorated in the modern

人家光降. 我曉得我的舅舅舅母〔也許是姨丈姨母〕. 有普博士作貴客. 一定歡喜欲狂的. 那主人夫婦聽見喊我的名字. 走上前來. 很客氣的歡迎我. 他們聽說我怎樣到他們家來的情景. 不禁一笑. 他們起初原要把那管家頭辭退. 我從旁說情. 也就饒了他.

雅諾先生夫婦. 一定留我住幾天. 他的姪女兒〔即威小姐〕. 原是我的學生. 受過我的教訓. 也來勸我. 我答應了. 到了晚上. 我就歇在一間很好的房子. 第二天早上. 威小姐同我在新式的花園散步. 指示各處有美

manner.   After some time
spent in pointing out the
beauties of the place, she
inquired with seeming un-
concern, when last I had
heard from my son George.

"Alas! madam," cried I,
"he has now been nearly
three years absent, without
ever writing to his friends
or me.   Where he is I
know not; perhaps I shall
never see him or happiness
more.   No, my dear mad-
am, we shall nevermore see
such pleasing hours as were
once spent by our fireside
at Wakefield.   My little
family are now dispersing
very fast, and poverty has
brought not only want,
but infamy upon us."
The good-natured girl let
fall a tear at this account;
but as I saw her possessed
of too much sensibility, I
forbore a more minute
detail of our sufferings.
It was, however, some
consolation to me to find
that time had made no
alteration in her affections,
and that she had rejected
several offers that had been
made her since our leaving
her part of the country.
She led me round all the

景的所在.他不卽不離
的問我兒子佐之的近
況.

我說道.哎呀.瑪當.
他走了將有三年.旣無
音信給朋友.也無音信
到家.我也不曉得他現
在何處.也許我永遠見
不着他.享不了快樂.我
們從前在維克村所享
的安樂日子.恐怕以後
永遠不能復見了.我的
小家庭.現在分散得很
快.窮困的境遇.不獨令
我們不得溫飽.還令我
們得不好的名譽.這位
溫柔的小姐聽我怎樣
說.也就滴下淚來.我見
他這樣的易受感觸.我
只好不詳細說我們的苦
況.他却並不因爲分離
久了.改變他的愛情.自
從我們搬家之後.有過
幾起人家向他求婚.他
都推辭了﹝開書至此才寫
威小姐用蜻蜓
點水法令人神
往傳神妙筆也﹞.我心裏

extensive improvements of the place, pointing to the several walks and arbors, and at the same time catching from every object a hint for some new question relative to my son.

In this manner we spent the forenoon, till the bell summoned us in to dinner, where we found the manager of the strolling company that I mentioned before, who was come to dispose of tickets for the "Fair Penitent,"[1] which was to be acted that evening, the part of Horatio by a young gentleman who had never appeared on any stage. He seemed to be very warm in the praises of the new performer, and averred that he never saw any one who bid so fair for excellence. Acting, he observed, was not learned in a day; "but this gentleman," continued he, "seems born to tread the stage. His voice, his figure, and

却覺得很安慰些.他領我看園內新佈置的地方.指出幾處散步的路.還有幾所軒榭.借故措辭.探問我兒子情狀.

我們這樣過了一早.等到聽見鐘響.才進屋吃飯.看見那雲遊戲班的經理人.來賣戲票.當天晚上.演的是一齣戲叫紅粉劍血記.演賀理紹的是一個少年.第一次登臺.他很恭維這個初出場的新戲子.說是向來未曾見過這樣一個絕頂的好手.他還說.演戲不是一天學得會的.這一位少年.好像是天生的一個好戲子.他的聲

---

1. "The Fair Penitent" (紅粉劍血記), 英人 Rowe 所製慘劇, 某貴族之女 Calista 結婚之日, 新郎 Lord Altamont 之戚 Horatio 以新娘與 Lothario 私通告, 新郎與姦夫決鬥, 姦夫 Lothario 被刺死俄而巷戰, 新娘之父又死, 新娘遂自刎死.

attitudes are all admirable. We caught him up accidentally in our journey down.''

This account, in some measure, excited our curiosity, and at the entreaty of the ladies, I was prevailed upon to accompany them to the playhouse, which was no other than a barn. As the company with which I went was incontestably the chief of the place, we were received with the greatest respect, and placed in the front seat of the theater, where we sat for some time with no small impatience to see Horatio make his appearance.

The new performer advanced at last, and let parents think of my sensations by their own, when I found it was my unfortunate son. He was going to begin, when turning his eyes upon the audience, he perceived Miss Wilmot and me, and stood at once speechless and immovable. The actors behind the scene, who ascribed this pause to his natural timidity, attempted

音身材架子.都是好的. 我們在路上.無意中得着他.

我們被他這話.引動我們好奇之性.幾位婦女勸我.我就陪他們去看.原來戲園就是拿存粮食的倉改的.我所陪的人.原是當地首屈一指的人家.到了那裏.衆人都極恭敬的歡迎.請我們坐在第一排.我們坐了一會.很不耐煩的要看賀理紹出臺.

後來這新戲子登場.我現在要請為父母的設身處地.替我想想我這個時候的感觸.那出場的新戲子.不是別人.就是我的兒子.他正要起演.看見威小姐同我.就同木雞一樣站在臺上.口說不出話.手脚也動不得.後臺的戲子們看見

to encourage him; but instead of going on, he burst into a flood of tears, and retired off the stage. I don't know what were my feelings on this occasion, for they succeeded with too much rapidity for description; but I was soon awakened from this disagreeable reverie by Miss Wilmot, who, pale, and with a trembling voice, desired me to conduct her back to her uncle's.

When we got home, Mr. Arnold, who was as yet a stranger to our extraordinary behavior, being informed that the new performer was my son, sent his coach and an invitation for him; and as he persisted in his refusal to appear again upon the stage, the players put another in his place, and we soon had him with us. Mr. Arnold gave him the kindest reception, and I received him with my usual transport; for I could never counterfeit false resentment. Miss Wilmot's reception was mixed with seeming neglect, and yet

他這樣.以為是初次出臺膽怯.在那裏鼓勵他.他却淚如泉湧的大哭.走回後臺去了.我轉瞬之間.接二連三的發生無限感觸.也說不出來.也不曉得是怎麼一回事.我正在彷彷彿彿作一場極敗興的似夢非夢.威小姐把我喚醒.他臉色灰白.聲音發抖.請我領他回舅舅家.

我們到了之後.雅諾先生不曉得為什麼我們有這樣的反常舉動.後來曉得那新戲子是我的兒子.打發車去請他接他我兒子一定不肯再登臺.戲班換了人頂他的脚色.他就到這裏來.雅諾先生很歡迎他.我接待他是非常高興.我是向來不會假裝怪責人的.威小姐接待他.外面看來像是不甚理他.然

I could perceive she acted a studied part. The tumult in her mind seemed not yet abated; she said twenty giddy things that looked like joy, and then laughed loud at her own want of meaning. At intervals she would take a sly peep at the glass, as if happy in the consciousness of irresistible beauty, and often would ask questions without giving any manner of attention to the answers.

而我却看出來. 不過是造作. 他心思紛亂. 這時還未沉靜下來. 他足足說了有二十句如顛似狂的話. 好像是歡喜. 說過又大笑. 笑他自己說無意識的話. 有時又偷偷的看鏡子. 好像是曉得自己是男子抵當不住的美. 覺得快樂. 有時問人一句話. 却毫不理會人家答他的話〈極力描寫〉.

威小姐却〈毫不費力〉.

CHAPTER XX

THE HISTORY OF A PHILOSOPHIC VAGABOND, PURSUING NOVELTY, BUT LOSING CONTENT

第 二 十 回

一個游手好閒無家可歸的哲學家去探
新奇反失去了厭足的心
（佐之途窮遊異地）

After we had supped, Mrs. Arnold politely offered to send a couple of her footmen for my son's baggage, which he at first seemed to decline; but upon her pressing the request, he was obliged to inform her, that a stick and a wallet were all the movable things upon this earth that he could boast of.

"Why, ay, my son," cried I, "you left me but poor, and poor I find you are come back; and yet I make no doubt you have seen a great deal of the world."

"Yes, sir," replied my son; "but traveling after fortune is not the way to

且說我們吃過晚飯.雅夫人很客氣的.打發兩個跟人去取我兒子的行李.我兒一定說不必.女主人一定要派人去取.我兒子只好告訴他.只有一個皮包.一根手杖.以外並無他物.

我說道.兒子呀.你離家的時候窮.你現在回來還是窮 ｛出門如是歸家亦如是一身之外無長物｝.但是你看見過世事.閱歷總該是富的.

他答道.父親.是的.但是旅行求富貴.是得不

225

secure her; and indeed, of late I have desisted from the pursuit."

"I fancy, sir," cried Mrs. Arnold, "that the account of your adventures would be amusing; the first part of them I have often heard from my niece; but could the company prevail for the rest, it would be an additional obligation."

"Madam," replied my son, "I promise you the pleasure you have in hearing will not be half so great as my vanity in repeating them; and yet in the whole narrative I can scarcely promise you one adventure, as my account is rather of what I saw than what I did.

"The first misfortune of my life, which you all know, was great; but though it distressed, it could not sink me. No person ever had a better knack at hoping than I. The less kind I found fortune at one time, the more I expected from her another; and being now at the bottom of her wheel, every new revolution might lift, but could

着富貴的.後來我只好不求了.

雅夫人道.先生.我看你這一番的閱歷.說來總該很有趣味.你最初的閱歷.我聽姪兒對我說過幾遍.現在在座的人.能彀得你把其餘的閱歷說一遍.那就更感激你.

我的兒子答道.瑪當.我很高興說一遍.我說我的閱歷.我覺得的快樂.還要倍於諸位要聽我說的快樂.不過我所說的.却無一件冒險的事因爲我只能說我之所見.並非說我所閱歷的事.

我平生第一件不幸的事.諸位已經曉得了.這總算是大不幸的事.我雖受了心上的痛苦.却並不灰心.我有永存希望的妙訣.是他人所無的.譬如這一次運氣不好.我希望第二次運氣要比第一次好得多.現在我在輪子的最低點.再一轉輪.我一定是

not depress, me. I proceeded, therefore, towards London in a fine morning, no way uneasy about tomorrow, but cheerful as the birds that caroled by the road, and comforted myself with reflecting that London was the mart where abilities of every kind were sure of meeting distinction and reward.

"Upon my arrival in town, sir, my first care was to deliver your letter of recommendation to our cousin, who was himself in little better circumstances than I. My first scheme, you know, sir, was to be usher at an academy, and I asked his advice on the affair.

"Our cousin received the proposal with a true sardonic grin. 'Ay,' cried he, 'this is indeed a very pretty career that has been chalked out for you. I have been an usher at a boarding school myself; and may I die by an anodyne necklace,[1] but I had rather be an underturnkey in Newgate. I

高升.不能把我再壓低了
〈歐美財神是位女神掌一輪
〈子人的運氣好就轉在輪上
運氣不好〉.於是有一天
轉在輪下〉
天氣好.我一早就向倫
敦走.却不管明天怎麼
過.我同路上唱歌的鳥.
一樣的高興.我心理想.
倫敦是個賣才能的市
場.只要有本事.總可以
享大名.得富貴.這麼一
想.我心裏就安慰.

一到了就把父親
給我的薦書.給我們的
老表.老表的景況.比我
稍微好些.我原意要當
一個學校的副教員.我
就請教老表.

老表聽了我這個主
意.很挖苦的一笑.說道.
人家替你劃的策.倒也
不錯.我曾在寄膳宿的學
校.當過副教員.我寧可
吊死.不然.我寧當監獄
裏的獄卒.也不當副教
員.當副教員的.無論日
夜一刻也不得閒.校長
給我惡嘴臉看.校長奶
奶討厭我的臉醜.在校

---

1. Anodyne necklace, 吊人之繩.

was up early and late; I was browbeat by the master, hated for my ugly face by the mistress, worried by the boys within, and never permitted to stir out to meet civility abroad. But are you sure you are fit for a school? Let me examine you a little. Have you been bred apprentice to the business? — No. Then you won't do for a school. Can you dress the boys' hair? — No. Then you won't do for a school. Have you had the smallpox? — No. Then you won't do for a school. Can you lie three in a bed? — No. Then you will never do for a school. Have you got a good stomach? — Yes. Then you will by no means do for a school. No, sir, if you are for a genteel, easy profession, bind yourself seven years as an apprentice to turn a cutler's wheel; but avoid a school by any means. Yet come,' continued he, 'I see you are a lad of spirit and some learning—what do you think of commencing author like me? You have read in books, no

裏是受學生的氣. 校長永不許我出校. 去見見世面. 你敢說. 你配當這個職事嗎. 讓我考試考試你. 你對於這件事. 當過學徒嗎. 我答道. 未曾當過. 他說道. 那嗎. 你不配到校裏去. 又問道. 你會替學生們理髮嗎. 我答道. 不會. 他說道. 你不配到校裏. 他又問道. 你出過天花嗎. 我答道. 未出過. 他答道. 你不配到校裏. 他又問道. 你受得了三個人同鋪嗎. 我答道. 我不能. 他答道. 你永遠不配到校裏. 他又問道. 你脾胃健嗎. 我答道. 很健. 他答道. 你無論怎麼樣. 都不配到校裏﹛校裏吃不飽也﹜. 總而言之. 你若要入一種斯文舒服的行業. 反不如跟打刀匠嘗磨刀輪. 替他轉七年的學徒. 千萬不要入學校﹛小學教員之不能當有如此者﹜. 他接着又說道. 來來. 你是個有志氣的少年. 也還有些學問. 你何妨作個著作家. 同我一樣呢. 你大約很有天才的人. 因為著書上說. 也曾讀過書. 有

228

THE VICAR OF WAKEFIELD 219

doubt, of men of genius starving at the trade. At present I'll show you forty very dull fellows about town that live by it in opulence. All honest jog-trot men, who go on smoothly and dully, and write history and politics, and are praised: men, sir, who, had they been bred cobblers, would all their lives have only mended shoes, but never made them.'

"Finding that there was no great degree of gentility affixed to the character of an usher, I resolved to accept his proposal; and, having the highest respect for literature, hailed the *antiqua Mater*[1] of Grub Street with reverence. I thought it my glory to pursue a track which Dryden and Otway trod before me. I considered the goddess of this region as the parent of excellence; and however an intercourse with the world might give us good sense, the poverty she entailed I supposed to be the nurse of genius!

餓死的.然而我現在就可以給你看有四十位大蠢材著書致富的〔文人厄運真有如此回所述者如美國之 Edgar Allen Poe 蘇格蘭之 Robert Burns 負天下重名幾乎窮餓而死作者以筆墨餬口屢受凍餒故寫所歷所見所聞極其淋漓盡致〕.這四十個人都是實實在在的.有精無神的.慢慢幹.著歷史政治.却很有人恭維他們.假使這班人當日學的是補鞋.他們一生只會補鞋.是不會作鞋的.

我一聽當副教員無甚體面.就依照他的條陳.我原是很奪敬文學的.我就很恭敬歡迎加拉街〔葛勒勃街作寒著名編輯儒所住之地〕編輯行業及政治歷史.我以爲追縱狄氏奧氏〔英國有名著作家〕.是一件最有榮耀的事.又以爲這個地方的女神.是生產最高等文字之母.况且同世界往來.可以增長知識.至於著作須要迫受饑寒.我以爲是培養才智之善法.我心

---

1. *Antiqua Mater*, 老母也, 此處指歷史政治及編輯而言.

Big with these reflections, I sat down, and finding that the best things remained to be said on the wrong side, I resolved to write a book that should be wholly new. I therefore dressed up three paradoxes[1] with some ingenuity.[2] They were false, indeed, but they were new. The jewels of truth have been so often imported by others, that nothing was left for me to import but some splendid things that at a distance looked every bit as well. Witness, you powers, what fancied importance sat perched upon my quill while I was writing. The whole learned world, I made no doubt, would rise to oppose my systems; but then I was prepared to oppose the whole learned world. Like the porcupine, I sat self-collected, with a quill pointed against every opposer."

"Well said, my boy," cried I; "and what subject did you treat upon? I

坐下的頂好的大思想.才曉得好些已經被人講完了.存了一看.剩下的都是不好的.我了一看.目.於是立意.寫一本最新題目.鮮的書.就把三條反對世人向來篤信不疑的道理.用些手段.粉飾起來.這幾條道理.誠然是假的.然而新鮮.眞理譬如珠寶.但是已經被人全數運輸入口了.我無法可想.只好運些假貨入口.人家遠遠的看見.也很像眞的 {維新著作之往往有／欺人者 如此者天下皆然} .你們看看呀.看我寫書的時候.我筆端上是多們要緊鄭重.我深信不疑天下的學者都要起來反對我的道理.我却預備反對天下的學者.我如同箭猪一樣.滾作一團.渾身周圍都是如箭的毛鋒.預備向四面八方射擊 {英國前／英從 有一報卽／名箭猪} .

'我聽了我兒子這番話.說道.說得好.你作的是什麼題目.我

THE VICAR OF WAKEFIELD 221

hope you did not pass over the importance of monogamy. But I interrupt; go on. You published your paradoxes; well, and what did the learned world say to your paradoxes?"

"Sir," replied my son, "the learned world said nothing to my paradoxes—nothing at all, sir. Every man of them was employed in praising his friends and himself, or condemning his enemies; and, unfortunately, as I had neither, I suffered the cruelest mortification—neglect.

"As I was meditating one day in a coffeehouse on the fate of my paradoxes, a little man happening to enter the room, placed himself in the box before me, and after some preliminary discourse, finding me to be a scholar, drew out a bundle of proposals, begging me to subscribe to a new edition he was going to give to the world of Propertius with notes. This demand necessarily produced a reply that I had no money, and that concession led him

盼望你不忘一夫一妻的要義. 你說下去罷. 我打了你的叉. 你登出你的反對世人相信的道理. 學者怎樣對付你呢.

我兒子答道. 父親. 學者對我的新道理. 一句話也不說. 簡直的是一字不提. 他們忙的是恭維朋友. 恭維自己. 攻擊異已 {可見當日學者之黨同伐異}. 最不幸的. 是我既無同志. 又無異已. 故此就沒得人理我. 眞是難過.

有一天. 我正在一個小咖啡店潛思我新道理的命運. 有一個小矮子剛好進來. 坐在我對面的小隔間. 彼此寒暄了幾句. 他曉得我是個學者. 從身上掏出一卷提議來. 原來他要新刻播氏拉丁詩注. 求我捐助刊貲. 我只好答我無錢. 這一答.

to inquire into the nature of my expectations. Finding that my expectations were just as great as my purse, 'I see,' cried he, 'you are unacquainted with the town—I'll teach you a part of it. Look at these proposals; upon these very proposals I have subsisted very comfortably for twelve years. The moment a nobleman returns from his travels, a Creolian[1] arrives from Jamaica, or a dowager[2] from her country seat, I strike for a subscription. I first besiege their hearts with flattery, and then pour in my proposals at the breach. If they subscribe readily the first time, I renew my request to beg a dedication[3] fee. If they let me have that, I smite them once more for engraving their coat of arms at the top. Thus,' continued he, 'I live by vanity, and laugh at it. But, between ourselves, I am now too well known,

引起他問我的前程希望. 聽見我說全無希望. 他說道. 我明白了. 你全不曉得倫敦情形. 我來教你一點罷. 你試看看我這一束的提議. 我靠這個提議. 過了十二年的飽暖日子. 只要遇着一位貴族從外國遊歷回來. 或是一位克利奧人從查美加來的. 或係鄉下邸宅來了一位貴族寡婦. 我就去求捐貲. 一下手. 我先恭維他. 巴結他. 叫他心裏高興. 只要看見有縫好鑽. 我就把提議掏出來. 他們若是第一次就樂捐. 我還再來求他們捐些題書費. 若是他們這一款也捐了. 我又求他讓我把他們的徽章. 刻在書上. 用這個法子. 一面用虛榮浮名去牢籠他們. 一面我就在背後笑他們{斯文／光棍}. 但是我要同你說句私話. 我耍這個把戲耍得日子太久. 臉

<hr>

1. Creolian, 克利奧人, 卽法國或西班牙人之後裔生長於美洲者. 2. Dowager, 貴族或富家寡婦之有權力或錢財者. 3. Dedication, 書成在卷首題某貴人或名人之名, 并加數語, 表示敬慕或感謝之意.

I should be glad to borrow your face a bit. A nobleman of distinction has just returned from Italy; my face is familiar to his porter; but if you bring this copy of verses, my life for it you succeed, and we divide the spoil.'"

"Bless us, George," cried I; "and is this the employment of poets now! Do men of their exalted talents thus stoop to beggary! Can they so far disgrace their calling, as to make a vile traffic of praise for bread?"

"Oh, no, sir," returned he, "a true poet can never be so base! for wherever there is genius there is pride.[1] The creatures I now describe are only beggars in rime. The real poet, as he braves every hardship for fame, so he is equally a coward to contempt; and none but those who are unworthy protection condescend to solicit it.

我來驗才看把見少分
原生
得生的臉纔你去多
許多人都認得
太熟了.你是初到的臉用用｛原生
我.要借你的臉用用有一位貴族.他的你帶去多少分
是可以｝
借用的｝
打意大利回來.他的你帶去多少分
門的認得我.只要你帶去多
我這鈔本的詩帶去
他.你只要捐到手多
錢.我們兩個人平
｛斯文光棍｝
｛太不要臉｝

我喊道.上帝保佑
我們佐之呀.現在的的這心殼把活
詩人.就是作這種才下能生
生涯嗎.他們天才下能身
樣的高.就肯低首他們人分作生
的去求乞辱文人結人作
這樣玷維人巴人嗎.
恭討飯吃嗎.

我兒子答道.父親.這
不然.眞詩人.不能一然人.文有困是班不痛上
個人.只要有天才.自的是得世中骨
就有身分.我所說之是難拒最的一才
不的叫化子.敢抗名.只有的那人
魄苦受值膽享侮護去求人
要臉的的去求
許多假詩人也不過自然有
外皆然眞詩人不自然

"Having a mind too proud to stoop to such indignities, and yet a fortune too humble to hazard a second attempt for fame, I was now obliged to take a middle course, and write for bread. But I was unqualified for a profession where mere industry alone was to insure success. I could not suppress my lurking passion for applause, but usually consumed that time in efforts after excellence which takes up but little room, when it should have been more advantageously employed in the diffusive productions of fruitful mediocrity. My little piece would therefore come forth in the midst of periodical publications, unnoticed and unknown. The public were more importantly employed, than to observe the easy simplicity of my style, or the harmony of my periods. Sheet after sheet was thrown off to oblivion. My essays were buried among the essays upon liberty, Eastern tales, and cures for the bite of a mad dog;

我是很顧身分.不肯學那樣卑賤.去作那丟臉的事.但是我既不名一錢.又不能再冒險去拿文字博聲譽.不得已.定一個酌中的辦法.靠寫作餬口.但是這種行業.非勤苦不能得法.我又怕作不來.我心理怦怦要博聲譽.按也按不住.於是把光陰都用在撰著最高妙的文章.所入自然無幾.若是把這光陰用在作凡庸文章.就易於成篇.收入較多.我把我的撰述.登在旬報上.竟無人理會.無人曉得.衆人在那裏忙別的要緊事.那裏有工夫注意我的文境清眞.句饒神韵呢.一張一張的登出來.都堙沒了.我所作的論說.都被什麽自由論東方故事治瘋狗咬的

while Philautos,[1] Philalethes, Phileluthheros, and Phiranthropos, all wrote better, because they wrote faster than I.

"Now, therefore, I began to associate with none but disappointed authors, like myself, who praised, deplored, and despised each other. The satisfaction we found in every celebrated writer's attempts was inversely as their merits. I found that no genius in another could please me. My unfortunate paradoxes had entirely dried up that source of comfort. I could neither read nor write with satisfaction; for excellence in another was my aversion, and writing was my trade.

"In the midst of these gloomy reflections, as I was one day sitting on a bench in St. James's Park, a young gentleman of distinction, who had been my intimate acquaintance at the university, approached me. We saluted each other with some hesitation, he

妙方壇沒了．同時什麼張三李四王六何九．比我寫得快．潤筆得的多
｛曲高和寡往往凍餓而死
庸庸碌碌者反享富貴｝．

我現在只有同一班失望的著作家往來．這班人互相恭維．互相憐惜．互相藐視．我們曉得．著作家的名譽．同他們的著作．往往成反比例．我不喜歡別人的才調．我新發明反對世人篤信的道理．不幸又無人過問．我自慰的來源．也就乾涸了．既不高興讀書．又不高興作文．既要拿文章賣錢．又不肯投世人所好．怎麼能自慰呢．

我正是滿肚憂思．有一日．我坐在公園櫈上．有一位清貴少年．原是我大學校的同學．走近我跟前．我們彼此見禮．都有

1. Philautos, etc., etc., 此是當時登報人所用的隱名

almost ashamed of being known to one who made so shabby an appearance, and I afraid of a repulse. But my suspicions soon vanished, for Ned Thornhill was at the bottom a very good-natured fellow."

"What did you say, George?" interrupted I.— "Thornhill, was not that his name? It can certainly be no other than my landlord."

"Bless me!" cried Mrs. Arnold; "is Mr. Thornhill so near a neighbor of yours? He has long been a friend in our family, and we expect a visit from him shortly."

"My friend's first care," continued my son, "was to alter my appearance by a very fine suit of his own clothes, and then I was admitted to his table, upon the footing of half friend, half underling. My business was to attend him at auctions, to put him in spirits when he sat for his picture, to take the left hand in his chariot when not filled by another, and

點遲疑. 他同我這樣襤褸的人拉交情. 很有點不好意思. 我同他拉交情. 恐怕他不理我. 但是來招呼的不是別人. 就是唐希爾. 性情很好的人. 我的疑團. 就立刻消滅了.

我攔住佐之說道. 佐之. 你說什麼. 你說那同學叫唐希爾嗎. 他不是別人. 一定就是我們的房東.

雅夫人聽了. 說道. 原來唐希爾是你的近鄰麼. 他是我們家的老朋友. 不久就要來探我們.

我兒子佐之接着說道. 他第一件事. 就是把他的衣服給我穿上. 改了我的外觀. 同他一桌吃飯. 當我是一半朋友. 一半走狗. 我的職事. 是陪他到拍賣場. 有時他坐下叫畫師替他寫眞的時候. 要我在旁邊想法. 引他高興. 他跑馬車. 若無他人相陪. 叫我坐在他的左邊. 他喜歡

to assist at tattering a kip,[1] as the phrase was, when he had a mind for a frolic. Besides this, I have twenty other little employments in the family. I was to do many small things without bidding; to carry the corkscrew; to stand godfather to all the butler's children; to sing when I was bid; to be never out of humor; always to be humble, and, if I could, to be very happy.

"In this honorable post, however, I was not without a rival. A captain of marines, who was formed for the place by nature, opposed me in my patron's affections. His mother had been laundress to a man of quality, and thus he early acquired a taste for pimping and pedigree. As this gentleman made it the study of his life to be acquainted with lords, though he was dismissed from several for his stupidity, yet he found many of them who were as dull as himself that permitted

開頑笑的時候 {接下一句不敢 強解大約是讓他開頑笑也}. 除此之外. 我還要在他家裏作許多事. 有許多不相干的小事. 不必他吩咐. 我就要作. 要我身上常帶酒鑽. 所有他的家人生了兒女. 都要我作乾爹. 他吩咐我唱. 我就得唱. 永遠不許我不高興. 永遠要我低首下心. (倘若我作得到) 同時還要我很快樂 {此寫外國篾片走狗似還還不如中國篾片走狗身分清高從此亦可略見中外人品格之不同}

我得了這樣一個有體面的席位 {注意此是反說}. 不料還遇着一位勁敵. 這個人是海軍大佐. 天生成他作走狗的. 他反對我. 同我爭寵. 這一個人. 一生只研究認識貴族. 雖然. 因爲他太蠢. 被貴族們閧走了好幾次. 却還有同他一樣蠢的貴族. 還喜歡讓他在身邊

----

1. Tattering a kip. (不敢強解) 英國坊刻本. 有删去此句者. 豈以其不可解歟.

his assiduities. As flattery
was his trade, he practiced
it with the easiest address
imaginable; but it came
awkward and stiff from
me; and as every day my
patron's desire for flattery
increased, so every hour,
being better acquainted
with his defects, I became
more unwilling to give it.
Thus, I was once more
fairly going to give up the
field to the captain, when
my friend found occasion
for my assistance. This
was nothing less than to
fight a duel for him, with
a gentleman whose sister
it was pretended he had
used ill. I readily complied
with his request; and
though I see you are dis-
pleased at my conduct, yet
as it was a debt indispensably due to friendship, I
could not refuse. I undertook the affair, disarmed
my antagonist, and soon
after had the pleasure of
finding that the lady was
only a woman of the town,
and the fellow her bully
and a sharper. This piece
of service was repaid with
the warmest professions of
gratitude; but as my friend

效勞. 巴結人就是他的
行業. 那巴結的法術. 練
到十二分純熟. 我的巴
結法術. 就來得太生硬.
我這個主人之好巴結
日見其甚. 我多在他左
右一點鐘. 就多窺見他
許多缺點. 我越不甘心
巴結他. 我打算快要不
幹了. 讓給那位大佐. 那
主人剛有一件事. 要我
都忙. 因爲他對不住一
個女人. 那女人的哥哥
要決鬬. 主人就要我去
替他決鬬. 我就替他去.
父親. 我看見你聽我這
話. 不高興. 但是我旣欠
朋友的情. 我不能不答
應他. 我擔任了這件事.
把敵人打敗了. 隨卽曉
得那個女人. 不過是個
妓女之流. 那個女人的
哥哥. 不過是個雇來的
土棍. 保護他. 替他打架
的. 我替他出了這番力.
他說了許多感激的話.

was to leave town in a few days, he knew no other method of serving me, but by recommending me to his uncle, Sir William Thornhill, and another nobleman of great distinction, who enjoyed a post under the government. When he was gone, my first care was to carry his recommendatory letter to his uncle, a man whose character for every virtue was universal, yet just. I was received by his servants with the most hospitable smiles; for the looks of the domestics ever transmit their master's benevolence. Being shown into a grand apartment, where Sir William soon came to me, I delivered my message and letter, which he read, and after pausing some minutes, 'Pray, sir,' cried he, 'inform me what you have done for my kinsman to deserve this warm recommendation? But I suppose, sir, I guess your merits—you have fought for him, and so you would expect a reward from me for being the instrument of his vices. I wish, sincerely

再過幾天.他要出京.把我薦給他叔叔威廉唐希爾爵士.一位很有名的貴族.在政府做官.他的道德很全備.而又公道.主人走了.我拿薦書去見這位爵士.他的家人見了我.都是很客氣的.凡主人對客人客氣的.家人見客人也客氣.我進去一間大屋子.威廉爵士不久就進來我把面說的話同薦信交代了.他讀信之後.停幾分鐘.問道.先生.請你告訴我.你替他出過什麼大力.他給你這樣結實的薦信.先生.我想我猜着你的功勞.你曾替他打過架.他利用你去為惡.却盼望我酬你的勞.我很懇切的盼望.我

wish, that my present refusal may be some punishment for your guilt; but still more, that it may be some inducement to your repentance.'—The severity of this rebuke I bore patiently, because I knew it was just. My whole expectations now, therefore, lay in my letter to the great man. As the doors of the nobility are almost ever beset with beggars, all ready to thrust in some sly petition, I found it no easy matter to gain admittance. However, after bribing the servants with half my worldly fortune, I was at last shown into a spacious apartment, my letter being previously sent up for his lordship's inspection. During this anxious interval, I had full time to look around me. Everything was grand and of happy contrivance; the paintings, the furniture, the gildings, petrified me with awe, and raised my idea of the owner. Ah, thought I to myself, how very great must the possessor of all these things be, who carries in his head the business of the state,

現在拒絕你．當作罰你的惡．更進一步說．我拒絕你．盼望你從此改過．他這樣嚴厲的面斥我．我曉得斥得公道．我只好忍受了．我這時候．毫無希望．只剩了一封給闊人的信．因爲闊人的門口．求事的人最多．人人都要塞一封求事信．要進門．是極不容易．我從身上餘存的錢．拿了一半．去賄那些家人．他們領我到一間大屋子．那封信是先呈上去了．我正在着急的等見．很有時候．看看周圍．所有陳設．無一不極其華麗奇巧．圖畫家具和舖金的東西把我驚呆了．那主人之闊．可想而知．我心裏就想．該這些好東西的人．不曉得是多大的偉人．他頭裏裝滿的．

and whose house displays half the wealth of a kingdom; sure his genius must be unfathomable! During these awful reflections I heard a step come heavily forward. Ah, this is the great man himself! No, it was only a chambermaid. Another foot was heard soon after. This must be he! No, it was only the great man's valet de chambre. At last his lordship actually made his appearance. 'Are you,' cried he, 'the bearer of this here letter?' I answered with a bow. 'I learn by this,' continued he, 'as how that'—But just at that instant a servant delivered him a card; and without taking further notice, he went out of the room, and left me to digest my own happiness at leisure. I saw no more of him till told by a footman that his lordship was going to his coach at the door. Down I immediately followed, and joined my voice to that of three or four more, who came like me to petition for favors. His lordship,

都是國家大事．家裏陳設的東西．富可敵半國．這個人的才能．自然是不可限量的了．我正在那裏想．忽聽見腳步很響．呀．這一定是闊人來了．原來不是的．不過是個女僕．不久又聽見有腳步響．這一定是他了．又不是的．這不過是闊人的隨身跟人．後來貴族眞出現了．問道．你就是帶信的來人麼．我鞠躬．答應一句是．闊人說道．這信裏說……剛好這時候．一個跟人遞給他一個名片．闊人什麼也不管．就走出去了．剩了我一個人．慢慢在那裏嚼嚼得見闊人的那種快樂的滋味．等到有一個下人來說．貴族在大門口上車．我立刻跟出去．就同着三四個求事的人．在那裏喊．不料那

however, went too fast for us, and was gaining his chariot door with large strides, when I hallooed out to know if I was to have any reply. He was by this time got in, and muttered an answer, half of which I only heard, the other half was lost in the rattling of his chariot wheels. I stood for some time with my neck stretched out, in the posture of one that was listening to catch the glorious sounds, till, looking round me, I found myself alone at his lordship's gate.

"My patience," continued my son, "was now quite exhausted. Stung with the thousand indignities I had met with, I was willing to cast myself away, and only wanted the gulf to receive me. I regarded myself as one of those vile things that nature designed should be thrown into her lumber room, there to perish in obscurity. I had still, however, half a guinea left, and of that I thought fortune herself should not deprive me; but in order to be sure of this, I was resolved to go instantly and

闊貴族走得太快. 大踏步的快到車邊. 我大聲喊問. 有無回信. 闊人此時已經上了車. 答了我一句話. 我却只聽見了半句. 那半句同那馬車轔轔的聲混在一起了. 我還站在那裏伸長頸子. 要聽闊人所說那句光寵的話. 我回頭一看. 闊人的大門口. 鬼也沒得一個. 只剩了我一個人 { 描寫之工 / 得未曾有 }.

我的兒子往下說道. 到了這個時候. 我的忍耐性是完全消滅了. 我受了千種的侮辱. 痛入心窩. 我寧願不要身命. 專等一個海灣把我淹沒了. 我自己當自己簡直是個最下賤無用的東西. 只配摔在木料廠的一邊. 慢慢的在黑暗裏去朽腐. 我雖困窮到這地步. 幸好還剩有半個金錢. 我想財神太太也不好意思連這半個金錢. 也要

spend it while I had it, and then trust to occurrences for the rest. As I was going along with this resolution, it happened that Mr. Crispe's office seemed invitingly open to give me a welcome reception. In this office Mr. Crispe kindly offers all his majesty's subjects a generous promise of thirty pounds a year, for which promise all they give in return is their liberty for life, and permission to let him transport them to America as slaves. I was happy at finding a place where I could lose my fears in desperation, and entered this cell, for it had the appearance of one, with the devotion of a monastic. Here I found a number of poor creatures, all in circumstances like myself, expecting the arrival of Mr. Crispe, presenting a true epitome of English impatience. Each untractable soul at variance with fortune, wreaked her injuries on their own hearts; but Mr. Crispe at last came down, and all our murmurs were hushed. He deigned to regard me with an air

趁我立刻就聽天由命罷了。我存了這個主意。正在路上走。看見克先生的店門大開。好像是很歡迎我進去的。克先生是個招工的他很慈愛慷慨的答應給國人一年三十鎊。得了他答應這三十鎊。只要報酬他兩宗事。一宗是性命自由交給他。一宗是讓他運到美洲當奴隸〔注意答應二字只是答應并不眞給〕。我倒喜歡找着一個地方。可以不害怕絕望。就走入這個小草庵（這個店像個草庵）。如同誠心修道的和尙一樣。我進去看見好些同我一樣的可憐蟲。等候克先生。等得極不耐煩。每位爲財神所反對而不甘受窮困的人。個個心裏在那裏切齒痛恨受財神的害。後來克先生到來。衆人嗟嘆呻吟之聲。都

奪丟我的。我立意

of peculiar approbation, and indeed he was the first man who for a month past talked to me with smiles. After a few questions, he found I was fit for everything in the world. He paused awhile upon the properest means of providing for me, and slapping his forehead, as if he had found it, assured me that there was at that time an embassy talked of from the synod of Pennsylvania to the Chickasaw Indians, and that he would use his interest to get me made secretary. I knew in my heart that the fellow lied, and yet his promise gave me pleasure, there was something so magnificent in the sound. I fairly, therefore, divided my half guinea, one half of which went to be added to his thirty thousand pounds, and with the other half I resolved to go to the next tavern, to be there more happy than he.

"As I was going out with that resolution, I was met at the door by the captain of a ship, with whom I had

停止了．他屈尊的特別看上我．近一個月來．還算是他第一個對我說話帶笑臉．問我幾句話之後．他說道．世界上．無論什麼職事．你都覺得上．想了一會．替我設法．後來拿手拍額．像是想出來了．說道．這時候．班西公司．正在商議派人去見赤加土人．我答應出力．替你謀一名祕書．我心裏明白這個人說謊．但是我很喜歡他的答應．因爲說得很好聽．我就同他平分我剩下來的半個金錢．一半添入他的三萬鎊之內．還剩下一半．我就立意花在飯店．要比他過得快樂．

我打好了這個主意．走出門．碰見認得的一位船主．我就拉他同去

THE VICAR OF WAKEFIELD 235

formerly some little acquaintance, and he agreed to be my companion over a bowl of punch. As I never chose to make a secret of my circumstances, he assured me that I was upon the very point of ruin in listening to the office keeper's promises, for that he only designed to sell me to the plantations. 'But,' continued he, 'I fancy you might by a much shorter voyage be very easily put into a genteel way of bread. Take my advice. My ship sails tomorrow for Amsterdam. What if you go in her as a passenger? The moment you land, all you have to do is to teach the Dutchmen English, and I'll warrant you'll get pupils and money enough. I suppose you understand English,' added he, 'by this time, or the deuce[1] is in it.' I confidently assured him of that, but expressed a doubt whether the Dutch would be willing to learn English. He affirmed with an oath

吃甜酒．我向來不隱藏我的景況．都告訴了他．他告訴我．若是相信了克先生的話．就精了．因爲那個人的詭計．不過是要把我賣去開墾．他又接着說道．你不必走這樣遠的路程．也還不難找一碗安樂飯吃．你聽我的話罷．我的船．明日就開駛往安斯頓．你何妨在我船上當搭客．你到了．一登岸．不必作別的．只要教荷蘭人讀英文．我可以保你學生也有了．錢也有了．這時候你英文總該懂得了．不然的話．你總是有了什麼毛病了．我告訴他．英文我很懂得．我却問他．荷蘭人是否要學英文呢．他破口的說道．荷

---

1. Deuce, 霓鬼．

that they were fond of it to distraction; and upon that affirmation I agreed with his proposal, and embarked the next day to teach the Dutch English in Holland. The wind was fair, our voyage short, and after having paid my passage with half my movables, I found myself, as fallen from the skies, a stranger in one of the principal streets of Amsterdam. In this situation I was unwilling to let any time pass unemployed in teaching. I addressed myself, therefore, to two or three of those I met whose appearance seemed most promising; but it was impossible to make ourselves mutually understood. It was not till this very moment I recollected, that in order to teach the Dutchmen English, it was necessary that they should first teach me Dutch. How I came to overlook so obvious an objection, is to me amazing; but certain it is, I overlooked it.

"This scheme thus blown up, I had some thoughts of fairly shipping back to

蘭人喜歡學英文.喜歡得要發狂.有他這一說.我就答應了.第二天上船去荷蘭教英文.遇着順風.不久就到了.拿了一半剩下的錢給了船錢.登岸.在安斯頓大街上.就如同天降下來的一般.作了個異鄉人.我現在到了這個景况.不能耽誤教書的光陰.我在街上遇見幾個人.好像是要學英文的.我就向前去問.但是彼此言語不通.這時候才明白.我若要教荷蘭人讀英文.我先要荷蘭人教我荷蘭文.這樣很明白的一件阻礙.我很詫異為什麼就想不起來.然而當日却眞想不起來.

這一個計策是炸了.行不通.我很想坐船

England again; but falling into company with an Irish student who was returning from Louvain, our conversation turning upon topics of literature (for, by the way, it may be observed that I always forgot the meanness of my circumstances when I could converse upon such subjects), from him I learned that there were not two men in his whole university who understood Greek. This amazed me. I instantly resolved to travel to Louvain, and there live by teaching Greek, and in this design I was heartened by my brother student, who threw out some hints that a fortune might be got by it.

"I set boldly forward the next morning. Every day lessened the burden of my movables, like Æsop and his basket of bread;[1] for I paid them for my lodgings to the Dutch as I traveled on. When I came to Louvain, I was resolved not to go sneaking

回國. 却碰見一位愛爾蘭學生. 從魯文大學來的. 我們談話談到文學上.(我要補說. 我談到文學上. 就自忘其檻褸.)他告訴我. 全校裏頭. 不過有兩人識希臘文. 我聽見. 非常詫異. 我立意立刻走到魯文. 到那裏教希臘文餬口. 他十分贊成. 還說了幾句話. 使我曉得教希臘文還可以發財.

第二天早上. 我很勇往的向前走. 在路上要花房飯錢. 我多走一天. 原來剩下的很有幾個錢. 更減少好些. 如同伊索寓言說的那一籃子麵包. 我到了魯文. 打定主義. 不要鬼頭鬼腦的去見下級教

---

1. Æsop and his basket of bread, 伊索拿麵包籃子, 一路走, 一路吃, 越吃籃子越輕.

to the lower professors, but openly tendered my talents to the principal himself. I went, had admittance, and offered him my service as a master of the Greek language, which I had been told was a desideratum[1] in this university. The principal seemed at first to doubt of my abilities; but of these I offered to convince him by turning a part of any Greek author he should fix upon into Latin. Finding me perfectly earnest in my proposal, he addressed me thus: 'You see me, young man,' continued he, 'I never learned Greek, and I don't find that I have ever missed it. I have had a doctor's cap and gown without Greek; I have ten thousand florins a year without Greek; I eat heartily without Greek; and in short,' continued he, 'as I don't know Greek, I do not believe there is any good in it.'

"I was now too far from home to think of returning,

員. 一直去見校長. 賣我的本事. 我去見着校長說. 聽見貴校想添希臘文科. 我自薦當希臘文教員. 校長起初疑心我的本事. 我就請他. 任從他挑選一段希臘文. 我繙作拉丁文. 他看見我很認真. 就對我說道. 少年. 你看看我. 我向來未學過希臘文. 我却不覺得有什麽缺憾. 我博士的長袍穿得. 我博士的帽子戴得. 向未用着希臘文. 我不懂得希臘文. 一年也得一萬個富羅令的束修. 我不懂得希臘文. 也一樣的吃飯. 總而言之. 我不懂希臘文. 我就不相信希臘文有什麽好處{校長說得得意洋洋. 目空一切. 可惜未曾打聽他是如何毅得上當. 校長的大約此時當校長是不靠學問}.

我這時候離家太遠. 就斷了回家的思想.

---

1. Desideratum, 所要需之事物.

THE VICAR OF WAKEFIELD 239

so I resolved to go forward.
I had some knowledge of
music, with a tolerable
voice, and now turned what
was once my amusement
into a present means of subsistence.[1]   I passed among
the harmless peasants of
Flanders, and among such
of the French as were poor
enough to be very merry;
for I ever found them
sprightly in proportion to
their wants.   Whenever I
approached a peasant's
house towards nightfall, I
played one of my most
merry tunes, and that procured me not only a lodg-
ing, but subsistence[2] for the
next day.   I once or twice
attempted to play for
people of fashion, but they
always thought my per-
formance odious and never
rewarded me even with a
trifle.   This was to me the
more extraordinary, as,
whenever I used in better
days to play for company
when playing was my a-
musement, my music never
failed to throw them into
raptures,   and   the   ladies

只好往前去.我原懂得
點音樂.唱得還好.現在
只好借重游戲消遣的
事去混飯吃｛文人末路說
得可憐是作
者自述
身世｝.我經過符蘭德.
法蘭西地方的鄉下.在
那些窮而能樂的鄉下
人隊裏往來.我常看見
他們越窮越樂.每逢日
落之後.我走近鄉下人
家.就奏一個令人快樂
的調.不獨可以得一夜
安眠的地方.並且還彀
明天吃食的用.有一兩
次.我試試奏給時髦人
聽.他們總以爲我奏得
不好.一點酬勞也不肯
給我.我見得這件事很
奇怪.因爲我從前景況
稍好的時候.每逢在應
酬場中奏樂消遣.他們
聽了.無不歡喜欲狂.婦

---

1. Means of subsistence, 生計.   2. Subsistence, 生活所需之物.

especially; but as it was now my only means, it was received with contempt; a proof how ready the world is to underrate those talents by which a man is supported.

"In this manner I proceeded to Paris, with no design but just to look about me, and then to go forward. The people of Paris are much fonder of strangers that have money than of those that have wit. As I could not boast much of either, I was no great favorite. After walking about the town four or five days, and seeing the outsides of the best houses, I was preparing to leave this retreat of venal hospitality, when passing through one of the principal streets, whom should I meet but our cousin to whom you first recommended me. This meeting was very agreeable to me, and I believe not displeasing to him. He inquired into the nature of my journey to Paris, and informed me of his own business there, which was to collect pictures, medals,

女聽了.是特別的歡喜.
現在我專靠音樂餬口.
人家就瞧不起.可見得
世人看不起餬口的本
事.這就是個憑據.

我就這樣子一路
向巴黎走.除了各處
看看之外.毫無主意.
只好到了一處.又向
前走.巴黎的人.很喜
歡有錢的外國人.不
甚喜歡有知識的外國
人.我既無甚知識.更無
什麼錢.故此沒得什麼
人喜歡我.我走了四五
天.在那些闊房子外面
看看.正想預備離開這
個腐敗地方.誰知在大
街上.碰見你教我去見
的那位老表.這一會面.
我們都喜歡.他問我來
巴黎作什麼.又告訴我.
他來收繪畫寶星寶石

THE VICAR OF WAKEFIELD 241

intaglios,[1] and antiques of all kinds for a gentleman in London, who had just stepped into taste and a large fortune. I was the more surprised at seeing our cousin pitched upon for this office, as he himself had often assured me he knew nothing of the matter. Upon asking how he had been taught the art of a cognoscento[2] so very suddenly, he assured me that nothing was more easy. The whole secret consisted in a strict adherence to two rules: the one, always to observe that the picture might have been better if the painter had taken more pains; and the other, to praise the works of Pietro Perugino.[3] 'But,' says he, 'as I once taught you how to be an author in London, I'll now undertake to instruct you in the art of picture buying at Paris.'

"With this proposal I very readily closed, as it was living, and now all my ambition was to live. I

及各種古董. 是替倫敦有一個人新近發了財講收藏的收買. 我從前聽見他說過. 並不識古董. 爲什麼去辦這種事. 我却以爲奇怪. 我問他. 何以忽然就學得收藏家的本事. 他說. 再容易也沒有. 全副的祕訣. 只在篤守兩條規則. 第一條是要說. 設使畫師多用點心. 那幅畫總應畫得好點. 第二條是要恭維畢魯氏的畫. 又說道. 我曾經教過你怎麼樣在倫敦當著作家. 我現在擔任教你怎麼樣在巴黎當買畫家.

我立刻照他的法子辦. 爲的是吃飯要緊. 我去到他的寓所.

---

1. Intaglios, 次等寶石. 2. Cognoscento, 識古董者. 3. Pietro Perugino, 十六世紀義大利有名畫師.

went therefore to his lodgings, improved my dress by his assistance, and after some time accompanied him to auctions of pictures, where the English gentry were expected to be purchasers. I was not a little surprised at his intimacy with people of the best fashion, who referred themselves to his judgment upon every picture or medal, as an unerring standard of taste He made very good use of my assistance upon these occasions; for when asked his opinion, he would gravely take me aside and ask mine, shrug, look wise, return, and assure the company that he could give no opinion upon an affair of so much importance. Yet there was sometimes an occasion for a more supported assurance. I remember to have seen him, after giving his opinion that the coloring of a picture was not mellow enough, very deliberately take a brush with brown varnish that was accidentally lying by, and rub it over the piece with great composure before all the

他幫我些忙.給我穿上兩件好看點的衣服.跟他到拍賣古畫的地方好幾次.那裏是英國人去買畫的多.他同那班闊人很熟.他們當他是個萬不會錯的老行家.見着古畫寶星.都請教他.遇着這種事體.他把我當作極有用的人.只要有人請教他.他很鄭重的把我拉在一邊.請教我.聳聳肩膀.裝出很有知識的樣子.隨後回到那一邊.去告訴衆人說.這件事體太重大.他不便出什麼主意〔凡是欺人的假內行往往有許多造作〕.有些時候.他却很有膽子.有一次我見他說.這幅畫的顏色不轂深.很斟酌的拿起畫筆來.蘸滿旁邊擺着的棕色油彩.從從容容的.對着衆人.在

THE VICAR OF WAKEFIELD   243

company, and then ask if he had no⁺ improved the tints.

"Wher he had finished h⸱   ssion in Paris, he left me strongly recommended to several men of distinction as a person very proper for a traveling tutor; and after some time I was employed in that capacity by a gentleman who brought his ward to Paris, in order to set him forward on his tour through Europe. I was to be the young gentleman's governor, with a proviso[1] that he should always be permitted to govern himself. My pupil, in fact, understood the art of guiding in money concerns much better than I. He was heir to a fortune of about two hundred thousand pounds, left him by an uncle in the West Indies; and his guardians, to qualify him for the management of it, had bound him apprentice to an attorney. Thus avarice was his prevailing passion; all his

畫上一塗. 還問衆人. 經他這一塗. 那畫的顏色是否好得多 { 可謂大膽妄 為大約無知 }

貴族反被他這一塗嚇 } 倒以為他是大畫家 } .

他在巴黎把事辦完了. 回國. 力薦我給好幾位闊人. 說我是一個極好的遊伴兼教讀. 不久就有一個人. 把他所保傅的少年. 帶來巴黎. 遊歷歐洲各國. 請我當遊伴兼教讀. 要我管着這少年. 却又說明. 要讓這少年自己管自己. 但是我這個學生. 對於管理銀錢. 比我在行得多. 他有一位叔伯 { 也許是姻 舅之類 } . 在西印度. 遺下二十萬鎊的財產交給他承受. 他的保傅要他曉得管理財產. 曾叫他跟律師當過徒弟. 他最大的嗜好

---

1. Proviso, 條件；除外之條件.

questions on the road were how money might be saved: which was the least expensive course of travel: whether anything could be bought that would turn to account when disposed of again in London. Such curiosities on the way as could be seen for nothing he was ready enough to look at; but if the sight of them was to be paid for, he usually asserted that he had been told they were not worth seeing. He never paid a bill that he would not observe how amazingly expensive traveling was; and all this though he was not yet twenty-one. When arrived at Leghorn, as we took a walk to look at the port and shipping, he inquired the expense of the passage by sea home to England. This, he was informed, was but a trifle compared to his returning by land; he was therefore unable to withstand the temptation; so paying me the small part of my salary that was due, he took leave, and embarked with only one attendant for London.

是貪財. 在路上所問的. 都是怎樣省錢的話. 怎樣的旅行最省. 在各處應該買什麼東西. 帶回倫敦可以賺錢. 路過的新奇物事. 不要花錢的. 他都看. 遇見是要花錢的. 他就說. 聽見有人講. 不值得一看. 每逢要還帳. 沒有一次他不說旅行是非常之花費. 他這時候年紀還不到二十一歲呢. 我們到了力干地方. 步行去看碼頭. 同那些出入口的船隻. 他就打聽從海路回英國的盤費. 人家告訴他. 水路比旱路省得多. 他抵抗不住省錢的心. 把欠我的薪水支給我. 只帶一個跟人. 乘船回國去了 ｛從水路回國是為省錢則無所謂遊歷矣｝

THE VICAR OF WAKEFIELD 245

"I now, therefore, was left once more upon the world at large; but then it was a thing I was used to. However, my skill in music could avail me nothing in a country where every peasant was a better musician than I; but by this time I had acquired another talent which answered my purpose as well, and this was a skill in disputation. In all the foreign universities and convents, there are, upon certain days, philosophical theses maintained against every adventitious[1] disputant; for which, if the champion opposes with any dexterity, he can claim a gratuity in money, a dinner, and a bed for one night. In this manner, therefore, I fought my way towards England, walked along from city to city, examined mankind more nearly, and, if I may so express it, saw both sides of the picture. My remarks, however, are but few: I found that monarchy

我現在又無事業.前路茫茫.但是我也嘗慣了這種滋味.這個國裏的鄉下人.個個會音樂.都比我好.我的音樂本事.到了這裏.是毫無用處.好在我現在新學了另外一種的本事.也可以餬口我說的就是辯駁的本事.因為那時候外國的大學校及大寺.常出哲學題目.定日期.開辯駁會.偶然走來的人.也可入場辯駁.只要敢出頭的人.辯駁得好.可以免費的一宿一餐.另外還得若干錢.我就這樣的囘國.一路的辯駁.穿市過鎮.研究風土人情.却十分親切.好的壞的.都研究到.如同看畫.正面背面都看過.我的心得.並無許多的幾句話.我所見到的是

---

1. Adventitious, 偶然; 碰巧; 外來的.

was the best government for the poor to live in, and commonwealths for the rich. I found that riches, in general, were in every country another name for freedom; and that no man is so fond of liberty himself as not to be desirous of subjecting the will of some individuals in society to his own.

"Upon my arrival in England I resolved to pay my respects first to you, and then to enlist as a volunteer in the first expedition that was going forward; but on my journey down, my resolutions were changed by meeting an old acquaintance who I found belonged to a company of comedians that were going to make a summer campaign[1] in the country. The company seemed not much to disapprove of me for an associate. They all, however, apprised me of the importance of the task at which I aimed; that the public was a many-headed

君主制度.宜於窮民.共和制度.宜於富人.我見得.無論在什麼國.有錢卽是自由.我又見得一個人.無論怎麼樣喜歡自由.無不喜歡強人從己的.限制他人的自由〔聊聊數語却把所謂國體憲法自由平等一切欺人之論發揮無餘〕.

我於是到了英國.原想先去見父親.然後投入第一個義勇隊.我到了鄉下.就改了宗旨.因爲遇見一個熟人.是詼諧劇班中的人.正要往鄉下演戲.我投入他們班中.他們却無不以爲然.他們都招呼我.說是.我所演的脚色.是要緊的.又告訴我說.看戲的人.是個多頭的怪物.要

---

1. Campaign, 打仗；政客演說；此處只作演戲解.

monster, and that only such as had very good heads could please it; that acting was not to be learned in a day; and that, without some traditional shrugs which had been on the stage, and only on the stage, these hundred years, I could never pretend to please. The next difficulty was in fitting me with parts, as almost every character was in keeping. I was driven for some time from one character to another, till at last Horatio was fixed upon, which the presence of the present company has happily hindered me from acting."

很有頭腦的人.才能叫他們喜歡.又說是.演戲不是一天可以學成的.近百年來演戲的人.一定要聳肩縮頸.除了戲臺上有這種狀態.別處是向來看不見的.你也要學他們聳肩縮頸.不然看戲的人.不會喜歡的{可見當時演戲是過於裝模作態以求入時人之眼又此回最長最臉炙人口}.第二件的為難是派我裝脚色.因為什麼脚色.都有人演了.於是一會叫我演這個.一會又叫我演那個.後來才派定我演賀理紹.因我見諸位進戲園.我就停演了.

CHAPTER XXI

THE SHORT CONTINUANCE OF FRIENDSHIP AMONGST THE VICIOUS, WHICH IS COEVAL ONLY WITH MUTUAL SATISFACTION.

第 二 十 一 回

同 惡 相 交 不 得 耐 久 不 相 滿 意
就 要 分 離
（投 小 店 父 女 相 逢）

My son's account was too long to be delivered[1] at once; the first part of it was begun that night, and he was concluding[2] the rest after dinner the next day, when the appearance of Mr. Thornhill's equipage[3] at the door seemed to make a pause in the general satisfaction. The butler, who was now become my friend in the family, informed me with a whisper that the squire had already made some overtures[4] to Miss Wilmot, and that her aunt and uncle seemed

且說我兒子所述的他那番閱歷.話語很長. 一次說不完.前半截是晚上說的.後半截是第二天飯後說的.那時候唐希爾的闊車馬已經到了門口.大衆都有點不甚滿意.那總管家同我很要好.附耳告訴我. 唐鄉紳已經向威小姐

1. Delivered, 說；交. 2. Concluding, 說完；收束. 3. Equipage. 此處作闊馬車解. 4. Overtures, 提議.

THE VICAR OF WAKEFIELD 249

highly to approve the match. Upon Mr. Thornhill's entering, he seemed, at seeing my son and me, to start back; but I readily imputed[1] that to surprise, and not displeasure. However, upon our advancing to salute him, he returned our greeting with the most apparent candor; and, after a short time, his presence served only to increase the general good humor.

After tea he called me aside to inquire after my daughter; but upon my informing him that my inquiry was unsuccessful, he seemed greatly surprised, adding that he had been since frequently at my house in order to comfort the rest of my family, whom he left perfectly well. He then asked if I had communicated her misfortune to Miss Wilmot or my son; and upon my replying that I had not told them as yet, he greatly approved my prudence and precaution, desiring me by

求過親. 雅諾先生夫婦. 好像很願意. 唐希爾一走進來. 看見我父子. 好像嚇一跳. 要往後退的樣子. 我以爲他是詫異. 並不是不喜歡我們. 我父子向前見禮. 他却像是很坦白的. 對我們還禮. 過了一會. 因爲他來了. 衆人却又高興起來.

吃過茶點後. 他把我拉開一邊. 探問我女兒的事. 我答他找尋無蹤. 他覺得很詫異. 他說曾經常到我家. 安慰我家裏的人. 並說他走的時候. 我家裏的人都很好. 他又問我. 曾否把這不幸之事告訴我兒子同威小姐. 我答他. 我還未曾告訴過他們. 他很以我

---

1. Imputed, 以爲.

all means to keep it a secret: "For at best," cried he, "it is but divulging one's own infamy, and perhaps Miss Livy may not be so guilty as we all imagine." We were here interrupted by a servant, who came to ask the squire in to stand up at country dances; so that he left me quite pleased with the interest he seemed to take in my concerns.[1]　His addresses, however, to Miss Wilmot were too obvious to be mistaken; and yet she seemed not perfctly pleased, but bore them rather in compliance to the will of her aunt than from real inclination. I had even the satisfaction to see her lavish some kind looks upon my unfortunate son, which the other could neither extort by his fortune nor assiduity.　Mr. Thornhill's seeming composure, however, not a little surprised me.　We had now continued here a week at the pressing instances of Mr. Arnold; but

小心謹慎爲然. 勸我守祕密. 說道. 毋論怎樣說. 這種算是家醜. 不必外傳. 況且奧維雅小姐. 或者不至如我們所料的那樣不幸 {唐希爾言動讀者須留意都是後文蛛絲馬跡餘仿此} 說到這裏. 一個家人來請他進去跳舞. 他對於我的家事. 這樣關切. 我心裏很歡喜. 至於他的親近威小姐要求親. 都是很明顯的. 一見便知. 但是威小姐却不甚喜歡他. 小姐自己. 原不願意. 不過遷就他長親的意思. 不能不忍受. 我並且很滿意的見威小姐兩眼. 對於我不幸的兒子. 常露深情. 唐希爾的富貴和他很費力的懇求. 却不能博得威小姐一顧. 然而唐希爾還是鎮靜如常. 我却覺得有點奇怪. 我們因爲雅諾先生之請. 在他府裏住了

---

1. Concerns, 此處作憂慮解.

each day the more tenderness Miss Wilmot showed my son, Mr. Thornhill's friendship seemed proportionably to increase for him.

He had formally made us the most kind assurances of using his interest to serve the family; but now his generosity was not confined to promises alone: the morning I designed for my departure, Mr. Thornhill came to me with looks of real pleasure to inform me of a piece of service he had done for his friend George. This was nothing less than his having procured him an ensign's commission[1] in one of the regiments that was going to the West Indies, for which he had promised but one hundred pounds, his interest having been sufficient to get an abatement of the other two.

"As for this trifling piece of service," continued the young gentleman, "I desire no other reward but the pleasure of having served my friend; and, as for the hundred pounds to be paid,

一星期. 但是越住得久. 威小姐對我兒子表示柔情也越深. 而唐希爾對我兒子交情也日好 ⟨不獨寫威小姐兼點明唐希 爾之所以設法薦佐之投軍 遠出係調 虎離山也⟩.

他從前曾經很結實的說過. 要替我們家裏幫忙. 從前不過是口頭答應. 現在却是實行. 我打算要走的那天早上. 唐希爾很歡喜的走來告訴我. 他替佐之謀了一件事. 就是有一團陸軍. 要赴西印度. 他替佐之謀得一個士官缺. 他只答應一百鎊 ⟨實缺軍官要花錢買⟩. 原要三百鎊的. 因為他的面子. 減讓了二百鎊.

他說道. 這點小事. 我不望酬謝. 不過替朋友出力. 博點歡喜罷了. 至於那一百鎊. 你若無

---

1. Commission, 職事；缺.

if you are unable to raise it yourselves, I will advance it, and you shall repay me at your leisure." This was a favor we wanted words to express our sense of; I readily, therefore, gave my bond for the money, and testified as much gratitude as if I never intended to pay.

George was to depart for town the next day to secure his commission, in pursuance of[1] his generous patron's directions, who judged it highly expedient[2] to use dispatch,[3] lest,[4] in the meantime, another should step in with more advantageous proposals. The next morning, therefore, our young soldier was early prepared for his departure, and seemed the only person among us who was not affected by it. Neither the fatigues and dangers he was going to encounter, nor the friends and mistress (for Miss Wilmot actually loved him) he was leaving behind, any

力籌款．由我代墊．你隨後得便還我．我領他這極大的情．說不出許多的感激．我寫一張借據交他．又說了許多感激的話．好像是我存了有借無還的心。

佐之聽唐希爾的指示．明日入京就職．他說要趕快的去．不然．別人多出錢．就先得到手．第二日早上．這位少年軍官．預備起程．只有他一個人．毫無感動．他這一去．要受許多辛苦．要遇許多危險．又與朋友及他心愛的女子遠離（威小姐原是眞愛他）．他却毫無委靡不振的神

---

1. In pursuance of, 依照. 2. Expedient, 便利；合法 (妙法). 3. Dispatch, 迅速. 4. Lest, 不然.

THE VICAR OF WAKEFIELD 253

way damped his spirits.
After he had taken leave
of the rest of the company,
I gave him all I had — my
blessing. "And now, my
boy," cried I, "thou art going to fight for thy country,
remember how thy brave
grandfather fought for his
sacred King, when loyalty
among Britons was a virtue.
Go, my boy, and imitate
him in all but his mis-
fortunes, if it was a misfortune to die with Lord
Falkland. Go, my boy;
and if you fall, though distant, exposed, and unwept
by those that love you, the
most precious tears are
those with which heaven
bedews the unburied head
of a soldier."

The next morning I took
leave of the good family
that had been kind enough
to entertain me so long,
not without several expres-
sions of gratitude to Mr.
Thornhill for his late
bounty. I left them in
the enjoyment of all that
happiness which affluence
and good breeding procure,
and returned towards
home, despairing of ever

色．同各人辭別之後．我
並無什麼東西給他．只
好保佑他．並吩咐他幾句
話．說道．我的孩子．你此
去是爲國攻敵．你要記
得．你的有勇的祖父．從
前是怎樣爲國王打仗．
那時候忠君．就是不列
顛人的道德．你去學他
樣樣都可以學他．却不
可學他的不幸．若是同
他那樣爲國王查理．而
與符爾克貴族同死．可
稱爲不幸｛査理第一與國
人戰大敗被擒
爲國人所殺
符爾克陣亡｝孩子．你去
罷．若是你陣亡．雖是離
家很遠．暴骨戰場．愛你
的人．不能撫屍痛哭．却
還有最可寶的淚．就是
上天垂憐．滴在無人收
葬陣亡人頭上的露水．
第二天．我同那深情
招待我住了多日的主
人們告辭．唐希爾新近
替我們很帮忙．我對他
很表示感激．我離開這
富而好禮享福的人們．
就首途回家．我曉得再

finding my daughter more, but sending a sigh to heaven to spare and forgive her. I was now come within about twenty miles of home, having hired a horse to carry me, as I was yet but weak, and comforted myself with the hopes of soon seeing all I held dearest upon earth. But the night coming on, I put up at a little public house by the roadside, and asked for the landlord's company over a pint of wine. We sat beside his kitchen fire, which was the best room in the house, and chatted on politics and the news of the country. We happened, among other topics, to talk of young Squire Thornhill, who, the host assured me, was hated as much as his uncle, Sir William, who sometimes came down to the country, was loved.

He went on to observe that he made it his whole study to betray the daughters of such as received him to their houses, and after a fortnight or three weeks' possession, turn them out unrewarded and

也找不着我的女兒.只求上天饒恕他.我此時身體還是未十分強健.雇了一匹馬走的.離家尚有六七十里的時候.自己安慰自己.不久就可以看見我的世上至寶了.天色將晚.住在路旁一間小店.請店主來相陪.店裏頂好地方.只有廚房.於是坐在廚房火爐邊.兩人談政治和國內新聞.偶然談到那少年鄉紳唐希爾.店主告訴我.這個少年是無人不怨恨的.他的叔叔威廉唐希爾爵士.却是無人不愛的.爵士有時也到這裏來.

他又說.唐希爾的全副精神.都用在誘惑人家的女兒.凡是接待他的人家.他總要想法去誘惑.那些女子.被他佔了兩三星期之後.就要被他趕走.被他遺棄.沒有麼什報答.

THE VICAR OF WAKEFIELD 255

abandoned to the world.

As we continued our discourse in this manner, his wife, who had been out to get change, returned, and perceiving that her husband was enjoying a pleasure in which she was not a sharer, she asked him in an angry tone what he did there; to which he only replied in an ironical way by drinking her health. "Mr. Symmonds," cried she, "you use me very ill, and I'll bear it no longer. Here three parts of the business is left for me to do, and the fourth left unfinished; while you do nothing but soak with the guests all day long; whereas if a spoonful of liquor were to cure me of a fever, I never touch a drop."

I now found what she would be at,[1] and immediately poured her out a glass, which she received with a curtsy, and drinking towards my good health.

我們兩人接下談話. 店主婆換錢回來. 看見 男人在那裏享福. 撇開 他. 那女人很生氣的問 他. 在那裏幹什麼. 店主 人舉杯吃酒. 同他祝壽. 反譏他. 店主婆喊道. 西 曼. 你刻薄我. 我不能再 受了. 店裏的事. 叫我作 了四分之三. 剩下四分 之一. 無人作. 你却終日 陪客人灌酒. 什麼也不 管. 即使有一匙酒可以 治我的熱病. 我却一點 也吃不到.

我聽了. 曉得他的意 思. 立刻倒一鍾酒請他 吃. 他很客氣的接過去. 同我祝壽.

---

1. What she would be at, 他意之所在; 他要什麼.

"Sir," resumed she, "it is not so much for the value of the liquor I am angry, but one cannot help it when the house is going out of the windows. If the customers or guests are to be dunned,[1] all the burden lies upon my back;[2] he'd as lief[3] eat that glass as budge after them himself. There now, above stairs, we have a young woman who has come to take up her lodgings here, and I don't believe she has got any money by her over civility. I am certain she is very slow of payment, and I wish she were put in mind of it."

"What signifies minding her?" cried the host, "if she be slow, she is sure."

"I don't know that," replied the wife; "but I know that I am sure she has been here a fortnight, and we have not yet seen the cross of her money."[4]

他說道. 我並不因為那酒值多少錢生氣. 店裏的事. 無人去管. 怎麼不令人生氣呢. 若是向客人討償. 他却不動. 總要我去討. 他寧願把酒鍾吞在肚裏. 也不願勤一勤. 現在樓上還住有一位少年女客. 他對我們非常客氣. 我就曉得他一個錢也沒有. 他還帳實在是還得太慢. 我看你得去討討看.

店主人答道. 不必去討. 他雖然還帳還得慢. 却是一定還的.

店主婆答道. 他來住已經有兩星期. 我還沒兒過他的錢面.

1. Dunned, 討帳. 2. All the burden lies upon my back, 所有責成都堆在我身上. 3. He'd as lief, 他寧願. 4. The cross of her money, 錢背上國王的徽章交加作十字形.

"I suppose, my dear," cried he, "we shall have it all in a lump."

"In a lump!" cried the other, "I hope we may get it anyway, and that I am resolved we will this very night, or out she tramps, bag and baggage."

"Consider, my dear," cried the husband; "she is a gentlewoman, and deserves more respect."

"As for the matter of that," returned the hostess, "gentle or simple, out she shall pack with a siserara.[1] Gentry may be good things where they take; but for my part, I never saw much good of them at the sign of the Harrow."[2] Thus saying, she ran up a narrow flight of stairs that went from the kitchen to a room overhead, and I soon perceived by the loudness of her voice and the bitterness of her reproaches, that no money was to be had from her lodger. I could hear her

店主人道. 我猜他是一次付清.

店主婆道. 一次付清麼. 我盼望我們可以得到手. 我們今天晚上向他討債. 若是不付清的話. 連人帶行李. 閗他出店.

店主人道. 我的寶貝. 他是個上等女人. 我們應該以禮相待.

店主婆答道. 上等也罷. 平常也罷. 立刻閗他走. 上等人原是好東西. 但是我們這裏. 看不見他們的什麼好處. 店主婆於是從小樓梯跑上去. 一會子. 我就聽見店主婆聲音極響極大. 怒斥得很利害. 我就曉得那女客人無錢

---

1. Siserara (a legal writ; any telling, effective act, as a blow), 一紙公文; 推廣作有力打擊; 閗走. 2. The sign of the Harrow, 本小店名.

remonstrances very distinctly: "Out, I say—pack out this moment—tramp thou infamous strumpet! or I'll give thee a mark thou won't be the better for this three months. What! you trumpery, to come and take up an honest house without cross[1] or coin to bless yourself with! Come along, I say."

"Oh, dear madam," cried the stranger, "pity me—pity a poor abandoned creature for one night, and death will soon do the rest."

I instantly knew the voice of my poor ruined child Olivia. I flew to her rescue, while the woman was dragging her along by the hair, and I caught the dear forlorn wretch in my arms.

"Welcome, anyway welcome, my dearest lost one, my treasure, to your poor old father's bosom! Though the vicious forsake thee, there is yet one in the world that will never forsake thee; though thou hadst ten thousand crimes

付帳.我聽見店主婆斥責的話很清楚.聽見說道.叫化子.你立刻收拾滾出去.不然.我就給你一個記號.三個月也好不了.你這個好看而不值錢的東西.你一文沒有.爲什麼跑來住在誠實好人家裏.走你的罷.

那女客人說道.瑪當.你可憐我一個困窮無人收留的人住一夜罷.以後我一死就完了.

我一聽.就曉得是我女兒奧維雅的聲音.那店主婆正在拖住他的頭髮.拉他走.我飛上樓去救他.兩手把我的至寶可憐的女兒抱住.

說道.我的失而復得的至寶呀.我歡迎你.無論你怎樣.我歡迎你傷靠在你老父的心胸.那犯罪惡的人.只管拋棄你.世界上還有一個人是永遠不拋棄你的.那

---

1. Cross, 錢面上之十字形.

to answer for, he will forget them all."

"Oh, my own dear,"—for minutes she could say no more—"my own dearest good papa! Could angels be kinder! How do I deserve so much! The villain, I hate him and myself, to be a reproach to such goodness. You can't forgive me. I know you cannot."

"Yes, my child; from my heart, I do forgive thee! Only repent, and we both shall yet be happy. We shall see many pleasant days yet, my Olivia!"

"Ah! never, sir, never. The rest of my wretched life must be infamy abroad and shame at home. But, alas! papa, you look much paler tban you used to do. Could such a thing as I am give you so much uneasiness? Surely you have too much wisdom to take the miseries of my guilt upon yourself."

"Our wisdom, young woman," replied I.

"Ah, why so cold a name, papa?" cried she. "This is the first time you

怕你犯了一萬次罪過. 他件件都忘了.

我女兒只說了半句我的至寶....有好幾分鐘.也說不下去.後來才接上說道.我的至寶爸爸呀.神仙也不能有你這樣慈愛.我不配享受這些慈愛.我痛我自己對不起你的慈愛.你不能恕我無罪.我曉得你不能.

我說道.我的孩子.我能恕你.我是從心裏恕你無罪.你只要悔過.我們還可以享受快樂.奧過維雅呀.我們還可以許多好過的日子.

他答道.父親.永遠不能的了.從此以後.我終身所過的愁苦日子.一定不過是在外得個醜名.在家我無面目見人.哎呀.爸爸呀.你臉色比向來灰白得多.我這樣一個不相干的人.能戳使你心裏那樣不安.麼爲什麼把我的愁苦.都拖在你自己身上呢.

我答道.少年女子呀.我們的智慧....

他問道.呀.爸爸.你爲什麼用這樣無情的稱

ever called me by so cold a name."

"I ask pardon, my darling," returned I; "but I was going to observe, that wisdom makes but a slow defense against trouble, though at last a sure one."

The landlady now returned to know if we did not choose a more genteel apartment; to which assenting, we were shown a room where we could converse more freely. After we had talked ourselves into some degree of tranquillity, I could not avoid desiring some account of the gradations that led to her present wretched situation.

"That villain, sir," said she, "from the first day of our meeting, made me honorable, though private, proposals."

"Villain, indeed," cried I; "and yet in some measure surprises me, how a person of Mr. Burchell's good sense and seeming honor could be guilty of such deliberate baseness, and thus step into a family to undo it."

呼. 這是第一次你對我用這個無情的稱呼.

我答道. 我的小寶貝. 你饒恕我. 我正在要說. 智慧抵抗愁苦. 雖是到底抵抗得住. 然而進步是很慢的.

這時候. 店主婆走來問我們是否要調換一間好點的屋子. 我說是要調換. 他就領我們到一間. 說話可以自由些. 我父女兩人說了些話. 心裏覺得比剛才安靜些. 我不免問他. 怎麼樣一步一步的走到現在這樣可憐的景況.

他說道. 那個陰毒人. 從第一次見面起. 就向我求為正式夫婦.

我喊道. 那人十分陰毒. 但是我却覺得有些詫異. 白且爾這個人. 原有善知識. 外面看去. 是講道德顧體面的. 怎麼樣能幹下這樣卑劣毒手. 走到我們家中. 害我們一家.

"My dear papa," returned my daughter, "you labor under a strange mistake; Mr. Burchell never attempted to deceive me; instead of that, he took every opportunity of privately admonishing me against the artifices of Mr. Thornhill, who I now find was even worse than he represented him."

"Mr. Thornhill!" interrupted I; "can it be?"

"Yes, sir," returned she; "it was Mr. Thornhill who seduced me, who employed the two ladies, as he called them, but who, in fact, were abandoned women of the town, without breeding or pity, to decoy us up to London. Their artifices, you may remember, would have certainly succeeded but for Mr. Burchell's letter, who directed those reproaches at them which we all applied to ourselves. How he came to have so much influence as to defeat their intentions still remains a secret to me; but I am convinced he was ever our warmest, sincerest friend."

他答道.爸爸.你錯了.白且爾向來並沒有設計騙我.每逢有機會.私下裏總勸戒我.不要上唐希爾的當.現在我才明白.唐希爾比白且爾告訴我的還要壞得多.

我攔住說道.是唐希爾麼.

他答道.父親.是他.唐希爾買出那兩個女人.說是良家女人.騙我們進京.其實他們是兩個妓女.既無教育.又無憐心.你還記得假使不是白且爾那封信.唐希爾的詭計.一定是行得通的.白且爾的信.是責備唐希爾他們一班人的.我們不曉得.誤作是責備我們的.白且爾怎麼能彀有這大的力量.打散他們的詭計.我至今還不能明白.但是我深信白且爾是我們的最熱心最眞誠的朋友.

"You amaze me, my dear," cried I; "but now I find my first suspicions of Mr. Thornhill's baseness were too well grounded: but he can triumph in security, for he is rich and we are poor. But tell me, my child—sure it was no small temptation that could thus obliterate[1] all the impressions[2] of such an education and so virtuous a disposition as thine?"

"Indeed, sir," replied she, "he owes all this triumph to the desire I had of making him, and not myself, happy. I knew that the ceremony of our marriage, which was privately performed by a popish priest, was no way binding, and that I had nothing to trust to but his honor."

"What!" interrupted I; "and were you indeed married by a priest, and in orders?"

"Indeed, sir, we were," replied she, "though we were both sworn to conceal his name."

我說道.我聽你這番話.十分詫異.現在我才曉得.我最初就疑心唐希爾是個惡劣小人.原來疑得不錯.他富我們窮.他作了惡事.還是一樣的得意安樂.我們奈何他不得｛富貴欺貧人貧受欺無處訴　貧人貧到處皆然｝.但是你受過教育.心向道德的.總有一件極有力量能引動你的事.才能使你都不顧.

他答道.他的詭計得行.實在是因為我要使他快樂.並不是我要快樂.我們是私下在教士面前行的結婚禮.我曉得是不算數的.我不靠別的.只靠他顧面子.

我攔住說道.什麼.是正式授過職的教士同你們結婚的麼.

他答道.是的.我們却發過誓.不說出他的名姓.

1. Obliterate, 磨滅.　2. Impressions, 印象；刻印.

"Why, then, my child, come to my arms again, and now you are a thousand times more welcome than before; for you are now his wife to all intents and purposes; nor can all the laws of man, though written upon tables of adamant, lessen the force of that sacred connection."

"Alas! · papa," replied she, "you are but little acquainted with his villainies: he has been married already by the same priest to six or eight wives more, whom, like me, he has deceived and abandoned."

"Has he so?" cried I; "then we must hang[1] the priest, and you shall inform against him to-morrow."

"But, sir," returned she, "will that be right, when I am sworn to secrecy?"

"My dear," I replied, "if you have made such a promise, I cannot, nor will I, tempt you to break it. Even though it may benefit the public, you must not inform against

我說道. 我的孩子. 你再過來. 我再偎抱你. 現在我比從前加千倍的歡迎你. 按居心及行事形式上論你是他的正式妻室. 凡是人所定的法律. 那怕寫在石上的. 都不能絲毫解散你們神聖不可侵犯成婚的締結.

他答道. 哎呀. 爸爸. 你不曉得他這個人的陰毒. 他用這個教士. 已經同六七個女人結過婚這幾個女人. 同我一樣. 先受他騙. 末後都被他拋棄了 {富貴人罪惡 有如此者}.

我說道. 旣是這樣. 我們先停止那教士的教職. 你明天告他 {揹唐 希爾}.

女兒問道. 我已經發過誓. 不露他的名姓. 我去告他. 對麼.

我答道. 你若發過誓. 我旣不能也不願意使你背誓. 若是告訴人. 原可以使大衆周知. 然而

---

1. Hang, 此處作停止解.

him. In all human institutions,[1] a smaller evil is allowed to procure a greater good: as in politics, a province may be given away to secure a kingdom; in medicine, a limb may be lopped off to preserve the body. But in religion, the law is written, and inflexible, *never* to do evil. And this law, my child, is right: for otherwise, if we commit a smaller evil to procure a greater good, certain guilt would be thus incurred, in expectation of contingent advantage. And though the advantage should certainly follow, yet the interval between commission and advantage, which is allowed to be guilty, may be that in which we are called away to answer for the things we have done, and the volume of human actions is closed forever. But I interrupt you, my dear; go on.''

"The very next morning," continued she, "I found what little expectations I was to have from

你不可告他.人世的事.往往有受小害而保存大體的.例如在政治上.棄一省而保一國.在醫學上.割一股而保全身.但是在宗教上.有一條不能通融的法律.就是永不作惡這一條.這條法律很對.不然的話.我們若是行小惡而得大利.就會因爲盼望不可必得的好處.去爲惡.那怕一定可以得着好處.但是在那行惡與得益之間.就許有來責問所作的事.還不是徒然枉作小人嗎｛語意不甚清晰｝.我打了你的叉.你只管往下說.

他說道.第二天早上.我就曉得他是全無眞心.那天早上他還介紹

---

1. Institutions, 建設.

his sincerity. That very morning he introduced me, to two unhappy women more, whom, like me, he had deceived, but who lived in contented prostitution. I loved him too tenderly to bear such rivals in his affections, and strove to forget my infamy in a tumult of pleasures. With this view, I danced, dressed, and talked; but still was unhappy. The gentlemen who visited there told me every moment of the power of my charms; and this only contributed to increase my melancholy, as I had thrown all their power quite away. Thus each day I grew more pensive, and he more insolent, till at last the monster had the assurance to offer me to a young baronet of his acquaintance. Need I describe, sir, how his ingratitude stung me? My answer to this proposal was almost madness. I desired to part. As I was going, he offered me a purse; but I flung it at him with indignation, and burst from him in a rage,

我見兩個女人. 這兩個也是受他騙的. 我實在是十分愛他. 也不管那兩個女人. 我就充量行樂. 極力要忘了我的醜行. 於是我只管跳舞. 穿好衣裳. 談話. 然而總是不樂. 到那個地方的男人們. 時時刻刻告訴我. 我怎樣有迷人的力量. 這些話. 不過令我更加憂愁. 因為我這種力量. 都拋棄於無用之地了. 於是我日見其愁懷不展. 他日見其無禮. 我不必細說他這種忘恩負義的行為. 使我心傷. 我於是要同他分離. 我臨走. 他給我一口袋的錢. 我很氣的摔在他身上. 大怒而去. 有好一會子. 我全不覺得我所處的境遇之愁苦. 後來我放眼一看. 才曉得我這個苦極的人. 天下之大. 無可哀告. 正在這個當口. 有一輛車走過. 我上了車. 那

that, for a while, kept me insensible of the miseries of my situation. But I soon looked round me, and saw myself a vile, abject, guilty thing, without one friend in the world to apply to. Just in that interval, a stage coach happening to pass by, I took a place, it being my only aim to be driven at a distance from a wretch I despised and detested. I was set down here, where, since my arrival, my own anxiety and this woman's unkindness, have been my only companions. The hours of pleasure that I have passed with my mamma and sister now grow painful to me. Their sorrows are much; but mine are greater than theirs, for mine are mixed with guilt and infamy."

"Have patience, my child," cried I, "and I hope things will yet be better. Take some repose to-night; and to-morrow I'll carry you home to your mother and the rest of the family, from whom you will receive a kind reception. Poor woman, this

時候. 我不過只要遠離我所深恨最看不起的人. 後來就在這裏下車. 自從到了這小店之後. 孤苦不堪. 只有這個店主婆的苛刻. 和我自己的焦慮. 同我作伴. 追想從前同母親妹妹過的快樂日子. 令我心痛. 他們的愁苦必重. 但是我的愁苦. 比他們的更重. 因爲我的愁苦裏. 還夾着醜名.

我說道. 孩子. 你忍耐些. 我盼望較好的前程. 你今晚略安歇. 明早我帶你回家. 你母親同弟妹一定歡迎你的. 可憐

has gone to her heart; but
she loves you still, Olivia,
and will forget it."

你 的 母 親. 這 件 事 很 傷
他 的 心. 但 是 他 還 是 愛
你 的. 把 前 事 都 忘 記 了.

CHAPTER XXII

OFFENSES ARE EASILY PARDONED WHERE THERE IS LOVE AT BOTTOM

第 二 十 二 回

為 愛 情 而 犯 之 過 易 於 寬 恕
（老 牧 師 住 宅 被 焚）

The next morning I took my daughter behind me, and set out on my return home. As we traveled along, I strove by every persuasion to calm her sorrows and fears, and to arm[1] her with resolution to bear the presence of her offended mother. I took every opportunity, from the prospect of a fine country through which we passed, to observe how much kinder Heaven was to us than we to each other, and that the misfortunes of nature's making were very few. I assured her that she should never perceive any change in my affections;

且說第二天早上．我們同騎一馬．女兒在我背後．一路回家．一面走．我一面極力勸他．不要愁苦．只管放心．又壯他的膽．預備見他得罪過的母親．我看見經過路上的好風景．乘機對他說．天待人．比人待人慈愛得多．天降於人的禍害．並不甚多 ｛天害人不見人害人害得兒｝．我叫他放心．我始

---

1. To arm, 授以抵禦之具；給軍械．

THE VICAR OF WAKEFIELD

and that during my life, which yet might be long, she might depend upon a guardian and an instructor. I armed her against the censure of the world, showed her that books were sweet, unreproaching companions to the miserable, and that, if they could not bring us to enjoy life, they would at least teach us to endure it.

The hired horse that we rode was to be put up that night at an inn by the way, within about five miles from my house; and as I was willing to prepare my family for my daughter's reception, I determined to leave her that night at the inn, and to return for her, accompanied by my daughter Sophia, early the next morning. It was night before we reached our appointed stage: however, after seeing her provided with a decent apartment, and having ordered the hostess to prepare proper refreshments, I kissed her, and proceeded towards home

And now my heart caught new sensations of pleasure the nearer I

終愛他.永無改變.我活在世上的日子還很長.還是要保護他教導他的.我又教他如何抵禦世人的詆毀.告訴他.書籍是愁苦人的好同伴.這種同伴.脾氣又好.又不斥責人.這種同伴.雖然不能使我們享受生人之樂.却能教我們忍受生人之苦.

這天晚上.就在路上一個小店下馬.那裏離家還有十多里路.我願意先通知家裏人.預備女兒回家.立意叫女兒住店.我再來.帶着二女兒素緋雅接他回家.我們到小店時.天已黑了.我看好他歇在一間舒服屋子.吩咐店主婆預備合宜飯菜.同女兒接過吻.我就先回家.

我離那安樂過日子的家庭越近.覺得異樣的歡喜.我離家時.如同離巢的

approached that peaceful mansion. As a bird that had been frighted from its nest, my affections outwent my haste, and hovered round my little fireside with all the rapture of expectation. I called up the many fond things I had to say, and anticipated the welcome I was to receive. I already felt my wife's tender embrace, and smiled at the joy of my little ones. As I walked but slowly, the night waned apace. The laborers of the day were all retired to rest; the lights were out in every cottage; no sounds were heard but of the shrilling cock, and the deep-mouthed watchdog at hollow distance. I approached my little abode of pleasure, and before I was within a furlong of the place, our honest mastiff came running to welcome me.

It was now near midnight that I came to knock at my door: all was still and silent: my heart dilated with unutterable happiness, when, to my amazement, I saw the house bursting out in a blaze of fire, and

受驚鳥. 現在我的慈愛心. 比我的身子已先到了家. 那心已經非常的快樂圍繞火爐左右. 我要說的慈愛話. 都湧上來. 又預料他們怎樣的歡迎我. 我已經覺得老妻之摟抱我. 見孩子們歡喜. 我對着他們微笑｛遠出的人將到快樂家庭時確有這種心境｝. 因爲我行得遲. 越走天越晚了. 所有白天作工的人. 都安歇了. 所過的村子. 燈火也都滅了｛若是金聖歎批必說從村子無燈火引起後文一片火光｝. 寂無人聲. 有時只聽見公雞高啼. 又聽見遠遠的狗吠. 我走近我的快樂家庭. 相離還不到一里路. 我家裏的狗就來歡迎.

這時候快到半夜. 我敲門. 家裏是寂然無聲. 也無動靜. 我覺得說不出來的快樂. 心裏大爲舒放. 忽然看見我的住宅起火. 心裏大驚. 只見

every aperture red with conflagration! I gave a loud, convulsive outcry, and fell upon the pavement insensible. This alarmed my son, who had till this been asleep; and he, perceiving the flames, instantly waked my wife and daughter; and all running out naked and wild with apprehension, recalled me to life with their anguish. But it was only to objects of new terror; for the flames had by this time caught the roof of our dwelling, part after part continuing to fall in, while the family stood with silent agony looking on, as if they enjoyed the blaze. I gazed upon them and upon it by turns, and then looked round me for my two little ones; but they were not to be seen. Oh, misery!

"Where," cried I— "where are my little ones?"

"They are burnt to death in the flames," says my wife, calmly; "and I will die with them."

That moment, I heard the cry of the babes within, who were just awakened

一片的火光.所有窗口都現紅光.我發抖的大喊一聲.倒在地上.不省人事.我的兒子原在睡夢中.被我這一喊驚醒.立刻喊醒他母親姊姊.一齊裸體跑出來.害怕得忘其所以.他們的悲痛呼號.把我叫醒過來.我一看都是令人可怕的新現象.因爲這時候.火燄已到房頂.一部分一部分的接二連三向裏傾倒.一家人心裏很悲苦的.站在那裏看.好像是愛看這一片火光.我看看他們.看看火.四圍找我那兩個最小的兒子.看不見.哎.苦呀.

我喊道.兩個小的在那裏.

我的女人道.他們已經被火燒死了.我要同他們死在一堆.

這時候我聽見兩個小的叫喊.因爲他們才

by the fire, and nothing could have stopped me.

"Where—where are my children?" cried I, rushing through the flames, and bursting the door of the chamber in which they were confined. "Where are my little ones?"

"Here, dear papa, here we are," cried they together, while the flames were just catching the bed where they lay. I caught them both in my arms, and snatching them through the fire as fast as possible, while just as I was got out, the roof fell in.

"Now," cried I, holding up my children—"now let the flames burn on, and all my possessions perish. Here they are—I have saved my treasures. Here, my dearest—here are our treasures, and we shall yet be happy!"

We kissed our little darlings a thousand times; they clasped us round the neck, and seemed to share our transports, while their mother laughed and wept by turns.

I now stood a calm spectator of the flames, and

被火驚醒. 這時候毋論什麼也攔不住我.

我從火堆裏竄過去. 推開他們被困的房門. 喊道. 孩子們在那裏. 孩子們在那裏.

兩個小的同時喊道. 爸爸. 我們在這裏. 那時候火燄剛到他們的牀. 我兩手抱住他們. 從火裏再逃出來. 那房頂全跌下來.

我把兩個孩子舉起來. 說道. 火只管燒. 凡是我們的東西. 都讓火燒光了罷. 我把寶貝救出來了. 他們都在這裏. 我的至寶呀. 我們的寶貝都在這裏. 我們還可以快樂.

我們同兩個小的接吻有一千次. 他們抱住我們的頸子. 好像同我們一樣的快活. 他們的母親. 一會子哭. 一會子笑.

我這時候是一個安閒無事的旁觀人. 站在

after some time began to perceive that my arm to the shoulder was scorched in a terrible manner. It was, therefore, out of my power to give my son any assistance, either in attempting to save our goods, or preventing the flames spreading to our corn.

By this time the neighbors were alarmed and came running to our assistance; but all they could do was to stand, like us, spectators of the calamity. My goods, among which were the notes I had reserved for my daughters' fortunes, were entirely consumed, except a box with some papers that stood in the kitchen, and two or three things more of little consequence, which my son brought away in the beginning. The neighbors contributed, however, what they could to lighten our distress. They brought us clothes, and furnished one of our outhouses with kitchen utensils; so that by daylight we had another, though a wretched dwelling, to retire to. My honest next neighbor and

那裏看火. 過了一會. 才曉得我一隻手直到肩上被火傷了. 傷得很利害. 我不能幫兒子搶救東西. 又不能阻止那火燒我們的粮食.

這時候鄰居聞警. 都來幫助. 他們也無法可施. 只好也同我們一樣. 站在那裏看. 我有些東西和紙幣. 存好了. 留給女兒的. 也都燒了. 只有廚房裏有一隻箱子. 內裏有些文件. 還有幾樣不相干的東西. 是我兒子早先搬出來的. 鄰居們大衆幫忙. 稍減輕我們現在的窘狀. 送些衣裳來我們穿. 搬幾樣家具同. 廚房用的東西來. 把我們外面另一間房. 稍爲布置. 到了天亮. 我們總算有一個很草草的地方. 作藏身之所. 我們

his children were not the least assiduous in providing us with everything necessary, and offering whatever consolation untutored[1] benevolence could suggest.

When the fears of my family had subsided, curiosity to know the cause of my long stay began to take place. Having therefore informed them of every particular, 1 proceeded to prepare them for the reception of our lost one; and, though we had nothing but wretchedness now to impart, I was willing to procure her a welcome to what we had. This task would have been more difficult but for our recent calamity, which had humbled my wife's pride and blunted it by more poignant[2] afflictions.

Being unable to go for my poor child myself, as my arm grew very painful, I sent my son and daughter, who soon returned, supporting the wretched delinquent, who had not the courage to look up at

緊靠的鄰居. 和他們的兒女們. 很出力的供給我們需用的東西. 還對我們說了許多出於至誠慈善的安慰話.

我家裏人受過驚恐. 心裏稍安之後. 就問起我爲什麼在外許久. 我把詳情說了一遍. 就預備接女兒回來. 我們現在只能分給他一分窮苦. 我却很願意歡迎他回家共享. 這一次天災. 把我女人的傲氣降低好些. 受過些刺骨痛苦. 把他傲氣的鋒芒. 也磨平了. 不然. 同他商量接女兒回家. 却有些爲難.

我重傷不能親去. 只好打發兒子女兒去接他. 不久他們回來. 扶着這個愁苦犯過的人. 不敢抬頭見他的母親. 無

---

1. Untutored, 非從教育得來的.　2. Poignant, 尖利.

her mother, whom no instructions of mine could persuade to a perfect reconciliation; for women have a much stronger sense of female error than men.

"Ah, madam," cried her mother, "this is but a poor place you are come to after so much finery. My daughter Sophy and I can afford but little entertainment to persons who have kept company only with people of distinction. Yes, Miss Livy, your poor father and I have suffered very much of late; but I hope Heaven will forgive you."

During this reception, the unhappy victim stood pale and trembling, unable to weep or to reply; but I could not continue a silent spectator of her distress; wherefore, assuming a degree of severity in my voice and manner, which was ever followed with instant submission, "I entreat, woman, that my words may now be marked once for all: I have here brought you back a poor deluded wanderer; her return to duty demands

論我如何說法.都不能勸我的女人.照舊的待遇這個女兒.因爲女人看得犯過.比男人重得多.

我女人對他這個女兒說道.瑪當.你經歷過多少繁華.你現在回來的.不過是個苦地方.我同我的女兒素緋雅.沒得什麼好的招待你這位只要同出色人來往的人.奧維雅小姊.你的可憐的父親同我.近來受罪也受得多了.但是我盼望上天赦你的罪.

當他們這樣接待他的時候.這個可憐被騙的人.站在那裏.臉色發青.哭也哭不出來.答也答不出來.但是我看見女兒如此的受痛苦.我不能不開口.我擺出很嚴厲的神色和聲音說.我每次如此.他無不立刻聽從的.我說道.女人.我勸你把我現在說的話.永遠記着.我現在把一個失足無所歸的人.帶回來給你.他旣回來.

the revival of our tender- ness. The real hardships of our life are now coming fast upon us; let us not, therefore, increase them by dissension among each other. If we live harmoni- ously together, we may yet be contented, as there are enough of us to· shut out the censuring world, and keep each other in countenance. The kind- ness of Heaven is promised to the penitent, and let ours be directed by the example. Heaven, we are assured, is much more pleased to view a repentant sinner than ninety-nine persons who have sup- ported a course of undeviat- ing rectitude. And this is right; for that single effort by which we stop short in the downhill path to perdition, is itself a greater exertion of virtue than a hundred acts of justice."

盡他女兒的職分. 我們就應該重新的慈愛他. 我們生活的實在痛苦. 現在來得很快. 我們不可以家裏不和睦. 加添痛苦. 我們若是能彀和睦. 還可以滿意. 因為我們人還多. 只要我們彼此都看得起. 就可以抵禦世人的非毀. 上天答應的. 凡是悔過的人. 都一體的待以慈愛. 我們可以學上天的樣子. 我們曉得的. 上天雖然喜歡看見有九十九個行為方正. 一點不走差的人. 但是尤其喜歡看見一個犯罪改悔的人. 這樣看法. 原是不錯的. 因為一次出力. 自己能攔住自己. 不再往下深入地獄. 比行一百次公道事. 費力得多.

CHAPTER XXIII

NONE BUT THE GUILTY CAN BE LONG AND COMPLETELY MISERABLE

第 二 十 三 回

惟 有 罪 人 是 完 全 愁 苦
（唐 希 爾 倚 勢 賴 婚）

Some assiduity was now required to make our present abode as convenient as possible, and we were soon again qualified to enjoy our former serenity. Being disabled myself from assisting my son in our usual occupations, I read to my family from the few books that were saved, and particularly from such as, by amusing the imagination, contributed to ease the heart. Our good neighbors, too, came every day with the kindest condolence, and fixed a time in which they were all to assist in repairing my former dwelling. Honest Farmer Williams was not last amongst these

且說我們要費些氣力. 才可以把現在住的地方布置利便. 不久又能殼同從前一樣過安閒日子. 我不能幫我的兒子照常工作. 我就把救出來的幾本書. 讀給家裏人聽. 特別挑那能頣養意境的書. 使他們聽了. 心境可以放寬些. 鄰居人家. 天天過來安慰我們. 又定了時刻. 幫忙補葺那被燒的房子. 威林也來願盡他的友誼.

287

visitors, but heartily offered his friendship. He would even have renewed his addresses to my daughter; but she rejected him in such a manner as totally repressed his future solicitations. Her grief seemed formed for continuing, and she was the only person of our little society that a week did not restore to cheerfulness. She now lost that unblushing innocence[1] which had once taught her to respect herself, and to seek pleasure by pleasing. Anxiety now had taken strong possession of her mind; her beauty began to be impaired with her constitution, and neglect still more contributed to diminish it. Every tender epithet bestowed on her sister brought a pang to her heart and a tear to her eye; and as one vice, though cured, ever plants others where it has been, so her former guilt, though driven out by repentance, left jealousy and envy behind. I strove a thousand

幫我們他還要求親．被我女兒拒絕．往後就不敢再求．我女兒的愁苦．總不能斷．過了一個星期．只有他一個人．仍是不高興的．他從前自知無過．自知無愧．曉得自愛．以令人歡喜．使自己歡喜．現在却不比從前了．自己知道慚愧．心裏總撇不開焦慮．身體漸不如從前康健．容貌自然不及從前．又不肯修飾．自然更差些．只要有人對他妹妹用個溫柔字眼．大女兒聽了就覺得傷心滴淚．大凡治好一種罪孽．往往又另在原地種一種罪孽．他悔過之後．把前次所犯之過逐出了．又留下妒忌．我用盡了一千個法子．

---

1. Unblushing innocence, 心地無虧；不知慚愧．

THE VICAR OF WAKEFIELD 279

ways to lessen her care, and even forgot my own pain in a concern for hers, collecting such amusing passages of history as a strong memory and some reading could suggest.— "Our happiness, my dear," I would say, "is in the power of One who can bring it about a thousand unforeseen ways that mock our foresight. If example be necessary to prove this, I'll give you a story, my child, told us by a grave, though sometimes a romancing,[1] historian.

"Matilda was married very young to a Neapolitan nobleman of the first quality, and found herself a widow and a mother at the age of fifteen. As she stood one day caressing her infant son in the open window of an apartment which hung over the river Volturna, the child, with a sudden spring, leaped from her arms into the flood below, and disappeared in a moment. The mother,

去減少他的憂慮. 因為照料他. 就忘了我自己痛苦. 凡我所記得的. 或因我讀書所想及的. 歷史內有趣的事. 收輯起來. 給他讀. 我對他說道. 我的寶貝. 我們的歡樂. 在上帝手上. 惟上帝有一千方法. 非人所預料的. 能使我們歡樂. 我們去預料. 也預料不出來. 你若要看一個榜樣. 我就讀一段古事給你聽. 這原是一位歷史家寫的. 他雖然有時不免杜撰. 却是一位很莊重的歷史家.

他說的是. 瑪提特. 很年青就嫁與一位尼蒲勒地方一位貴族. 十五歲就寡了. 只有一個孤子. 有一天. 他在臨河一個窗口. 撫弄這個兒子. 這孩子忽然一跳. 跳入河裏. 立刻就看不見了.

---

1. Romancing, 杜撰；以意為之.

struck with instant surprise, and making an effort to save him, plunged in after; but far from being able to assist the infant, she herself with great difficulty escaped to the opposite shore, just when some French soldiers were plundering the country on that side, who immediately made her their prisoner.

"As the war was then carried on between the French and Italians with the utmost inhumanity, they were going at once to perpetrate those two extremes suggested by appetite and cruelty. This base resolution, however, was opposed by a young officer, who, though their retreat required the utmost expedition, placed her behind him, and brought her in safety to his native city. Her beauty at first caught his eye; her merit, soon after, his heart. They were married; he rose to the highest posts; they lived long together, and were happy. But the felicity of a soldier can never be called permanent; after an interval of several years.

那母親大驚. 因要救那兒子. 自己也跳入河裏. 兒子是救不來. 他自己很費力才到了對岸. 剛好有些法國兵在那裏擄掠. 就把這女人擄去.

那時候. 正是法國同義大利打仗. 兩方都是慘無人道的. 那些法國兵就要動手. 作那極端暴虐的行為. 却有一位少年軍官不答應. 雖是正在敗退的時候. 少年軍官把女人放在他身後. 一路送去自己家鄉. 這女人的美貌. 先動這少年的眼. 這女人的德行. 更深入這少年的心. 兩人結了婚. 少年超升到最高級軍官. 兩人很歡樂. 相處很久. 但是軍官的歡樂. 是難以永久的. 過了數年. 他所帶的

THE VICAR OF WAKEFIELD

the troops which he commanded having met with a repulse, he was obliged to take shelter in the city where he had lived with his wife. Here they suffered a siege, and the city at length was taken. Few histories can produce more various instances of cruelty than those which the French and Italians at that time exercised upon each other. It was resolved by the victors upon this occasion to put all the French prisoners to death, but particularly the husband of the unfortunate Matilda, as he was principally instrumental in protracting the siege. Their determinations were in general executed almost as soon as resolved upon. The captive soldier was led forth, and the executioner with his sword stood ready, while the spectators in gloomy silence awaited the fatal blow, which was only suspended till the general, who presided as judge, should give the signal. It was in this interval of anguish and expectation, that Matilda came to take

軍隊敗退. 逃到一個地方. 是他夫婦曾經住過的. 敵軍來包圍. 不幸失守. 那時法義兩軍. 彼此對待的殘暴慘酷. 是歷史上所罕見的. 這一次得勝之軍. 要把所獲的法軍俘虜. 都要殺死. 他們最恨的是瑪提特的丈夫. 因爲是他主張死守的. 他們一商定這種慘酷辦法. 立刻就要實行. 於是把俘虜牽上前. 劊子手舉刀候令. 旁觀的只顧看殺人. 義國軍長當裁判官. 只要暗號一發. 劊子手就揮刀殺人. 正在這個慘酷的當口. 瑪提特走來. 同他的

her last farewell of her husband and deliverer, deploring her wretched situation, and the cruelty of fate, that had saved her from perishing by a premature death in the river Volturna, to be the spectator of still greater calamities. The general, who was a young man, was struck with surprise at her beauty, and pity at her distress; but with still stronger emotions when he heard her mention her former dangers. He was her son, the infant for whom she had encountered so much danger. He acknowledged her at once as his mother, and fell at her feet. The rest may be easily supposed, the captive was set free, and all the happiness that love, friendship, and duty could confer on each was united."

In this manner I would attempt to amuse[1] my daughter, but she listened with divided attention; for her own misfortunes engrossed[2] all the pity she

救命的丈夫永遠長辭. 這時候瑪提特自傷他的苦境. 嘆自己的命苦. 說道. 從前在河裏是萬死一生. 幸而遇救. 不料到了這個時候. 還要親眼目覩更慘酷的大禍. 那裁判的軍長. 是個少年. 一見瑪提特美貌. 很驚異. 又憐他這樣悽慘. 聽見他說從前所遇的危險. 更爲驚異. 這位軍長. 原來就是瑪提特的兒子. 瑪提特因爲他受了多少危險. 他立刻就認瑪提特作母親. 跪在地下. 後來的事. 是容易猜的. 那被俘的瑪提特的丈夫. 自然是釋放了. 各人彼此對待. 都能盡愛情友誼職分. 同過歡樂日子.

我就是怎樣的設法娛悅我的女兒. 他却不能專心的聽. 他從前是很能憐憫他人的不幸.

---

1. To amuse, 娛人; 使人心有所寄.   2. Engrossed, 聚精會神.

THE VICAR OF WAKEFIELD

once had for those of another, and nothing gave her ease. In company, she dreaded contempt; and in solitude she only found anxiety. Such was the color[1] of her wretchedness, when we received certain information that Mr. Thornhill was going to be married to Miss Wilmot, for whom I always suspected he had a real passion, though he took every opportunity before me to express his contempt both of her person and fortune. This news only served to increase poor Olivia's affliction; such a flagrant[2] breach of fidelity was more than her courage could support. I was resolved, however, to get more certain information, and to defeat, if possible, the completion of his designs, by sending my son to old Mr. Wilmot's with instructions to know the truth of the report, and to deliver Miss Wilmot a letter intimating Mr.

現在是他自己不幸.來不及憐憫他人.故此無論怎麼樣.他的心境總不能安.同衆人在一起.他是怕人不齒他.獨自一個的時候.就悶坐憂慮.這就是他悽慘困苦的情狀.有一天.我們得了消息.說是唐希爾快要同威小姐結婚.唐希爾雖屢次告訴我.他看不起威小姐這個人.也看不起他的財產.我却常疑心唐希爾是眞愛威小姐.我女兒聽見這消息.更加痛心.這樣悍然不顧的賴婚.如何能受得住.我打定主意.叫兒子去威府.打聽眞情.並帶一封信.給威小姐.把

1, Color, 此處作光景或情狀解. 2. Flagrant, 悍然不顧; 公然爲惡.

Thornhill's conduct in my family. My son went in pursuance of my directions; and in three days returned assuring us of the truth of the account, but that he had found it impossible to deliver the letter, which he was therefore obliged to leave, as Mr. Thornhill and Miss Wilmot were visiting round the country. They were to be married, he said, in a few days, having appeared together at church the Sunday before he was there, in great splendor, the bride attended by six young ladies, and he by as many gentlemen. Their approaching nuptials filled the whole country with rejoicing, and they usually rode out together in the grandest equipage that had been seen in the country for many years. All the friends of both families, he said, were there, particularly the squire's uncle, Sir William Thornhill, who bore so good a character. He added, that nothing but mirth and feasting were going forward, that all the country praised the young bride's beauty, and the

唐希爾對待我女兒的情形.告訴他.我這個意思.一來是要打探實情.二來.若是我辦得到.我要破壞這件事.我兒子奉命前去.三日回頭.說.消息是眞的.但是無法投遞那封信.只好留在那裏.因爲唐希爾同威小姐在附近地方遊覽上一個星期日.他們兩人同到教堂.鋪排得很闊.威小姐有六位少年女人陪伴.唐希爾是六個少年男子陪伴.聽說數日內.就要行結婚禮附近一帶人家.聽了這個喜信.都十分歡喜.他們兩個人.常同坐一輛極華麗的馬車出遊.鄉下地方許久不看見這樣的闊排場.我兒子又說道.男家女家的親友.都到了.很特別的一件事.就是唐希爾的叔叔.威廉唐希爾爵士.也來了.這一位的名譽甚好.又說道.那裏的人.除了尋樂同歡宴之外.並無別事.那一帶地方的人.都恭維威小姐怎樣的一個美女人.唐希爾怎

THE VICAR OF WAKEFIELD

bridegroom's fine person, and that they were immensely fond of each other; concluding that he could not help thinking Mr. Thornhill one of the most happy men in the world.

"Why, let him if he can," returned I; "but, my son, observe this bed of straw and unsheltering roof; those moldering walls and humid floor; my wretched body thus disabled by fire, and my children weeping round me for bread: you have come home, my child, to all this; yet here—even here—you see a man that would not for a thousand worlds[1] exchange situations. Oh, my children, if you could but learn to commune with your own hearts, and know what noble company you can make them, you would little regard the elegance and splendor of the worthless. Almost all men have been taught to call life a passage, and themselves the travelers. The similitude still may be improved

樣的一個美男子. 兩個人的愛情極深. 最後我兒子還說. 唐希爾是世界上第一個快樂人 { 這一段是借老牧師兒子口中暗寫一番人熱鬧奧維雅小姐却是一個人獨自傷心聞之自不傷痛欲死 }.

我答道. 唐希爾還能作人. 就讓他去作. 兒子. 你看看我睡的乾草鋪的牀. 上頭是不蔽風雨的房頂. 你看看四面發霉的牆. 發潮濕的地面. 看看我是受了火傷. 動不得. 兒女們圍住我啼哭求食. 你到威家去. 看見的是何等華麗歡樂. 你回來看見的. 是何等窮困愁苦. 然而你却要看看. 這裏還有一個人. 那怕拿一千個世界給我. 我也不肯同威家調換. 兒女們呀. 你們各人. 只要能殼同你們自己的心. 作個神交. 要曉得自己的心. 是一個極高貴的同伴. 你們就不大理會無價值的人的繁華富貴. 世上有許多人曉得. 浮生如過路. 人呢.

---

1. For a thousand worlds, 毋論什麼.

when we observe that the good are joyful and serene, like travelers that are going towards home: the wicked but by intervals happy, like travelers that are going into exile."

My compassion for my poor daughter, over-powered by this new dis-aster, interrupted what I had further to observe. I bade her mother support her, and after a short time she recovered. She ap-peared from that time more calm, and I imagined had gained a new degree of resolution; but appearances deceived me; for her tran-quillity was the languor of overwrought resentment. A supply of provisions, charitably sent us by my kind parishioners, seemed to diffuse new cheerfulness amongst the rest of the family, nor was I dis-pleased at seeing them once more sprightly and at ease. It would have been unjust to damp their satisfactions, merely to condole with resolute melancholy, or to burden them with a sadness they did not feel. Thus once more the tale went

不過是個過客. 這個比喻. 還可以改良些. 不如說. 好人心安而又樂. 如行客之歸家. 惡人不過有時快樂. 却如行客之遠戍.

再說. 這一個最不好的消息. 我女兒聽見. 更加難過. 暈過去了. 我十分可憐他. 只好不再往下說. 吩咐他的母親. 扶住他. 過了一會. 女兒醒過來. 好像是心裏安靜些. 我以爲他是新得了多幾分的鎮靜. 誰知不然. 不過因爲他痛恨過度. 疲乏已極. 反現出安靜來. 我教職屬下的人. 發了慈善心. 供給我們些食物. 我家裏的人. 除女兒之外. 都帶點高興之色. 我看見他們重新安閒活潑. 心裏也安些. 若是他們滿意. 我去抑遏他. 或是他們的憂悶. 是牢不可破的. 我去憐憫他. 或係我去添加他們並不曾覺得的愁苦. 完全都可以不必. 於是

round, and the song was demanded, and cheerfulness condescended to hover round our little habitation.

他們又是有說有笑的. 重新又說些古事. 唱唱歌. 我們這個小小的茅舍. 居然重見高興日子.

CHAPTER XXIV

FRESH CALAMITIES

第 二 十 四 回

新 禍 殃

（唐 希 爾 討 債 嚇 牧 師）

The next morning the sun arose with peculiar warmth for the season; so that we agreed to breakfast together on the honeysuckle bank: where, while we sat, my youngest daughter, at my request, joined her voice to the concert on the trees about us. It was in this place my poor Olivia first met her seducer, and every object served to recall her sadness. But that melancholy which is excited by objects of pleasure, or inspired by sounds of harmony, soothes the heart instead of corroding it. Her mother, too, upon this occasion, felt a pleasing distress, and wept, and loved her daughter as before. "Do, my pretty

再說第二天早上.太陽一出.比往常特別的暖.我們都到那金銀花堆旁吃早餐.我們坐在那裏的時候.我要我的小女兒唱歌.同樹上的鳥相和.當日奧維雅第一次遇着那負心的人.就在這裏.四圍景物.都令他傷心.但是令人歡喜的景物.或悅耳之聲.所觸發的愁懷.是安人心的.不是傷人心的.這一次他的母親.也覺得有一種苦中之樂.一面滴淚.一面仍同舊日.愛他的女兒.說道.我的美

THE VICAR OF WAKEFIELD

Olivia," cried she, "let us have that little melancholy air your papa was so fond of: your sister Sophy has already obliged us. Do, child; it will please your old father." She complied in a manner so exquisitely[1] pathetic as moved me.

貌奧維雅. 你唱那老父喜歡的淒涼短調. 你的妹妹已經唱過一調. 你也唱唱. 使老父喜歡. 他聽了這話. 果然就唱. 唱得十分悲哀動人.

When lovely woman stoops to folly,
　And finds too late that men betray,
What charm can soothe her melancholy,
　What art can wash her guilt away?

The only art her guilt to cover,
　To hide her shame from every eye,
To give repentance to her lover,
　And wring his bosom, is—to die.

當一個美貌女子. 已墮落. 作了失檢的行爲. 受了欺騙. 等到覺得晚了. 以什麼的手段. 可以安慰他的愁. 自慚以洗遮人看. 唯一的術. 要各人看不見他的羞辱. 使他的罪過. 並使他的愛人. 悔過傷心. 那唯一的方法. 只有一死.

As she was concluding the last stanza, to which an interruption in her voice from sorrow gave peculiar softness, the appearance of Mr. Thornhill's equipage at a distance alarmed us all, but particularly increased the uneasiness of my eldest daughter, who, desirous of shunning her betrayer, returned to the house with her sister. In a few minutes he was alighted from

他快唱完末一段. 聲音爲哀情所阻. 音調特別柔和. 我們遠遠看見唐希爾的車馬. 未免一驚. 我大女兒更覺不安. 不願同那負心人見面. 同他妹妹躲在屋裏. 過了幾分鐘. 他下了車. 走向

---

1. Exquisitely, 十分.

his chariot; and making up to the place where I was still sitting, inquired after my health with his usual air of familiarity.—"Sir," replied I, "your present assurance only serves to aggravate the baseness of your character; and there was a time when I would have chastised your insolence for presuming thus to appear before me. But now you are safe; for age has cooled my passions, and my calling[1] restrains them."

"I vow, my dear sir," returned he, "I am amazed at all this; nor can I understand what it means! I hope you don't think your daughter's late excursion with me had anything criminal in it."

"Go," cried I; "thou art a wretch—a poor, pitiful wretch, and every way a liar; but your meanness secures you from my anger! Yet, sir, I am descended from a family that would not have borne this! And so, thou vile thing, to

我坐的地方. 很慣熟的樣子問候我. 我答道. 先生. 你這樣的厚臉皮. 不過替你的卑劣人格加重些. 若是從前的話. 你這樣膽敢來見我. 我是要懲罰你的無禮行為. 現在我又老了. 消耗了火氣. 我又是個教士. 禁阻我. 你却沒得怕的.

他答道. 我聽得很詫異. 又不懂你什麽意思. 我盼望你不要想我前者同你的女兒出外. 有什麽犯刑事的行為.

我說道. 你是個下流可憐的惡人. 完全是個說謊的人. 你這種卑劣行為. 保全你不致受我的譴怒. 你須曉得. 我的先人是不受的. 你這個

---

1. Calling, 行業; 職業.

gratify a momentary pas-
sion, thou hast made one
poor creature wretched for
life, and polluted a family
that had nothing but
honor for their portion."[1]

"If she or you," returned
he, "are resolved to be
miserable, I cannot help
it. But you may still be
happy: and whatever
opinion you may have
formed of me, you shall
ever find me ready to
contribute to it. We can
marry her to another in
a short time: and, what
is more, she may keep her
lover beside; for I protest,
I shall ever continue to
have a true regard for[2]
her."

I found all my passions
alarmed at this new de-
grading proposal; for
though the mind may often
be calm under great in-
juries, little villainy can at
any time get within the
soul and sting it into rage.

"Avoid my sight, thou
reptile," cried I, "nor continue to insult me with thy

下流人. 因爲解你一時
的渴慾. 就不顧把一個
可憐的女子. 害了終身.
汙辱了一個最顧體面
的寒家.

他答道. 或是他. 或是
你. 一定要愁苦. 我也無
法. 然而你還可以歡樂.
無論你當我怎麼樣壞.
我永遠可以出力使你
歡樂. 再過些時. 你可以
把他嫁與他人. 我認眞
的說. 我永遠還是眞以
好意待他的 { 唐希爾的話
實在不中聽
富貴人爲惡眞是行所無事近
世的離婚案仍是以金錢了事
者爲
多 }.

我一聽他這卑鄙的
話. 我的怒意大作. 一個
人受了極大的傷害. 倒
能鎮靜. 較小的惡劣行
爲. 反能深刺腦筋. 令人
生氣.

我說道. 你這個畜類.
你走開. 不要再在我面

---

1. Portion, 妝奩; 產業. 2. Have a regard for, 關切; 以禮相待; 好意相待.

presence. Were my brave son at home, he would not suffer this; but I am old and disabled, and every way undone."

"I find," cried he, "you are bent upon obliging me to talk in a harsher manner than I intended. But as I have shown you what may be hoped from my friendship, it may not be improper to represent what may be the consequences of my resentment. My attorney, to whom your late bond has been transferred, threatens hard, nor do I know how to prevent the course of justice, except by paying the money myself, which, as I have been at some expenses lately, previous to my intended marriage, is not so easy to be done. And then my steward talks of driving for the rent: it is certain he knows his duty; for I never trouble myself with affairs of that nature. Yet still I could wish to serve you, and even to have you and your daughter present at my marriage, which is

前辱我. 若是我有勇的兒子在家. 他一定不受你這番汙辱. 但是我老了. 又動不得. 奈何你不得.

他說道. 原來你一定要我對你說兇話. 我已經告訴過你. 你當我是個朋友. 還可以盼望我幫你. 我又不能不告訴你. 你若得罪我. 又是一樣的結果. 你前些日子交給我的借據. 我已交與我的律師. 他追這筆款. 追得很緊. 除了把錢還清. 我却無法攔阻他們照正法律而行. 我快要結婚. 花錢已經不少. 要我完清那筆款. 却很不容易. 我的帳房又說過. 要捉你的牲畜抵債. 這種事我向來是不管的. 我的帳房曉得他應辦的事. 然而我還願意替你出力. 還願意你同你的女兒來看我結婚 {此一冊}{請毋}

THE VICAR OF WAKEFIELD

shortly to be solemnized[1] with Miss Wilmot; it is even the request of my charming Arabella herself, whom I hope you will not refuse."

"Mr. Thornhill," replied I, "hear me once for all; as to your marriage with any but my daughter, that I will never consent to; and though your friendship could raise me to a throne, or your resentment sink me to the grave, yet would I despise both. Thou hast once woefully, irreparably deceived me. I reposed my heart upon thine honor, and have found its baseness. Never more therefore expect friendship from me. Go, and possess what fortune has given thee— beauty, riches, health, and pleasure. Go, and leave me to want, infamy, disease and sorrow. Yet, humbled as I am, shall my heart still vindicate its dignity; and though thou hast my forgiveness, thou shalt ever have my contempt."

乃辱人太甚 } 我不久. 就要同威小姐行結婚禮. 這却是威小姐的意思. 我望你不要拒絕不來.

我答道. 唐希爾. 你聽我最末後的一番話. 你除了同我女兒結婚之外. 毋論你同什麼人結婚. 我都不答應. 那怕你的交情. 可以抬舉我做皇帝. 那怕你懷恨我. 逼壓我入墳墓. 我兩樣都看不起. 你已經一次騙我. 騙得我很慘. 騙得我很無法補救. 我存心原當你是個有道德顧體面的人. 誰知你是個惡劣人. 你永遠不要盼望我當你是朋友. 你去罷. 你去享受錢財能買來的美貌奢華康健快樂. 你走罷. 讓我受我的損失名譽疾病困苦罷. 我雖貧賤. 我的可敬的心地端正. 仍是要維持的. 你雖然得我的恕宥. 我永遠是看不起你.

---

1. Solemnized, 敬謹行禮.

"If so," returned he, "depend upon it you shall feel the effects of this insolence, and we shall shortly see which is the fittest object of scorn— you or me." Upon which, he departed abruptly.

My wife and son, who were present at this interview, seemed terrified with the apprehension. My daughters, also, finding that he was gone, came out to be informed of the result of our conference, which, when known, alarmed them not less than the rest. But as to myself, I disregarded the utmost stretch of his malevolence; he had already struck the blow, and now I stood prepared to repel every new effort; like one of those instruments[1] used in the art of war, which, however thrown, still presents a point to receive the enemy.

We soon, however, found that he had not threatened in vain; for the very next morning his steward came to demand my annual rent,

他答道. 既然如此. 你看罷. 你要受這樣無禮的結果. 你不久就要曉得還是我被人看不起. 還是你被人看不起. 說完. 他掉過頭走了 ｛欺人太甚 氣逼｝.

我同他會面的時候. 我女人我兒子都在場. 聽見他這番恐嚇話. 很害怕. 我兩女兒知道他走了. 出來. 聽見我們會面的結果. 也同他們一樣害怕. 我呢. 都不管他恩將仇報到什麼地步. 他是痛擊了一下. 現在我預備抵抗他再打. 如同有一種東西. 雖然倒在地下. 還突出一個尖子. 對待敵人.

不久他就實行他的恐嚇. 第二天早上. 他的帳房就來討租. 因爲接

---

1. Those instruments, 指鐵蒺藜.

THE VICAR OF WAKEFIELD 295

which, by the train of accidents already related, I was unable to pay. The consequence of my incapacity was his driving my cattle that evening and their being appraised and sold the next day for less than half their value. My wife and children now therefore entreated me to comply upon any terms, rather than incur certain destruction. They begged of me to admit his visits once more, and used all their little eloquence to paint the calamities I was going to endure—the terrors of a prison in so rigorous a season as the present, with the danger that threatened my health from the late accident that happened by the fire. But I continued inflexible.[1]

"Why, my treasures," cried I,—"why will you thus attempt to persuade me to the thing that is not right? My duty has taught me to forgive him; but my conscience will not permit me to approve.

連出了幾件事.我不能給租.當日將晚時候.那帳房果然把我的牲口趕走.第二天估價賣了.只賣得原價一半.我女人同兒女們.勸我寗可依照唐希爾無論什麼的辦事.免得把家都毀了.他們還求我讓唐希爾再來我們家一次.他們還用盡他們演說的本事.把我將來所受的苦.說得十分利害.現在天氣嚴寒.入監是要受無限若干的苦.況且新近又受過火傷.身體是要受危險的.他們雖然說了這許多可怕的話.我總是不聽.

我答道.我的寶貝們.你們為什麼設法勸我做不對的事呢.我的職分.教我恕他的罪.但是我的良心.不讓我以他

---

1. Inflexible, 不肯通融.

Would you have me applaud to the world what my heart must internally condemn? Would you have me tamely sit down and flatter our infamous betrayer; and, to avoid a prison, continually suffer the more galling bonds of mental confinement? No—never. If we are to be taken from this abode, only let us hold to the right, and wherever we are thrown, we can still retire to a charming apartment, when we can look round our own hearts with intrepidity and with pleasure."

In this manner we spent that evening. Early the next morning, as the snow had fallen in great abundance in the night, my son was employed in clearing it away, and opening a passage before the door. He had not been thus engaged long when he came running in with looks all pale, to tell us that two strangers, whom he knew to be officers of justice, were making towards the house.

Just as he spoke, they came in: and approaching

的行事爲然．我心裏不以他．爲然的事．你們要我對天下人讚美他麼．你們要我安安靜靜的坐下來巴結這個喪失名譽陷害我們的人麼．因爲要免得入監．身體被困．你們要我繼續去受靈魂被縛的加重痛苦麼．這是我永遠不能作的．倘若我們被逐出這個住宅．我們只要抱住正道．無論人家把我們摔在什麼地方．我們還可以退到一所美宅｛大約指良心曰｝．我們還可以很大膽很歡樂的看我們的心｛大約是指雖然無家可歸却是問心無愧之意｝．

這天晚上．我們就是這樣過的．第二天早上．因爲昨夜下了大雪．我的兒子在門前掃雪．掃了不過一會．忽然臉都青了．跑進來說．有兩個生人．他曉得他們是衙役．向我們家裏來．

他說話時候．這兩個人走進來．走近我的牀

the bed where I lay, after previously informing me of their employment and business, made me their prisoner, bidding me prepare to go with them to the county jail, which was eleven miles off.

"My friends," said I, "this is severe weather in which you have come to take me to a prison; and it is particularly unfortunate at this time, as one of my arms has lately been burnt in a terrible manner, and it has thrown me into a slight fever, and I want clothes to cover me, and I am now too weak and old to walk far in such deep snow: but if it must be so—"

I then turned to my wife and children, and directed them to get together what few things were left us, and to prepare immediately for leaving this place. I entreated them to be expeditious, and desired my son to assist his eldest sister, who, from a consciousness that she was the cause of all our calamities, was fallen, and had lost anguish in insensibility. I

邊.告訴我他們是什麼. 爲什麼來的.把我拘捕. 叫我預備入獄.那監獄 離家有三十多里地.

我說道.朋友們.正是 嚴寒天氣.你們來拘我 時候.又特別的不湊巧. 因爲我兩手新近才受 過火傷.現在微微的發 熱.我要披上些衣裳.天 冷雪深.我又老又病.難 以遠行.倘若一定這 樣....

我回頭吩咐女人兒 女收拾幾樣剩下的東 西.預備立刻就走.我還 勸他們趕快收拾.叫兒 子去扶大女兒.因爲他 曉得自己是我們受害 的禍根.暈倒了.他失了 知覺.就忘了心痛.我的

encouraged my wife, who, pale and trembling, clasped our affrighted little ones in her arms, that clung to her bosom in silence, dreading to look round at the strangers. In the meantime my youngest daughter prepared for our departure; and as she received several hints to use dispatch, in about an hour we were ready to depart.

女人臉青發抖. 兩個小孩看見生人害怕. 倒在他母親懷裏. 不敢響. 我女人兩手緊緊的抱住這兩個小的. 我只好說話安慰我的女人. 當下我的二女兒收拾東西. 預備我們離家. 他屢屢被催. 有一點鐘光景. 預備好了.

CHAPTER XXV

NO SITUATION, HOWEVER WRETCHED IT SEEMS, BUT
HAS SOME SORT OF COMFORT ATTENDING IT

第 二 十 五 回

人 的 境 遇 無 論 怎 樣 的 困 苦 也 還 短 不
了 有 些 舒 服
（老 牧 師 監 獄 遇 故 人）

We set forward from this peaceful neighborhood and walked on slowly. My eldest daughter, being enfeebled by a slow fever, which had begun for some days to undermine her constitution, one of the officers, who had a horse, kindly took her behind him; for even these men cannot entirely divest themselves of humanity. My son led one of the little ones by the hand, and my wife the other, while I leaned upon my youngest girl, whose tears fell not for her own but my distresses.

We were now got from my late dwelling about two

且 說 我 們 離 開 這 個 安 樂 地 方. 慢 慢 往 前 走. 我 的 大 女 兒 發 微 熱. 暗 傷 他 的 身 體. 慢 慢 的 軟 弱 下 來. 有 一 個 衙 役 有 一 匹 馬. 讓 他 騎 在 背 後. 可 見 這 種 人 也 不 是 全 無 人 道. 我 兒 子 領 着 一 個 小 的. 我 的 女 人 也 領 着 一 個. 我 靠 着 二 女 兒 走. 他 見 我 愁 苦. 爲 我 滴 淚.

我 們 走 了 有 六 七 里 路. 看 見 一 羣 人 追 來 大

miles, when we saw a crowd running and shouting behind us, consisting of about fifty of my poorest parishioners. These, with dreadful imprecations, soon seized upon the two officers of justice; and swearing they would never see their minister go to jail while they had a drop of blood to shed in his defense, were going to use them with great severity. The consequence might have been fatal had I not immediately interposed, and with some difficulty rescued the officers from the hands of the enraged multitude. My children, who looked upon my delivery now as certain, appeared transported with joy, and were incapable of containing their raptures. But they were soon undeceived, upon hearing me address the poor deluded people who came, as they imagined, to do me service.

"What, my friends!" cried I; "and is this the way you love me? Is this the manner you obey the instructions I have given you from the pulpit?

喊. 大約有五十多人. 都是我教屬下最貧的人. 滿嘴是很可怕的詛咒的話. 捉住兩個衙役. 禱咒的說. 只要他們還有一滴血. 也要保護他們的牧師. 不能瞪着眼. 看他們的牧師捉將官裏去. 正要動手難為兩個衙役. 假使不是我立刻干預. 不知要鬧到什麼地步〔鄉愚有義氣〕. 很費了事. 才把兩個衙役救了. 不致遭這班鄉下人的毒手. 我的兒女們. 以為我一定遇救的. 很高興. 禁不住十分歡喜. 這班鄉下人無知. 以為這一來可以救我. 我就對這羣不曉事的人解說明白. 我的兒女們. 也才曉得不對.

我對這班鄉下人說道. 我的朋友們. 這是你們愛我麼. 我在教堂裏講臺上. 是什麼樣教你

Thus to fly in the face of justice, and bring down ruin on yourselves and me! Which is your ringleader? Show me the man that has thus seduced you. As sure as he lives, he shall feel my resentment. Alas! my dear deluded flock,[1] return back to the duty you owe to God, to your country, and to me. I shall yet, perhaps, one day see you in greater felicity here, and contribute to make your lives more happy. But let it at least be my comfort when I pen my fold for immortality,[2] that not one here shall be wanting."

They now seemed all repentance; and melting into tears, came one after the other to bid me farewell. I shook each tenderly by the hand; and leaving them my blessing, proceeded forward without meeting any further interruption. Some hours before night, we reached the town, or rather village; for it consisted but of a few

們的.你們聽我的教訓是這樣的麼.你們現在是違抗法律.害我.兼害你們自己.你們爲首的是誰.是誰引你們走錯路的.他一定受我的怪責.哎.我的寶貝走錯路的牧羣呀.你們應盡你們的職分對上帝.對國家.對我.將來總還要有一天.我看見你們比現在快樂.我還要盡點力.使你們略加歡樂.但是我收攬我的牧羣.歸入永遠長存的時候.我盼望今日在這裏的人.一個也不差.我就心安了.

他們聽了.才後悔.都笑起來.一個一個的走過來送別.我每人都同他拉手.保佑他們.然後向前走.並無別的攔阻.天還未黑.我們就到了那市鎮.其實不過是個鄉村.從前的富麗都沒有了.只剩下不多的幾

---

1. Flock, 羊羣；牧羣；受牧師教導之人衆. 2. Pen my fold for immortality, 此一句極爲人所傳誦指末日受判而言.

mean houses, having lost all its former opulence, and retaining no marks of its ancient superiority but the jail.

Upon entering, we put up at an inn, where we had such refreshments as could most readily be procured; and I supped with my family with my usual cheerfulness. After seeing them properly accommodated for that night, I next attended the sheriff's officers to the prison, which had formerly been built for the purposes of war, and consisted of one large apartment, strongly grated and paved with stone, common to both felons and debtors at certain hours in the four-and-twenty. Besides this, every prisoner had a separate cell where he was locked in for the night.

I expected, upon my entrance, to find nothing but lamentations and various sounds of misery; but it was very different. The prisoners seemed all employed in one common design— that of forgetting thought in merriment or clamor, I was apprised of the usual

間窮房子.古時高等建築的古蹟都完了.只剩了一個監獄.

我們到了這地方.先在小客店住下.吃了點現成的食物.我同家裏人吃晚飯.還是照常的高興.我把他們安頓好.過這一夜.我就跟着衙役入了牢監.這個地方是從前爲打仗築的.有一間大房子.石板鋪地.四面都有鐵條.重囚兇犯和債犯.每天有幾點鐘同聚這裏.每個犯人.另四一個小牢.晚上加鎖.

我初進去的時候.盼望聽見的是哀號愁歎之聲.誰知不然.所有的犯人.都是一樣的用意.不是快樂.就是叫喊.把什麼思想都忘了.我一進去.他們就告訴我.初

perquisite[1] required upon these occasions; and immediately complied with the demand, though the little money I had was very near being all exhausted. This was immediately sent away for liquor, and the whole prison soon was filled with riot, laughter, and profaneness.

"How?" cried I to myself; "shall men so very wicked be cheerful, and shall I be melancholy? I feel only the same confinement with them, and I think I have more reason to be happy."

With such reflections, I labored to become cheerful; but cheerfulness was never yet produced by effort, which is itself painful. As I was sitting, therefore, in a corner of the jail, in a pensive posture, one of my fellow prisoners came up, and sitting by me, entered into conversation. It was my constant rule in life never to avoid the conversation of any man who seemed to desire it; for,

進監是要花例錢的. 我雖然剩了幾個錢. 也快要用完了. 只好拿出來給他們. 他們拿到這點錢. 立刻就買酒吃. 不到一會工夫. 全個監裏都是亂打亂鬧. 大笑. 和褻瀆神聖的話.

我對自己說道. 他們這種惡人. 都能高興. 我爲什麼反去憂愁. 我與他們相同的. 不過是同監在一個地方. 我一想. 我很有許多道理. 應該比他們歡樂得多.

我心裏這樣想過之後. 我就竭力的也要高興. 但是費力去求高興. 是高興不來的. 一費力就是苦痛. 我一個人坐在監裏的一個角頭. 在那裏想念. 有一個同監的人走來. 坐在我身邊. 同我交談. 我向來的規則. 是只要有人想同我談. 我是無不同他談的. 我

___

1. Perquisite, 例錢; 陌規; 例得好處.

if good, I might profit by his instruction; if bad, he might be assisted by mine. I found this to be a knowing man of strong, unlettered sense, but with a thorough knowledge of the world, as it is called—or, more properly speaking, of human nature on the wrong side. He asked me if I had taken care to provide myself with a bed, which was a circumstance I had never once attended to.

"That's unfortunate," cried he; "as you are allowed here nothing but straw, and your apartment is very large and cold. However, you seem to be something of a gentleman; and as I have been one myself in my time, part of my bedclothes are heartily at your service."

I thanked him, professing my surprise at finding such humanity in a jail in misfortunes: adding, to let him see that I was a scholar, that "the sage ancient seemed to understand the value of company in affliction when he said, 'Ton kosmon aire, ei dos

的意思是. 若是他談得好. 我領他的教. 他若談得不好. 是他領我的教. 我覺得現在這個人. 是個曉事的. 頗有不從學問得來的見識. 有有力量的見識. 人情世故. 是很深透明白. 所謂世情說破了. 就是世人的惡劣性情心理. 他問我預備好竝沒有. 這一層. 我却並朱想到.

他答道. 這却是不幸. 你的牢是很大很冷. 他們這裏. 只給你些乾草. 但是你像是個上等人. 我從前也是個上等人. 我的被褥. 你可以用.

我謝謝他說. 想不到在不幸人堆裏. 又是在監獄裏. 居然有講人道的. 我要他曉得. 我是個學者. 又說道. 有一位古人. 曉得患難朋友之可貴. 曾說過. 你只要把我的朋友留下給我. 你可

THE VICAR OF WAKEFIELD

ton etairon';[1] and, in fact," continued I, "what is the world if it affords only solitude?"

"You talk of the world, sir," returned my fellow prisoner; "*the world is in its dotage, and yet the cosmogony, or creation of the world, has puzzled the philosophers of every age. What a medley of opinions have they not broached upon the creation of the world. Sanconiathon, Manetho, Berosus, and Ocellus Lucanus, have all attempted it in vain. The latter has these words, 'Anarchon, ara kai atelutaion to pan,' which implies*"—"I ask pardon, sir," cried I, "for interrupting so much learning; but I think I have heard all this before. Have I not had the pleasure of once seeing you at Welbridge Fair, and is not your name Ephraim Jenkinson?" At this demand he only sighed. "I suppose you must recollect," resumed I, "one Dr.

以把什麼東西都拿去.接着又說道.倘若人生在世.沒得一個朋友.還要什麼世界呢.

他答道.你談到世界.世界已經到了老糊塗的程度了.然而世界是如何創造的.歷來的哲學家都迷惑了.對於這個問題.發表了一大堆東拉西扯七雜八湊的意見〔以下是一希臘短句 此是第十四回老頭子騙子對牧師說過的話這次又說牧師記性好聽了一牛就打叉盤問他〕.我說道.我打叉打斷這些學問.求你恕我.這些話我好像從前聽過.是不是我從前在某處同你會過.你是不是叫伊法雷金京森麼〔見第十四回〕.我這一問.他歎了一口氣.我接着說

---

1. *Ton kosmon aire, ei dos ton etairon*, 只要有朋友, 世界都可以不要.

Primrose from whom you bought a horse?"

He now at once recollected me; for the gloominess of the face and the approaching night had prevented his distinguishing my features before. "Yes, sir," returned Mr. Jenkinson, "I remember you perfectly well; I bought a horse, but forgot to pay for him. Your neighbor Flamborough is the only prosecutor I am any way afraid of at the next assizes; for he intends to swear positively against me as a coiner.[1] I am heartily sorry, sir, I ever deceived you, or indeed any man; for you see," continued he, showing his shackles, "what my tricks have brought me to."

"Well, sir," replied I, "your kindness in offering me assistance when you could expect no return shall be repaid with my endeavors to soften or totally suppress Mr. Flamborough's evidence, and I will send my son to him

道. 你還記得普博士麼. 你買過他一匹馬.

他立刻就記得. 大約因爲天色將晚. 監房裏黑暗. 故此他起初不認得我. 金京森答道. 先生. 我很記得你. 我買一匹馬. 忘記付錢 {這兩句說騙了一匹馬不過說得好聽些}. 下次開堂告我的人. 我只怕你鄰居法林巴. 因爲他要告我用假支票. 我很惋惜我騙你. 和騙別人. 他指脚鐐給我看. 接着說道. 我因爲行騙弄到這個地步.

我答道. 好呀. 先生. 你並不盼望什麽報酬. 願意帮助我. 我却要報答你. 我出力勸法林巴. 或是減輕或是壓住告你的證據. 我一有機會. 就打發我的兒子去見法林巴

---

1. Coiner, 私鑄犯；此處指用假支票.

for that purpose the first
opportunity; nor do I in
the least doubt but he will
comply with my request;
and as to my own evidence,
you need be under no un-
easiness about that."

"Well, sir," cried he,
"all the return I can make
shall be yours. You shall
have more than half my
bedclothes to-night, and
I'll take care to stand your
friend in the prison, where
I think I have some in-
fluence."

I thanked him, and could
not avoid being surprised at
the present youthful change
in his spect,[1] for at the
time I had seen him before
he appeared at least sixty.

"Sir," answered he,
"you are little acquainted
with the world; I had at
that time false hair, and
have learned the art of
counterfeiting every age
from seventeen to seventy.
Ah! sir, had I but bestowed
half the pains in learning
a trade that I have in
learning to be a scoundrel,
I might have been a rich

辦這件事. 我絲毫無疑.
法林巴可以聽我勸. 至
於我的見證. 請你放心.
不必憂慮{寫老牧師之寬厚}.

他說道. 好呀. 先生.
所有我的一切報酬. 都
是你的. 今晚我分給你
多半的被褥 我在監裏.
有點勢力. 我留意作你
的朋友. 帮助你.

我謝謝他. 看見他現
在變得很年輕. 倒有點
詫異. 因爲初會他的時
候. 他的面貌至少有六
十歲.

他答道. 先生. 你不甚
曉得世故. 我初見你的
時候. 披上假頭髮. 我學
會了假裝年歲. 從十七
歲到七十歲. 我都會裝
哎. 先生. 我費了多少苦
心. 去學行騙. 假使我只
費一半苦心. 去務正業.
到了這個時候. 我可以

---

1. Aspect, 景象; 風景; 狀貌.

man at this day. But, rogue as I am, I may still be your friend, and that, perhaps, when you least expect it."

We were now prevented from further conversation by the arrival of the jailer's servants, who came to call over the prisoners' names, and to lock up for the night. A fellow also, with a bundle of straw for my bed, attended, who led me along a dark, narrow passage into a room paved like the common prison; and in one corner of this I spread my bed, and the clothes given me by my fellow prisoner; which done, my conductor, who was civil enough, bade me a good night. After my usual meditations, and having praised my Heavenly Corrector, I laid myself down and slept with the utmost tranquillity till morning.

作個富翁了. 我雖是個騙子. 到你想不到的時候. 我還可以作你的朋友.

這時候. 獄卒來了. 我們談話就停住. 獄卒是來點名. 把犯人關鎖通夜. 又來了一個人. 拿把乾草. 領我走過一條黑暗過道. 進去一間平常監房. 我在房角上作一個鋪. 把金京森給我的被褥鋪上. 那個人還很客氣的說一聲請安睡. 我就同向來一樣. 想念一會子. 禱謝了上帝躺下安眠. 睡至天亮.

CHAPTER XXVI

A REFORMATION IN THE JAIL—TO MAKE LAWS COMPLETE, THEY SHOULD REWARD AS WELL AS PUNISH

第 二 十 六 回

犯 人 悔 過　　定 法 律 須 有 賞 有 罰
（牧 師 講 道 勸 囚 犯）

The next morning early I was awakened by my family, whom I found in tears at my bedside. The gloomy strength of everything about us, it seems, had daunted them. I gently rebuked their sorrow, assuring them I had never slept with greater tranquillity: and next inquired after my eldest daughter, who was not among them. They informed me that yesterday's uneasiness and fatigue had increased her fever, and it was judged proper to leave her behind. My next care was to send my son to procure a room or two to lodge the family in, as near the prison as conveniently could be found. He

且說第二天早上. 我被家裏的人來驚醒. 我看見他在我牀邊滴淚. 大約是看見四圍慘淡情景. 受了一驚. 我稍為責備他們. 為什麼憂愁. 又告訴他們. 我向來未有如昨夜的安睡. 因為大女兒未來. 我問他怎麼樣. 他們說. 因為昨天心裏不安. 又受了些勞頓. 熱度略增. 只好留他在店裏. 我又打發兒子去租一兩間屋子. 暫住家眷. 要離得監獄極近.

obeyed, but could only find one apartment, which was hired at a small expense for his mother and sisters, the jailer, with humanity, consenting to let him and his two little brothers lie in the prison with me. A bed was therefore prepared for them in a corner of the room, which I thought answered very conveniently. I was willing, however, previously to know whether my little children chose to lie in a place which seemed to fright them upon entrance.

"Well," cried I, "my good boys, how do you like your bed? I hope you are not afraid to lie in this room, dark as it appears?"

"No, papa," says Dick; "I am not afraid to lie anywhere where you are."

"And I," says Bill, who was yet but four years old, "love every place best that my papa is in."

After this, I allotted to each of the family what they were to do. My daughter was particularly directed to watch her declining sister's health; my wife was to attend me; my

他奉命去找.只找着一間屋子.花些少房錢住女眷們.管監的有點慈心.讓我三個兒子同我宿在牢裏.就在牢的一角鋪了牀.也還便當.我却預先問孩子們.他們一進監有點害怕.現在宿在監裏.願意不願意.

我說道.好孩子們.你看你們的牀.好不好.屋裏是很黑的.你們不害怕嗎.

狄克答道.爸爸.我不怕.你所在的地方.我不怕睡.

比勒那時才四歲.說道.我頂愛爸爸所在的地方.

我以後分派家屬每人應作的事.我叫二女兒特別留心他姊姊日見沉重的病體.我的女人招呼我.兩個小的讀

little boys were to read to me; "And as for you, my son," continued I, "it is by the labor of your hands we must all hope to be supported. Your wages as a day laborer will be fully sufficient, with proper frugality, to maintain us all, and comfortably, too. Thou art now sixteen years old, and hast strength, and it was given thee, my son, for very useful purposes; for it must save from famine your helpless parents and family. Prepare, then, this evening, to look out for work against to-morrow, and bring home every night what money you earn for our support."

Having thus instructed him, and settled the rest, I walked down to the common prison, where I could enjoy more air and room. But I was not long there when the execrations, lewdness, and brutality, that invaded me on every side, drove me back to my apartment again. Here I sat for some time, pondering

書給我聽.我對摩西說道.至於你呢.我們只好靠你兩手作工養我們的了.你每天作散工的工錢.雖不多.若是省儉的用.也彀養我們.並且很舒服的了.你今年十六歲.也有氣力.氣力是極有用處的.你要用來救你的無告的父母同手足.免得捱飢餓.你今晚就去預備找明天的工作.每天晚上.把工錢帶回來養家.

我吩咐了他.又安排好餘人的事.我就走到眾囚犯聚會的大屋子去.享受空氣.那裏也寬敞些.到那裏不久.四面八方都是呪罵的話.下賤無恥的行為.和兇暴的舉動.我實在是受不慣.只好跑回我自己的牢裏坐下.思想了好一

upon the strange infatuation[1] of wretches who, finding all mankind in open arms against them, were laboring to make themselves a future and a tremendous enemy.

Their insensibility excited my highest compassion, and blotted my own uneasiness from my mind. It even appeared a duty incumbent[2] upon me to attempt to reclaim them. I resolved, therefore, once more to return, and in spite of their contempt, to give them my advice, and conquer them by perseverance. Going, therefore, among them again, I informed Mr. Jenkinson of my design, at which he laughed heartily, but communicated it to the rest. The proposal was received with the greatest good humor, as it promised to afford a new fund of entertainment to persons who had now no other resource for mirth but what could be derived from ridicule or debauchery.

會.這班可憐的惡人.深陷於罪.看見世人無不忿恨反對他們.他們也竭力的作成世人將來的大仇敵.

他們這樣無知無識.激動我憐憫之心.把我自心的不安.都刷得淨盡.我還得去設法感化他們.這是我分內的事.我於是立意再出去.無論他們怎麼樣羞辱我.我還是勸導他們.憑我百折不回的志願.降伏他們.我走到他們隊裏.把我的意思.告訴金京森.他聽了大笑.却告訴了大衆.大衆聽了我這個意思.却也還很高興.因爲這班人.什麼開頑笑尋樂的方法都試遍了.只好靠挖苦嘲笑.或作壞事.好去開心.

---

1. Infatuation, 此處作深陷於罪解. 2. Incumbent, 分內;在職

I therefore read them a portion of the service with a loud, unaffected voice, and found my audience perfectly merry upon the occasion. Lewd whispers, groans of contrition burlesqued, winking and coughing, alternately excited laughter. However, I continued with my natural solemnity to read on, sensible that what I did might mend some, but could itself receive no contamination from any.

After reading, I entered upon my exhortation, which was rather calculated at first to amuse them than reprove. I previously observed that no other motive but their welfare could induce me to this; that I was their fellow prisoner, and now got nothing by preaching. I was sorry, I said, to hear them so very profane; because they got nothing by it, but might lose a great deal. "For be assured, my friends," cried I, "for you are my friends, however the world may disclaim your friendship—though you swore twelve thousand oaths in a day,

我對他們讀一段宣講文.聲音是自然響亮.聽的人都在那裏頑笑取樂.有的附耳說無恥下流的話.有的裝作悔過的呻吟.有的咳嗽瞬眼.接續大笑.我却不管.還是自然嚴肅往下讀.我覺得這樣辦法.我沾染不着什麼壞處上身.也許能感化幾個人.

讀完了.我就勸誡他們.我的用意.起初先娛樂他們.却不去責備他們.我先說明我勸誡他們.別無用意.不過是為他們的好.我不過是監獄裏的同伴.宣講是無進款的.我說.我聽見他們這樣的蔑教.很難過.因為這樣.不獨得不了什麼.還要損失好些.我說道.我的朋友.你們該相信....世界雖然不認你們作朋友.你們都是我的朋友.你們要曉得.那怕你們每天呪罵一千次.也得不了一文銅錢

it would not put one penny in your purse. Then what signifies calling every moment upon the devil, and courting his friendship, since you find how scurvily he uses you? He has given you nothing here, you find, but a mouthful of oaths and an empty belly, and by the best accounts I have of him he will give you nothing that's good hereafter.

"If used ill in our dealings with one man, we naturally go elsewhere. Were it not worth your while, then, just to try how you may like the usage of another master, who gives you fair promises, at least, to come to him? Surely, my friends, of all stupidity in the world, his must be the greatest, who, after robbing a house, runs to the thief takers for protection. And yet how are you more wise? You are all seeking comfort from one that has already betrayed you—applying to a more malicious being than any thief taker of them all; for they only decoy, and then hang you; but he decoys, and hangs, and,

到你的口袋裹．那嗎爲
什麼時時刻刻都要請
出那魔鬼來．巴結他．同
他拉攏．你們是曉得的．
魔鬼待你們是很不好．
你們曉得魔鬼沒得什
麼好東西給你們．只給
了你們滿嘴的呪罵．一
肚子的飢餓．我很曉得
魔鬼的行事．以後他給
你們的．沒得好事．

譬如我們同人交．這
一個待我們不好．我們
自然去同別人交．你們
想想看．值得不值得試
試同另外一個主人
{指上帝} 交．看他怎樣的
待我們．這位主人．至少
也曾很公道的答應你
們．讓你們去找他．我的
朋友們．世上最愚蠢的
人．也蠢不過一個作賊
的．偷了一家人家．却跑
去投捕快求保護．你們
的行爲．能比這一個人
聰明些嗎．人家還去找
當上．他們你們所求的捕快．求的
安樂．你們比什麼捕快不
個人．陰險得多．捕後吊死你．這要過是這魔
先騙你．後吊死你．

what is worst of all, will not let you loose after the hangman has done."

When I had concluded, I received the compliments of my audience, some of whom came and shook me by the hand, swearing that I was a very honest fellow, and that they desired my further acquaintance. I therefore promised to repeat my lecture next day, and actually conceived some hopes of making a reformation here; for it had ever been my opinion that no man was past the hour of amendment, every heart lying open to the shafts of reproof, if the archer could but take a proper aim. When I had thus satisfied my mind, I went back to my apartment, where my wife prepared a frugal meal, while Mr. Jenkinson begged leave to add his dinner to ours, and partake of the pleasure, as he was kind enough to express it, of my conversation. He had not yet seen my family—for as they came to my apartment by a door in the narrow passage already described, by

鬼. 不獨騙你. 吊死你還不干休. 他把你吊死之後. 還不放鬆的.

我說完. 衆人來恭維我. 有些走來同我拉手說. 我是個誠實人. 願意多同我相見. 我答應明天再宣講. 頗有點希望. 可以感化他們. 我一向以爲毋論什麼惡人的心. 都是攤開. 同箭靶子一樣. 可以受好的教訓. 只要那善射的. 射得中. 可見世人無有不能悔過的. 我宣講了一番. 很滿意回去牢裏. 我女人預備很省儉的飯菜. 金京森把他自己的那一份湊在一起. 他說很歡喜聽我談話. 我家眷進

this means they avoided the common prison. Jenkinson, at the first interview, therefore, seemed not a little struck with the beauty of my youngest daughter, which her pensive air contributed to heighten; and my little ones did not pass unnoticed.

"Alas, doctor!" cried he; "these children are too handsome and too good for such a place as this!"

"Why, Mr. Jenkinson," replied I, "thank Heaven my children are pretty tolerable in morals; and if they be good, it matters little for the rest."

"I fancy, sir," returned my fellow prisoner, "that it must give you great comfort to have this little family about you."

"A comfort, Mr. Jenkinson!" replied I; "yes, it is indeed a comfort, and I would not be without them for all the world: for they can make a dungeon seem a palace. There is but one way in this life of wounding my happiness, and that is by injuring them."

來是另由一小道. 不走過那大屋子. 故此金京森尚未見着他們. 他第一次見面. 就很驚訝我二女兒的美貌. 又帶愁思的神色. 更顯得貌美. 我的兩個小兒子. 金京森也留意看.

金京森說道. 哎呀. 博士. 你的兒女們. 長得太好看. 不宜在監獄裏.

我答道. 金先生. 我謝上天. 我的兒女們道德還過得去. 只要道德好. 別的就可以不必管了.

他答道. 你有家裏人在你身邊. 我想你覺得很心安.

我答道. 金京森. 是的. 我很心安. 無論什麼. 我總要他們在我身旁. 有了他們. 監獄就變了王宮. 只有傷害他們. 就是傷害我的歡樂.

THE VICAR OF WAKEFIELD 317

"I am afraid, then, sir," cried he, "that I am in some measure culpable; for I think I see here" (looking at my son Moses) "one that I have injured, and by whom I wish to be forgiven."

My son immediately recollected his voice and features, though he had before seen him in disguise; and taking him by the hand, with a smile forgave him. "Yet," continued he, "I can't help wondering at what you could see in my face to think me a proper mark for deception."

"My dear sir," returned the other, "it was not your face, but your white stockings and the black riband in your hair, that allured me. But no disparagement to your parts.[1] I have deceived wiser men than you in my time; and yet with all my tricks, the blockheads have been too many for me[2] at last."

"I suppose," cried my son, "that the narrative of

他說道.我恐怕我多少犯了傷害他們的罪.他看着摩西說道.我曉得.我曾傷害過他.我求他赦罪.

我的兒子.從前雖然是見看他改裝的樣.現在一聽他的聲音.看見他的面貌.立刻就認得他.摩西拉住他的手.微笑.饒恕了他.接着說道.我却想不出來.你看我臉上那一處.是可以受騙的記號.

金京森答道.却不是我的臉.還是你穿的白襪子.頭上結的黑帶子.引我騙你的.我却並不是說.看不起你的精明.比你精明多的人.也曾上過我的當.但是我騙人的本事雖然好.到底還吃了這班蠢人的虧.

我兒子說道.你把你一生這樣的行事.說出

---

1. No disparagement to your parts, 并非看不起你的本事. 2. Too many for me, 我敵不過.

such a life as yours must
be extremely instructive
and amusing."

"Not much of either,"
returned Mr. Jenkinson.
"Those relations which describe the tricks and vices
only of mankind, by in-
creasing our suspicion in
life, retard our success.
The traveler that distrusts
every person he meets, and
turns back upon the ap-
pearance of every man that
looks like a robber, seldom
arrives in time[1] at his
journey's end.

"Indeed, I think from
my own experience, that
the knowing one is the
silliest fellow under the
sun. I was thought cun-
ning from my very child-
hood: when but seven years
old, the ladies would say
that I was a perfect little
man; at fourteen, I knew
the world, cocked my hat,
and loved the ladies; at
twenty, though I was per-
fectly honest, yet everyone
thought me so cunning,
that no one would trust me.
Thu I was at last obliged

來. 必然很有趣味. 很令
人聽了增長多少知識.

金京森答道. 都不見
得. 凡是說人的詭詐. 說
人的罪惡的話. 令人聽
了. 更使人多疑. 就阻礙
成功. 譬如一個旅行的
人. 見一個人. 疑一個人.
看見有人面貌像是盜
賊. 就要回頭. 就很少能
彀及時走到旅行的末
站 ｛此話何常無理善處事者
　莫如能用這種人其次莫
如善防之多
疑原難成事 ｝.

據我自己的閱歷而
論. 天下最愚的人. 就是
精明人. 我從小兒起. 人
家就說我狡猾. 到了七
歲. 女人們都說我很像
完完全全的一個小男
子. 到了十四歲. 我就曉
得世情. 歪戴帽子. 愛女
人. 到了二十歲. 我還是
一個完全誠實人. 但是
人人都以為我狡猾. 無
人相信我. 到後來我沒

及時.

to turn sharper in my own defense, and have lived ever since, my head throbbing with schemes to deceive, and my heart palpitating with fears of detection. I used often to laugh at your honest, simple neighbor Flamborough, and, one way or other, generally cheated him once a year. Yet still, the honest man went forward without suspicion and grew rich, while I still continued tricksy and cunning, and was poor without the consolation of being honest. However," continued he, "let me know your case, and what has brought you here; perhaps, though I have not skill to avoid a jail myself, I may extricate my friends."

In compliance with his curiosity, I informed him of the whole train of accidents and follies that had plunged me into my present troubles, and my utter inability to get free.

After hearing my story, and pausing some minutes, he slapped his forehead as

得法. 只好當騙子自衞. 自此以後. 都是當騙子. 頭裏撲突撲突的想計策騙人. 心裏總是跳. 怕被人看破我的手段. 我常常笑你的鄰居. 單簡老實的法林巴. 每年我總要想法騙他一次. 這個老實人. 還是一樣的向前辦他的事. 一點也不疑心他人. 却是很發財. 我還是一味狡猾. 還是一樣的窮 ｛竊鈎者誅 竊國者侯 毋怪其然｝. 又不能說我因爲老實而窮的. 安慰我自己. 雖然. 你何妨告訴我. 你犯的什麼罪. 爲什麼到監裏來. 我雖然無本事免我自己入監. 也許我有本事拔朋友出監.

他旣是好奇. 要曉得我入監的緣故. 我就把一切的天災人禍. 陷我入於現在的窘境. 和我完全無法出獄的情形. 告訴他.

他聽了之後. 想了好幾分鐘. 拿手拍額. 好像

if he had hit upon some-
thing material,[1] and took
his leave, saying he would
try what could be done.

是想出些重要事. 說了
一句他去盡力想法. 就
告辭了.

---

1. Material, 重要.

CHAPTER XXVII

THE SAME SUBJECT CONTINUED

第 二 十 七 回

同 前
(憤 酷 刑 牧 師 論 改 律)

The next morning I communicated to my wife and children the scheme I had planned of reforming the prisoners, which they received with universal disapprobation, alleging[1] the impossibility and impropriety of it; adding, that my endeavors would no way contribute to their amendment, but might probably disgrace my calling.

"Excuse me," returned I; "these people, however fallen, are still men, and that is a very good title to my affections. Good counsel rejected returns to enrich the giver's bosom; and though the instruction I communicate may not

且說第二天早上．我把想法感化囚犯的主意．告訴我女人同兒女．他們都不以為然．說是不必作．也作不到．又說我只管盡力．不獨不能使他們改過．還怕把我牧師身分打低了．

我答道．你們聽我說．囚犯雖然是人格降低了．然而總還是人．既然是人．就值得我愛他們．我用好言相勸．他們不聽．那好言還回頭來．使我自己心裏受益．我告訴他們的話．即使不能

---

1. Alleging, 據說；姑說 (是非確實未定).

331

mend them, yet it will assuredly mend myself. If these wretches, my children, were princes, there would be thousands ready to offer their ministry;[1] but, in my opinion, the heart that is buried in a dungeon is as precious as that seated upon a throne. Yes, my treasures, if I can mend them, I will; perhaps they will not all despise me. Perhaps I may catch up even one from the gulf, and that will be great gain; for is there upon earth a gem so precious as the human soul?"

Thus saying, I left them, and descended to the common prison, where I found the prisoners very merry, expecting my arrival, and each prepared with some jail trick to play upon the doctor.

Thus, as I was going to begin, one turned my wig awry, as if by accident, and then asked my pardon. A second, who stood at some distance, had a knack of spitting through his

叫他們遷善. 却能使我自己遷善. 我的兒女們. 假使這羣可憐蟲. 是一班王公. 自然有幾千人把宗教道理同他們說 {原來宗教家} {也這樣勢利}. 不過我以爲沉埋在監獄的人心. 同那坐在帝王殿上的人心. 是同樣的可寶貴. 我的寶貝呀. 我果能勸他們改過遷善. 我願意勸他們. 也許他們不藐視我. 也許我能彀從苦海裏救出一個來. 那就是一件好事. 世界上的至寶. 無過於人的靈魂.

說完. 我就走到那囚犯聚合的大屋子. 看見他們很快樂的盼望我來. 每人都預備把監獄裏的把戲. 同我開頑笑. 我正要開講. 就有一個人. 把我戴的假髮. 拉歪了. 他還裝作是無意拉歪的. 求我恕他. 又有一個. 站得離我遠些. 他善於從牙縫間噴唾沫. 把我的書都噴

---

1. Ministry, 政府之一專部; 教士之辦公地; 教士所辦之事.

teeth, which fell in showers upon my book. A third would cry "Amen!" in such an affected[1] tone as gave the rest great delight. A fourth had slily picked my pocket of my spectacles. But there was one whose trick gave more universal pleasure than all the rest; for, observing the manner in which I had disposed my books on the table before me, he very dexterously displaced one of them, and put an obscene jest book of his own in the place.

However, I took no notice of all that this mischievous group of little beings could do, but went on, perfectly sensible that what was ridiculous in my attempt would excite mirth only the first or second time, while what was serious would be permanent. My design succeeded; and in less than six days, some were penitent, and all attentive.

It was now that I applauded my perseverance and address[2] at thus giving

滿了. 又有一個. 用怪聲音喊亞曼. 衆人聽了就大樂. 又有一個. 偷偷的從我口袋裏. 把我的眼鏡掏出來. 更有一個. 他耍的把戲. 耍得比人特別. 引了最多人發笑. 他留心看見把幾本書放在桌上的樣子. 他偷了一本. 另外把他自己的一本誨淫的笑話書擺上｛寫監犯行爲 不曾目睹｝.

我却不去理會這班好惹事的小人. 在那裏耍把戲開頑笑. 我還是講我的. 我深曉得他們要同我開頑笑. 也不過第一二次可以引人笑. 至於正言莊論. 是可以持久的. 我的用意. 居然收效. 不到六天. 大衆都留心聽我講. 還有幾個居然悔過.

我自己讚美我的耐性. 同我的妙法. 居然能

1. Affected, 假裝的.　2. Address, 巧妙.

sensibility to wretches divested[1] of every moral feeling, and now began to think of doing them temporal[2] services also, by rendering their situation somewhat more comfortable. Their time had hitherto been divided between famine and excess, tumultuous riot and bitter repining. Their only employment was quarreling among each other, playing at cribbage, and cutting tobacco stoppers. From this last mode of idle industry I took the hint of setting such as chose to work at cutting pegs for tobacconists and shoemakers, the proper wood being bought by a general subscription, and, when manufactured, sold by my appointment; so that each earned something every day—a trifle indeed, but sufficient to maintain him.

I did not stop here, but instituted fines for the punishment of immorality,

令這班全無道德的可憐蟲．有了感覺．我又着手使他們生活上受益．使他們舒服些．從前他們不是吃得太多．就是捱餓．不是亂吵亂鬧．就是煩惱怨恨．終天就是彼此相爭相吵．鬪紙牌．削木塊塞菸草入烟斗．我從他們削木塊的手工．就想出法子．叫他們削木塊賣給菸店鞋店．木料是衆人湊錢買的．製好木塊之後．我指點他們按期出賣．每人每天就可以賺幾個錢．進項雖是極小．也可以毀自養了

我還要進一步．同他們定賞罰．無道德的受罰．勤力工作的受賞．

---

1. Divested, 脫 (衣服)；此處作失去解．　2. Temporal, 俗；與世俗相關；此處指生活；spiritual 與 temporal 相對待，spiritual 指與靈魂或宗教相關，temporal 指與身體或飲食飽暖或世事相關．

and rewards for peculiar industry. Thus, in less than a fortnight, I had formed them into something social and humane, and had the pleasure of regarding myself as a legislator, who brought men from their native[1] ferocity into friendship and obedience.

And it was highly to be wished that legislative power would thus direct the law rather to reformation than severity — that it would seem convinced that the work of eradicating[2] crimes is not by making punishments familiar,[3] but formidable. Then, instead of our present prisons, which find or make men guilty — which inclose wretches for the commission of one crime, and return them, if returned alive, fitted for the perpetration of thousands — we should see, as in other parts of Europe, places of penitence and solitude, where the accused might be attended by such

不到兩星期. 竟辦到他們有了社交. 彼此相處. 總算有些人道. 我很歡喜當我自己是個立法家. 竟把生性殘暴的人. 改到彼此以友誼相待. 且能聽我的教訓.

可見立法之權. 不宜趨於嚴酷. 只宜趨於能令人改過遷善. 凡要芟除世界罪惡. 刑法宜使人畏懼. 不宜使人易犯. 現在監獄制度. 不過教人犯罪. 犯人入監時候. 犯的不過一條罪. 收監之後. 若猶幸而不死. 釋放出來. 反造成他可以再犯一千條罪. 我們應仿照歐洲他國制度. 設有遷善所. 或獨自一人的小牢. 派人去勸化

---

1. Native, 與生俱生的；天生的. 2. Eradicating, 除根；芟除.
3. Familiar, 狎習；相熟；此處作易犯解.

as could give them repentance, if guilty, or new motives to virtue, if innocent.
And this, but not the
increasing punishments, is
the way to mend a state;
nor can I avoid even ques-
tioning the validity of that
right which social combinations have assumed of capi-
tally punishing offenses of
a slight nature.　In cases
of murder, their right is
obvious, as it is the duty
of us all, from the law
of self-defense, to cut
off that man who has
shown a disregard for the
life of another.　Against
such all nature rises in
arms; but it is not so
against him who steals my
property.　Natural law
gives me no right to take
away his life, as, by that,
the horse he steals is as
much his property as mine.
If, then, I have any right,
it must be from a compact
made between us, that he
who deprives the other of
his horse shall die.　But
this is a false compact;
because no man has a
right to barter his life
any more than to take it
away, as it is not his own.

或罪益社會，對〔例如恐小樹上，令一株先伐〕。悔罪，能勸能嚴刑聯合起來。犯罪的人，勸之自新之路，能勸人遷善改過，不應一味嚴刑。勸人於國會上的人，於小過處以極刑〔例寫：以小過處以極刑。信訧、竊錢、竊物、一隻兔子，在五砍伐，先令一株，均處極刑〕。

我要詰問：他們有這種大權嗎？他們有處而律我，有顯命殺我，是所我天殺馬，是於產權以偷我的。他們原是生命要他，至於財之授，他也是守律許說。這自衛人殺的，偷殺他，並未為他產。行兇殺人，他們的權這是自衛來有，以殺的作是他不應。可作過有並律權。民天然財產此〔初日天有此明，謂人不行意〕。

若是我過約，一定過誰，誰從偷罪；但是這種人的權，死假約，因為無去換有奪東西。把生命，人生命這件西，也生命自己的，不是〔換言之是上帝給的〕。

THE VICAR OF WAKEFIELD 327

And, besides, the compact is inadequate,[1] and would be set aside even in a court of modern equity,[2] as there is a great penalty for a very trifling inconvenience: since it is far better that two men should live than that one man should ride. But a compact that is false between two men is equally so between a hundred, or a hundred thousand; for as ten millions of circles can never make a square, so the united voice of myriads cannot lend the smallest foundation to falsehood It is thus that reason speaks, and untutored nature says the same thing. Savages that are directed by natural law alone are very tender of the lives of each other; they seldom shed blood but to retaliate former cruelty.

Our Saxon ancestors, fierce as they were in war, had but few executions in times of peace; and in all

況且這種約. 也不相當. 卽使到現在廷尉衙門. 也不能憑這種約斷案. 因爲失去的物產太輕. 而科罪太重. 與其一個人有馬騎. 不如兩人有生命. 旣然兩個人定的約是假的. 不能算數. 卽使百人十萬人定的約. 也不能算數. 因爲十兆個圓圈. 永遠湊不成一個四方. 故此恆河沙數的人. 衆口同聲. 也不能說假的就是眞的. 就可以算數. 是以遇着這種問題. 是道理說話. 未受過教育. 天然的理想. 也是這樣說. 野人生番只受天然法律者. 對於人的生命. 是很慈愛的. 若不是報前仇. 是少得殺人流血的.

我們的薩克遜種遠祖. 打仗的時候. 雖是殘暴. 在太平時代. 却不輕

---

1. Inadequate, 不相當; 不相抵; 不足. 2. Court of equity, 廷尉 (中國西漢制度).

commencing governments that have the print of nature still strong upon them, scarcely any crime is held capital.[1]

It is among the citizens of a refined community that penal laws, which are in the hands of the rich, are laid upon the poor. Government, while it grows older, seems to acquire the moroseness of age; and as if our property were become dearer in proportion as it increased, as if the more enormous our wealth the more extensive our fears, all our possessions are paled up with new edicts every day, and hung round with gibbets to scare every invader.

I cannot tell whether it is from the number of our penal laws, or the licentiousness of our people, that this country should show more convicts in a year than half the dominions of Europe united. Perhaps it is owing to both; for they mutually produce each

殺人. 凡是種族之富有天然性情者. 其初建之政府. 定的死罪極少.

世界所謂文明種族所定的刑律. 是在富人掌握中. 施於貧人的 {可見欲稍平貧富階級先從 刑律始英美刑律全為富人 所定偏重 於保財產}. 這種刑法. 好像是越老越嚴酷. 也同老年人每多恣怒. 又好像財產積得越多. 本來價值越增. 又好像財產越多. 害怕之心越廣. 所有的財產. 每天總頒新律保護 {從前英國刑律定 死罪者不過六十 餘條自佐治第二在位 之後又加增六十餘條 處處都建有縊殺盜竊犯的架. 恐嚇人不要侵犯財產 {第十八世紀英國境 內縊殺架頗多作者 當猶及見之}.

我不曉得是因為我們的刑律太繁. 抑或是我們的人好為惡. 每年犯罪的人. 比半個歐洲合計起來還要多. 也許是兩種原因都有. 因為這兩件事. 是互

---

1. Capital crime, 殺頭的罪; 死罪.

THE VICAR OF WAKEFIELD

other. When by indiscriminate[1] penal laws a nation beholds the same punishment affixed to dissimilar degrees of guilt, from perceiving no distinction in the penalty, the people are led to lose all sense of distinction in the crime, and this distinction is the bulwark of all morality: thus the multitude of laws produce new vices, and new vices call for fresh restraints.

It were to be wished, then, that power, instead of contriving new laws to punish vice — instead of drawing hard the cords of society till a convulsion come to burst them — instead of cutting away wretches as useless before we have tried their utility — instead of converting correction into vengeance — it were to be wished that we tried the restrictive arts of government, and made law the protector, but not the tyrant, of the people. We should then find that creatures, whose

為因果的. 凡一個國. 定了不分輕重的刑律. 國人只見過犯有輕重. 却一樣的處以重刑. 因為這樣. 人民就全不能辨過犯之輕重. 須知人民惟能辨罪之輕重然後能保全道德. 故此法律越繁. 則新出之惡行越多. 新出之惡行越多. 則禁之之法越密.

然則與其定新法以罰罪. 與其束縛人民太急. 以致暴動橫溢. 與其不先試人民之有用與否. 而橫殺許多可憐蟲. 以為無用而不可惜. 與其棄悔過遷善良法. 專行報仇主義. 不如試用收窄縮小之治民良法. 把法律改為保民之具. 而廢強霸兇殘之虐政. 我們那時候才曉得. 從前當人民之靈魂. 如鎔爐之渣滓. 現在不過要良匠鍊冶修治. 便成器

---

1. Indiscriminate, 無分別.

souls are held as dross, only wanted the hand of a refiner; we should then find that creatures, now stuck up for long tortures,[1] lest luxury should feel a momentary pang, might, if properly treated, serve to sinew the state[2] in times of danger; that as their faces are like ours, their hearts are so too; that few minds are so base as that perseverance cannot amend; that a man may see his last crime without dying for it; and that very little blood will serve to cement our security.

皿.我們那時候才曉得.從前奢侈人家.不忍一刻之苦.就把許多人受長久刑在獄裏.叫他們受{當時法網之慘不覺痛／罰之慘}之痛.其言{}.這被監禁的多人.現在只要用合宜事方法待遇.可以保國家.我們的面貌與他們的心.他們一樣.人心無論去遷.人心耐的改過.並不能再犯.人若犯罪才曉得.用不着殺他.要流血太多才能保護財產.

---

1. Stuck up for long tortures, 長久監禁. 2. To sinew the state, 保國；爲國家柱石.

CHAPTER XXVIII

HAPPINESS AND MISERY RATHER THE RESULT OF PRU-
DENCE THAN OF VIRTUE IN THIS LIFE; TEMPORAL
EVILS OR FELICITIES BEING REGARDED BY HEAVEN
AS THINGS MERELY IN THEMSELVES TRIFLING, AND
UNWORTHY ITS CARE IN THE DISTRIBUTION.

第 二 十 八 回

人生苦樂是治產得法與否之結果並不關
於道德　　上天視世人之悲樂作爲無
足重輕不足介意不必善爲分派
(牧師倒運又遭殃)

I had now been confined more than a fortnight, but had not since my arrival been visited by my dear Olivia, and I greatly longed to see her. Having communicated my wishes to my wife, the next morning the poor girl entered my apartment, leaning on her sister's arm. The change which I saw in her countenance struck me. The numberless graces that once resided there were now fled, and the hand of death seemed to have molded every feature to

且說我被禁在監. 已經過了兩星期. 奧維雅還未曾來見我. 我很想見他. 我把意思告訴了我的女人. 第二日早上. 奧維雅扶着他妹妹. 進來見我. 他臉上已經改變了許多. 我見了一驚. 從前他臉上有無數秀媚動人的神色光采. 現在都沒有了. 臉上現出

341

alarm me. Her temples were sunk, her forehead was tense, and a fatal paleness sat upon her cheek.

"I am glad to see thee, my dear," cried I; "but why this dejection, Livy? I hope, my love, you have too great a regard for me to permit disappointment thus to undermine a life which I prize as my own. Be cheerful, child, and we yet may see happier days."

"You have ever, sir," replied she, "been kind to me, and it adds to my pain that I shall never have an opportunity of sharing that happiness you promise. Happiness, I fear, is no longer reserved for me here; and I long to be rid of a place where I have only found distress. Indeed, sir, I wish you would make a proper submission to Mr. Thornhill; it may in some measure induce him to pity you, and it will give me relief in dying."

"Never, child," replied I, "never will I be brought to acknowledge my daughter a prostitute; for, though the world may look upon your offense with

都是將死的氣色. 令我見了害怕. 兩額角都凹進去. 眉間緊窄. 臉色死白色.

我說道. 我喜歡見你. 奧維雅. 你為什麼這樣憂愁. 我盼望你盡孝於我. 不使失望的事體. 陷害你的生命. 我寶貴你的生命. 如同寶貴我自己的生命一樣. 你開心罷. 我們還可以見歡樂日子.

他答道. 父親向來是慈愛我. 你答應我有歡樂日子過. 我恐怕永遠沒有機會享. 我更難過. 我恐怕在這個世界上. 沒有什麼歡樂保留給我享. 我只見這世界上都是愁苦. 很望離開了. 父親. 我願意你對於唐希爾作合宜讓步罷. 多少可以動他可憐你. 那嗎我死了也心寬些.

我答道. 毋論怎樣. 我不能承認我的女兒犯了不是. 世人雖然看你犯了罪. 看你不起. 我當

scorn, let it be mine to regard it as a mark of credulity, not of guilt. My dear, I am no way miserable in this place, however dismal it may seem; and be assured that while you continue to bless me by living, he shall never have my consent to make you more wretched by marrying another."

After the departure of my daughter, my fellow prisoner, who was by at this interview, sensibly enough expostulated upon[1] my obstinacy in refusing a submission which promised to give me freedom. He observed that the rest of my family was not to be sacrificed to the peace of one child alone, and she the only one who had offended me.

"Besides," added he, "I don't know if it be just thus to obstruct the union of man and wife, which you do at present by refusing to consent to a match you cannot hinder, but may render unhappy."

你走差了.是由於你信人太過.並不是你有意犯罪.我的寶貝.監裏雖然是個悽慘的地方.我却一點也不覺得愁苦.你可以放心.只要你活在世上.保佑我.我萬不讓唐希爾再娶別人.使你更愁苦.

金京森在場聽見我父女談話.我女兒走過之後.金京森很有理的責備我.既是讓步就可自由.不應該倔彊到底.不允讓步.又說.得罪我的是一個女兒.不能因為一個女兒.犧牲家裏其餘的人.使他們不安.

他又說道.況且阻撓男女結婚.也不見得是公道.你既無力禁止人家結婚.又不許他們結婚.不過令人家不歡樂.

---

1. Expostulated upon, 以友誼責備.

"Sir," replied I, "you are unacquainted with the man that oppresses us. I am very sensible that no submission I can make could procure me liberty even for an hour. I am told that even in this very room a debtor of his, no later than last year, died for want. But, though my submission and approbation could transfer me from hence to the most beautiful apartment he is possessed of, yet I would grant neither, as something whispers me that it would be giving a sanction to adultery. While my daughter lives, no other marriage of his shall ever be legal in my eye. Were she removed, indeed, I should be the basest of men, from any resentment of my own, to attempt putting asunder those who wish for an union. No, villain as he is, I should then wish him married to prevent the consequences of his future debaucheries. But now, should I not be the most cruel of all fathers

我答道.先生.你不曉得那個拿勢力逼壓我們的人.我很曉得這個人.假使我讓了步.也是不能得一點鐘的自由.有人告訴我.去年有一個欠他債的人.被禁在這個牢裏.因窮困死在這裏的.那怕我讓了步.許了他們結婚.我就可以從監牢搬到他所有的極華麗房屋.我也不能.因為我良心上告訴我.倘若我讓了步.許了他結婚.就是我許他犯惡罪.只要我女兒活在世上.毋論唐希爾同什麼人結婚.我都以為不合法律.倘若我女兒不在世.我若因為一人懷恨.還阻攔他們結婚.我就是極卑劣的人.他雖是個惡人.我女兒死後.我卻願意他結婚.因為可以免得他將來再作許多壞事{牧師此數語讀者宜注意}.假使我為的是要出監.

THE VICAR OF WAKEFIELD 335

to sign an instrument [1] which must send my child to the grave, merely to avoid a prison myself; and thus, to escape one pang, break my child's heart with a thousand?"

He acquiesced in the justice of this answer, but could not avoid observing that he feared my daughter's life was already too much wasted to keep me long a prisoner.

"However," continued he, "though you refuse to submit to the nephew, I hope you have no objections to laying your case before the uncle, who has the first character in the kingdom for everything that is just and good. I would advise you to send him a letter by the post, intimating all his nephew's ill usage; and my life for it that in three days you shall have an answer."

I thanked him for the hint, and instantly set about complying; but I wanted paper, and unluckily all our money had

在一紙約據上簽了字. 把我女兒的性命送了. 豈不是我因爲要免了 我自己的一種痛苦. 反 令一千種的痛苦. 破毀 了我女兒的心. 我豈不 成了最殘忍的父親嗎.

他聽了很以爲我答 他的話是公道. 但是他 禁不住說. 他恐怕我女 兒病已過重. 不見得致 我久關監牢.

他又說道. 你雖然不 肯對姪子讓步. 何妨把 你這宗事. 對他的叔父 陳說呢. 他的叔父. 人又 好. 又公道. 是國內第一 種人格. 我勸你寫封信. 寄給他的叔父. 詳說他 姪兒種種不正當行爲. 我肯擔保. 三天之內. 你 一定可以得回信.

我謝他這個主意. 立 刻就辦. 我却找不着紙. 又不幸那天早上. 我的

---

1. Instrument, 此處作憑據契約合同之類解.

been laid out that morning
in provisions; however, he
supplied me.

For the three ensuing
days I was in a state of
anxiety to know what re-
ception my letter might
meet with; but in the
meantime was frequently
solicited by my wife to
submit to any conditions
rather than remain here,
and every hour received
repeated accounts of the
decline of my daughter's
health.　The third day and
the fourth arrived, but I
received no answer to my
letter: the complaints of a
stranger against a favorite
nephew were no way likely
to succeed; so that these
hopes soon vanished like
all my former.　My mind,
however, still supported
itself, though confinement
and bad air began to make
a visible alteration in my
health, and my arm that
had suffered in the fire grew
worse.　My children, how-
ever, sat by me, and while
I was stretched on my
straw read to me by turns,
or listened and wept at my

幾個餘錢.買了火食.他
却供給我一切.

以後三天.我很着急
的等回信.當下我的女
人.屢次求我讓步.不要
久住監獄.又每點鐘都
得到報告.說我女兒病
狀越深.等到第三天第
四天.還未有回信.一個
素不相識的人.反對人
家歡喜的姪子.那叔叔
自然不會聽的.這一次
的希望.同從前的幾種
希望一樣.都無結果.
雖然被困在監.空氣
又不好.我的身體自此
不如從前的康健.我受
了火傷的膀子.比前更
甚.我的心却還受得住.
我的兒子們陪我坐.當
我躺在乾草上.他們讀
書給我聽.我有時教他

instructions. But my daughter's health declined faster than mine; every message from her contributed to increase my apprehensions and pain.

The fifth morning after I had written the letter which was sent to Sir William Thornhill, I was alarmed with an account that she was speechless. Now it was that confinement was truly painful to me; my soul was bursting from its prison to be near the pillow of my child — to comfort, to strengthen her — to receive her last wishes, and teach her soul the way to heaven!

Another account came. She was expiring, and yet I was debarred the small comfort of weeping by her. My fellow prisoner some time after came with the last account. He bade me be patient. She was dead! The next morning he returned, and found me with my two little ones, now my only companions, who were using all their innocent efforts to comfort me. They entreated to read to

們. 他們聽着滴淚. 但是我女兒的身體. 日見其弱. 比我更快. 每次我得了消息. 都添我的憂慮. 添我的心痛.

寫信給唐希爾爵士之第五天. 我得了家人報告. 說是我的女兒已經不能言語了. 我很驚懼. 到了這個時候. 我真覺得被禁在監的苦. 我的靈魂. 要衝出監獄去. 走近我女兒的枕邊. 去安慰他. 扶持他. 聽他臨終有什麼吩咐. 指示他的靈魂上天之路.

又一個消息來說. 是他快斷氣了. 我還是不能去在他身邊哭一場稍以自慰. 過了一會金京森來報最後的消息. 勸我耐煩些. 女兒已經死了〔大女兒之死是用虛寫〕 第二天早上. 他回來. 見我的兩個小兒子陪我. 我只有這兩個同伴. 他們費了許多孩子們的心思. 安慰我. 他們苦求讀書

me, and bade me not to cry, for I was now, too old to weep.

·'And is not my sister an angel now, papa?" cried the eldest; "and why, then are you sorry for her? I wish I were an angel out of this frightful place. if my papa were with me."

"Yes," added my youngest darling, "Heaven, where my sister is, is a finer place than this, and there are none but good people there and the people here are very bad."

Mr. Jenkinson interrupted their harmless prattle by observing that now my daughter was no more, I should seriously think of the rest of my family, and attempt to save my own life, which was every day declining for want of necessaries and wholesome air. He added that it was now incumbent on me[1] to sacrifice any pride or resentment of my own to the welfare of those who depended on me for support; and that I was now. both

給我聽．勸我不要哭．因為我年紀太大．不可哭了．

那大的小孩子說道．爸爸，姊姊現在不是做了仙女啦嗎．你為什麼還要為他傷心呢．假使爸爸同我在一起．我寧可離開這可怕的地方．去做仙童．

那小的孩子說道．是的．姊姊不是上了天嗎．天上比這裏好．天上都是好人．這裏的人很不好．

金京森攔住他們說孩子話．對我說．你的女兒是死了．你要替其餘的家裏人打算．也要設法自救性命．因為日給不足．加以不好空氣．你身體很不強健．又說．這時候．你應該犧牲個人的倔疆傲骨同怨恨．要替依靠你養活的家人設想．按公道說．按道理

---

1. Incumbent on me, 我應該；我負責.

by reason and justice, obliged to try to reconcile my landlord.

"Heaven be praised," replied I, "there is no pride left me now I should detest my own heart if I saw either pride or resentment lurking there. On the contrary. as my oppressor has been once my parishioner, I hope one day to present him up an unpolluted soul at the eternal tribunal No, sir, I have no resentment now; and though he has taken from me what I held dearer than all his treasures, though he has wrung my heart — for I am sick almost to fainting. very sick. my fellow prisoner—yet that shall never inspire me with vengeance. I am now willing to approve his marriage, and if this submission can do him any pleasure, let him know that if I have done him any injury I am sorry for it."

Mr. Jenkinson took pen and ink and wrote down my submission nearly as I have expressed it, to which I signed my name. My son was enployed to

說. 都不得不設法同房東講和.

我答道. 我讚美上天. 現在我什麼傲骨都完了. 假使我看見我現在還懷怨恨. 還藏有傲骨. 我就要憎惡我自己. 我不獨不懷恨. 我因為欺凌我的人. 從前原是在我的教屬. 我還盼望有一天. 我可以送他到天上受最後審判時. 仍是個清淨未受汙點的靈魂. 先生. 我現在並無怨恨. 他雖然把我的至寶奪去. 他雖然傷了我的心.... 現在我很難過快要暈倒了. 我的同伴. 我很難過.... 我却永不報仇. 我現在願意許他結婚. 倘若我這樣退讓. 能使他歡喜. 我願意讓他曉得. 若是我曾經作過傷害他的事. 我很惋惜

> 牧師所說是篤守基督教
> 人的話然而痛女心切離
> 之篤亦排壓不住故發現
> 信道要暈倒情狀人理與天性交
> 將有如是者非大
> 戰筆力不能寫出

金京森紙筆在手. 把我讓步的話寫下來. 我簽了字. 叫我兒子拿字

carry the letter to Mr.
Thornhill, who was then
at his seat in the country.
He went, and in about
six hours returned with a
verbal answer. He had
some difficulty, he said, to
get a sight of his landlord.
as the servants were in-
solent and suspicious; but
he accidentally saw him as
he was going out upon
business, preparing for his
marriage, which was to be
in three days. He con-
tinued to inform us that he
stepped up in the humblest
manner and delivered the
letter, which, when Mr.
Thornhill had read, he said
that all submission was
now too late and unneces-
sary; that he had heard
of our application to his
uncle, which met with the
contempt it deserved; and
as for the rest, that all
future applications should
be directed to his attorney,
not to him. He observed,
however. that as he had
a very good opinion of the
discretion of the two young
ladies, they might have
been the most agreeable
intercessors.

據送給唐希爾.他這時
候住在鄉間的宅子.我
兒子去了六點鐘.帶口信
回來說.起初很不容易見
房東的面.因爲那羣底
下人旣懷疑.又無禮.碰
巧房東出門辦事.才見
了面.房東是預備辦喜
事.三天就是吉期.我兒
子又說.很客氣的走向
前遞交這信.唐希爾讀
畢.說是讓步太遲了.現
在也用不着.又說曉得
我們求他的叔叔.叔叔
那裏看得起我們.其餘
的事.無論求他什麼.只
好同他的律師說話.又
說雖是這樣.他看我們
家裏兩位小姐.都很好.
很聰明機靈的.在早應
該叫兩位小姐來說情.
最爲合宜 {兩語寫盡唐希爾之惡毒}.

"Well, sir," said I to my fellow prisoner, "you now discover the temper of the man who oppresses me. He can at once be facetious and cruel; but let him use me as he will, I shall soon be free, in spite of all his bolts to restrain me. I am now drawing towards an abode that looks brighter as I approach it: this expectation cheers my afflictions; and though I leave a helpless family of orphans behind me, yet they will not be utterly forsaken; some friend, perhaps, will be found to assist them for the sake of their poor father, and some may charitably relieve them for the sake of their Heavenly Father."

Just as I spoke, my wife, whom I had not seen that day before, appeared with looks of terror, and making efforts, but unable to speak.

"Why, my love," cried I—"why will you thus increase my afflictions by your own? What though no submissions can turn our severe master—though he has doomed me to die

我對金京森說道.先生.現在你才曉得欺凌我的人是什麼脾氣.他旣好騙人.性又殘忍.隨他怎樣待我.只管他處處攔阻我.我不久也就自由了.我現在一步一步的走近一個地方.這地方我越走近越顯得有光明.我這種盼望.減輕我的愁苦.我雖然遺下幾個無告的孤寡.尙不至於無人照料.他們也還有朋友.因爲他們的老父都助他們.也有因爲天父.發慈善心.救他們的困苦.

我才說完.我昨天起未看見我的女人.這時候他走來.滿臉驚怕.要說話.也說不出來.

我喊道.你爲什麼愁苦.令我再加愁苦.我無論如何退讓.也不能改變那嚴酷的主人〈指唐希爾〉.那怕他致我死

in this place of wretched-ness, and though we have lost a darling child—yet still you will find comfort in your other children when I shall be no more."

"We have indeed lost," returned she, "a darling child. My Sophia, my dearest, is gone—snatched from us—carried off by ruffians!"

"How! madam," cried my fellow prisoner, "Miss Sophia carried off by ruffians? Sure it cannot be."

She could only answer with a fixed look and a flood of tears. But one of the prisoner's wives, who was present, and came in with her, gave us a more distinct account: she informed us that as my wife, my daughter, and herself were taking a walk together on the great road a little way out of the village, a post chaise and pair drove up to them, and instantly stopped. Upon which a well-dressed man, but not Mr. Thornhill, stepping out, clasped my daughter round the waist, and forcing her in, bade the postilion drive

在監裏.那怕是我們喪失一個女兒.我死之後.你還有幾個兒女安慰你.

我女人答道.我們當真是丟了一個女兒.我的至寶素緋雅.也丟了.搶走了.被匪徒搶走了〔才死一個女兒又被匪搶了〕〔一個女兒眞是苦了牧師〕.

金京森喊道.瑪當.怎麼樣.素緋雅小姐被無賴搶走了麼.這是一定不能的.

我的女人不能答.只是兩眼不動.大哭却有一個囚犯的女人.他曾眼見.同我的女人同時進來.說得還淸楚.他告訴我們.說是我的女人女兒.同他在大路上同走.離村子還不甚遠.有一輛雙馬車趕上來.忽然停住.有一個穿得很好的人.却不是唐希爾.走出來.雙手抱住素緋雅小姐的腰.強逼他上了車.吩咐馬夫快趕車

on, so that they were out of sight in a moment.

"Now," cried I, "the sum of my miseries is made up, nor is it in the power of anything on earth to give me another pang. What! not one left!—not to leave me one! The monster! The child that was next my heart! She had the beauty of an angel, and almost the wisdom of an angel. But support that woman, nor let her fall. Not to leave me one!"

"Alas! my husband," said my wife, "you seem to want comfort even more than I. Our distresses are great, but I could bear this and more if I saw you but easy. They may take away my children, and all the world, if they leave me but you."

My son, who was present, endeavored to moderate her grief; he bade us take comfort, for he hoped that we might still have reason to be thankful.

"My child," cried I, "look round the world, and see if there be any happiness left me now. Is not every ray of comfort shut

往前走．不過一會子．馬車同人就看不見了．

我喊道．我的愁苦是到了盡頭．無可再加了．無論世人用什麽力量．也不能再加我的痛苦了．一個女兒也不留下給我．一個也不留．你這個窮兇極惡的人呀．我最愛的女兒呀．他有仙女的美貌．有仙女的智慧……你們扶那女人．不要讓他暈倒了……一個女兒也不留給我．

我女人說道．我的丈夫．你的心好像比我還不安．我們的愁苦是多極了．只要我看見你安靜些．我還能再多受痛苦．他們那怕把我們的兒女們都搶走了．把世界都拿走了．我只求把你留下給我．

我的兒子竭力的拿話去勸他母親．要減輕他母親的痛苦．又勸我們安心些．因爲他盼望我們還可以有感謝的道理．

我說道．我的孩子．你試把世界一看．看看還有什麽歡樂留下給我．

out, while all our bright prospects only lie beyond the grave!"

"My dear father," returned he, "I hope there is still something that will give you an interval of satisfaction; for I have a letter from my brother George."

"What of him, child?" interrupted I; "does he know our misery? I hope my boy is exempt from any part of what his wretched family suffers."

"Yes, sir," returned he; "he is perfectly gay, cheerful, and happy. His letter brings nothing but good news; he is the favorite of his colonel, who promises to procure him the very next lieutenancy that becomes vacant!"

"And are you sure of all this?" cried my wife. "Are you sure that nothing ill has befallen my boy?"

"Nothing, indeed, madam," returned my son; "you shall see the letter, which will give you the highest pleasure; and if anything can procure you comfort, I am sure that will."

是不是一線的安慰都沒有了. 我們光明的前程. 都在埋骨以後了.

他答道. 我的父親. 我盼望還有些事. 可以使你滿意幾時. 我接着佐之哥哥的一封信.

我攔住問道. 孩子. 他怎麼樣了. 他曉得我們的愁苦嗎. 我盼望他免受我們的愁苦.

他答道. 父親. 是的. 他很風流很得意很快樂. 他的信說的都是好消息. 他的大佐很喜歡他. 答應他遇有缺出就補他中尉.

我的女人問道. 這話靠得住嗎. 你曉得的確. 他未遇着什麼不好的事嗎.

他答道. 母親. 的確沒有. 你可以看信. 你看過一定歡喜. 別的若不能彀令你歡喜. 這封信一定能彀使你歡喜.

THE VICAR OF WAKEFIELD 345

"But are you sure," still repeated she, "that the letter is from himself, and that he is really so happy?"

"Yes, madam," replied he; "it is certainly his, and he will one day be the credit and the support of our family!"

"Then I thank Providence," cried she, "that my last letter to him has miscarried. Yes, my dear," continued she, turning to me, "I will now confess that though the hand of Heaven is sore upon us in other instances, it has been favorable here. By the last letter I wrote my son, which was in the bitterness of anger, I desired him, upon his mother's blessing, and if he had the heart of a man, to see justice done his father and sister, and avenge our cause. But thanks be to Him that directs all things, it has miscarried, and I am at rest."

"Woman," cried I, "thou hast done very ill, and at another time my reproaches might have been more severe. Oh! what a tremendous gulf hast thou

他母親又問道. 是他的親筆信嗎. 他當真的是快樂嗎.

他答道是的. 一定是他自己寫的信 {牧師女人懷疑 却有緣故觀下文便知}. 將來他定能光大家門. 能助我們一家.

我女人說道. 謝謝上天. 我最後一封信. 達不到他. 又回頭對我說道. 我現在供認. 別的事體. 上天待我們. 未免太苦. 對於我的兒子. 却是很好. 我最後寫給他的信. 我是怒氣騰騰的. 我給他的信. 說是母親保佑他. 他若是有人心的話. 要替我們報仇. 替父親姊姊出口氣. 使父親姊姊得公道待遇. 但是. 凡事都有天作主. 我謝上帝. 這封信達不到他. 我放心了.

我喊道. 女人. 你大錯了. 若是在別的時候. 我責備你的話. 還要重得多. 幸而你逃出大海了.

escaped, that would have buried both thee and him in endless ruin. Providence, indeed, has here been kinder to us than we to ourselves. It has reserved that son to be the father and protector of my children when I shall be away. How unjustly did I complain of being stripped of every comfort, when I still hear that he is happy and insensible of our afflictions; still kept in reserve to support his widowed mother, and to protect his brothers and sisters. But what sisters has he left? He has no sisters now; they are all gone, robbed from me, and I am undone."

"Father," interrupted my son, "I beg you will give me leave to read this letter; I know it will please you." Upon which, with my permission, he read as follows:

"HONORED SIR,—I have called off my imagination of a few moments from the pleasures that surround me, to fix it upon objects that are still more pleasing—the dear little fireside at home. My fancy draws

不然是要把你.連你的兒子.淹沒在大海裏.永遠不得出來.天待我們.比我們自待.還厚些.天現在保留這個兒子.等到我死後.他就是我的兒女們的父親.保護他們.我還常出怨言.說是我的安樂.都剝奪淨盡了.是怨得很不公道.因爲我還聽見我的大兒子還是歡喜的.還不曉得我們的愁苦的寡母保在世.扶持他的小兄弟護他的姊姊們.還有姊姊們.但是他那裏還得姊姊姊呢.他現在沒得了.都被人搶走了.我算是完了.

我的兒子打叉說道.我求你讓我讀信給你聽.你聽了必歡喜.我就讓他讀.他讀道.

父親大人.我左右前後.都被快樂事包圍住了.我的心完全埋在歡樂裏頭.我只好把這種思想暫時撇開.把我的心擺在更令我歡樂的的事物上....我的心現在到了家裏的火爐邊.我心裏描

that harmless group as listening to every line of this with great composure. I view those faces with delight which never felt the deforming hand of ambition or distress! But whatever your happiness may be at home, I am sure it will be some addition to it to hear that I am perfectly pleased with my situation, and every way happy here.

"Our regiment is countermanded, and is not to leave the kingdom; the colonel, who professes himself my friend, takes me with him to all companies where he is acquainted, and after my first visit I generally find myself received with increased respect upon repeating it. I danced last night with Lady G——, and could I forget you know whom, I might be perhaps successful. But it is my fate still to remember others while I am myself forgotten by most of my absent friends; and in this number, I fear, sir, that I must consider you; for I have long expected the pleasure of a

---

我想畫家裏衆人靜聽我這信裏的一字一句。聽得心裏極舒服的景象。凡是人好安想富貴，或受過愁苦，臉上是要減少色澤的。我們家裏向來不如是。我看見家裏面貌是非常之歡喜。但是無論你們怎樣的歡樂，你們若是聽見我說，我很歡喜我現在所處的境地，我們在這裏很快樂，你們聽了自然更加高興。

我們這一團人，奉命停止開赴外國。大佐是我的好朋友，凡是他所認得的人有應酬宴會，他都帶我去。我只要去過一次，其後再去，他都敬我有加。昨晚我同某貴族小姐跳舞。有曉望成功。假使我能忘記這個人你記得是誰，我或者可以成功。〔假使他能忘了他向小姐求婚可望成功也〕但是我別記人，而忘了我的算。人們卻忘記我。在忘記頭裏，我的父親也算一個。因爲我久已盼

letter from home to no purpose. Olivia and Sophia too promised to write, but seem to have forgotten me. Tell them they are two arrant little baggages, and that I am this moment in a most violent passion with them; yet still, I know not how, though I want to bluster a little, my heart is respondent only to softer emotions. Then tell them, sir, that, after all, I love them affectionately, and be assured of my ever remaining

"YOUR DUTIFUL SON."

"In all our miseries," cried I, "what thanks have we not to return, that one at least of our family is exempted from what we suffer. Heaven be his guard, and keep my boy thus happy, to be the supporter of his widowed mother, and the father of these two babes, which is all the patrimony I can now bequeath him. May he keep their innocence from the temptations of want, and be their conductor in the paths of honor!"

望得一家信. 也是枉然. 兩位姊姊. 答應寫信. 也不寫. 好像是把我全忘了. 告訴他們說. 是我說的. 他們兩個人. 簡直的是兩個粗鴉頭. 我此刻很同他們生氣. 雖是這樣說. 我不曉得怎樣的. 我雖稍微責備幾句. 我的心仍然是爲柔情所感化. 請你告訴他們. 我還是極愛他們. 　　兒稟.

我聽完了信. 說道. 我們愁苦到這樣. 我們家裏. 還有一個免了受我們所受的愁苦. 這是應該感謝的. 我求天保衛他. 仍使他歡樂. 扶持他的已寡老母. 作兩個小兒子的父親. 這就是我遺留給他的家產. 盼望他保全他們. 不致因困窮而爲惡. 引他們走正道.

I had scarcely said these words, when a noise like that of a tumult seemed to proceed from the prison below; it died away soon after, and a clanking of fetters was heard along the passage that led to my apartment. The keeper of the prison entered holding a man all bloody, wounded, and fettered with the heaviest irons. I looked with compassion on the wretch as he approached me, but with horror when I found it was my own son. "My George!—my George! And do I behold thee thus? Wounded! Fettered! Is this thy happiness? Is this the manner you return to me? O that this sight could break my heart at once and let me die!"

"Where, sir, is your fortitude?" returned my son with an intrepid voice. "I must suffer, my life is forfeited, and let them take it."

I tried to restrain my passions for a few minutes in silence, but I thought I should have died with the effort.

我剛把這話說完. 忽聽見有吵鬧之聲. 好像是從底下監獄來的. 一會子又不響了. 再一聽. 是脚鐐的聲響. 一直向我牢裏來. 獄卒進來. 捉住一個人. 受了傷. 滿身是血. 上了極重的脚鐐. 當這個人走近前來. 我很可憐他. 細看. 原來是我的兒子. 大驚.

我喊道. 我的佐之呀. 我的佐之呀. 你為什麼這樣受傷. 上了脚鐐. 這是你的歡樂嗎. 你這樣回來見我嗎. 這樣光景令我心碎. 讓我死了罷

〔蕭佐之家信如何令全家人快樂接着就是佐之受傷被禁又是作者善用反襯法〕

我的兒子毫不畏懼的答道. 父親. 你的堅忍那裏去了. 我一定受苦. 我的性命是拚丟的了. 讓他們把我的性命拿去.

我用力把感情按住. 有幾分鐘不說話. 我以為非死是按不下去的.

"Oh, my boy, my heart weeps to behold thee thus, and I cannot, cannot help it. In the moment that I thought thee blessed, and prayed for thy safety, to behold thee thus again! Chained, wounded! And yet the death of the youthful is happy. But I am old—a very old man, and have lived to see this day. To see my children all untimely falling about me, while I continue a wretched survivor in the midst of ruin! May all the curses that ever sunk a soul fall heavy upon the murderer of my children! May he live, like me, to see—"

"Hold, sir," replied my son, "or I shall blush for thee. How, sir, forgetful of your age, your holy calling, thus to arrogate the justice of Heaven, and fling those curses upward that must soon descend to crush thy own gray head with destruction! No, sir, let it be your care now to fit me for that vile death I must shortly suffer; to arm me with hope and resolution, to give me courage

我說道.我的孩子.我看見你這種模樣.我心要哭.我實在禁不住自己.我剛才正在以爲你蒙天保佑.祈禱你的平安.忽然看見你這樣帶上鎖鏈脚鐐.又受了傷.雖然死在壯年.是歡樂的.但是我老了.我是很老的人.活了這些年.看今天這種的日子.看見我的兒女們.一個個未到時候.都倒地了.只留我一個可憐蟲.還活在家散人亡殘景中.我但求上天.把一切沉埋靈魂的禍災.都降在殺我兒女的人身上.我望他同我一樣.活在世上.看見....

我的兒子攔住我.說道.父親.不要再說下去了.不然.我替你慚愧.父親爲何忘了你這大的年紀.忘了你是個牧師.擅行僭奪上天賞罰之權.對上蒼說了好些詛呪的話.將來不久.上天降禍於你.把你老年人毀滅了.父親.你不要如此.我不久就要受死刑.你這時候應該爲我預

to drink of that bitterness which must shortly be my portion."

"My child, you must not die; I am sure no offense of thine can deserve so vile a punishment. My George could never be guilty of any crime to make his ancestors ashamed of him."

"Mine, sir," returned my son, "is, I fear, an unpardonable one. When I received my mother's letter from home, I immediately came down, determined to punish the betrayer of our honor, and sent him an order to meet me, which he answered, not in person, but by dispatching four of his domestics to seize me. I wounded one who first assaulted me, and I fear desperately; but the rest made me their prisoner. The coward is determined to put the law in execution against me; the proofs are undeniable; I have sent a challenge, and as I am the first transgressor upon the statute, I see no hopes of pardon. But you have often charmed me with

備. 我好去死. 令我有希望. 有決心. 壯我的膽. 好去受苦.

我答道. 我的孩子. 你一定不死. 我敢說你不能犯受死刑的罪. 我的佐之. 斷不能犯罪. 玷辱祖宗.

我兒子答道. 我恐怕我犯的是不能赦的罪. 我一接到母親來信. 我立刻就來. 決意懲罰傷害我們名譽的人. 我送他一封信. 要他會我. 他却自己不來. 打發四個家人. 把我捉住. 第一個來攻打我的. 被我打傷了. 我很害怕. 其餘三個人把我捉住. 那個無勇的懦夫. 立意拿法律來對待我. 憑據是無可賴. 我同他挑戰. 按律是我首先犯事. 我看不出有什麼赦罪的希望. 但是你屢次以堅忍敎我. 我

your lessons of fortitude; let me now, sir, find them in your example."

"And, my son, you shall find them. I am now raised above this world, and all the pleasures it can produce. From this moment, I break from my heart all the ties that held it down to earth, and will prepare to fit us both for eternity. Yes, my son, I will point out the way, and my soul shall guide yours in the ascent, for we will take our flight together. I now see, and am convinced, you can expect no pardon here, and I can only exhort you to seek it at that greatest tribunal where we both shall shortly answer. But let us not be niggardly in our exhortation, but let all our fellow prisoners have a share: good jailer, let them be permitted to stand here while I attempt to improve them."

Thus saying, I made an effort to rise from my straw, but wanted strength, and was able only to recline

聽過都心醉. 現在讓我拿你作榜樣求堅忍.

我答道. 你一定求得着. 我現在已超出人世之外了. 毋論世上什麼歡樂. 也動不了我. 從這刻起. 把一切什麼羈絆我的心留戀人世的葛藤. 一刀斬斷. 預備你我兩人與世永遠長辭. 我的兒子. 我指示你的正路. 我的靈魂. 領你的靈魂登天. 因為我同你兩人. 一同飛去. 我現在也曉得. 也相信. 你不能盼望這個世界能救你. 我只勸你向最大的法庭〈即所謂末　後審列也〉望赦. 我們不久都要到那裏去對質. 但是只有我們互相勸勉. 未免太過吝嗇. 也讓那些同被監禁的人. 受些勸勉之益. 好獄卒你讓所有犯人. 都走來. 聽我勸他們.

我說完. 用力從我的乾草鋪裏站起來. 但是

against the wall. The prisoners assembled themselves according to my directions, for they loved to hear my counsel; my son and his mother supported me on either side; I looked and saw that none were wanting, and then addressed them with the following exhortation.

我已經很衰弱．站不起來．只能斜靠牆上．同時被禁的囚犯．果然聽我說．都來了．他們很喜歡聽我教訓．我的女人兒子．兩旁扶我．我一看．所有犯人都到齊了．一個也不少．我就把下回的話勸勉他們．

CHAPTER XXIX

THE EQUAL DEALINGS OF PROVIDENCE DEMONSTRATED WITH REGARD TO THE HAPPY AND THE MISERABLE HERE BELOW — THAT FROM THE NATURE OF PLEASURE AND PAIN, THE WRETCHED MUST BE REPAID THE BALANCE OF THEIR SUFFERINGS IN THE LIFE HEREAFTER.

第 二 十 九 回

證 明 人 世 苦 樂 上 天 分 得 很 勻 的
以 苦 樂 的 本 性 而 論 在 人 世 受 苦 的 死 後
應 享 快 樂
（勸 囚 徒 牧 師 講 大 道）

My friends, my children, and fellow sufferers, when I reflect on the distribution of good and evil here below, I find that much has been given man to enjoy, yet still more to suffer. Though we should examine the whole world, we shall not find one man so happy as to have nothing left to wish for; but we daily see thousands who by suicide show us they have nothing left to hope. In this life, then, it appears that we cannot be entirely blessed,

且 說. 我 對 衆 囚 犯 說 道. 我 的 朋 友 們. 我 的 兒 子 們. 我 的 受 苦 同 伴 們. 我 想 到 人 世 上 苦 樂 的 分 配. 就 曉 得 有 許 多 是 給 人 享 福 的. 然 而 使 人 受 苦 的 更 多. 即 使 我 們 把 全 個 人 世 都 查 遍 了. 也 找 不 出 一 個 人. 是 享 盡 了 福 再 無 所 求 的. 天 天 却 看 見 千 人 萬 人 自 殺. 可 見 這 許 多 人 是 絕 望 的 了. 這 個 世 上. 好 像

THE VICAR OF WAKEFIELD 355

but yet we may be completely miserable.

Why man should thus feel pain; why our wretchedness should be requisite in the formation of universal felicity; why, when all other systems are made perfect by the perfection of their subordinate parts, the great system should require for its perfection parts that are not only subordinate to others, but imperfect in themselves; these are questions that never can be explained, and might be useless if known. On this subject Providence has thought fit to elude our curiosity, satisfied with granting us motives to consolation.

In this situation man has called in the friendly assistance of philosophy; and Heaven, seeing the incapacity of that to console him, has given him the aid of religion. The consolations of philosophy are very amusing, but often fallacious. It tells us that life is filled with comforts, if we will but enjoy them; and on the other hand,

人是不能享全福的．却是人人都可完全受苦．

一個人爲什麼要受痛苦．爲什麼受過愁苦．然後才能享福．爲什麼其餘的組織．只要把分部做得完全無缺．那全體也就完全無缺．惟有我們這世界．是不完全的分部做成的．這幾個問題．是永遠解說不通的．假使解說通了．也許無甚用處．說到這個題目．上天不讓我們好奇之心窺見祕妙．只許我們有感觸以求心安〔宗教哲學都不能解說得通〕．

旣是這樣．人就求哲學相助．上天曉得．哲學仍是不能使人心安．故助以宗教．哲學安慰人心．很有可娛人之處．而往往無眞理．哲學說的是．世界上到處都有樂境．只要人曉得怎樣尋

that though we unavoidably have miseries here, life is short, and they will soon be over. Thus, do these consolations destroy each other; for if life is a place of comfort, its shortness must be misery; and if it be long, our griefs are protracted. Thus philosophy is weak, but religion comforts in a higher strain. Man is here, it tells us, fitting up his mind, and preparing it for another abode. When the good man leaves the body and is all a glorious mind, he will find he has been making himself a heaven of happiness here, while the wretch that has been maimed and contaminated by his vices, shrinks from his body with terror, and finds that he has anticipated[1] the vengeance of Heaven.

To religion, then, we must hold in every circumstance of life for our truest comfort; for if already we are happy, it is a pleasure to think that

樂.至於苦境.世人雖不能免.好在人生在世.爲時甚短.一會子就過了.這兩層的自慰話.是不能相容的.因爲世界若是個樂境.而浮生却甚短.則樂境旣不能久處.豈不又是苦境了嗎.若是在世甚久.豈不是把苦境拖長了嗎.可見哲學力量很弱.惟有宗教慰人.入人較深｛此兩語宜注意｝.宗教說的是.人生在世.好像是個預備科.先把心教練好.預備到另一世界.好人離開肉體的時候.那心全是光明的.就曉待他久已在此爲自己創造一個快樂世界.惡人已因爲惡而得殘廢.受了污穢.畏離肉體.才曉得預先已受上天的報仇.

是故無論一個人.所處的環境如何.一定要'抱住宗教.才求得最眞的心安.因爲我們若是已經歡樂.就想到將來

---

1. Anticipated, 預期；預享.

we can make that happiness unending; and if we are miserable, it is very consoling to think that there is a place of rest. Thus to the fortunate, religion holds out a continuance of bliss; to the wretched, a change from pain.

But though religion is very kind to all men, it has promised peculiar rewards to the unhappy; the sick, the naked, the houseless, the heavy-laden, and the prisoner have ever most frequent promises in our sacred law. The Author of our religion everywhere professes Himself the wretch's friend, and, unlike the false ones of this world, bestows all His caresses upon the forlorn. The unthinking have censured this as partiality, as a preference without merit to deserve it. But they never reflect that it is not in the power even of Heaven itself to make the offer of unceasing felicity as great a gift to the happy as to the miserable. To the first, eternity is but a single blessing, since at most it

我以自示永以改苦境為樂境．我想到自然也可以安心．宗教示有幸福的人以接續永享幸福．示不幸的人以

宗教雖對於人都是以慈愛．惟對於苦人．許以法律．對於病人．無衣服穿的人．無家可歸的人．負重累的人．被禁在監的人之主．到處都說過．他是世上可憐人的真朋友．所有的扶持愛護．都施於世上的可憐人．與世上的假朋友．絕不相同．假朋友只去巴結富貴人｛作者之基督教理略見於此篇大議論然不甚能自圓其說｝．無思想的人．却有責言．以此為有所偏愛．以為是可憐人無德以當此．這些人却從未想到．即使把同樣的永無止境的歡樂．就是上天自己也無力量．能過於苦人樂所得這樂境．能過於無限所前所覺富人．只覺得與從享

的歡樂是永無止境．我若是愁苦．就還有歇息的地方．

367

but increases what they already possess. To the latter, it is a double advantage; for it diminishes their pain here, and rewards them with heavenly bliss hereafter.

But Providence is, in another respect, kinder to the poor than the rich; for, as it thus makes the life after death more desirable, so it smooths the passage there. The wretched have had a long familiarity[1] with every face of terror. The man of sorrows lays himself quietly down, without possessions to regret, and but few ties to stop his departure: he feels only nature's pang in the final separation, and this is no way greater than he has often fainted under before; for, after a certain degree of pain, every new breach that death opens in the constitution, nature kindly covers with insensibility.

Thus Providence has given the wretched two advantages over the happy

的仍是一件事.無甚進步.因為他們曾經享過福.以後不過是添福而已.苦人則不然.却覺得有兩層好處.一則減輕在世之苦.二則受以後的天賜.

另從一方面看.上天還有一層.對苦人慈愛得多.因為表示以後的世界更好.就把從這個世界到那個世界的過道.先鋪平了.苦人是無論什麼苦.都已飽受過.納頭便倒地.並無財產之類牽掛.也無多少親眷.不讓他走.是不會捨不得走的.最後離開這世界時.只覺得一陣天然之痛.並不比他向來常受痛到暈絕的苦.有什麼大分別.因為受痛苦.到了一種的限度.將死的時候.身體上發生的各種苦痛.老天可憐.自然禁壓住.使他無知無覺.

可見上天給世上的苦人.比給富人.多兩種

---

1. Long familiarity, 相識已久; 此處作飽嘗解

in this life—greater felicity in dying, and in heaven all that superiority of pleasure which arises from contrasted[1] enjoyment.

And this superiority, my friends, is no small advantage, and seems to be one of the pleasures of the poor man in the parable; for, though he was already in heaven, and felt all the raptures it could give, yet it was mentioned as an addition to his happiness, that he had once been wretched, and now was comforted: that he had known what it was to be miserable, and now felt what it was to be happy.

Thus, my friends, you see religion does what philosophy can never do: it shows the equal dealings of Heaven to the happy and the unhappy, and levels all human enjoyments to nearly the same standard. It gives to both rich and poor the same happiness hereafter, and equal hopes to aspire after it; but if the rich have the

利益. 一. 死得安心些. 二. 因為在世上已受過苦. 死後到天堂享福. 覺得加倍歡樂.

我的朋友們. 這一層好處不小這就是寓言所說苦人所享歡樂中之一 {見路加福音[十六]一九至三一}. 因為他雖已到天堂. 覺得天堂所有的種種歡樂. 書上說. 因他曾經受過苦. 現在安心. 更覺得歡樂. 又說. 他曉得受苦是那麼樣. 現在曉得享福是這麼樣.

朋友們可以明白. 宗教作得到的. 哲學永遠作不到. 宗教告訴我們. 上天是不管在這世界受苦的或是享福的. 都是一樣的待遇. 把人類一切的享受. 都鋪平了. 歸到一個標準. 不問受苦的享福的. 死後給的都是一樣的樂. 同給一樣的希望 {此段語意卻與新約不合}. 若是在這個世界. 富人

---

1. Contrasted, 以兩相反對事比較; 反襯.

advantage of enjoying pleasure here, the poor have the endless satisfaction of knowing what it was once to be miserable, when crowned with endless felicity hereafter; and even though this should be called a small advantage, yet being an eternal one, it must make up by duration what the temporal happiness of the great may have exceeded by intenseness.

These are, therefore, the consolations which the wretched have peculiar to themselves, and in which they are above the rest of mankind; in other respects they are below them. They who would know the miseries of the poor, must see life and endure it. To declaim on the temporal advantages[1] they enjoy is only repeating what none either believe or practice. The men who have the necessaries of living are not poor, and they who want them must be miserable. Yes, my friends, we must

有享快樂的利益.貧人
却曾經受過苦.到後來
曉得享受無限快樂.有
無限的滿意.雖說這不
過是小利益.然而却是
無窮無盡的.苦人的樂
境長.富人的樂境深.一
定可以相抵. .

這就是貧人特別所
有可以自慰之處.只這
一件.却是勝過他人.其
餘的却不及他人.凡人
若要曉得貧人的苦况.
須要出來問世.身受其
苦 {作者是飽歷貧人 苦境故說得出} . 光
是拿嘴去說.不要世上
富貴.既沒得人相信.也
沒得人肯去實行.凡人
既有生活所需.就不是
貧.連生活所需都沒有.
那才是苦 {詩人患此病 者多樂觀派
'亦然} . 朋友們.我們都要
受受苦.無論費盡多少

---

1. Temporal advantages, 世人所享利益,富貴尊榮是也.

be miserable. No vain efforts of a refined imagination can soothe the wants of nature, can give elastic sweetness to the dank vapor of a dungeon, or ease the throbbings of a broken heart. Let the philosopher from his couch of softness tell us that we can resist all these. Alas! the effort by which we resist them is still the greatest pain! Death is slight, and any man may sustain it; but torments are dreadful, and these no man can endure.

To us, then, my friends, the promises of happiness in heaven should be peculiarly dear; for if our reward be in this life alone, we are then, indeed, of all men the most miserable. When I look round these gloomy walls, made to terrify as well as to confine us; this light that only serves to show the horrors of the place; those shackles that tyranny has imposed, or crime made necessary; when I survey these emaciated looks, and hear those

奧妙思想也不能穀抵飢禦寒，也不能穀把監獄裏頭的潮濕發徵的壞氣味變作怡神的新氣，也不能穀使受傷的心不撲同撲同的跳。只管讓哲學家坐在輭的交椅上，大發其議論，勸人抵禦種種的苦。可惜我們一件用力去抵禦，就是一件最苦。死原算不了什麼，人都可以受；痛苦是最可怕，無論什麼人都受不了。〔可見痛苦是眞的，空言安慰都不相干，亦徒自欺而已。〕

我的朋友們，我們對於上帝所許在天的歡樂，應該看得特別寶貴；假使我們的賞報只在這個世界，那我們眞是最苦的人了。我四面一看，圍禁我們這些造得光的牆，這光只照見這地方的兇暴，這些霸加在我們身上的，或是各人罪惡弄成必需的腳鐐；我看各人的黃瘦餓死的臉，再聽那一

groans, oh! my friends, what a glorious exchange would heaven be for these. To fly through regions unconfined as air, to bask in the sunshine of eternal bliss, to carol over endless hymns of praise, to have no master to threaten or insult us, but the form of Goodness Himself forever in our eyes! When I think of these things, death becomes the messenger of very glad tidings; when I think of these things, His sharpest arrow becomes the staff of my support; when I think of these things, what is there in life worth having? when I think of these things, what is there that should not be spurned away? Kings in their palaces should groan for[1] such advantages; but we, humbled as we are, should yearn for them.

And shall these things be ours? Ours they will certainly be if we but try for them; and what is a comfort, we are shut out

派愁歎呻吟之聲. 我的朋友們呀. 拿天堂來換這些愁苦景況. 豈不是立變悽慘黑暗爲光榮顯赫嗎. 我想到在那無限無邊如在空氣中飛行. 飽受永遠歡樂中的日光. 唱不盡讚美的詩歌. 絕無主人恐嚇我們. 侮辱我們. 永遠只見上帝的聖容. 我想到這幾件樂事的時候. 看得死這件事. 不過是來報喜信的使者. 我想到這幾件樂事的時候. 死的最鋒利的箭矢. 變作我的拐杖. 我想到這幾件樂事的時候. 人世上有什麼值得要的呢. 我想到這幾件樂事的時候. 人世上那一件不是可以踢開不要的呢. 住在宮殿的帝王們. 那個不很想要這種好處. 何況我們卑賤. 更應想得這種好處.

我們旣然想得這種好處. 我們能彀得着不不能呢. 我們只要去試. 一定是能得着的. 我們

---

1. Groan for, 求; 很想.

from many temptations that would retard our pursuit. Only let us try for them, and they will certainly be ours, and, what is still a comfort, shortly too; for, if we look back on a past life, it appears but a very short span; and, whatever we may think of the rest of life, it will yet be found of less duration; as we grow older the days seem to grow shorter, and our intimacy with time ever lessens the perception of his stay. Then let us take comfort now, for we shall soon be at our journey's end; we shall soon lay down the heavy burden laid by Heaven upon us; and though death, the only friend of the wretched, for a little while mocks the weary traveler with the view, and like his horizon, still flies before him, yet the time will certainly and shortly come when we shall cease from our toil; when the luxuriant great ones of the world shall no more tread us to the earth; when we shall think with pleasure of our sufferings below;

貧苦的人.既無財無力.不能爲許多外物所誘.阻止我們的進步.這一層我們是可以放心的.我們只要出力去求那些好處.一定是我們的.並且用不着久候.這又是一層可以放心的.我們只要追想巳過的日子.還不是很短的嗎.再想想將來的日子.那是更短了.我們的年紀一年長一年.日子覺得一年短一年.見其多了.我們經過的日子.也習慣了.日子過得快.我們覺得現在放心罷.我們的路程.不久就可以走完了.把天給我們的很重的負累放下來.我們這一羣可憐蟲.無朋友.只有死是我們的朋友.我們死怕好得走.受苦也受戮了.死雖然有時在前頭.拿可好的面目.戲弄我們.又像越趨近他.他越退遠.然而不久.一定要一時再把一切勞苦.一齊放下.那時世上的豪富大人.再也不能踐踏我們.那時世上四周圍.我們歡心的追想苦況.那時候四周都是朋友.不然也以朋友相待的.值得我們享的人.那時候我們

when we shall be sur-
rounded with all our
friends, or such as deserved
our friendship; when our
bliss shall be unutterable,
and, still, to crown all,
unending.

是口不能說的歡樂. 還
有最好的一層. 就是我
們所享的歡樂. 是無窮
無盡的｛說實人苦況淋漓
盡致亦惟有一死
可以了之宗教哲｝.
學亦無如之何

CHAPTER XXX

HAPPIER PROSPECTS BEGIN TO APPEAR—LET US BE INFLEXIBLE, AND FORTUNE WILL AT LAST CHANGE IN OUR FAVOR.

第 三 十 回

歡 樂 光 景 開 始 出 現　我 們 只 要 不 遷 就
到 後 來 一 定 有 好 運 氣
（救 牧 師 白 且 爾 露 眞 相）

When I had thus finished, and my audience was retired, the jailer, who was one of the most humane of his profession, hoped I would not be displeased, as what he did was but his duty, observing that he must be obliged to remove my son into a stronger cell, but that he should be permitted to visit me every morning. I thanked him for his clemency, and, grasping my boy's hand, bade him farewell, and be mindful of the great duty that was before him.

I again, therefore, laid me down, and one of my

且說.我講完之後.衆囚犯都散了.那個最慈善的獄卒.對我說.請我不要不高興.因爲他所作的事.不過是要盡他的職.他說不得不把我的兒子.收禁在堅固的牢裏.但是仍可以讓他每早同我相見.我謝他一番的憐憫.我同兒子抓手.吩咐他不要忘了眼前應作的本分事.

我於是再躺下.一個小兒子坐在我牀邊讀

little ones sat by my bedside reading, when Mr. Jenhinson entering, informed me that there was news of my daughter; for that she was seen by a person about two hours before in a strange gentleman's company, and that they had stopped at a neighboring village for refreshment, and seemed as if returning to town. He had scarcely delivered this news, when the jailer came, with looks of haste and pleasure, to inform me that my daughter was found. Moses came running in a moment after, crying out that his sister Sophy was below, and coming up with our old friend Mr. Burchell.

Just as he delivered this news, my dearest girl entered; and with looks almost wild with pleasure, ran to kiss me in a transport of affection. Her mother's tears and silence also showed her pleasure.

"Here, papa," cried the charming girl—"here is the brave man to whom I owe my delivery; to this

書. 金京森走進來告訴我. 我的二女兒有了下落. 因為有人兩點鐘前. 看見他同一位不知名姓的上等人在一起. 在隔村吃飯. 好像是要回來. 他剛說完. 獄卒走來. 臉上很匆忙. 很喜歡. 告訴我. 我的女兒已經找着了. 摩西一會子也跑進來說. 素緋雅姊姊在下面. 正同我們的朋友白且爾上來.

他正在說話. 我的至寶女兒進來. 臉上是歡喜欲狂的. 跑來同我接吻. 樂不可支. 他的母親歡喜到流淚. 說不出話來.

我的女兒說道. 爸爸. 這就是那位勇敢的人. 我虧他救我的. 我虧得

gentleman's intrepidity I am indebted for my happiness and safety."

A kiss from Mr. Burchell, whose pleasure seemed even greater than hers, interrupted what she was going to add.

"Ah, Mr. Burchell," cried I, "this is but a wretched habitation you now find us in; and we are now very different from what you last saw us. You were ever our friend: we have long discovered our errors with regard to you, and repented of our ingratitude. After the vile usage you then received at my hands, I am almost ashamed to behold your face; yet I hope you'll forgive me, as I was deceived by a base ungenerous wretch, who, under the mask of friendship, has undone me."

"It is impossible," replied Mr. Burchell, "that I should forgive you, as you never deserved my resentment. I partly saw your delusion then; and as it was out of my power to restrain, I could only pity it!"

他的勇氣.才得今日平安歡樂.

白且爾同我女兒接吻.攔住他.不叫他往下說.那白且爾好像比素緋雅還要快樂.

我說道.白且爾先生.你現在看見我們住的是極苦的地方.我們現在比不得從前你看見我們的時候了.你向來是我們的好朋友.我們早已明白我們看錯你了.我們忘恩負義.很覺得後悔.從前我們家裏那樣不好的待你.我現在很慚愧的見你面.我却盼望你寬恕我們.因為我被一個卑劣無義的小人騙了.這個人戴了一個好朋友的假面具.把我毀了.

白且爾答道.我向來不怨恨你.我就無所謂寬赦你.我當日也看出一點.你上了人家的當.我却無力阻止.我只好可憐你.

"It was ever my conjecture," cried I, "that your mind was noble; but now I find it so. But tell me, my dear child, how hast thou been relieved, or who the ruffians were who carried thee away."

"Indeed, sir," replied she, "as to the villain who carried me off, I am yet ignorant. For as my mamma and I were walking out, he came behind us, and almost before I could call for help, forced me into the post chaise, and in an instant the horses drove away. I met several on the road to whom I cried out for assistance, but they disregarded my entreaties. In the meantime, the ruffian himself used every art to hinder me from crying out: he flattered and threatened by turns, and swore that if I continued but silent he intended no harm.

In the meantime I had broken the canvas that he had drawn up; and whom should I perceive at some distance, but your old friend Mr. Burchell, walking along with his usual

我答道. 我向來忖度你的心地是高貴的. 我現在曉得你是的確如此. 我回頭問女兒道. 我的好孩子. 你告訴我. 那些匪人是怎樣刼你的, 你怎樣遇救的.

我的女兒答道. 刼我的匪人. 我現在究不曉得是誰. 當日我母親同我在路上走. 那個人從背後來. 我還來不及叫喊. 他就把我抓到車上. 那馬車就立刻趕走了. 在路上雖碰見幾個人. 我大叫. 向他們求救. 他們都不管﹛白晝擄女人可見當時貴族之橫行﹜. 那時候那個匪類用許多法子 不讓我喊. 一會兒恭維我. 一會兒又恐嚇我. 又發誓的說. 只要我不喊. 他無意傷害我.

當下我把他掛起來的一張帆布帷子撕破了. 我遠遠看見一個人. 却不是別人. 就是你的老友白且爾先生. 在路上同向來一樣的走

swiftness, with the great stick for which we used so much to ridicule him. As soon as we came within hearing, I called out to him by name, and entreated his help.

"I repeated my exclamation several times; upon which, with a very loud voice, he bade the postilion stop; but the boy took no notice, but drove on with still greater speed. I now thought he could never overtake us, when in less than a minute I saw Mr. Burchell come running up by the side of the horses, and with one blow knock the postilion to the ground. The horses when he was falling soon stopped of themselves, and the ruffian stepped out, with oaths and menaces, drew his sword and ordered him at his peril to retire; but Mr. Burchell, running up, shivered his sword to pieces, and then pursued him for near a quarter of a mile; but he made his escape.

"I was at this time come out myself, willing to assist my deliverer, but he soon

得很快.手上還拿着大手杖.我們向來很笑他這個手杖的.我等到走得相近.他可以聽得見喊.我就喊他的名字.求他打救.

我一連喊了好幾聲.他很大聲的叫那趕車的停住.那車夫不理.向前趕.趕得更快.我這時候心裏叫苦.恐怕他永遠趕不上馬車.誰知不到一分鐘工夫.白先生趕到馬的身邊.用大力一擊.把馬夫打倒在地下.馬夫一倒.那些馬也就停住了.匪人跳出車來.滿嘴亂罵.滿嘴恐嚇.拔出刀來.叫白先生退後.不然.就要他的命.白先生走向前.把那把刀打碎了好幾塊.追趕那匪人.趕了差不多有一里路.那匪人逃走了.

我這時候也走上去.要助白先生.他一會子得勝了.回頭來.這時候

returned to me in triumph. The postilion, who was recovered, was going to make his escape too; but Mr. Burchell ordered him at his peril to mount again and drive back to town. Finding it impossible to resist, he reluctantly complied, though the wound he had received seemed to me at least to be dangerous. He continued to complain of the pain as we drove along, so that he at last excited Mr. Burchell's compassion, who, at my request, exchanged him for another at an inn where we called on our return."

"Welcome, then," cried I, "my child, and thou her gallant deliverer—a thousand welcomes. Though our cheer is but wretched, yet our hearts are ready to receive you. And now, Mr. Burchell, as you have delivered my girl, if you think her a recompense, she is yours; if you can stoop to an alliance with a family so poor as mine, take her; obtain her consent, as I know you have her heart, and you have mine And let me

馬夫醒過來．正在也要逃走．白先生叫他再上車．不然．就要他的命．叫他上車．趕回村裏．他一看不能抗拒．滿肚子不舒服．上了車．那馬夫受的傷．却是很重的．他一面趕．一面說痛．後來白先生見他可憐．我就勸白先生在我們回來時候所住的那個小客店內．另找了一個馬夫．

我說道．我的孩子．我歡迎你．你這位有勇的救難的人．我一千倍的歡迎他．我們雖然並無令你高興的招待．我們的心．都是很歡迎你．白且爾先生．你旣經救了我的女兒．你若以爲我的女兒可以抵得過你的解救．我願意把女兒嫁與你爲妻．倘若你能屈尊俯就．同我們這樣窮苦人家結親．你就娶他．我曉得你已經得了他的心．也得了我的心．

tell you, sir, that I give you no small treasure: she has been celebrated for beauty, it is true, but that is not my meaning: I give you up a treasure in her mind."

"But I suppose, sir," cried Mr. Burchell, "that you are apprised of my circumstances, and of my incapacity to support her as she deserves?"

"If your present objection," replied I, "be meant as an evasion[1] of my offer, I desist: but I know no man so worthy to deserve her as you; and if I could give her thousands, and thousands sought her from me, yet my honest, brave Burchell should be my dearest choice."

To all this his silence alone seemed to give a mortifying refusal; and without the least reply to my offer, he demanded if he could not be furnished with refreshments from the next inn; to which being answered in the affirmative, he ordered them to

你只要問他願意與否. 我還要告訴你. 我把女兒給你. 是給你一個至寶. 他的美貌很出名. 這是可以不必說的了. 這也不是我的意思. 我說的是他的心地是至寶.

白且爾說道. 先生. 我揣度. 你已經曉得我的光景. 你也曉得他應該享受的一切. 我無力量供給他.

我答道. 你現在種種的不願意. 若是推諉的話. 我就不勉強你. 但是我曉得. 除了你之外. 再無別人. 配得上他. 假使我能給他千千萬萬的妝奩. 那怕有千千萬萬的人來求婚. 我還是挑選誠實有勇的白且爾作女婿.

我說到這種話. 他一味的不響. 我見得好像是他是無可挽回的拒絕. 我願意把女兒給他. 他一句也不答｛將遇好事偏用筆故推曲折白且爾借故推宕成｝. 只問最近的小客店有什麼吃的

---

1. Evasion, 躲閃話；避重就輕或避名就實.

send in the best dinner that could be provided upon such short notice. He bespoke also a dozen of their best wine, and some cordials for me; adding, with a smile, that he would stretch a little for once; and though in a prison, asserted he was never better disposed to be merry. The waiter soon made his appearance with preparations for dinner; a table was lent us by the jailer, who seemed remarkably assiduous; the wine was disposed in order, and two very well-dressed dishes were brought in.

My daughter had not yet heard of her poor brother's melancholy situation, and we all seemed unwilling to damp her cheerfulness by the relation. But it was in vain that I attempted to appear cheerful; the circumstances of my unfortunate son broke through all efforts to dissemble;[1] so that I was at last obliged to damp our mirth by

沒有. 有人答他說有. 他吩咐人們把最好的大餐送來. 又定了十二瓶頂好的酒. 又專為我定些甜酒. 還微笑的說. 要破戒一次. 又說. 雖是在監獄裏. 他卻願意熱鬧一番. 一會子. 店裏的跑堂來了. 預備大餐. 獄卒借給我們一張桌子. 非常的出力張羅. 酒都擺好了. 送來兩樣很好的菜.

我女兒還不曉得他兄弟的慘狀. 衆人都不願意告訴他. 敗他的興頭. 無論我怎樣裝高興. 也高興不來. 無論怎樣裝假. 我也禁不住把我兒子的情形說出來. 後

---

1. Dissemble, 不露眞意; 裝假; 作僞.

relating his misfortunes, and wishing that he might be permitted to share with us in this little interval of satisfaction. After my guests were recovered from the consternation my account had produced, I requested also that Mr. Jenkinson, a fellow prisoner, might be admitted, and the jailer granted my request with an air of unusual submission. The clanking of my son's irons was no sooner heard along the passage than his sister ran impatiently to meet him; while Mr. Burchell, in the meantime, asked me if my son's name was George, to which replying in the affirmative, he still continued silent. As soon as my boy entered the room, I could perceive he regarded Mr. Burchell with a look of astonishment and reverence.

"Come on," cried I, "my son; though we are fallen very low, yet Providence has been pleased to grant us some small relaxation from pain. Thy sister is restored to us, and there

來不得不敗他們的興頭.把兒子被禁的事說了.我還說我願意兒子出來.同我們一齊宴會.同席的人聽過了.驚魂稍定之後.我還要把金京森也請來同吃.獄卒很服從的.都答應了.一聽見過道裏我兒子腳鐐聲響.他的姊姊很不耐煩.就跑出去會他.當下白且爾問我兒子的名字是否叫佐之.我答是的.他就不響.我的兒子一進牢來.他看見白且爾.一驚.却現出很尊敬他的神氣. •

我說道.兒子.我們雖然墮落得很低.上天却許我們稍爲止痛.你的姊姊尋回來了.這一位

is her deliverer; to that brave man it is that I am indebted for yet having a daughter; give him, my boy, the hand of friendship; he deserves our warmest gratitude."

My son seemed all this while regardless of what I said, and still continued fixed at respectful distance.

"My dear brother," cried his sister, "why don't you thank my good deliverer? The brave should ever love each other."

He still continued his silence and astonishment, till our guest at last perceived himself to be known, and, assuming all his native dignity, desired my son to come forward. Never before had I seen anything so truly majestic[1] as the air he assumed upon this occasion. The greatest object in the universe, says a certain philosopher, is a good man struggling with adversity; yet there is still a greater, which is the good man that comes to relieve it.

就是打救他的人．我是很虧這位有勇的人．使我還有一個女兒．我的孩子．你伸手給他．他應該受我們最熱心的感激．

這個時候．我的兒子不管我說什麼．只遠遠站在那裏不動．

他的姊姊說道．你為什麼不謝謝救我的人．凡是有勇的人．都應該相愛．

我的兒子．還是一樣的驚奇．還是不響．後來我們的客人白且爾曉得有人認得他的真相．就露出他本來的氣概．叫我的兒子走向前．我見人也見得多．向來未曾見過這時候白且爾流露出來的那一種尊嚴威重氣概．有一位哲學家曾說過．宇宙間偉大的事．無過於好人同禍患奮鬪．然而還有一件更偉大的事．就是好人來解除禍患．

1. Majestic, 尊嚴.

After he had regarded my son for some time with a superior air, "I again find," said he, "unthinking boy, that the same crime——" But here he was interrupted by one of the jailer's servants, who came to inform us that a person of distinction, who had driven into town with a chariot and several attendants, sent his respects to the gentleman that was with us, and begged to know when he should think proper to be waited upon.

"Bid the fellow wait," cried our guest, "till I shall have leisure to receive him;" and then turning to my son, "I again find, sir," proceeded he, "that you are guilty of the same offense for which you once had my reproof, and for which the law is now preparing its justest punishments. You imagine, perhaps, that a contempt for your own life gives you a right to take that of another; but where, sir, is the difference between a duelist, who hazards a life of no value, and the murderer, who acts

白且爾現出很高貴的神色.很看了我的兒子一會.說道.你這個無思想的莽孩子.我又看見你又犯一樣的罪....說到這裏.獄卒走來打叉.說是有一位闊人.坐了馬車.帶了好幾個跟人來到.同這裏的一位貴人請安.求貴人給他一句話.吩咐他幾時可以晉見.

我們的客人說道.叫他在底下等.等到我幾時有空再見他.白且爾吩咐完.接着對我兒子說道.我又看見你犯同樣的罪.我從前曾經戒責你不要再犯的.現在法律就預備公道的罰你.你大約以為你把自己的性命看得輕.就可以隨便要人家的性命.我來問你.一個決鬥的人.拿自己無價值的性命去冒險.又有一個殺人

with greater security? Is it any diminution of the gamester's fraud, when he alleges that he has staked a counter?"[1]

"Alas! sir," cried I, "whoever you are, pity the poor misguided creature; for whatever he has done was in obedience to a deluded mother, who, in the bitterness of her resentment, required him upon her blessing to avenge her quarrel. Here, sir, is the letter which will serve to convince you of her imprudence, and diminish his guilt."

He took the letter, and hastily read it over. "This," says he, "though not a perfect excuse, is such a palliation of his fault as induces me to forgive him.

"And now, sir," continued he, kindly taking my son by the hand, "I see you are surprised at finding me here; but I have often visited prisons upon occasions less interesting. I am now come to see

的人. 自己却站在安穩地方. 然後殺人. 這兩個人. 有什麼分別. 譬如有一個賭徒. 自稱他是用假幣去賭. 這一解說. 能彀減輕他行騙的罪嗎.

我說道. 先生. 我不問你是誰. 我求你憐憫他是被人引去走差路. 他爲的是奉老母之命去作的. 他的母親懷恨甚深. 一時糊塗. 保佑他的兒子. 要他報仇. 先生. 這就是他母親的信. 你一讀就可以相信他母親的輕率行爲. 可以減輕他兒子的罪.

他把信接過去. 匆匆的一讀. 說道. 這封信雖不能替他完全解脫清楚. 却把他的罪過減輕許多. 我可以寬恕他.

於是他很慈愛的拉着我兒子的手. 說道. 你看見我在這裏. 很詫異. 但是我因事探視監獄的時候很多. 却不如這次有意味. 我這次來. 是對

---

1. Counter, 假幣.

justice done a worthy man, for whom I have the most sincere esteem. I have long been a disguised spectator of thy father's benevolence. I have at his little dwelling enjoyed respect uncontaminated by flattery, and have received that happiness that courts could not give, from the amusing simplicity round his fireside. My nephew has been apprised of my intentions of coming here, and, I find, is arrived; it would be wronging him and you to condemn him without examination; if there be injury, there shall be redress; and this I may say without boasting, that none have ever taxed[1] the injustice of Sir William Thornhill."

We now found the personage whom we had so long entertained as a harmless, amusing companion was no other than the celebrated Sir William Thornhill, to whose virtues and singularities scarce any were strangers.[2] The poor

於我所真誠尊敬的人來的. 使他得公平的待遇. 免他受屈. 我曾經久已改裝. 親見你父親行善. 我在他的小住宅. 享受過未沾染過諂媚的敬意. 我也曾在他家裏圍爐. 享受過娛人的天倫之樂. 這是王侯第宅所未有的{專務富貴好出鋒頭的人那知有此}. 我的姪子得了信. 曉得我有意到這裏. 現在他到了. 若是不把他審問清楚. 就定他的罪. 未免對他不起. 也對你不起. 若是有傷害. 一定有賠償傷害的辦法. 我不是說好吹的話. 向來無人說過威廉唐希爾爵士不公道.

我們這時候. 才曉得原來我們款待了許久的一個老實無害很有趣的白且爾先生. 就是有名的威廉唐希爾爵士. 這個人的道德. 同他的癖性. 大概是無人不

---

1. Taxed, 此處作指謫責問解.　2. Strangers, 此處作不曉得的人解

Mr. Burchell was in reality a man of large fortune and great interest, to whom senates listened with applause, and whom party heard with conviction; who was the friend of his country, but loyal to his king. My poor wife, recollecting her former familiarity, seemed to shrink with apprehension; but Sophia, who a few minutes before thought him her own, now perceiving the immense distance to which he was removed by fortune, was unable to conceal her tears.

"Ah, sir," cried my wife, with a piteous aspect, "how is it possible that I can ever have your forgiveness? The slights you received from me the last time I had the honor of seeing you at our house, and the jokes I audaciously threw out—these jokes, sir, I fear, can never be forgiven."

"My dear, good lady," returned he with a smile, "if you had your joke, I had my answer; I'll leave it to all the company, if mine were not as good as

曉得的. 那個貧窮的白且爾. 原來是一位大富人. 許多大事業同他都有關係. 議院聽他說話是要喝采的. 政黨也信他的話. 他却是忠君愛國. 我的女人記得從前太不客氣. 好像畏懼到縮起來 {可見英國貴族之威權氣酸}.

素緋雅前幾分鐘. 以為白且爾是他的了. 現在覺得貧富相差太遠. 以為無望. 禁不住流淚. {前此寫白且爾不肯痛快說此顧與素緋雅結婚此次却寫素緋雅因貧富太差其勢不能與白且爾結婚固是好事多磨亦行文曲折應有之筆}.

我的女人很可憐的. 說道. 我怎麼樣能彀得你寬恕我呢. 末了一次. 你在我們家中. 你受了我許多藐視. 我並且很大膽同你開頑笑. 先生. 我恐怕你永遠不能寬恕我那些笑話.

他微笑答道. 你有你的笑話. 我有我的對答. 我請在座衆位批評. 是不是我的笑話. 也有你

yours. To say the truth, I know nobody whom I am disposed to be angry with at present but the fellow who so frighted my little girl here. I had not even time to examine the rascal's person so as to describe him in an advertisement. Can you tell me, Sophia, my dear, whether you should know him again?"

"Indeed, sir," replied she, "I can't be positive; yet, now I recollect, he had a large mark over one of his eyebrows."

"I ask pardon, madam," interrupted Jenkinson, who was by; "but be so good as to inform me if the fellow wore his own red hair?"

"Yes, I think so," cried Sophia.

"And did your honor," continued he, turning to Sir William, "observe the length of his legs?"

"I can't be sure of their length," cried the Baronet, "but I am convinced of their swiftness; for he outran me, which is what I thought few men in the kingdom could have done."

的好.我老實說.我同誰都不生氣.只同那個驚嚇我的小女孩的人生氣.我當日來不及細看那匪類的面貌身材.好爲將來登告白尋他.素緋雅.我的寶貝.你能告訴我.你能再認得他麽.

素緋雅答道.先生.我不能說一定認得他.我只記得他有一大塊疤.在一邊眉毛上.

金京森從旁說道.瑪當.你能告訴我.他頭上是眞的紅頭髮麽.

素緋雅答道.我想是的.

又回頭對威廉爵士說道.大人曾否留意.那個人的腿是很長的.

爵士答道.我不能說實在他的腿是很長.我却曉得那兩條腿跑得飛快.他跑得比我快.我心裏還想.國內沒得幾個人跑得過我的.

"Please your honor," cried Jenkinson, "I know the man; it is certainly the same—the best runner in England; he has beaten Pinwire of Newcastle; Timothy Baxter is his name. I know him perfectly, and the very place of his retreat this moment. If your honor will bid Mr. Jailer let two of his men go with me, I'll engage to produce him to you in an hour at farthest." Upon this, the jailer was called, who instantly appearing, Sir William demanded if he knew him.

"Yes, please your honor," replied the jailer, "I know Sir William Thornhill well; and everybody that knows anything of him will desire to know more of him."

"Well, then," said the Baronet, "my request is, that you will permit this man and two of your servants to go upon a message by my authority; and as I am in the commission of the peace, I undertake to secure you."

"Your promise is sufficient," replied the other;

金京森說道. 大人. 我曉得這個人. 一定是他. 英國境內第一個能跑的. 他跑贏某處的某人. 他名叫巴士特. 我很曉得他這個人. 他現時躲在什麼地方. 我也曉得. 倘若大人吩咐獄卒讓他的手下兩個人同我去. 最多在一個鐘頭以內. 我一定將他交到你面前來. 於是把獄卒傳了來. 威廉爵士問獄卒道. 你可認得我.

獄卒答道. 大人. 我認得你是威廉唐希爾爵士. 凡是認得他的人. 都願意多認得他.

爵士說道. 很好. 我今要你讓這個人. 同你的手下兩個人. 奉我命去辦事. 我原是一位地方官. 我擔保你不受損失.

獄卒答道. 只要你答應就是了. 大人只要吩

"and you may at a minute's warning send them over England whenever your honor thinks fit."

In pursuance of the jailer's compliance, Jenkinson was dispatched in search of Timothy Baxter, while we were amused with the assiduity of our youngest boy Bill, who had just come in and climbed up to Sir William's neck in order to kiss him. His mother was immediately going to chastise his familiarity, but the worthy man prevented her; and taking the child, all ragged as he was, upon his knee, "What, Bill, you chubby rogue," cried he, "do you remember your old friend Burchell?—and Dick, too, my honest veteran,[1] are you here?—you shall find I have not forgot you." So saying, he gave each a large piece of gingerbread, which the poor fellows ate very heartily, as they had got that morning but a very scanty breakfast.

咐下來.無論什麼時候你要他們走遍一個英國都使得.

獄卒奉了命.派人同金京森去找巴士特.剛好我們最小的孩子比勒走進來.爬到威廉爵士膝上.同他接吻.我們看着這小孩很忙的.很開心.他的母親.立刻要斥責他太不客氣.爵士倒攔着.把這個衣衫襤褸的小孩.抱在膝上.說道.比勒.你這個小胖子光棍.你還認得你的老朋友白且爾嗎.狄克.你這個老實的老將.你也在這裏嗎.你們曉得我並沒忘記你們.一面說.一面一個孩子給一塊餅.可憐這兩個孩子.早上未乞飽.把餅接過來.吃得開心.

---

1. Veteran, 老將; 老手.

We now sat down to dinner, which was almost cold; but previously, my arm still continuing painful, Sir William wrote a prescription, for he had made the study of physic his amusement, and was more than moderately skilled in the profession; this being sent to an apothecary who lived in the place, my arm was dressed, and I found almost instantaneous relief. We were waited upon at dinner by the jailer himself, who was willing to do our guest all the honor in his power.　But before we had well dined, another message was brought from his nephew, desiring permission to appear in order to vindicate his innocence and honor; with which request the Baronet complied, and desired Mr. Thornhill to be introduced.

我們於是坐下吃大餐. 這時候菜都快涼了. 剛才我的手很疼. 威廉爵士學醫消遣. 醫道還好. 替我開方子. 買了藥敷上. 立刻止痛. 獄卒當了我們的侍者. 他很出力巴結我們的貴客. 我們還未吃完. 爵士的姪子. 又打發人來請示. 幾時可以晉見. 辯明他無罪. 辯明他並無作不顧廉恥的事. 爵士准他晉見. 叫人帶他來.

CHAPTER XXXI

FORMER BENEVOLENCE NOW REPAID WITH
UNEXPECTED INTEREST

第 三 十 一 回

由 從 前 的 行 善 收 今 日 意 外 的 利 益
（唐 希 爾 弄 假 成 眞）

Mr. Thornhill made his appearance with a smile, which he seldom wanted, and was going to embrace his uncle, which the latter repulsed with an air of disdain. "No fawning, sir, at present," cried the Baronet, with a look of severity; "the only way to my heart is by the road of honor; but here I only see complicated instances of falsehood, cowardice, and oppression. How is it, sir, that this poor man, for whom I know you professed a friendship, is used thus hardly? His daughter vilely seduced as a recompense for his hospitality, and he himself thrown into

且 說. 唐 希 爾 含 笑 走 進 來. 他 向 來 是 很 難 得 不 帶 這 一 笑 的. 正 要 向 前 摟 抱 他 的 叔 父. 他 的 叔 叔 很 輕 視 他. 不 理 他. 拒 絕 他 摟 抱. 爵 士 嚴 厲 說 道. 你 現 在 不 要 諂 媚 我. 要 走 光 明 正 大 的 路. 才 能 達 到 我 的 心 裏. 我 在 這 裏. 只 看 見 你 重 重 疊 疊 的 奸 謀 懦 怯. 欺 凌 這 一 位 可 憐 人. 我 曉 得 你 嘴 裏 說 以 友 誼 相 待 的. 你 爲 什 麼 這 樣 慘 酷 的 待 他. 他 好 好 的 以 上 賓 款 待 你. 你 却 把 他 的 女 兒 拐 走 了 報 答 他. 他 大 約 不 過 報 復

393

prison, perhaps but for re-
senting the insult? His
son, too, whom you feared
to face as a man——"

"Is it possible, sir,"
interrupted his nephew,
"that my uncle could ob-
ject that as a crime, which
his repeated instructions
alone have persuaded me
to avoid?"

"Your rebuke," cried Sir
William, "is just; you have
acted in this instance prudently and well, though
not quite as your father
would have done. My
brother, indeed, was the
soul of honor; but thou—
yes, you have acted in this
instance perfectly right,
and it has my warmest
approbation."

"And I hope," said his
nephew, "that the rest of
my conduct will not be
found to deserve censure.
I appeared, sir, with this
gentleman's daughter at
some places of public
amusement: thus, what
was levity, scandal called
by a harsher name, and
it was reported that I had
debauched her. I waited
on her father in person,
willing to clear the thing

你玷辱他家門.你却把
他關了監.你丟了人格.
不敢見他的兒子....

他的姪子攔住說道.
你屢次教訓我.勸我不
要同人決鬪.你現在為
什麼坐我的罪.

爵士答道.這一層你
駁得我不錯.這一次你
算是謹慎.辦得還好.你
的父親在日.却不這樣
作.我的哥哥.眞是光
明磊落.最顧名譽的.但
是你...是的.這一次你
作得很對.我很以為然
{爵士之意仍以決鬪為然不
過有教訓在先不便出爾反
爾觀其語
意可知}.

他的姪子答道.我盼
望.其餘我所作所為.也
不應受貶責.叔父.我同
這位先生的女兒.到過
幾處公共娛樂地方.說
我輕浮失檢則有之.造
謠言的人.就妄加難聽
的字眼.我自己親去見
他的父親.願意把這件
事辦清楚.使他父親滿

THE VICAR OF WAKEFIELD

to his satisfaction, and he received me only with insult and abuse. As for the rest, with regard to his being here, my attorney and steward can best inform you, as I commit the management of business entirely to them. If he has contracted debts, and is unwilling or even unable to pay them, it is their business to proceed in this manner, and I see no hardship or injustice in pursuing the most legal means of redress."

"If this," cried Sir William, "be as you have stated it, there is nothing unpardonable in your offense; and though your conduct might have been more generous in not suffering this gentleman to be oppressed by subordinate tyranny, yet it has been at least equitable."

"He cannot contradict a single particular," replied the squire; "I defy[1] him to do so, and several of my servants are ready to attest what I say. Thus, sir,"

意.他父親只是斥責我. 羞辱我.至於其餘的事 體.他為什麼被監在這 裏.我的律師.我的帳房. 可以對你說清楚.管理 產業的事體.我完全交 給他們.他若欠了債.不 願意還.或無力還.按照 法律辦.原是他們的事 體.用正當法律討債.我 却不見得有什麼刻薄. 有什麼不公道.

爵士說道.若如你所 說.你所犯的並不是不 可赦之罪.你原可以寬 厚些.不令這位先生受 你手下的人逼壓.然而 你的辦法.也不能算不 公道.

鄉紳答道.我所說的 詳情.他無一件能駁我. 我不相信他能駁我.我 的跟人們.預備作證.他

---

1. **Defy,** 挑戰；不信他人有能力；抗命.

continued he, finding that I was silent—for in fact I could not contradict him—"thus, sir, my own innocence is vindicated; but though at your entreaty I am ready to forgive this gentleman every other offense, yet his attempts to lessen me in your esteem excite a resentment that I cannot govern. And this, too, at a time when his son was actually preparing to take away my life; this, I say, was such guilt that I am determined to let the law take its course. I have here the challenge that was sent me, and two witnesses to prove it; one of my servants has been wounded dangerously, and even though my uncle himself should dissuade me, which I know he will not, yet I will see public justice done, and he shall suffer for it."

"Thou monster," cried my wife; "hast thou not had vengeance enough already, but must my poor boy feel thy cruelty? I hope that good Sir William will protect us, for my son is as innocent as a child:

聽見我不響.我實在是不能駁他.他又接着說道.叔父.我證明我無罪.我雖是聽你的勸.預備寬赦他.然而他在你面前.想躋蹝我.使你看輕我.我却制不住我的怨恨.況且他的兒子.還要我的命.我決意要任從法律辦他兒子的罪.他挑我決鬬的信.還在我這裏.還有兩個人作證.有一個還受了重傷.我曉得我的叔叔不會勸我不打官司的.假使叔父勸我不打.我還是要按法律辦理.他的兒子是要受刑罰的.

我的女人喊道.你這個怪物.你報仇還報不彀嗎.你還要我的兒子嘗你的殘酷手段嗎.我盼望威廉爵士保護我們.我的兒子老實無害.

I am sure he is, and never did harm to man."

"Madam," replied the good man, "your wishes for his safety are not greater than mine; but I am sorry to find his guilt too plain; and if my nephew persists——"

But the appearance of Jenkinson and the jailer's two servants now called off our attention, who entered, hauling in a tall man, very genteelly dressed, and answering the description already given of the ruffian who had carried off my daughter.

"Here," cried Jenkinson, pulling him in, "here we have him; and if ever there was a candidate for Tyburn,[1] this is one."

The moment Mr. Thornhill perceived the prisoner, and Jenkinson who had him in custody, he seemed to shrink back with terror. His face became pale with conscious guilt, and he would have withdrawn; but Jenkinson, who perceived his design, stopped

同個小孩一樣．我很曉得他．他從來沒害過人

爵士答道．瑪當．你願意你的兒子平安．不能比過我的同樣心願．但是我見得他所犯的罪．是很明顯的．我覺得難過．我的姪子若是一定要辦....

說到這裏．金京森．同獄卒的伙計走進來．我們的精神．都注在他們身上．這幾個人．拖一個人進來．這人身材很高．穿得很文雅．同剛才所說擄我女兒的人．身材面貌一樣．

金京森把這個人拖進來．說道．我們捉着他了．這就是殺人場考取合格的一位．

唐希爾一看見金京森．同他所捉住的犯人．立刻驚懼．要往後退．這時候．他曉得自己的罪惡無可逃．臉上立變了灰白色．正想退出．金京森曉得他的意思．攔阻

---

1. Tyburn，倫敦之殺人場．

him. "What, squire," cried he, "are you ashamed of your two old acquaintances, Jenkinson and Baxter? But this is the way all great men forget their friends, though I am resolved we will not forget you. Our prisoner, please your honor," continued he, turning to Sir William, "has already confessed all. This is the gentleman reported to be so dangerously wounded: he declares that it was Mr. Thornhill who first put him upon this affair; that he gave him the clothes he now wears to appear like a gentleman, and furnished him with the post chaise. The plan was laid between them, that he should carry off the young lady to a place of safety, and that he should threaten and terrify her; but Mr. Thornhill was to come in in the meantime, as if by accident, to her rescue, and that they should fight a while, and then he was to run off, by which Mr. Thornhill would have the better opportunity of

他.說道.鄉紳.你見了兩位老朋友.金京森同巴士特.有什麼不好意思.但是闊人的派頭.總是忘記了老朋友.我却是打定主意.不忘記你.回頭對爵士說道.大人.這個犯人.一切都招供了.這就是報告所說受重傷的人.他供的是.唐希爾叫他去辦這件事.給他一套好衣服穿上.像個上等人.還給他馬車坐.他現在身上穿的.就是那套衣服.他們定的計策.是叫他把那位小姐搶到一個安穩地方.恐嚇他.當下唐希爾好像是無意中走進來.打救小姐.兩個人還要裝作假打一場.他假作打他不過.先逃走.好叫唐

gaining her affections himself under the character of her defender."

Sir William remembered the coat to have been worn by his nephew, and all the rest the prisoner himself confirmed by a more circumstantial account;[1] concluding that Mr. Thornhill had often declared to him that he was in love with both sisters at the same time.

"Heavens!" cried Sir William; "what a viper have I been fostering in my bosom! And so fond of public justice, too, as he seemed to be! But he shall have it: secure him, Mr. Jailer. Yet hold, I fear there is not legal evidence to detain him."

Upon this, Mr. Thornhill, with the utmost humility, entreated that two such abandoned wretches might not be admitted as evidences against him, but that his servants should be examined.

"Your servants!" replied Sir William, "wretch, call

希爾有機會作打救人.贏小姐的愛情.

威廉爵士認得巴士特現時所穿的衣服.是他姪子穿過的.其餘的詳細情形都由巴士特證實巴士特末後還說.唐希爾說過多次.他同時戀愛牧師兩位小姐.

爵士大聲說道.上天呀.我爲什麼這些年.抱着這一條毒蛇在我懷裏.他還好像是很喜歡司法公平的{指唐希爾剛才說依照法律辦理的話}我要他受刑罰.獄卒.把他拘起來...且慢.我恐怕照着法律.還不能拘留他.

唐希爾於是很低首下心的哀求.說道.不應該憑這兩個爲世所不齒的惡人作見證.定他的罪.要求審問他自己的底下人.

威廉爵士答道.你的底下人嗎.你這個惡人呀.他們不是你的底下

1. Circumstantial account, 細情;環境詳情.

them yours no longer: but come, let us hear what those fellows have to say; let his butler be called."

When the butler was introduced, he soon perceived by his former master's looks that all his power was now over.

"Tell me," cried Sir William, sternly, "have you ever seen your master and that fellow dressed up in his clothes in company together?"

"Yes, please your honor," cried the butler, "a thousand times; he was the man that always brought him his ladies."

"How," interrupted young Mr. Thornhill; "this to my face!"

"Yes," replied the butler, "or to any man's face. To tell you a truth, Master Thornhill, I never either loved or liked you, and I don't care if I tell you now a piece of my mind."

"Now then," cried Jenkinson, "tell his honor whether you know anything of me."

"I can't say," replied the butler, "that I know

人了.來.我且聽聽這些底下人.有什麼說的.喊總管事來.

有人把那總管帶進來.那總管一看他主人的神色.就曉得他的權勢都完了.

爵士很嚴厲的問道.告訴我.你向來曾見過這個人穿了你主人的衣服.同你的主人在一起麼.

那總管答道.大人.我見過有一千次.

唐希爾攔住說道.怎麼呀.當住我的面.說這個話嗎.

總管答道.是的.無論對什麼人.我也是這樣說.唐希爾主人呀.我老實對你說.我向來不愛你.不喜歡你.我不怕把我心裏的話告訴你.

金京森說道.你告訴大人.你曉得我作過些什麼事.

總管答道.我却不能說你這個人作過些什

much good of you. The night that gentleman's daughter was deluded to our house, you were one of them."

"So then," cried Sir William, "I find you have brought a very fine witness to prove your innocence: thou stain to humanity! to associate with such wretches!" (But continuing his examination) "You tell me, Mr. Butler, that this was the person who brought him this old gentleman's daughter."

"No, please your honor," replied the butler, "he did not bring her, for the squire himself undertook that business; but he brought the priest that pretended to marry them."

"It is but too true," cried Jenkinson; "I cannot deny it; that was the employment assigned me, and I confess it to my confusion."

"Good heavens!" exclaimed the Baronet; "how every new discovery of his villainy alarms me. All his guilt is now too plain, and I find his prosecution

麼好事. 那天晚上. 這位先生的小姐. 被騙到我們府裏. 就有你一份.

爵士說道. 我才曉得你帶來一個很好的證人. 來證你無罪. 你這個人中的敗類. 同這種的惡人為伍. 回頭再審那總管. 問他道. 總管. 你才說是這個人. 把這位老先生的小姐帶去交你主人的.

總管答道. 大人. 不是的. 是鄉紳自己帶那位小姐. 金京森帶來的是那個教士. 替他們行假結婚禮.

金京森說道. 千眞萬眞. 我不抵賴. 鄉紳派我作的. 就是這件事. 我供認.

爵士嘆道. 層層發現出來他的罪孽. 使我害怕. 現在他所犯的罪很明顯了. 原來他之所以

was dictated by tyranny, cowardice, and revenge; at my request, Mr. Jailer, set this young officer, now your prisoner, free, and trust to me for the consequences. I'll make it my business to set the affair in a proper light to my friend the magistrate who has committed him. But where is the unfortunate young lady herself? Let her appear to confront this wretch; I long to know by what arts he has seduced her. Entreat her to come in. Where is she?"

"Ah, sir," said I, "that question stings me to the heart; I was once indeed happy in a daughter; but her miseries——"

Another interruption here prevented me; for who should make her appearance but Miss Arabella Wilmot, who was next day to have been married to Mr. Thornhill. Nothing could equal her surprise at seeing Sir William and his nephew here before her, for her arrival was quite accidental. It happened that she and the old gentleman, her

控告人. 全是爲暴虐怯懦復仇起見. 獄卒. 我要你把這位少年軍官釋放. 餘事有我負責. 收禁他的縣官. 是我的朋友. 我要把這件事對他說個明白. 那位可憐的小姐在那裏. 請他出來面質. 我很要曉得他用什麼詭計. 引誘小姐去的. 勸小姐進來. 他在那裏.

我答道. 先生. 你這一問. 直刺我的心. 我從前有女兒爲樂. 但是他的愁苦....

我說到這裏. 又有一件事攔住我. 這時候進來一個人. 却不是別人. 就是威小姐. 原定的是明日同唐希爾結婚的. 他原是偶然到這裏的. 一看見威廉爵士叔姪. 都在這裏. 非常之詫異. 原來威小姐同他的

father, were passing through the town, on the way to her aunt's, who had insisted that her nuptials with Mr. Thornhill should be consummated[1] at her house; but, stopping for refreshment, they put up at an inn at the other end of the town. It was there from the window that the young lady happened to observe one of my little boys playing in the street, and instantly sending a footman to bring the child to her, she learned from him some account of our misfortunes, but was still kept ignorant of young Mr. Thornhill's being the cause. Though her father made several remonstrances on the impropriety of going to a prison to visit us, yet they were ineffectual; she desired the child to conduct her, which he did, and it was thus she surprised us at a juncture[2] so unexpected.

Nor can I go on without a reflection on those accidental meetings, which, though they happen every

父親.要到他姨母 { 或舅 / 母等 } 家行婚禮.路過此地.就在一個店裏打尖.威小姐碰巧在窗子裏.看見我的小孩子在街上玩.立刻叫跟人把小孩帶進去.一問.才曉得我們遇了許多不幸的事.却不曉得都是唐希爾製造出來的.威小姐一定要到監裏看我們.他父親力阻無效.就叫我的小孩子領他來.是以威小姐這一來很是出乎我們意料之外的.

我說到這裏.禁不住想起.世上無日不有偶然相遇之事發生.平常都不覺得奇怪.遇了非常之事.才覺得奇怪.我

---

1. Consummated, 完全辦好. 2. Juncture, 時會

day, seldom excite our surprise but upon some extraordinary occasion. To what a fortuitous[1] concurrence do we not owe every pleasure and convenience of our lives! How many seeming accidents must unite before we can be clothed or fed! The peasant must be disposed to labor, the shower must fall, the wind fill the merchant's sail, or numbers must want the usual supply.

We all continued silent for some moments, while my charming pupil, which was the name which I generally gave this young lady, united in her looks compassion and astonishment, which gave new finishings to her beauty. "Indeed, my dear Mr. Thornhill," cried she to the squire, who she supposed was come here to succor, and not to oppress us, "I take it a little unkindly that you should come here without me, or never inform me of the

們在世所享的歡樂. 及各種便利. 那一樣不是從偶然巧合得來的呢. 有多少好像是偶然之事巧合起來. 然後我們才有衣有食. 例如須得農人心願工作. 又要遇着有雨. 又要遇着順風滿帆. 諸如此類的事甚多. 不然. 就有許多人得不着吃的.

再說. 我們停了一會子. 都不響. 當下我的明媚的女學生. 這是我向來對威小姐的稱呼. 他臉上又是詫異. 又是憐憫我們. 襯出他分外貌美. 他還以爲唐希爾到這裏來. 是打救我們. 不是來逼壓我們的. 說道. 我的寶貝唐希爾. 你一個人走來. 不帶着我. 我

---

1. Fortuitous, 偶然.

situation of a family so dear to us both; you know I should take as much pleasure in contributing to the relief of my reverend old master here, whom I shall ever esteem as you can. But I find that, like your uncle, you take a pleasure in doing good in secret."

"He find pleasure in doing good!" cried Sir William, interrupting her. "No, my dear, his pleasures are as base as he is. You see in him, madam, as complete a villain as ever disgraced humanity. A wretch who, after having deluded this poor man's daughter — after plotting against the innocence of her sister — has thrown the father into prison, and the eldest son into fetters, because he had courage to face her betrayer. And give me leave, madam, now to congratulate you upon an escape from the embraces of such a monster."

"Oh, goodness!" cried the lovely girl, "how have I been deceived! Mr. Thornhill informed me for certain

以為你有些不體念我. 你我都是很親愛這家人的. 你又向來沒告訴過我他們的困苦. 我很喜歡出我一份的力量. 救濟我所尊敬的老師. 也同你一樣. 你是曉得的. 我這才曉得. 你同你的叔叔. 是一樣的喜歡祕密作好事. 不願人曉得.

爵士攔住答道. 他歡喜好事嗎. 不是的. 他的快樂事. 同他的人格. 一樣卑劣. 瑪當. 他完全是個惡人. 玷辱人類. 這個惡人. 騙了這位可憐人的女兒. 又設計謀毀他的妹妹. 又把他們的父親關在監裏. 這位先生的兒子. 很有勇氣. 要同這個好行歎騙的惡人決鬪. 又被這惡人把他鎖禁起來. 瑪當. 讓我同你賀喜. 幸而你從這個惡怪手裏. 脫逃出來.

威小姐說道. 我怎麽樣被他騙了許久. 唐希爾告訴我說. 這位先生

that this gentleman's eldest son, Captain Primrose, was gone off to America with his new-married lady."

"My sweetest miss," cried my wife, "he has told you nothing but false-hoods. My son George never left the kingdom, nor ever was married. Though you have forsaken him, he has always loved you too well to think of anybody else, and I have heard him say he would die a bache-lor for your sake."

She then proceeded to expatiate[1] upon the sin-cerity of her son's passion; she set his duel with Mr. Thornhill in a proper light; from thence she made a rapid digression[2] to the squire's debaucheries, his pretended marriages, and ended with a most insulting picture of his cowardice.[3]

"Good heavens!" cried Miss Wilmot; "how very near have I been to the brink of ruin! Ten thou-sand falsehoods has this gentleman told me! He

的大兒子.普大佐.的確帶了他的新娘子.往美國去了.

我的女人說道.我的好小姐.他告訴你的.全是謊話.我的兒子佐之.從來未離開英國.也並未娶親.你雖然不要他.他太戀愛你.心裏並無別人.我聽他說過.爲你起見.他永不娶親{此數語一來責備威小姐二來表白佐之的真愛情}.

我的女人.還說了許多話.說他大兒子怎樣的真誠愛威小姐.他自己怎樣要大兒子決鬪復仇.從此離開本題.說到唐希爾的假結婚.最後把唐希爾的懦怯卑劣行爲.細數一遍.說得極其不堪.

威小姐說道.上天呀.我怎樣幾乎被毀了.這個人告訴我.足有一萬件的謊話.最後他極詭

1. Expatiate, 多說; 多寫. 2. Digression, 離本題說話. 3. Cow-ardice, 此字雖只作怯懦無勇解, coward 雖只作懦夫解,却是斥人極重之字.

had, at last, art enough to persuade me that my promise to the only man I esteemed was no longer binding, since he had been unfaithful. By his falsehoods I was taught to detest one equally brave and generous!"

But by this time my son was freed from the encumbrances of justice, as the person supposed to be wounded was detected to be an impostor. Mr. Jenkinson also, who had acted as his valet-de-chambre, had dressed up his hair and furnished him with whatever was necessary to make a genteel appearance. He now, therefore, entered, handsomely dressed in his regimentals, and, without vanity (for I am above it), he appeared as handsome a fellow as ever wore a military dress. As he entered, he made Miss Wilmot a modest and distant bow, for he was not as yet acquainted with the change which the eloquence of his mother had wrought in his favor. But no decorums

謊的說到我相信我答應了我最重視的人的話. 可以不算數. 因爲這個人先失信. 我信了他的謊話. 就厭惡那位又有勇又慷慨大度的人

到了這時候. 當初所謂被傷的人. 現在曉得原是假裝的. 故此把我大兒子的脚鐐解放了. 金京森當作他的底下人. 同他把髮理好. 供給他各樣應用物件. 把他打扮得很像樣. 於是走進來. 穿上很好看的軍服. 毋論什麼人穿了軍服. 我的大兒子都比得上他們好看. 我却不是呵好的話 (因我不重外觀). 他一進來. 向威小姐不卽不離的鞠躬. 他還不知道他母親說了一番話. 把威小姐的意思變過來了. 威小姐心裏是很着急的. 要我大

could restrain the impa-
tience of his blushing mistress to be forgiven.   Her
tears, her looks, all contributed to discover the
real sensations of her heart
for having forgotten her
former promise, and having
suffered herself to be deluded by an impostor.   My
son appeared amazed at her
condescension, and could
scarce believe it real.

"Sure, madam," cried
he, "this is but delusion;
I can never have merited
this!   To be blessed thus
is to be too happy."

"No, sir," replied she;
"I have been deceived —
basely deceived; else nothing could ever have made
me unjust to my promise.
You know my friendship,
you have long known it;
but forget what I have
done; and, as you once
had my warmest vows of
constancy, you shall now
have them repeated; and
be assured that if your
Arabella cannot be yours
she shall never be an-
other's."

"And no other's you
shall be," cried Sir William,

兒子原諒他.什麼社會
上的規矩.也蓋不住他
合羞臉紅.威小姐滴的
眼淚.同臉上的神色.都
現出他心裏是十分難
過.不守婚約.上了一個
騙子的當.我的兒子見
他這樣的屈尊自怨自
艾.反詫異起來.好像還
有點不相信.

他對威小姐說道.我
莫非是迷蒙未醒嗎.我
不配你這樣相待.我如
此的荷天降福.我是很
歡樂.

威小姐答道.不然.我
是上了當.被人騙得很
慘.不然.我是絕不肯背
約的.你曉得我待你的
交情.你是曉得許久的
了.請你把我以往所作
的事.忘記了.你從前得
過我極眞誠的許愿.我
永不改變.現在我許愿.
你可以放心.我若是不
嫁你.我也不嫁別人.

威廉爵士說道.威小
姐.倘我有運動你父親

"if I have any influence with your father."

This hint was sufficient for my son Moses, who immediately flew to the inn where the old gentleman was, to inform him of every circumstance that had happened. But in the meantime, the squire, perceiving that he was on every side undone, now finding that no hopes were left from flattery or dissimulation, concluded that his wisest way would be to turn and face his pursuers. Thus laying aside all shame, he appeared the open, hardy villain.

"I find, then," cried he, "that I am to expect no justice here; but I am resolved it shall be done me. You shall know, sir,"—turning to Sir William—"I am no longer a poor dependent upon your favors. I scorn them. Nothing can keep Miss Wilmot's fortune from me, which, I thank her father's assiduity, is pretty large. The articles and a bond[1] for her fortune

的力量．你一定不能嫁與別人．

我的兒子摩西．一聽這話．很曉得話裏的意思．立刻跑到客店．把一切情形．報告與威小姐的父親．唐希爾這時候一看．什麼破綻都被人看透了．巴結或說謊．都無希望．一打算．最妙無過於翻過臉．對付窮追他的人．於是把什麼羞恥都不顧．公然盡露他的老光棍眞相．

說道．我曉得在這裏得不着公道的了．我却決意你們還要把公道還我．回頭來．對威廉爵士說道．你該曉得．我現在用不着靠你給我什麼好處．我也全看不起那些好處．毋論怎麼樣．你們禁不住我得着威小姐的一份家產．我倒要謝謝他老子的一生辛苦．那份家產．却是很大的．那分配財產的條據．是簽過字的．在我手

---

1. Articles and a bond, 定婚或將婚時分配財產之條款文據．

are signed, and safe in my possession. It was her fortune, not her person, that induced me to wish for this match; and possessed of the one, let who will take the other."

This was an alarming blow. Sir William was sensible of the justice of his claims, for he had been instrumental in drawing up the marriage articles himself. Miss Wilmot, therefore, perceiving that her fortune was irretrievably lost, turning to my son, she asked if the loss of fortune could lessen her value to him. "Though fortune," said she, "is out of my power, at least I have my hand to give."[1]

"And that, madam," cried her real lover, "was indeed all that you ever had to give; at least, all that I ever thought worth the acceptance. And I now protest, my Arabella, by all that's happy, your want of fortune this moment increases my pleasure,

裏.當日所以引動我同威小姐定親的.並不是因爲我愛他這個人.我愛的是他的財產.我旣得了他的財產.誰願意娶他就娶他 ｛唐眞是希爾要臉是不爲威小姐聽了這話殊難情威小姐同佐之的親事至此又生一波折 ｝.

他這一打擊.令人一驚.威廉爵士.覺得他姪子要財產的話.原是公道.因爲當日定條款.他是與聞的.威小姐曉得這一份財產是全丟了.再也無法可收得回來.回過頭來.問我的兒子說.財產是沒有了.問我的兒子.還能看重他否.又說道.我雖不能許你以財產.我却能許你以身.

我兒子答道.瑪當.我只要你個人.我向來以爲最值得承受的.就是你個人.我很誠懇的對你立誓說.你此時丟了財產.更加我的歡喜.因

---

1. I have my hand to give, 我以身許人.

as it serves to convince my sweet girl of my sincerity."

Mr. Wilmot now entering, he seemed not a little pleased at the danger his daughter had just escaped, and readily consented to a dissolution of the match. But finding that her fortune, which was secured to Mr. Thornhill by bond, would not be given up, nothing could exceed his disappointment. He now saw that his money must all go to enrich one who had no fortune of his own. He could bear his being a rascal, but to want an equivalent to his daughter's fortune was wormwood.[1] He sat, therefore, for some minutes employed in the most mortifying speculations, till Sir William attempted to lessen his anxiety.

"I must confess, sir," cried he, "that your present disappointment does not entirely displease me. Your immoderate passion for wealth is now justly punished. But though the

爲這樣可以使你相信我的眞誠.

這時候威勒模先生進來. 好像喜歡他女兒幸免陷入危險. 預備答應廢除婚約. 但是一見他女兒的財產. 已經簽給唐希爾. 不能取回來. 却很失望. 只好望着他自己的錢財. 白送給這個自己無財產的人. 白叫他發財. 唐希爾是個棍徒. 他還可以受得. 但是再不能給他女兒一份柏等財產. 他却心裏苦得難過. 他坐下有好幾分鐘. 在那裏胡思亂想. 後來還是威廉爵士設法減輕他的憂慮.

說道. 先生. 我供認你現在的失望. 我見了. 却不是完全使我不高興. 因爲你向來太過好財. 現在你才受罰〈此是挖苦威勒模好財〉. 你的小姐雖然

---

1. Wormwood, 木名, 味苦.

young lady cannot be rich, she has still a competence[1] sufficient to give content. Here you see an honest young soldier who is willing to take her without fortune; they have long loved each other, and for the friendship I bear his father, my interest shall not be wanting in his promotion. Leave, then, that ambition which disappoints you, and, for once, admit that happiness which courts your acceptance."

"Sir William," replied the old gentleman, "be assured I never yet forced her inclinations, nor will I now. If she still continues to love this young gentleman, let her have him with all my heart. There is still, thank heaven, some fortune left, and your promise will make it something more. Only let my old friend here (meaning me) give me a promise of settling six thousand pounds upon my girl if ever he should come to his fortune, and

不能富.但是足彀飽食暖衣.亦可以心足.你看這位真誠少年軍官.願意娶你的女兒.不要財產.他們兩人相愛日久.因爲我同他父親的交情起見.不能不替他設法.你原來志在同貴人聯姻.已經失望.你可以撇開了.現在只要你答應.你不如就答應了.也享一次的歡樂.

那老先生答道.威廉爵士.我向來不勉強我女兒擇夫.我現在也不勉強他.他若是現在仍愛這個少年.我很願意他嫁與他.我謝謝上天.我還剩下些財產.又承你答應設法.那財產更多些.只要我的老朋友(指我也)答應分六千鎊給我女兒.這是說他將來有錢的話.我今天

---

1. Competence, 彀過活之財產；彀資格；有勝任之才能.

THE VICAR OF WAKEFIELD 403

I am ready this night to be the first to join them together."

As it now remained with me to make the young couple happy, I readily gave a promise of making the settlement he required, which, from one who had such little expectations as I, was no great favor. We had now, therefore, the satisfaction of seeing them fly into each other's arms in a transport.

"After all my misfortunes," cried my son George, "to be thus rewarded! Sure this is more than I could ever have presumed to hope for! To be possessed of all that's good, and after such an interval of pain! My warmest wishes could never rise so high!"

"Yes, my George," returned his lovely bride; "now let the wretch take my fortune; since you are happy without it, so am I. Oh, what an exchange have I made from the basest of men to the dearest, the best! Let him enjoy our fortune. I can now be happy even in indigence."

晚上.我就是第一個要他們締婚的人.

現在只爭在我一個人使這兩個少年人歡喜.我就答應了那分給六千鎊的話.想到我前程有限.就是答應了.也算不了什麼實惠.於是我們這時候親眼見這兩個少年人.歡喜欲狂的.飛走向前.互相摟抱.

我兒子佐之說道.我受了多少愁苦之後.居然有這樣報酬.實在是我不敢希望的.中間受了多少痛苦之後.現在所有好處.都是我的.我最親切的志願.從來未達到這個高點.

那位最美最可愛的新娘子答道.我的佐之.讓那個惡人拿我的財產.你既然無那財產也能歡樂.我亦能歡樂.我脫離一個最卑鄙的人.得了一個最好最可寶貴的人.這是什麼變局.讓他享受我們的財產.我現在卽使是貧窮.也是歡樂的.

"And I promise you," cried the squire, with a malicious grin, "that I shall be very happy with what you despise."

"Hold, hold, sir," cried Jenkinson; "there are two words to that bargain. As for that lady's fortune, sir, you shall never touch a single stiver[1] of it. Pray, your honor," continued he to Sir William, "can the squire have this lady's fortune if he be married to another?"

"How can you make such a simple demand?" replied the Baronet; "undoubtedly he cannot."

"I am sorry for that," cried Jenkinson; "for as this gentleman and I have been old fellow supporters, I have a friendship for him. But I must declare, well as I love him, that his contract is not worth a tobacco stopper, for he is married already."

"You lie like a rascal!" returned the squire, who seemed roused by this insult; "I never was legally married to any woman."

唐希爾滿肚的惡意. 笑道. 你看不起的財產. 我卻很喜歡享受.

金京森說道. 且慢. 對於這條款有兩句話可講. 這位小姐的財產. 你唐希爾一文也不能到手 { 這一轉如 / 天外奇峰 }. 接着問威廉爵士道. 大人. 我請問你. 倘若唐希爾娶過別位女人. 他還能得這宗財產麽.

爵士答道. 你爲什麽問這樣一句最易答的話. 自然不能.

金京森答道. 我心裏有些替唐希爾難過. 唐希爾同我兩人. 是同頑同樂的老朋友. 我是很念交情的. 但是我雖然愛他. 我卻不能不宣布明白. 他已經娶過別的女人. 剛才所說的婚約. 是不值一個烟斗的塞子.

唐希爾. 被他這一羞辱. 發怒起來. 答道. 你同騙子一樣的說謊. 我從來未正式同什麽女人結過婚.

---

1. Stiver, 荷蘭小銅錢名.

"Indeed, begging your honor's pardon," replied the other, "you were, and I hope you will show a proper return of friendship to your own honest Jenkinson who brings you a wife; and if the company restrain their curiosity a few minutes, they shall see her."

So saying he went off with his usual celerity, and left us all unable to form any probable conjecture as to his design.

"Ay, let him go," cried the squire, "whatever else I may have done, I defy him there. I am too old now to be frightened by squibs."[1]

"I am surprised," said the Baronet, "what the fellow can intend by this. Some low piece of humor, I suppose."

"Perhaps, sir," replied I, "he may have a more serious meaning. For when we reflect on the various schemes this gentleman has laid to seduce innocence, perhaps some one more artful than the rest has been found able

金京森答他道.大人不要怪.你曾經正式結過婚.你的眞誠老友金京森帶給你一位夫人.你該好好的酬謝他才是.我請衆位稍爲按住好奇之心.略等幾分鐘.就可以見見這位夫人.

他說完.趕快就走了{情節離奇}.我們都猜不出他的用意.

唐希爾說道.讓他去.我什麼事都許作過.我却未娶過親.我不是小孩子.不怕小火箭.

爵士說道.那個人跑去作什麼.我覺得詫異.也許是不相干的開頑笑.

我答道.先生.也許他有極深的用意.不是開頑笑因爲我們只要細想.這個鄉紳用盡許多詭計欺騙良家女子也許有個最善於行詐的大騙子.把鄉紳也騙在裏頭

---

1. Squibs, 手拋之小火箭 (此處借喻倜儺), 又作極利害之挖苦話解.

to deceive him. When we consider what numbers he has ruined, how many parents now feel with anguish the infamy and contamination which he has brought into their families, it would not surprise me if some one of them— Amazement! Do I see my lost daughter? Do I hold her? It is, it is my life, my happiness. I thought thee lost, my Olivia, yet still I hold thee—and still thou shalt live to bless me."

The warmest transports of the fondest lover were not greater than mine, when I saw him introduce my child, and held my daughter in my arms, whose silence only spoke her raptures.

"And art thou returned to me, my darling," cried I, "to be my comfort in age!"

"That she is," cried Jenkinson, "and make much of her, for she is your own honorable child, and as honest a woman as any in the whole room, let the other be who she will. And as for you,

我們只要想到.他毀了多少人.多少作父母的覺得他汙辱家庭的苦痛 {唐希爾之 / 罪惡如是}. 也許有人…怪事.怪事.這不是我巳死的女兒嗎.我抱的不是他嗎.是他是他.是我的性命.是我的歡樂.我的奧維雅呀.我以爲你死了.我現在還抱住你.你還要活着.保佑我 {突如其來令 / 人不可捉摸}.

我一看見金京森.把我女兒帶進來.就是最相戀愛的情人相見.也比不上我的狂喜.我雙手把女兒抱住.他也是狂喜.說不出話.

我說道.我的至寶.你回來了.安慰我的暮年.

金京森說道.是的.他回來了.你們要好好的看待他.他是你的貞潔女兒.別的女人.我們只好不管.這一位比得上這屋內無論什麼女人.

squire, as sure as you stand there, this young lady is your lawful wedded wife. And to convince you that I speak nothing but truth, here is the license by which you were married together." So saying, he put the license into the Baronet's hands, who read it, and found it perfect in every respect.

"And now, gentlemen," continued he, "I find you are surprised at all this; but a few words will explain the difficulty. That there squire of renown, for whom I have a great friendship — but that's between ourselves — has often employed me in doing odd little things for him. Among the rest, he commissioned me to procure him a false license and a false priest, in order to deceive this young lady. But as I was very much his friend, what did I do but went and got a true license and a true priest, and married them both as

回頭對唐希爾說道. 鄉紳. 這一位是你按照法律行結婚禮的正式夫人. 的確無疑. 我要使你相信我說的是真話. 這就是你們結婚的證書. 一面說. 一面把證書遞與爵士. 爵士一讀. 果然是完全證書.

金京森又說道. 諸位覺得詫異. 我說幾句話解釋. 諸位就可以無疑難了. 這位著名的鄉紳. 我同他很有交情的. (這却是我們兩人彼此心照的.) 他時常用我替他作零碎小事. 就中有一件. 就是派我去找一紙假婚證請一位假教士. 要騙這位小姐. 但是我是鄉紳的好朋友. 我怎麼辦呢. 我只好找了一份真證書. 請了一位真教士. 那教士趕快的爲他

fast as the cloth¹ could
make them. Perhaps
you'll think it was generosity that made me do all
this. But no. To my
shame I confess it, my only
design was to keep the
license, and let the squire
know that I could prove it
upon him whenever I
thought proper, and so
make him come down when-
ever I wanted money."

A burst of pleasure now
seemed to fill the whole
apartment; our joy reached
even to the common room,
where the prisoners them-
selves sympathized,

And shook their chains
In transport and rude harmony.

Happiness was expanded
upon every face, and even
Olivia's cheek seemed
flushed with pleasure. To
be thus restored to reputation, to friends and fortune
at once, was a rapture
sufficient to stop the progress of decay, and restore
former health and vivacity.
But perhaps among all

們行了結婚禮.你們也
許以為我這樣辦法.是
出於好意.其實不然.我
不怕難為情.供出來罷.
我的用意.是把婚證藏
起來.毋論什麼時候.我
要錢用.我就把婚證拿
出來.證明他曾經正式
結婚.訛他幾個錢用.

　說到這裏.滿屋子人
都歡樂起來.這一傳出
來.連監裏的大屋子所
有的囚犯.都替我歡喜.
嘗有一段古哥說過.

囚犯搖動脚鐐鍊
子的聲響.同歡樂
之聲相和成調.

這有點像我們此時
的情景.人人臉上都是
喜色.奧維雅的臉.也是
一片的歡樂.這樣一來.
立刻把名譽也恢復了.
朋友也有了.財產也有
了.這一歡.喜把病都截
住.恢復從前的健康活
潑.但是衆人中的歡樂.

---

1. Cloth, 此處作教士解.

there was not one who felt sincerer pleasure than I. Still holding the dear loved child in my arms, I asked my heart if these transports were not delusion.

"How could you," cried I, turning to Mr. Jenkinson—"how could you add to my miseries by the story of her death? But it matters not, my pleasure at finding her again is more than a recompense for the pain."

"As to your question," replied Jenkinson, "that is easily answered. I thought the only probable means of freeing you from prison, was by submitting to the squire, and consenting to his marriage with the other young lady. But these you had vowed never to grant while your daughter was living; there was therefore no other method to bring things to bear but by persuading you that she was dead. I prevailed on your wife to join in the deceit, and we have not had a fit opportunity of undeceiving you till now."

大抵都比不上我.我這時候.還摟着我的女兒.我還自問.這一場歡樂.莫非是一場好夢麽.

回頭問金京森.你爲什麼造謠言.說我的女兒死了.使我更加愁苦.現在是不要緊了.我現在有了女兒.這場歡樂.不止抵過我所受的痛苦.

金京森答道.我很容易答你這一問.我當日想到.大約只有勸你服從了鄉紳.答應他娶威小姐.才能救你出獄.但是你曾發過誓說.只要你的女兒還在世上.你不能答應他們結婚.那嗎.除了告訴你女兒死了之外.是沒得別的法子好想.我就勸你的女人串同造謠言.一直等到這時候.才有好機會.把眞情告訴你.

In the whole assembly now there only appeared two faces that did not glow with transport. Mr. Thornhill's assurance had entirely forsaken him: he now saw the gulf of infamy and want before him, and trembled to take the plunge. He therefore fell on his knees before his uncle, and, in a voice of piercing misery, implored compassion. Sir William was going to spurn him away, but at my request he raised him; and after pausing a few moments, "Thy vices, crimes, and ingratitude," cried he, "deserve no tenderness; yet thou shalt not be entirely forsaken; a bare competence shall be supplied to support the wants of life, but not its follies. This young lady, thy wife, shall be put in possession of a third part of that fortune which once was thine, and from her tenderness alone thou art to expect any extraordinary supplies for the future."

He was going to express his gratitude for such kindness in a set speech; but

現在衆人裏頭.只有兩個人的臉.並無喜色.唐希爾自己以爲他的詭計很有把握的.現在全發露了.曉得損失名譽同財產的苦況就在眼前.在那裏害怕到發抖.不敢嘗試這苦況.於是跪在他的叔父跟前.說了好些可憐的話.哀求他叔叔.威廉爵士正要踢開他.不管他.還是我替他求.他叔父才把他拉起來.歇了一會子.說道.你的罪惡.你的忘恩負義的行爲.不配憐憫.但是我却不使你受飢寒.我給你幾個錢.剛穀你過活.不穀你荒唐.這一位你的妻室.我給他你原應享受的財產三分之一.將來你若另要用錢.全憑你女人的慈心.酌量供給你.

唐希爾正要把想好的一番話.感謝他叔叔.

the Baronet prevented him by bidding him not aggravate his meanness, which was already but too apparent. He ordered him at the same time to be gone, and from all his former domestics to choose one such as he should think proper, which was all that should be granted to attend him.

As soon as he left us, Sir William very politely stepped up to his new niece with a smile, and wished her joy. His example was followed by Miss Wilmot and her father; my wife, too, kissed her daughter with much affection, as, to use her own expression, she was now made an honest woman of. Sophia and Moses followed in turn; and even our benefactor, Jenkinson, desired to be admitted to that honor. Our satisfaction seemed scarce capable of increase. Sir William, whose greatest pleasure was in doing good, now looked round with a countenance open as the sun, and saw nothing but joy in the looks of all except that of my

他的叔叔却攔住他.不要再作下賤樣子.他的下賤.被衆人都看穿了.叫他走.在從前的老家人中.挑一個去服待他.

唐希爾走了之後.威廉爵士.很有禮的.含笑走到他的姪婦{即奧維雅}.跟前.同他賀喜.跟住就是威小姐.威小姐的父親.都同奧維雅賀喜.我的女人很慈愛的.同女兒接吻.後來是素緋雅同摩西.我們的恩人金京森.也要賀喜.我們滿意到極點了.無可復加了.

威廉爵士.向來是以做好事爲樂的.他四圍的一看.臉上光明正大.好像是個太陽.一看衆人都是滿臉的歡笑.只

daughter Sophia, who for some reasons we could not understand, did not seem perfectly satisfied.

"I think now," cried he, with a smile, "that all the company, except one or two, seem perfectly happy. There only remains an act of justice for me to do. You are sensible, sir," continued he, turning to me, "of the obligations we both owe Mr. Jenkinson. And it is but just we should both reward him for it. Miss Sophia will, I am sure, make him very happy, and he shall have from me five hundred pounds as her fortune, and upon this I am sure they can live very comfortably together. Come, Miss Sophia, what say you to this match of my making? Will you have him?"

My poor girl seemed almost sinking into her mother's arms at the hideous proposal.

"Have him, sir!" cried she faintly. "No, sir— never."

"What!" cried he again; "not have Mr. Jenkinson,

有素緋雅一個人. 我們不曉得. 他為什麼好像是不十分滿意.

威廉爵士. 帶笑說道. 現在只剩一件事. 我要辦得公道. 回頭對我說道. 你曉得我同你兩個. 人. 都應很感激金京森. 我們兩個人. 都應酬謝他. 我很曉得素緋雅可以嫁他. 我給他五百鎊. 作素緋雅的妝奩. 我看. 有五百鎊. 他們兩人. 可以過安樂日子. 來來來. 素緋雅小姐. 你看我這個媒. 做得怎麼樣. 你願意嫁他麼.

我的女兒聽見了這種可厭的條陳. 氣的幾乎倒在他母親懷裏. 素緋雅聲音很低微的說道. 嫁他麼. 我永不嫁他.

爵士說道. 什麼呀. 你不嫁金京森麼. 他是你

your benefactor—a handsome young fellow, with five hundred pounds and good expectations!"

"I beg, sir," returned she, scarce able to speak, "that you'll desist, and not make me so very wretched."

"Was ever such obstinacy known," cried he again, "to refuse a man whom the family has such infinite obligations to, who has preserved your sister, and who has five hundred pounds? What, not have him!"

"No, sir—never," replied she angrily; "I'd sooner die first."

"If that be the case, then," cried he—"if you will not have him, I think I must have you myself." And so saying, he caught her to his breast with ardor. "My loveliest—my most sensible of girls!" cried he, "how could you ever think that your own Burchell could deceive you, or that Sir William Thornhill could ever cease to admire a mistress that loved him for himself alone! I have for some years sought

的恩人.他是個美貌少年.還有五百鎊又有好前程.

素緋雅幾乎說不出聲.答道.請你不要強我.不要使我難受.

爵士又說道.你們聽見過有這樣倔強性子的人嗎.他家裏受了這個人無限的深恩.他救你姊姊.又有五百鎊的財產.這樣人還不願嫁麼{威廉爵士要同素緋雅金是京森做媒亦出入意外是 作者巧弄其狡獪之筆若平鋪直敘威廉爵士同素緋雅締婚則索然無味奕然而論文雖是曲折論事則太不近人情}

素緋雅含怒答道.我寧願先死.我永不嫁他.

爵士說道.如果這樣.你既不願嫁他.我看還是我娶你罷.於是把素緋雅拖到懷裏.說道.我的最可愛最有知識的女孩呀.你怎麼能彀想.你的白爾能騙你呀.威廉爵士能彀不仰慕一位只愛他本人.不是貪富貴的小姐麼.我已經尋了許

for a woman, who, a stranger to my fortune, could think that I had merit as a man. After having tried in vain, even amongst the pert and the ugly, how great at last must be my rapture to have made a conquest over such sense and such heavenly beauty!"

Then turning to Jenkinson, "As I cannot, sir, part with this young lady myself, for she has taken a fancy to the cut of my face, all the recompense I can make is to give you her fortune, and you may call upon my steward tomorrow for five hundred pounds."

Thus, we had all our compliments to repeat; and Lady Thornhill underwent the same round of ceremony that her sister had done before. In the meantime, Sir William's gentleman appeared, to tell us that the equipages were ready to carry us to the inn, where everything was prepared for our reception. My wife and I led the van, and left those gloomy mansions of sorrow. The

多年．要尋一個女子．不知道我有錢．只知我這個人還有所長的．我尋了許久．都尋不着．我從醜怪女子中．放肆無禮的女子中．都找過．後來我居然得了一位極有知識貌如天仙的女子愛我．我是歡樂極了｛至此才說出他微服往來改名換姓的苦心｝．

回頭對金京森說道．我既不能把這位小姐讓給你．因為他喜歡我的臉．我只能把給他的財產．轉給你作賠補．你明天去找我的帳房要五百鎊．

我們於是重新賀喜．現在是威廉唐希爾的貴夫人受賀．也同剛才他姉姉受賀一樣．當下爵士左右的人．走來報告．說是馬車都預備好．送我們到客店．那裏已經預備好歡迎我們．我夫婦兩人在前．離開這愁苦監獄．這位慷慨爵士，

generous Baronet ordered forty pounds to be distributed among the prisoners; and Mr. Wilmot, induced by his example, gave half that sum. We were received below by the shouts of the villagers, and I saw and shook by the hand two or three of my honest parishioners who were among the number. They attended us to our inn, where a sumptuous entertainment was provided, and coarser provisions were distributed in great quantities among the populace.

After supper, as my spirits were exhausted by the alternation of pleasure and pain which they had sustained during the day, I asked permission to withdraw; and leaving the company in the midst of their mirth, as soon as I found myself alone, I poured out my heart in gratitude to the Giver of joy as well as of sorrow, and then slept undisturbed till morning.

吩咐拿四十鎊分給衆囚犯. 威勒模學他的樣子. 賞囚犯們二十鎊. 底下是一羣鄉下人高聲的歡迎. 內中還有我教屬的兩三個人. 我看見他們. 同他們拉手. 他們陪我們到客店. 那裏已預備好大排筵宴. 分了許多稍粗的食物. 給村裏的人.

我這一天. 因悲喜相接而來. 精神困倦. 吃過晚飯. 我就先告饒. 退去歇息. 讓其餘的人快樂. 我獨自一人的時候. 我感謝上帝. 賜我的苦樂. 一夜安睡到天亮.

CHAPTER XXXII

THE CONCLUSION

第 三 十 二 回

結 局

不 過 是 一 派 結 婚 聲

The next morning, as soon as I awaked, I found my eldest son sitting by my bedside, who came to increase my joy with another turn of fortune in my favor. First having released me from the settlement that I had made the day before in his favor, he let me know that my merchant who had failed in town was arrested at Antwerp, and there had given up effects[1] to a much greater amount than what was due to his creditors. My boy's generosity pleased me almost as much as this unlooked-for good fortune. But I had some doubts whether I ought in

第二天早上.我一醒就看見我大兒子坐在我牀邊.他來告訴我.又轉到好運氣了.使我更加歡喜.他先把我昨日簽給他的財產放棄.隨即告訴我.在倫敦破產的商人.茬安和地方被捕.就在那裏.把拐逃的財產都交出來.比抵償還有餘.我兒子的慷慨.使我喜歡.差不多也同想不到欠債有着一樣的歡喜.但我心裏却躊躇.應

---

1. Effects, 財產.

justice to accept his offer. While I was pondering upon this, Sir William entered the room, to whom I communicated my doubts. His opinion was, that as my son was already possessed of a very affluent[1] fortune by his marriage, I might accept his offer without any hesitation. His business, however, was to inform me, that as he had the night before sent for the licenses, and expected them every hour, he hoped that I would not refuse my assistance in making all the company happy that morning.

A footman entered while we were speaking, to tell us that the messenger was returned; and as I was by this time ready, I went down, where I found the whole company as merry as affluence and innocence could make them. However, as they were now preparing for a very solemn ceremony, their laughter entirely displeased me.

否收受我兒子放棄的財產．我正在盤算這一層．威廉爵士進來．我把我的疑團告訴他．他以爲我兒子因締婚得了很豐厚的妝奩．我可以收受他願放棄的財產．不必懷疑．但是爵士來見我．爲的是昨晚已打發人去取婚證．現在可以快到了．他盼望我不要不答應．今早都忙湊熱鬧．

我們說話的時候．有一個跟人進來說．出差的回來了．我這時候也都收拾好．我就下去．看見人人都歡喜．人人也都有了錢．人人心地都是光明．自然能放懷儘情歡樂．然而現在他們正在預備行人生最鄭重的禮節．我有點不甚喜歡他們大笑．

---

1. Affluent, 富厚.

I told them of the grave, becoming,[1] and sublime[2] deportment they should assume upon this mystical occasion, and read them two homilies[3] and a thesis[4] of my own composing, in order to prepare them. Yet they still seemed perfectly refractory and ungovernable. Even as we were going along to church, to which I led the way, all gravity had quite forsaken them, and I was often tempted to turn back in indignation. In church a new dilemma[5] arose, which promised no easy solution. This was, which couple should be married first; my son's bride warmly insisted that Lady Thornhill (that was to be) should take the lead; but this the other refused with equal ardor, protesting she would not be guilty of such rudeness for the world. The argument was supported for some time between both with equal obstinacy and good breeding.

我告訴他們.這是一件神祕的事.理應存一種莊重合理肅態度.我就對他們讀了我自製的兩篇經解.一篇經論.好預備他們行大禮〔行結婚禮仍先讀經解經論牧師拘迂故態復萌〕.他們簡直的是不聽.我也管不了他們.當我先行領他們到教堂的時候.他們簡直的把莊重兩字全忘了.我有好幾次要生氣回去.我們到了教堂又出了一件爲難的事.頗不容易解決.因爲這時候有兩起結婚.究竟誰應先行禮呢.我的新媳婦.一定要讓唐希爾貴夫人(成禮後的稱呼)先行禮.唐希爾貴夫人.一定不肯.說是他不能這樣無禮.兩方辯起理來.辯得很客氣.各有各的理.旗鼓相當.兩不相下.

---

1. Becoming, 合禮; 適合. 2. Sublime, 高遠或高深; 使人肅然起敬或使人驚奇. 3. Homilies, 經解. 4. Thesis, 經論; 論說. 5. Dilemma, 兩難.

But as I stood all this time with my book ready, I was at last quite tired of the contest, and shutting it, "I perceive," cried I, "that none of you have a mind to be married, and I think we had as good go back again; for I suppose there will be no business done here to-day." This at once reduced them to reason. The Baronet and his lady were first married, and then my son and his lovely partner.

I had previously that morning given orders that a coach should be sent for my honest neighbor Flamborough and his family, by which means, upon our return to the inn, we had the pleasure of finding the two Miss Flamboroughs alighted before us. Mr. Jenkinson gave his hand to the eldest, and my son Moses led up the other (and I have since found that he has taken a real liking to the girl, and my consent and bounty he shall have, whenever he thinks proper to demand them).

我早已把聖經打開. 都預備好了. 站在那裏老等. 後來我不耐煩. 把聖經關了. 說道. 據我看來. 你們是無意結婚. 我們不如回去罷. 這裏今天是無事可辦的了. 這一說. 他們才明白過來. 爵士同我的女兒先行結婚禮. 隨後就是我兒子同威小姐行禮.

我早已吩咐. 派車去接我的老實鄰居法林巴. 和他的眷屬. 等到我們回到客店. 剛好那兩位法林巴小姐的車也到了. 金京森扶大小姐下車. 摩西領的是二小姐（我以後才曉得. 摩西很愛這位小姐. 只要他來問我. 我就允許他結親. 分給他財產）.

We were no sooner returned to the inn, but numbers of my parishioners, hearing of my success, came to congratulate me; but among the rest were those who rose to rescue me and whom I formerly rebuked with such sharpness. I told the story to Sir William, my son-in-law, who went out and reproved them with great severity; but finding them quite disheartened by his harsh reproof, he gave them half a guinea apiece to drink his health, and raise their dejected spirits.

Soon after this we were called to a very genteel entertainment, which was dressed by Mr. Thornhill's cook. And it may not be improper to observe with respect to that gentleman, that he now resides in quality of companion at a relation's house, being very well liked, and seldom sitting at the side table, except when there is no room at the other; for they make no stranger of him. His time is pretty much taken up in keeping his relation, who is a little

我們才到客店．有許多我教屬的人．聽見我得意．來同我賀喜．其中還有激於義憤．要打救我的人．當日被我一番嚴屬言語阻止住的．我把這件事告訴我的女壻威廉爵士．他走出去．很嚴詞屬色的再責備他們一番．這羣鄉下人．被他這一責備．人人都神色很頹喪的．爵士賞他們每人半個金錢．去吃酒．替他祝壽．提提他們的精神．

再過一會子．就有人來請我們吃喜酒．酒席是鄉紳唐希爾的廚子辦的．我應該趁這個機會說唐希爾的近況．他住在一個親戚家．算是這親戚的陪伴．那家人家．也還喜歡他．也不把他當作外人看待．正桌人滿．才叫他坐在旁桌．不然．也許他同在正桌吃飯．他這個親戚．有點神經煩惱．唐希爾時刻的陪伴他．有空閒的時

melancholy, in spirits, and in learning to blow the French horn. My eldest daughter, however, still remembers him with regret; and she has even told me, though I make a great secret of it, that when he reforms she may be brought to relent.

But to return, for I am not apt to digress thus, when we were to sit down to dinner, our ceremonies were going to be renewed. The question was, whether my eldest daughter, as being a matron, should not sit above the two young brides; but the debate was cut short by my son George, who proposed that the company should sit indiscriminately,[1] every gentleman by his lady.

This was received with great approbation by all, excepting my wife, who I could perceive was not perfectly satisfied, as she expected to have had the pleasure of sitting at the head of the table, and carving all the meat for all

候. 學吹喇叭（順手一筆代唐希爾交下／落說得無聊不堪意在言外）. 我的大女兒. 仍然是怨恨他. 却有一件祕密事. 我是不告訴人的. 我的女兒曾對我說過. 唐希爾若是改過遷善. 他也許寬恕他的罪過. 這是後事. 暫且不提. 再說我們快要入席的時候. 重新又講起禮節來.

這次的問題. 是我的大女兒先嫁的. 是否應該上坐. 這一層的辯論. 被我大兒子很痛快的解決了. 他提議眾人隨便坐. 新娘坐在新郎身旁.

這個提議. 人人贊成. 惟有我的女人. 不甚滿意. 我曉得他要坐主位. 割肉分與各人. 雖有這

1. Indiscriminately, 無分別.

the company. But not-withstanding this, it is impossible to describe our good humor. I can't say whether we had more wit among us now than usual; but I am certain we had more laughing, which answered the end as well. One jest I particularly remember: old Mr. Wilmot drinking to Moses, whose head was turned another way, my son replied, "Madam, I thank you."

Upon which the old gentleman, winking upon the rest of the company, observed that he was thinking of his mistress. At which jest I thought the two Miss Flamboroughs would have died with laughing. As soon as dinner was over, according to my old custom, I requested that the table might be taken away, to have the pleasure of seeing all my family assembled once more by a cheerful fireside. My two little ones sat upon each knee, the rest of the company by their partners. I had nothing now on this

一層的辯論.而坐中都是非常之歡樂.非筆墨所能形容的.我不能說.我們這一次.比向來說的俏皮話是否多些.我却曉得人人大笑.比向來笑得多.也還罷了.有一句笑話.我是特別記得清楚.威勒模老先生對摩西舉杯.摩西的臉却反向對方.答道.瑪當.我謝謝你.

那老先生對席上人瞬目示意.說摩西在那裏想他的所愛.那兩位法林巴小姐.聽了大笑.幾乎笑死.散席之後.我還照着我向來的老例.搬開桌子.要家裏人再圍爐歡談一次.我兩個小孩坐在我膝上.餘人靠近同伴坐.我在世上.是無可要求的了.現在

THE VICAR OF WAKEFIELD 423

side of the grave[1] to wish for; all my cares were over, my pleasure was unspeakable. It now only remained that my gratitude in good fortune should exceed my former submission in adversity.

我是無憂無慮．樂不可言．只有感謝餘年的厚福．深於忍受從前的憂患 {所謂雷霆雨露 都是天恩也} ．

---

1. This side of the grave, 未死之先．

隱　士　吟 ＊

王　蓴　農　譯

（轉載英文雜誌第八卷第十二號）

隱士且迴身
前路導余獨
有燈似歡迎
熒熒燦幽谷

我本失路人
力弱行躑躅
曠野渺無垠
修途益綿邈

隱士呼少年
愼莫再前去
魍魅喜人過
陰燐當路舞

蝸廬幸不遠
爲客開蓬戶
供給雖不周
願作東道主

今夕復何夕
共此田家樂
草塲飯粗糲
高臥亦清福

谷中多野羊
戒殺不戮牲
天意憐衆生
我亦愛牲畜

山麓草萋萋
素食富採擷
蔬果盛一囊
酌以泉水潔

願君泯世慮
世慮皆誤失
人生無多求
百年但一瞥

＊原文見本書第八回 (pages73-78)

435

曉露降太虛
喻此溫存語
再拜納嘉言
追隨至山廬

平楚色蒼然
寂寥橫廣墅
貧隣及孤客
於此安居處

室中無長物
環堵不須守
翛然脫扃入
主客同攜手

夜深羣動息
沉沉聽更漏
主人起剪燭
慰客開笑口

野蔌列筵前
笑勸加餐飯
主人熟故事
清談消夜緩

一室滿太和
貍奴傍人戀
蟋蟀鳴壁間
炭爐爆餘烈

多慟窮途客
繁愁無術解
淚下如泉湧
云何仍抱憂

隱士詢客情
神驚心亦聳
問客胡為乎
摧胸絕沉痛

將毋背人羣
獨行違心索
友誼與愛情
不答轉懷楚

吁嗟富與貴
其樂何足數
榮華倏凋謝
斯人更微窳

交誼原空名
愚弄厚不覺
富貴託人蔭
貧賤同聲哭

愛情虛更虛
羣雌徒粥粥
何處覓真情
定巢輸羽族

嗟爾少年人
毋自貽羞為
主詞方云畢
客顏頰如醉

儀態驚萬方
艷質轉秀媚
煥若餘霞綺
光采映天際

綽態蕩酥胸
倉卒愈局促
頓現女兒身
喬裝顏如玉

宛轉乞主憐
哀鳴恕見辱
純潔君子堂
著我不潔足

願更進一言
儂生落情網
欲求安樂土
翻使儂失望

儂家太因河
阿父懋爵賞
膝下更無人
獨我珠擎掌

內助覬我賢
玉臺爭下聘
厚幣諛我美
伴作多情證

時復雜沓來
百朋陳文錦
獨有愛德文
私情不輕請

衣飾僕且素
絕無財及勢
獨富慧與德
儂心實最喜

伴儂居深谷
和鳴樂心意
吹氣如芳蘭
嬌歌悅嘉卉

日中花蕊放
天畔露華吐
清潔比郎心
郎心更堪慕

燦爛而無恆
喻彼花間露
燦爛郎情眞
無恆妾心苦

儂常肆薄技
無謂而脅迫
郎情投儂意
郎苦儂意得

郎忍無可忍
避我驕餘觸
尋幽不復返
寂死形影獨

儂今悔不追
誓以死相報
願尋郎去處
同穴諧偕老

野曠望寥廓
瘞玉埋香好
郎死旣爲儂
儂拚爲郎槁

隱士擁女懷
呼天勿云此
回首女欲嗔
擁者夫壻是

吾愛安琪兒
試復凝神視
闊別愛德文
深情愛重贈

THE VICAR OF WAKEFIELD　429

好合終吾生
和諧若琴瑟
卿莫再歎傷
卿悲我悽惻

貯卿在心頭
温馨萬慮息
永結無盡緣
終身毋離逖

瘈犬之輓歌 ※

平海瀾譯

（轉載英文雜誌第十卷第六號）

凡爾諸君子
我歌傾耳聽
倘嗤我短章
亦勿羈君行

益史林頓鎮
衆口有聞人
操行號聖潔
見諸祈禱辰

慈懷好周恤
無間友與敵
衣被衆蒼生
身外非所涉

同地多黃耳
咻咻猶狗國
有犬亦凡庸
與衆初無別

始與若人善
忽乃起爭執
爲謀遂所私
猖獗恣狂嚙

奔走相告語
羣情殊喧囂
是畜失其常
桀犬竟吠堯

僉謂創痛深
觸目成悽哽
謂犬已癲狂
被嚙必無幸

無何事大白
衆喙徒紛呶
其人傷旋復
犬則委蓬蒿

※原文見本書第十七回（pages174-175）

民國二十一年一月二十九日
敝公司突遭國難總務處印刷
所編譯所書棧房均被炸燬附
設之涵芬樓東方圖書館尙公
小學亦遭殃及盡付焚如三十
五載之經營燬於一旦迭蒙
各界慰問督望速圖恢復詞意
懇摯銜感何窮敝館雖處境艱
困不敢不勉爲其難因將需要
較切各書先行覆印其他各書
亦將次第出版惟是圖版裝製
不能盡如原式事勢所限想荷
鑒原謹布下忱統祈　垂詧
上海商務印書館謹啓

中華民國十八年十一月初版
民國二十二年
一月印行國難後第一版
（二七六四）

維克斐牧師傳譯註
THE VICAR OF WAKEFIELD

每冊定價大洋貳元伍角
（外埠酌加運費匯費）

原著者　Oliver Goldsmith
譯註者　伍光建
印刷者　上海商務印書館
發行兼
發行所　商務印書館　上海及各埠

二六三〇

書名: 維克斐牧師傳譯註
系列: 漢英對照經典英文文學文庫
主編: 潘國森、陳劍聰
原作者:歌士米
漢譯:伍光健

出版: 心一堂有限公司
地址: 香港九龍旺角彌敦道610號
　　　荷李活商業中心18樓1805-06室
電話號碼: (852) 6715-0840
網址: www.sunyata.cc
　　　publish.sunyata.cc
電郵: sunyatabook@gmail.com
心一堂讀者論壇: http://bbs.sunyata.cc
網上書店: http://book.sunyata.cc

香港發行: 香港聯合書刊物流有限公司
香港新界大埔汀麗路36號中華商務印刷
大廈3樓
電話號碼: (852)2150-2100
傳真號碼: (852)2407-3062
電郵: info@suplogistics.com.hk

台灣發行: 秀威資訊科技股份有限公司
地址: 台灣台北市內湖區瑞光路七十六巷
　　　六十五號一樓
電話號碼: +886-2-2796-3638
傳真號碼: +886-2-2796-1377
網絡書店: www.bodbooks.com.tw
心一堂台灣國家書店讀者服務中心:
地址: 台灣台北市中山區松江路二〇九號1樓
電話號碼: +886-2-2518-0207
傳真號碼: +886-2-2518-0778
網址: www.govbooks.com.tw

中國大陸發行 零售:
　　　　深圳心一堂文化传播有限公司
深圳: 中國深圳羅湖立新路六號東門
　　　博雅負一層零零八號
電話號碼: (86)0755-82224934
北京: 中國北京東城區雍和宮大街四十號
心一堂官方淘寶流通處:
http://sunyatacc.taobao.com/

版次: 2019年1月初版

　　　HKD 178
定價: NT　698

國際書號　978-988-8582-18-1

Title: The Vicar of Wakefield
 (with Chinese translation)
Series: Classic English Literature
Collections with Chinese Translation
Editor: POON, Kwok-Sum(MCIoL,
DipTranCIoL), CHEN, Kim
byOliver Goldsmith
Translated and Annotated (in Chinese)
by Woo Kwang-Kien

Published in Hong Kong by Sunyata Ltd
Address: Unit 1805-06, 18/F, Hollywood Plaza,610
Nathan Road, Mong Kok, Kowloon, Hong Kong
Tel: (852) 6715-0840
Website: publish.sunyata.cc
Email: sunyatabook@fmail.com
Online bookstore: http://book.sunyata.cc

Distributed in Hong Kong by:
SUP PUBLISHING LOGISTICS(HK)
LIMITED
Address: 3/F, C & C Buliding,
36 Ting Lai Road, Tai Po, N.T.,
Hong Kong
Tel: (852) 2150-2100
Fax: (852) 2407-3062
E-mail: info@suplogistics.com.hk

Distributed in Taiwan by:
Showwe Information Co. Ltd.
Address: 1/F, No.65, Lane 76, Rueiguang
Road, Neihu District, Taipei, Taiwan
Website: www.bodbooks.com.tw

First Edition 2019
HKD 178
NT 698

ISBN: 978-988-8582-18-1